Ab

Three-time Golden Heart® Award finalist **Tina Beckett** learned to pack her suitcases almost before she learned to read. Born to a military family, she has lived in the United States, Puerto Rico, Portugal, and Brazil. In addition to travelling, Tina loves to cuddle with her pug, Alex, spend time with her family and hit the trails on her horse. Learn more about Tina from her website or friend her on Facebook.

With a background of working in medical laboratories and a love of the romance genre, it's no surprise that **Sue MacKay** writes medical romance stories. She wrote her first story at age eight and hasn't stopped since. She lives in New Zealand's Marlborough Sounds where she indulges her passions for cycling, walking, and kayaking. When she isn't writing she also loves cooking and entertaining guests with sumptuous meals that include locally caught fish.

After completing a degree in journalism, then working in advertising and mothering her kids, **Robin Gianna** had what she calls her awakening. She decided she wanted to write the romance novels she'd loved since her teens, and now enjoys pushing her characters toward their own happily-ever-after's. When she's not writing, Robin's life is filled with a happily messy kitchen, a needy garden, a wonderful husband, three great kids, a drooling bulldog and one grouchy Siamese cat.

The Surgeon Collection

The Surgeon's Secret

TINA BECKETT

SUE MacKAY

ROBIN GIANNA

MILLS & BOON

First Published in Great Britain 2023
by Mills & Boon, an imprint of HarperCollins*Publishers* Ltd,
1 London Bridge Street, London, SE1 9GF

www.harpercollins.co.uk

HarperCollins*Publishers*
Macken House, 39/40 Mayor Street Upper,
Dublin 1, D01 C9W8, Ireland

The Surgeon's Secret © 2023 Harlequin Enterprises ULC.

The Surgeon's Surprise Baby © 2019 Tina Beckett
Surgeon in a Wedding Dress © 2011 Sue MacKay
Second Chance with the Surgeon © 2019 Robin Gianakopoulos

ISBN: 978-0-263-31967-5

THE SURGEON'S SURPRISE BABY

TINA BECKETT

To my husband:
thank you for my chickens!

PROLOGUE

"WELL, I'M NO longer your boss."

Luca Venezio stared at her as if she'd lost her mind. No longer his boss? Was that all she had to say to him? The obvious relief in her voice told him that she'd been anxious to wield that particular ax. Only she'd just done it in a room full of his colleagues, who had suffered a similar fate. He'd stayed behind after the others had all filed out dejectedly.

She was perched on her desk, looking just as gorgeous as she had a year ago, when he'd first stepped into her neurology department. It had taken him a while, but he'd finally convinced her to look past her reservations about engaging in a workplace relationship and see what they could be like together.

And it had been good. So very good.

He took a step closer. "Is that all you have to say to me, Elyse?"

Her head tilted as if she truly couldn't understand what the problem was. Was this an American thing that he hadn't yet grasped? Just when he thought he was understanding this culture, the woman in front of him threw something into the mix that had him reeling.

Italy was suddenly beckoning him home. But he wasn't leaving without a fight.

She slid from her desk and stood in front of him. "Don't you see? This could be a good thing."

No. He didn't see it. No matter how he looked at it.

She drove him insane. With want. With need. And now was no different.

"Do you want me gone, is that it?"

She took his hands in hers, before her hands slid up his forearms. "Are we talking about from the hospital? Or from my life?"

It was one and the same to Luca. It felt like they'd been trapped in a game of tug-of-war ever since their first date. The harder he pulled her toward him, the more she seemed to resist letting him get close to her, and he didn't understand why. They were in a relationship, only nothing was easy. Except the sex.

And that had been mind-blowing. Maybe part of that was the uncertainty of it all. Maybe it had lent an air of desperation to their lovemaking.

Her green eyes stared into his, and the crazy thing was, he could swear he saw a hint of lust in there, even though she'd just fired him. Had she gotten off on delivering that death blow to all those people?

No. That wasn't the Elyse he'd known these past few months.

"What is it you want from me, Elyse?"

"Don't you know?"

He didn't. Not at all, but he was tired of playing guessing games with her. He cupped her face, trying to make sense of it all, but the swirling in his head gave him no time to think. No time to ask any questions. Instead, the refuge they'd sought after each fight opened its door and whispered in his ear, promising it would all be okay.

He no longer believed it. But his blood was stirring in his veins, sending waves of heat through him. Even as her lips tilted up, telling him what she wanted, he was already there, the kiss scorching hot, just as it always was. His tongue met hers, his hands going under her ass and sitting her back on her desk. The sound of her shoes hitting the floor one at a time and her hands going to his waist and tugging him forward between her legs answered his earlier question about what she wanted.

Hell. There was no question as to that. *Grazie a Dio* he'd locked the door behind him, thinking that what he'd had to say to her he wanted said in private. Right now, though, the last thing he wanted to do was talk.

And he was so hot. So ready. Just as he always was for her.

The desk was wide, the middle bare of anything.

Made for sex.

He grabbed hold of her wrists and tugged her hands away so that he could take a step back to unzip.

The sight of Elyse licking her lips was his undoing.

He came back to her, reaching under her skirt to yank her boy shorts down, tossing them away. Then he eased her down until her back was flat against her desk, her breasts jutting upward, the outline of her nipples plainly visible beneath the thin white blouse.

"Do you want me?" His hands palmed the smooth skin of her hips and tugged her to the very edge of the desk.

She bit her lip, her legs twining around his until he was pressed tight against her, his hard flesh finding a wet heat that destroyed any hopes of prolonging this. He drove home, her sharp cry ending on a moan, her hips moving as if to seat him even deeper.

"*Dio*, Elyse…" His eyes closed, trying to grasp at any shred of control and finding nothing there.

His thumb moved from her hip to her center, hoping to help things along, but the second he touched her, she exploded around him, her gasped "Yes," sending him over the edge. Bracing his hands on the desk, he plunged home again and again, his body spasming so hard his vision went white for a brief instant. Still he thrust, unwilling for the moment to end.

Because that's exactly what it would do. What it needed to do.

His movements slowed, reality slowly filtering back in. *Hell.* As good as this was, it had solved nothing.

Nothing.

The job had been the thing that had held him there, made him keep trying, even as she burned hot and then cold.

But now she'd killed the job. And in doing that, the relationship. What they said about goodbye sex was evidently true.

He didn't try to kiss her, just moved away, zipping himself back in, even as she sat up on the desk.

"What's wrong?"

Was she really asking him that? Everything was wrong. But he was about to make it right.

"Did you put my name on that list of people to be fired?"

She frowned, coming off the desk, retrieving her undergarment, turning away from him as she slid them over her legs. She didn't answer as, with her back still turned, she pushed her feet into her shoes, black high-heeled pumps that he had always found so sexy.

By the time she finally turned around, his last shred of patience had disappeared and he no longer needed a response. "You know what? It doesn't matter. You've been pushing me away ever since I got here, so I'm finally giving you your wish. I'm leaving. Going back to Italy. You actually did me a favor in firing me, so thank you."

He put a hand on the doorknob, half thinking she would

call his name and tell him it was all a big mistake. Tell him that she didn't want him to go. He tensed, knowing that even if she did he was no longer willing to go on as they had been. Maybe he'd revisit that decision in a week…in a month. But right now, he needed time to think things through.

Except there was no sound from behind him as he opened the door. As he stepped through it. As he closed it.

Maybe that was all the thinking he needed to do.

So he started walking. And kept on walking until he was away from the hospital and on his way out of her life.

CHAPTER ONE

"I'M FINALLY GIVING you your wish."

Elyse Tenner hesitated, those words ringing in her ears just as fresh and sharp today as they'd done a little over a year ago.

Luca leaving hadn't been what she'd wanted. But it had evidently been what he'd wanted.

The entry door to the upscale clinic—complete with ornate scrollwork carved into the stone around it—was right in front of her. But she couldn't make herself open it.

Not yet.

It had been easier to find him than she'd thought. And yet it was the hardest thing she'd ever done in her life. Well, almost. A part of her whispered she should get back on that plane…he would never be any the wiser. And yet she couldn't, not now. The weight of the baby on her hip reminded her exactly why she'd come here.

She needed him to know. Needed to see his face. Get this whole thing off her conscience. And then she'd be done.

"Scusi."

The unfamiliar word reminded her that she was far from home.

"Sorry," she murmured, stepping aside to let the man

pass. Unfortunately, he then held the door for her, forcing her to make a quick decision. Leave? Or stay?

Then she was through the door, the black marble floor as cold and hard as the words she'd said to a group of people at work thirteen months ago.

The man didn't rush off like she expected him to do, but said something else to her in Italian. She shook her head to indicate she didn't understand, shifting Annalisa a bit higher on her hip.

"English?" he asked.

"Yes, do you speak it?"

"Yes, can I help you find something?" He glanced at the baby and then back at her. "Are you a patient?"

"No, I'm looking for…"

Her eyes skated to the wall across from her, where pictures of staff members were displayed along with their accreditation. And there he was: Hair as black as night. His eyes that were just as dark. But unlike the chilly floors beneath her feet, his had always been warm, flashing with humor. The eyes in the picture, however, were somber, the laugh lines that had once surrounded them barely noticeable.

Elyse swallowed. Had she done that to him?

Of course she had. But her back had been up against a wall. She'd had a choice to make. It had obviously been the wrong one.

She'd chosen the coward's way out. Just as she'd done nine months earlier. But she was here to make amends, if she could. Not in their relationship. That was certainly gone. Destroyed by her pride, her stupidity, and her fear of history repeating itself. But she could at least set one thing right. What he did with that information was up to him.

"You're looking for…?"

The man in front of her reminded her of her reason for coming.

What if he wasn't here yet? It was still early.

Oh, he was here. He worked notoriously long hours. "I'm actually looking for an...old friend. He used to work at the same hospital that I did in the States."

"Luca?"

Relief swamped her. "Yes. Do you know where I can find him?"

He glanced at her, a slight frown marring his handsome face. "Refresh my *memoria*. Which hospital?"

"Atlanta Central Medical Center."

"Ah, I see." Something about the way he said it made her wonder exactly what Luca had said about his exit from the hospital. It didn't matter. Nothing he could have said would be worse than the truth. Although she hadn't orchestrated the layoffs, perhaps she also hadn't fought them as hard as she could have. At the time, a tiny part of her had wondered whether, if she and Luca weren't working together, it might be a way to repair some of the rifts that had been growing between them. Rifts she knew she had caused. But scars from a previous relationship had made her extremely wary of workplace romances.

And Luca hadn't been able to see how their dating could complicate their jobs, even after they'd erupted in a fierce argument during a meeting, disagreeing over the diagnosis of a patient and causing the whole room to stare at them. Kind of like this man was doing now.

"I'm sorry," he said, as if realizing his gaffe. "Come. I'll take you to Luca."

"Thank you. I'm Elyse Tenner, by the way." She shifted Anna yet again. She'd gotten her directions wrong, leaving the bus a few stops too early, and the heat was taking its toll on her. So much for going in looking cool and unruffled.

"Nice to meet you. I'm Lorenzo Giorgino. I work with Luca here at the clinic. I'm one of the neurosurgeons." He held out his arms. "Why don't you let me take her? You look tired."

Yet another blow to her confidence. But he was right. She was exhausted, both physically and emotionally. Between jet lag and the long walk, she could use a place to sit down.

She hesitated for a moment, then he said, "I promise not to break her. I have two...*nipoti*. What's your word for it? Nieces?"

Smiling, she held Anna out to him. She should have brought her baby sling, but she hadn't been able to think straight since the plane had touched down. Nerves. Fear.

Hadn't Luca told her he was in no hurry to have children? He had. More than once, in fact. She swallowed hard, even as this doctor's hands cradled the baby like an old pro, speaking to her in Italian.

He glanced at Elyse, just a hint of speculation in his eyes. "Ready?"

Not at all, but she wasn't going to make her confessions to anyone other than Luca himself. So she lied.

"I am. Lead the way." In handing Anna over, the die had been cast and her decision made. She was going to walk into Luca's office with her head held high and tell him that Anna was his daughter, and then hope that, in doing so, she'd made the right decision.

Luca stared at the EEG readings in front of him. Taken from a six-year-old boy, they showed the typical running waves of a Rolandic seizure. Benign. Filippo would more than likely outgrow them. Great news for his parents, who were worried out of their minds. It was always a relief to have a case where there was no threat to life. Just a temporary bump in the road.

Kind of like his time in the US had been. One big bump in the road, followed by a wave of smaller ones that still set him back on his ass at odd moments. But he thought it was getting better. His mind dwelt on her less. Or maybe it was just that he kept himself so busy that he didn't have time to think about her.

Kind of like he was doing now?

"Porca miseria!"

A second or two after the words left his mouth, there was a knock on the door to his office. Great. He hadn't mean to swear quite that loudly.

"Yes?"

Lorenzo appeared in the doorway, holding a baby.

Shock stilled his thoughts. "Everything okay?"

"Someone is here to see you."

It was obviously not the baby, so he raised his brows in question.

"She said she worked with you in Atlanta."

A section of his heart jolted before settling back into rhythm. He'd worked with a lot of people at Atlanta Central.

"Does this person have a name?"

"I'd probably better let her tell you herself." Lorenzo switched to English.

This time the jolt was stronger. Lasted longer. Surely it wasn't… But the look on his friend's face told him all he needed to know.

He hadn't dated since he'd returned to Italy and didn't see himself doing so anytime in the near future. And those plans to revisit his decision to leave Atlanta permanently?

Put off over and over until it was far too late to do anything about it.

He hadn't been able to stomach going back to his hospital in Rome either. His parents and two sisters lived there, and he hadn't felt like answering a million questions. Oh, there'd still been the worried texts and phone calls about why he'd suddenly returned to Italy, but since they hadn't been able to see his face, he was pretty sure he'd put their fears to rest. As far as they knew, he'd simply decided to practice in his own country. A short tenable statement. One he'd stuck to no matter how hard it was to force those words past his lips.

He ignored the churning in his stomach. "Okay, where is she?"

Instead of answering, Lorenzo pushed the door farther open and came into the room, revealing the woman who'd driven him out of the States and back to Italy.

Hell!

Chaotic memories gathered around, all of them pointing at the figure in front of them. He swallowed hard in an effort to push them back.

"Elyse? What are you doing here?" There was a slight accusation in his tone that he couldn't suppress. A defense mechanism, another way to hold back the wall of emotion.

Dio. He'd fallen for this woman, once upon a time, and then she'd gone and stabbed him in the back in the worst possible way. Better to let her know up front that he hadn't forgotten.

But why was she in Italy?

When she didn't answer, Lorenzo turned and handed her the baby. Shock flared up his spine. He looked from one to the other as a sudden horrible thought came to him. Did the two of them know each other? Was that why she'd made sure he was fired?

No. Of course not. Lorenzo had never been out of Italy as far as he knew. There was no way the two of them could have met.

"I'll go so you can talk." Lorenzo glanced at Elyse. "It was very nice meeting you."

"Thank you. You as well."

Then he backed out of the room and closed the door behind him with a quiet click.

Something in Luca's brain had frozen in place, the gears all stuck for several long seconds. His ass was also still firmly in his chair, something his mother would have frowned about.

But the memories were still doing their work, each one stabbing his heart and sticking there, like darts on a dartboard.

She ventured closer to the desk. "Luca?"

Somehow he dislodged his tongue, making a careful sidestep around the biggest question in his head while he puzzled through it. "How's your mother?"

He glanced at the baby. Elyse didn't have any siblings, so that wasn't a niece she was holding. Had she adopted a child after he'd left?

"She's still hanging in there. The Parkinson's progression has remained slower than average."

They'd tried an experimental treatment a few years back that had helped tremendously, even if it hadn't rolled back the clock.

"Good." Of course she hadn't traveled all this way just to report on her mother's condition. That left one question: Why was Elyse Tenner standing in the middle of his office, holding a baby? He nodded toward the seat in front of the desk. "Would you like a coffee?"

She sank into one of the chairs with what looked like relief. "I would love one, thank you."

"When did you arrive?" He got up and measured grounds into his coffee press and turned on the kettle to heat the water. The mindless task gave his fuzzy brain time to work through a few of the more obvious items: yes, she was really here, and he was pretty sure she wouldn't be if he'd simply left his toothbrush at her place. So it had to be something important. Important enough to travel across the ocean to see him.

His eyes went to the baby again before rejecting the thought outright. She would have told him before now.

"My flight arrived this morning."

"You have a hotel?"

And if she didn't? There was always his place. His thoughts ventured into dangerous territory.

Not happening, Luca.

He carried the pot with its water and coffee to the desk and set it down before retrieving two cups off the sideboard.

"Yes, I stopped at the hotel first, before coming here."

He poured the coffees and reached into the small fridge beside his desk, hiding his disappointment by concentrating on the mundane task before him. She'd always taken her coffee like he did, with a splash of milk. He added some to both, stirring a time or two before pushing one across toward her.

He studied her face. It was pale and drawn, her cheekbones a little more pronounced than they'd been a year earlier. "So what brings you to Italy?"

There was a marked hesitation before she answered. "You, actually. I need to tell you something."

That jolt he'd experienced earlier turned into an earthquake, pushing all other thoughts from his head except for the one staring him in the face.

"You do?"

"Yes." Elyse slowly turned the baby to face him. "This is Annalisa." Her eyes closed, and her throat moved a time or two before she went on. "She's your—she's *our* daughter, Luca."

A hundred emotions marched across that gorgeous face over the course of the next few seconds, ranging from confusion to shock before finally settling on anger. His hands came together, fingers twining tightly, the knuckles going white. "My what?"

The words were dangerously soft.

He'd heard what she'd said. He just didn't believe it. And Elyse wondered for the thousandth time if it wouldn't have been better just to leave well enough alone. To raise Anna on her own and let Luca stay in the dark about his part in her existence. But she owned it to Annalisa and, if she was honest, to Luca himself, to own up to the circumstances behind their daughter's birth. If he rejected her claim outright, then at least she'd tried.

She probably should have tracked him down during her pregnancy, but it had been a difficult time. She'd been so caught up in grief over his leaving that she hadn't realized she was pregnant until she'd missed her third period. A test had revealed the worst. And she knew exactly when it had happened. That day in her office. The day he'd left the States forever.

She had been going to call and tell him, but each time she'd picked up the phone, she'd gotten cold feet, afraid that hearing his voice would undo any tiny bits of healing that had taken place. She'd kept telling herself she'd do it tomorrow. Except a month of tomorrows had gone by, and then things had suddenly started to go wrong with her pregnancy. She'd been placed on bed rest. Her parents had come to the house to help her. Her mom had been a trouper, despite her own medical issues.

Elyse wasn't even sure the baby would survive at that point, so she'd elected to keep the news to herself in case the worse happened.

And now she couldn't…would never be able to…

Annalisa was the only chance she would ever have to do this right. She swallowed back her fear.

"It's true, Luca. She's yours. I thought you should know." She settled the baby against her shoulder once again.

He swore. At least she thought it was a swear word, from his tone of voice.

God, she'd been right. He didn't want Anna.

She'd been wrong to come. Wrong to tell him.

"You *kept* this from me? All this time? You come waltzing into my office with Lorenzo, who is holding a baby that I think is his niece?" He drew an audible breath. "Only he hands the baby to you. And now you tell me she's *mine*?"

Her chin went up in confusion. "It isn't like it was easy. You left, and you had no intention of coming back, isn't that right?"

"Yes."

"And didn't you insist more than once that you didn't want children?"

That had him sitting back in his chair, his eyes going to Anna. "I did, but that was—"

"I didn't think you'd even *want* to know."

"You didn't think I'd… *Mio Dio.* Well, you were wrong. And my statement about kids, if I remember right, included the phrase 'not right now.' The word 'never' was not mentioned. Ever."

How was she supposed to know that? There were men

who would be just as happy to never father a child and who wouldn't want to know even if they did.

But as she'd taken that choice away from him, he had every right to be angry with her.

"I'm sorry. Things were tenuous at the time." She didn't go into the particulars of the precarious pregnancy or the fact that she would never give birth to another child. Anna might be his concern, but the other stuff? Not so much, since they were no longer a couple.

And that fact hurt more than it should have, especially after all this time.

"Tenuous." His brows drew together. "*Tenuous?* You let a colleague of mine hold my child before I get a chance to, and that's all you can say?"

Yep, she was right. He was mad. Livid, even, and she couldn't blame him. She held Anna close against the tirade.

He noticed it, and his eyes closed. "Dammit, I'm sorry."

The sudden ache in her chest made her reach out and touch the edge of his desk with fingers that trembled.

"No, *I'm* sorry, Luca. It just never seemed like the right time and I couldn't… I didn't want to tell you over the phone." She didn't want to admit how afraid she'd been to hear his voice. And after Annalisa's birth she'd had a recovery period that most new mothers didn't have to worry about. It had delayed any travel plans she might have made. So here they were. In the present.

"When?"

She withdrew her hand. What was he asking? When Anna was born? When she was conceived? That was the kicker. They'd had sex in the aftermath of the announced downsizing, when there had been anger on both sides. Their coming together had been volatile and passionate. But the erotic coupling had solved nothing and only after her missed periods had she remembered that they hadn't used protection.

In the end, the layoffs that she'd hoped would save their relationship—by removing the work dynamics that had bothered her so much—had done the opposite. She hadn't wanted anyone to think she played favorites, and Luca had never asked for special treatment.

But memories of a former boyfriend's behavior had loitered in the background, ready to pounce, warning her of what had happened in the past. Of what could happen again if she weren't careful. Kyle had also been a colleague. He had asked—and expected—her to make allowances for things at work, most of them small and unimportant. But with each instance she'd gotten more and more uncomfortable with the relationship. Just as she'd been ready to break things off, he'd asked her to overlook a mistake he'd made with a patient. She hadn't, and he'd been fired.

She told herself she'd never put herself in that position ever again. Except then Luca had come along and all those warnings had been in vain.

Remembering his question, she decided on the simplest answer possible. If he wanted to do the math, he could. "Anna is four months old."

"Four months." He placed his hands flat on the desk. "I want to spend time with her. Did you come by yourself?"

He didn't ask if she was sure Anna was his. A lump formed in her throat.

"And I want you to spend time with her. That's part of why I came. No, I didn't come alone. Peggy came with me. You remember my aunt?" If her mom had been well enough, Elyse would have asked her to come, but since she couldn't, this was the next best thing. She'd needed the moral support or she might have backed out entirely.

As many times as Luca had asked her out, she might

have held firm to her resolve that there would be no more work relationships after Kyle. Until the day Luca had come out of one of the surgical suites after monitoring a patient's brain waves, white-faced, a grim look of defeat on his face. It had done her in. She'd walked over to him, laid a hand on his arm and asked him out.

He'd said yes. The rest was history. A history peppered with moments of beauty and the sting of pain.

But the way he made love…

The realization that her eyes were tracking over his broad shoulders made her bite her lip and force herself to look away.

God! The attraction was still there—still very real. Even if the fairy tale had crashed to dust around her feet.

But from that rubble had come her baby girl. She would go through every bit of that pain all over again if she was the end result.

"After all this time, why come at all? You could have let things be. Never told me at all," Luca pressed.

The very things she'd told herself as she'd booked her flight.

"It was the right thing to do." Her hand went to Anna's head, rocking her subconsciously, still shielding her.

He looked at the baby for a second and walked over to the window, staring out, hands thrust in his pockets, shoulders hunched. "*La cosa giusta?* The right thing would have been to tell me long before she was born."

"Would it have changed things?"

He swung back around to face her. "I don't know. I wasn't given that choice, was I?"

"No." Maybe she needed to tell him at least a little of the circumstances. "When I said things were tenuous, I meant it. The doctors weren't sure Anna was going to make it for a while. And I didn't see any reason to say anything if…"

All the color drained out of his face, and he walked back to the desk. "*Dio.* What happened? Is she okay?"

She rushed to put his mind at ease. "She's fine. Now. I had placenta previa. It didn't resolve and there were a couple of incidents of bleeding, heavy enough to cause worry." And in the end it had been life-threatening to both of them when it had ruptured. "I wasn't going to do anything that might put her at even more risk."

"And telling me would have done that?" He dragged a hand through his hair.

"I was talking more about physical stress but, yes. Inside I think I was afraid of jinxing the pregnancy. As if telling you might cause everything to fall apart, and I'd lose her. I didn't see any reason for us both to grieve if she didn't survive."

Not that she'd been sure he would. Because she'd convinced herself that he'd be horrified to have fathered a child in the first place.

"And after she was born? Why wait four months?"

She wasn't quite ready to share more than she already had.

"Does it really matter? I'm here now."

He crouched in front of her and touched the baby's arm with his index finger. "I can hardly believe she's mine."

"She is." She wasn't sure if he was questioning Anna's parentage, but either way she understood. Here came a woman who shows up over a year after they break up, claiming he'd fathered her child. "We can do a paternity test, if you want."

"No, I know she's mine." He looked up into her face. "Can I see her?"

She realized Anna was sound asleep, but the baby was still facing away from him.

A tiny flutter of relief mixed with fear went through

her midsection. While she hadn't thought Luca would reject his own daughter outright once he knew she existed, she hadn't been sure what his actual reaction would be.

She carefully turned the baby, cradling her in her arms so that he could see her tiny face. A muscle worked in his jaw and he stroked her hair. "How long are you here?"

"I have a little time left of my medical leave. I want you to get to know her. But…" she hesitated "…I want to have some ground rules in place. Come to an agreement first."

His fingers stilled. "The only agreement we need is that we have a child." There was a hard edge to his voice that told her he wasn't going to let her call all the shots here. And she wasn't trying to.

"I know that, Luca. I'm hoping we can—"

"A daughter. My daughter." The anger had melted away and in his voice was a sense of awe. "Annalisa."

A dangerous prickling behind her eyes made her sit up, teeth coming together in a way that forced it back.

"Yes."

His head came up. "I have a few ground rules of my own. First we are going to figure out our schedules and come up with a plan."

His fingers flipped pages on his phone for a moment, probably looking at his caseload. "I have some free time right now, in fact. So I can drive you back to your hotel, and then we'll sit down and talk about any concerns you might have. But I want to make one thing perfectly clear. I *will* be a part of my daughter's life. No matter how much you might dislike me personally."

CHAPTER TWO

PEGGY SLIPPED OUT of the room as soon as the greetings were exchanged. She promised to be back in an hour.

A prearranged signal to keep Elyse from enduring his company?

His gut tightened in anger, even as his eyes soaked in the sight of his daughter. Now that the shock was wearing off, he could finally look beyond his own emotions and see Anna for who she was.

Unlike her *mamma*'s silky blond locks, which had always driven him to distraction, the baby's hair was black and thick and stuck up around her head at odd angles that made him smile. A red satin bow gathered one of the bunches onto the very top of her head, where it did a tiny loop-the-loop. As dark as her hair was, her skin was Elyse's through and through. It was as pale as the sand on the beaches of Sardinia. When she grew up, she'd probably blush just like her *mamma* too.

Cieli, he'd loved the way Elyse's cheeks had bloomed to life when he'd whispered to her at night. Realizing his gaze had moved from the baby to the green eyes of the woman holding her, he gave a half smile when color swooped into her face. Right on cue. Some things never changed.

And neither did his reaction to them.

Elyse cleared her throat and looked away, jiggling the baby in her arms. "So her full name is Annalisa Marie."

Maybe coming back to her hotel hadn't been such a good idea after all. But he'd wanted this discussion to happen in a more private setting. He didn't want Lorenzo or anyone walking in on them and asking questions before he had some answers.

"Marie. After your mother?"

Her attention turned back to him. "Yes."

He liked the nod to a woman he had come to admire in the few times they'd met, but there was also the sense of lost time…lost opportunities. He hadn't even been able to help choose his own child's name. Hadn't been there to see the first time she'd rolled over—if she had yet—and whatever other milestones four-month-olds normally achieved.

"You gave her an Italian name."

"It was only right. She's half-Italian." She smiled, although there was an uncertainty to it. Had she honestly thought he wouldn't want his own child? Just because of some offhand comment he'd made? His reasons for saying it had had more to do with not scaring Elyse off—he hadn't wanted her to think he was rushing her to deepen their relationship. He did want kids. Just hadn't needed them right that second.

And now he had one. He was already in love, after only knowing her for an hour.

"Do you want to hold her?"

The question made him stop. Did he? His jaw tightened. Another thing he'd missed: holding her at birth.

He could worry about that later, though. Right now, he needed to concentrate on what was in front of him, not what was out of his control, as difficult as that might be.

And, yes, he wanted to hold her. He held out his arms and Elyse carefully placed their daughter in them. Looping an arm beneath her legs to support her, he held the baby against his chest, her baby scent tickling his nose. A sense of awe went through him.

He glanced at Elyse, who had taken a step back and stood watching them, arms wrapped tight around her midsection. There was a look on her face that he couldn't decipher. Despite the bitterness and chaos of their breakup thirteen months ago, he and Elyse had at least done something right. They'd made this tiny creature. Murmuring to her in Italian, so her *mamma* wouldn't understand, he turned and walked toward the hotel's window and looked out over the city.

"You don't know me yet, Annalisa, but I promise you will." Was that even realistic? How long was Elyse planning to be in Italy? She'd said she had a little medical leave left but hadn't specified how much.

When would she be back?

Bile washed up his throat when he thought of going months or a year between visits. But how could it be any different than that? Atlanta and Florence might as well be on separate planets.

He looked through the window at the city below. "This is part of your heritage, Anna. I want you to see Italy. To grow up speaking its language." He was going to make that happen, somehow.

A sound behind him made him look back. Elyse had moved to the front door, as if ready to push him out of his daughter's future before he'd even planted himself into her present. What he'd said was the truth, though. He was going to be a part of her life.

He could start by making sure they were all under the same roof for the duration of her stay. "You should come stay at the house, instead of at the hotel. I have some spare bedrooms. Your aunt will come as well, of course."

"I don't know." She bit her lip. "It might be better if we stayed here at the hotel."

"Why?"

He was already booked solid with appointments at the hospital for the next month. He couldn't just blow them all off and take a vacation. Especially not a couple of the patients who were set to undergo treatment in the coming days.

He crossed the room. "You've had Annalisa to yourself for four months. I'd like you to be there when I get home. When I get up."

Hell, was he talking about wanting Anna there? Or Elyse? He'd better make it clear. "I want as much time with her as possible. And there's a kitchen and more room to spread out than you have here. It'll make it easier on everyone."

"I don't…"

He shifted the baby into one arm, tilting Elyse's face with the crook of his index finger. "Say yes. It would mean a lot to me."

Something flickered through her green eyes before she said, "Are you sure? It'll be for a whole month."

A month. Said as if it were an eternity, when really it was only a millisecond. But at least now he knew how long he had with his baby. "A month is nothing."

The weight of his daughter in his arms felt right. Good. He didn't want to give that up. Not in a month. Not in a year. Not in a lifetime.

With her head still tilted, they stared at each other.

"Is it?" Her words came out breathy, lips still slightly parted.

Damn. His midsection tightened in warning. A warning he ignored, leaning closer even as she seemed to stretch up toward him.

Annalisa chose that moment to squirm, and fidget, giving a soft cry. The spell was broken, and he stepped back.

"Sorry," she said. "She's getting hungry." The breathiness was gone, replaced by a wariness he didn't like.

He handed the baby over, watching as Elyse went to the bed and sat, unbuttoning her blouse and helping the baby latch on.

The fact that she did it right in front of him made the tenseness in his chest release its hold.

He'd been her lover, for God's sake. Why should he be surprised?

What did surprise him was that she'd come to Italy at all. Did she really care about him getting to know his daughter? Or was she simply assuaging any future guilt she might feel if Annalisa asked questions about who her father was?

Did it matter?

Yes, it did. Because her motivation behind this trip would set the tone for their future encounters. If she was just looking for the occasional photo op to show that she'd made the effort, she was going to be sorely disappointed. He wanted—no, he *intended*—to have an actual relationship with Anna. He would not be content with being the type of absentee father who did nothing more than send an occasional gift at birthdays or Christmas.

Adorable snuffling sounds came from the bed, where the baby still nursed. Suddenly he couldn't bear to watch anymore, looking on from the outside.

"I'm going down to get a drink. Do you want anything?"

Elyse looked up, the slight smile that had been on her lips fading. "A water, if it's not too much trouble?"

"No trouble at all."

A few steps later, he was opening the door, tossing one last look over his shoulder as he exited. But not before his eyes met hers and he saw the one thing he'd never wanted to see in them: fear. What was she afraid of? That he might try to take Annalisa away from her? He would never do that. But he also wasn't going to simply step back and pretend his child didn't exist.

The elevator ride gave him the little bit of space and time he needed. It unclogged the lump in his throat and eased the ache in his chest. At least for the moment.

She'd agreed to come to the house. That was something. She hadn't refused outright.

There was no sign of Peggy in the empty lobby where he asked for a coffee and Elyse's water. It made sense. The Peggy he'd known in the States was kind and considerate. She might make it a point to stay away for more than an hour, if she thought they needed the time to work out stuff with the baby.

Luca had juggled some of his calendar, but he still had appointments this afternoon, so he wouldn't be able to stay long as it was.

Dammit. He could just clear his calendar for the rest of the day—or a week, for that matter—but it wasn't fair to the clinic's patients. And even shuffling the cases to other neurophysiologists in the area would be a challenge. He was sure everyone else was just as slammed as he was. This was tourist season and a busy one for most of the doctors and clinicians in the city.

So what did he do?

All he could do. Make sure he used his time with Elyse and Annalisa wisely and hope that he could find a compromise that would suit all of them. She'd agreed to move into his house. They'd start with that.

Why had she agreed to stay at his home?

The expression on his face when he'd looked at her,

that's why. The raw emotions that had streamed through her. The way he'd gripped his daughter tightly as if afraid to let her go. None of that fit with the man who'd said with such confidence that he didn't want children.

It was one of the million and one excuses she'd told herself every time she'd picked up the phone to call him and then set it back down again. She hadn't been sure how Luca would react to the news that he'd fathered a daughter, which was why she'd finally decided to come to Italy and look him in the eye. If he'd shown any hint of horror or rejection at the news, Elyse would have been devastated. She would have turned back around and caught the first flight out of Italy to save her daughter the pain of having a father who didn't want her.

But he hadn't rejected her, had insisted he wanted to be a part of her life. The distance between Italy and her homeland was going to make that extremely hard.

If he were still in Atlanta, it would have been so much easier.

Would it have been?

It wasn't like she'd could have hidden the weight gain from him. He'd have known. Plus the added stress of having him right there might have made an already difficult pregnancy worse.

And knowing Anna was going to be her only child?

None of this was easy, and having him stand there as she'd nursed had driven that point home. It was a relief to have him leave. It gave her enough time to finish up, since Annalisa was barely hanging on, her long dark lashes fluttering as she got sleepy.

Moving the baby to the crook of her arm, she quickly closed herself back up before lifting the baby to her chest and gently rubbing her back until she burped. And a good burp it was too. Elyse chuckled and got up to put the baby in the portable crib she'd brought on the flight with her.

Anna shifted in her sleep, raising small fists that slowly floated back down until they were at her sides.

Wow. She could stare at her daughter all day long. There were times she found herself forgetting what she was supposed to be doing because of it. Once she started back at the hospital, that would all change and life would become chaotic once again.

One month. That's all she had left.

She didn't want to think about how long it would be until Luca could see Anna again. Elyse would be able to follow the minuscule day-to-day developments of their daughter's personality and physical growth.

He would miss out on so much.

But she didn't know how to make it better.

Maybe he could move back to the States.

And do what? Her hospital's neurology department was still operating on a skeleton crew and they weren't looking to expand that area. But there were other hospitals and other clinics. Surely he could find a place at one of those, just like she'd thought he would do all those months ago.

Why would he, though? She'd been awestruck at the little bit of Florence she'd seen as she'd come in. The city was gorgeous, with true old-world charm that couldn't be matched. The Florence Cathedral and its domed roof was one of the most beautiful buildings she'd seen in her life. She needed to make a point to get a closer look at it. Then there was the Pitti Palace and so many other historic sites that she wanted to explore. Maybe while Luca was at the hospital, working, she, Peg and the baby could do some sightseeing.

After seeing where he came from, she couldn't imagine him wanting to move back to Atlanta. But maybe the baby would change that.

Did she want it to? It was hard seeing him again. The punch to her senses had been just as jolting as the first time she'd laid eyes on him. And when he'd tipped up her face... God. For a second, she had been sure he was going to kiss her. Had wanted him to so badly.

How much worse would that be if they lived a half-hour apart? Or maybe even closer than that? Or saw each other every day? She was obviously not as over him as she'd thought.

There was a quiet knock at the door and then Luca came in, holding a coffee in one hand and a water in the other. Suddenly she was wishing she'd asked for one of those instead of the water. "Thank you," she said as she took the bottle, her eyes still on his cup.

He must have noticed her wistful gaze because he said, "Did you want coffee?"

"No. It's okay. I'll just have water." She uncapped her bottle and took a quick slug, the cold liquid making her stomach clench as it hit. She couldn't repress the slight grimace. She drank water because it was good for her, but it had never been her favorite beverage.

"Are you sure you don't want some? It has milk. Just like you like."

Something about that sent a rush of moisture to her eyes. She wasn't even sure why. He'd given her coffee in his office too. It had to be the stress of the trip and everything that went with it. Before she could stop herself, she blurted out, "Could I? Just a sip."

"You're the one who introduced me to milk in my coffee." He smiled and handed her the cup, the heat of it in her hands a welcome change from the incessant blowing of the air conditioner. She took a tiny sip.

Oh! That was good. Rich and dark and full of flavor. She took a second sip and then a third before finally forcing herself to hand the cup back.

"Are you sure you don't want more?"

"Positive. But that was delicious."

He smiled. "Italian. Hard to beat."

Yes, it was. And not just the coffee. She'd missed him. Missed the good times. The lovemaking. The laughter. But she didn't miss what had come toward the end. That huge fight during the meeting about the patient's diagnosis had caused a major rift between them. Add that to her growing uneasiness about their relationship, her fear that she would repeat the mistakes she'd made with Kyle. And then the final blow of the downsizing. She hadn't even been able to warn Luca about it before it happened due to that same fear of showing him preferential treatment.

It was easier with him gone. She kept telling herself that, even though easier didn't necessarily mean better. It was just less complicated.

Less complicated? Was she kidding? They had a baby now. She shook that thought away, washing the coffee down with another sip of water, as if that would take care of the predicament she found herself in. If she'd had an abortion she wouldn't be here right now.

And yet... Her eyes went to the baby's crib. There's no way she'd give any of this up, even if she could.

"Remind me to buy some Italian roast coffee before I go back to the States."

"It won't be the same as drinking it here."

No, it wouldn't. Life itself wasn't the same since he'd left. But he'd made it pretty obvious back then that he wasn't interested in working things out.

Maybe they'd been similar in all the wrong ways. They were both neurologists, even if their respective specialties had subtle differences to them. Elyse treated patients, and while Luca dealt with patients as well, his side was more involved in testing, interpreting and diagnosing. But the two subspecialties overlapped. A lot. And there had been times she'd been certain of a diagnosis and had spoken her mind. Luca had never challenged her.

Until that one difficult case, when he'd done so during a staff meeting. If he'd been a nurse, a tech, or even another doctor, it might have been a nonissue. She could have listened and then made a decision based on the evidence at hand. That would have been that. But because it was Luca, she'd found herself wanting to defer to him. Not because she thought he was necessarily right but because of their relationship. And she knew herself well enough to know it would happen again. Why? Because she'd been there once before with Kyle.

If she and Luca had worked at different hospitals, those murky situations wouldn't have arisen in the first place. They could have...

She sighed, cutting herself off. All the might-haves in the world wouldn't change the reality of what was. Or the fact that he'd clearly found it easy to leave Atlanta—and her—behind.

Luca sat in one of the two club chairs in the room, backed by a wall that was thickly textured, like those in many of the buildings she'd seen. Elyse perched on the edge of one of the two beds. Thank goodness the maid service had already been and tidied up. It might have made an already awkward situation even more unbearable.

Elyse decided to tackle the elephant in the room. "So where do we go from here, Luca?"

"I don't know." He glanced at the crib, where the baby was currently sleeping. "Right now, I'm wishing I had more than a month with her."

"I know. I wish you did too. But my maternity leave is going to end. I don't see how I can extend it." She didn't add that she hadn't been sure of his reaction.

The fact that he was sitting here saying he wanted more time with Anna created an entirely different problem.

She went on. "If you have any ideas—other than my leaving her behind—I'm open to suggestions." She hadn't meant it as a jab at the past, but the quick tightening of his lips said he'd taken it as one.

"I would never ask you to leave her."

"I know that."

His elbows landed on his knees, hands dangling between his strong thighs. Thighs that she'd once…

Nope. No going down that path, Elyse. That's what had gotten her in trouble in the first place.

Luca had captured her attention from the moment he'd walked onto her floor at the hospital. Only she had just gotten out of a difficult relationship with Kyle a year earlier and hadn't been anxious to repeat the experience. She'd resisted going out with him, feeling proud of herself, until he'd walked out of that surgical suite that day looking like a beaten man. He'd touched her heart, and the rest was history. She'd told herself the attraction would eventually burn itself out. It hadn't.

Even now, she knew she still wanted him.

He looked up. "I think we're overlooking the obvious solution."

Her heart leaped in her chest. Was he saying he wanted to get back together?

And if he did?

She swallowed. He lived here, and she lived in Atlanta. Besides, the damage had been done. He'd never forgive her for firing him. He'd made that pretty clear when he'd left.

"I guess I'm still overlooking it, because I don't see an obvious solution at all."

"We could get married."

Her mouth, which had been open to make a completely different suggestion, snapped shut again. Surely she hadn't heard him correctly?

"I'm sorry?" Maybe he *was* saying he wanted to get back together. But marriage? Um, no. Not a possibility.

She hurried to send the conversation in a completely different direction. "Maybe you could just move back to the States? We could work out an agreement for visitation."

Why had she said that? Maybe because that was the only obvious thing her brain could catch hold of. They could work at different hospitals and be aloofly friendly. Like those famous divorced couples who managed to get along for the sake of their kids.

"That's not quite what I had in mind."

"I can't marry you. We don't even like each other anymore." She forced out the words, even though they were a lie. She did like him. A little too much, in fact.

"You can't marry me? Or you won't?" Luca got up from his chair and went over to stand by the crib. He leaned over, fingers sliding over the baby's forehead, pushing back some dark locks of hair. Then he twirled the tiny ponytail in a way that made her stomach clench. Watching him with their baby girl set up an ache she couldn't banish.

It wasn't something she was likely to see every day as Annalisa grew up. But she couldn't marry him. Aside from the fact that he didn't love her—he'd as much as said so by not challenging her comment that they didn't even like each other—she couldn't have any more children. She had barely had time to grieve over that fact herself, much less tell anyone else.

Lord, she shouldn't have come here.

"Both. Getting married just because of Anna would be wrong. And not fair to either of us."

He turned to face her with a frown. "Is there someone else?"

"What? No, of course not." She gave a nervous laugh. "I've just had a baby. There's no time for romance."

"But there would be if the timing were better?"

"That's not what I'm saying."

"Well, I can't move back to the States right now. Not with my caseload."

Disappointment winged through her even though she knew he was right. He couldn't just pick up and leave at a moment's notice. "It was just a suggestion."

He looked up, his gaze holding hers in a way that made her swallow. "You're currently on maternity leave. No patients or boyfriends waiting in the wings, right?"

Something began unfurling inside of her. Something she hadn't thought about. Something she hadn't even wanted to think about. Was he going to ask her to marry him again? If so, would she be able to resist?

"No, but the no-patients thing is only for a month, and then I have to be back."

"What if you didn't?"

"Sorry?"

"What if you didn't go? Instead of me moving to the States, what if you stayed here—in Italy—instead?"

CHAPTER THREE

PEG ARRIVED BEFORE Elyse could give him an answer to the staying-in-Italy question.

But the look of horror on his ex's face said that marriage was off the table. For good. He wasn't even sure why he'd asked that. It had just come to him as the easiest solution as he'd stood over his daughter's crib. But Elyse had made it clear that the chances of a marriage between them working were just about nil: they didn't even like each other. He could only assume she was speaking for herself.

Although he hadn't liked her very much either when she'd kicked him and the others out of their jobs. But after arriving back in Italy, he'd been the one doing the kicking…and it was his own behind. He should have stayed and finished that last fateful conversation—even if it had only been to gain closure. But he'd been so hurt and utterly furious that he couldn't have found the words in English to express any of it.

"Everything okay?" Peg looked from one to the other, a worried expression on her face.

Her niece gave her a smile that didn't quite reach her eyes. "Great."

It wasn't great. It was frustrating. He felt totally impotent to change things right now. But he was going to. Was going to fight, if necessary, to be involved in his daughter's life. Elyse marrying him would have made sure that happened. Maybe she was right to refuse. Kids were pretty intuitive nowadays. Annalisa would have eventually seen right through the sham, setting them up for a messy divorce down the road.

So no tying the knot. But surely they could live in the same vicinity. Or at least the same country. If she could put off going back to work for three months or maybe even six, he might be able to swing moving back to the US. Even if that prospect didn't thrill him like it once had.

Only with Elyse explaining to Peggy that they were going to be staying at his house, the chance to talk about things was gone. For now. He'd just have to pull her aside or sit them down when they didn't have an audience and hash it out.

And afterward? If she agreed to stay in Italy? She would have to remain in his house for the duration, because she wouldn't be able to afford a villa or even an apartment without working.

Luca wasn't at all sure how he felt about that. Especially after the way he'd reacted to her a few minutes ago.

He scribbled down the address and handed it to Elyse. "Just ask a cab to take you to this address. I'll let my housekeeper know to get a couple of rooms ready."

"Housekeeper?"

The way she said the word made him uneasy. "Emilia. She doesn't live there. Just comes during the week to clean the place up. Today happens to be one of those days. She won't mind. And she normally fixes a couple of meals and puts them in the fridge for me. There's a ton of food, so don't worry about cooking."

"That was part of the reason you wanted us to stay at your place, though, because you had a kitchen we could use."

He smiled. She'd caught him. "I said you could use it, but I didn't say you had to cook in it."

"No, you didn't."

But her voice said she was beginning to have some misgivings, so maybe it was time to make himself scarce before she changed her mind. She'd already turned down his proposal of marriage, he didn't want her backing out of anything else. "I would go with you, but I have a patient scheduled in half an hour."

Peg spoke up. "We'll be fine. And thank you for letting us stay in your house. It will be a lot more comfortable for the baby than the hotel...won't it, Elyse?"

"Yes. Thank you."

The prodding and the reluctance of Elyse's response made his smile widen. He had an odd ally in Peggy, but if it got him closer to his goal—having his daughter within reach—it was worth it.

"I should be home before dinner. Just rest. The recovery time for jet lag is one day per hour of time difference."

"In that case, we'll be well recovered by the time..."

She let the sentence trail away, and he wasn't sure if that was a good thing or a bad thing. Was she thinking about staying longer than a month? Or warning him that she would soon be leaving?

He was sure she and Peggy were going to have quite a discussion once he walked out of that door. Going over to the crib one last time, he murmured to Annalisa, telling her he would see her in a few hours. And hopefully his time with her would be measured in years, rather than just a few short weeks.

"Mary Landers, aged forty-three, a tourist from the US who has been having seizures over the last two weeks.

She's in the MRI machine right now. The team could use a second look."

The receptionist at the front desk had already alerted him of that fact when he'd arrived. But his favorite nurse always liked to chat for a minute. His scheduled patient had already been advised that he'd be a few minutes late.

"I'll head up there now. Anything else I should know?"

With her silvery hair and friendly personality, he and Thirza had hit it off immediately. He could count on her to give him additional information on patients if he needed it, rather than having to look things up in the system. The fact that she had an eidetic memory was a great asset for the clinic.

"She got a workup at one of the neighboring hospitals and they suspected a brain tumor because of the cluster of symptoms that came with the seizures, but their scan didn't turn up anything concrete. They've added contrast to the one done here, hoping to get a better view of the way the vessels are laid out."

"Do you remember the cluster of symptoms?"

She brandished a slip of paper and a smile. "Of course. I wrote them down for you."

"Grazie."

He was glad of the work. It would take his mind off the fact that he would once again be living with Elyse. Only temporarily, though, and he'd decided that was a good thing. Elyse was right. Marriage would have been a mistake.

Going up the stairs, because waiting for the elevator had never been his style, he exited through the door on the third floor and went to the imaging section. Once there, he used his passkey to get into the observation area.

"Luca, glad to see you. We still have about ten minutes before the scan is finished."

"Where's Lorenzo?"

"He's in surgery. He'll be down as soon as he finishes up."

The city of Florence was a tourist magnet, and they treated people of many nationalities. It helped that several of the doctors at the clinic spoke English with varying degrees of fluency. Faster communication meant faster treatment.

He glanced down at the paper in his hand: Seizures, double vision in the left eye, tremor on that same side, muscle weakness. He could see why the other clinic had initially thought she had a brain tumor. They did present with similar symptoms.

"Hey! Stop!" One of the techs was staring down at the patient. "She's seizing!"

The whole room went into action. They retracted the sliding table from the imager, while multiple staff members rushed into the room. Thank God they didn't allow family to observe the procedures.

A few minutes later, after administering an injection of lorazepam, they were able to stabilize her. She slowly regained consciousness, totally unaware of what had happened. She remembered a momentary sense of confusion just before the seizure hit.

Luca frowned. "How close were we to getting those scans finished?"

"About seven minutes."

"Before putting her back in the tube, let me look at what you have. Maybe we won't have to finish it."

Going back into the control room, they scrolled through the scans, the contrast agent helping to visualize blood vessels.

Dannazione! Everything looked pretty normal.

Wait.

"Can we replay those last images?"

The tech backed the slides up and slowly went through them again.

"There." He tapped a pen to the screen where a small, hyper-dense lesion nestled in the left ventricle. "See that?"

"I do. And I can understand how the other hospital missed it. Cavernoma?"

"It looks that way."

A cavernous malformation wasn't like an arteriovenous malformation, where the high pressure in the vessels put the patient at risk of a stroke or brain bleed. Cavernomas were normally asymptomatic, in fact. But since this patient had presented with both seizures and neurological deficits, the cavernoma was probably the cause and would have to be treated.

The problem was, the ventricles were deep in the brain and traditional microsurgery in those areas didn't always go well.

Elyse would love to sit in on this case.

Maybe she could. And it might be a way to coax her into staying longer. There was no reason she couldn't observe or weigh in with an opinion, was there? As long as she wasn't actually treating the patient, it should be fine.

"What do you think Dr. Giorgino will want to do?"

"I think he'll want to do a combined approach. Ventriculoscopy followed by microsurgery."

"Tricky," said the tech.

"Yes, but by getting an actual look at it, rather than just an MRI image, there's a better chance of success. I saw one of them done when I was in the States." It had actually been one of Elyse's patients. She'd performed the surgery and successfully removed the cavernoma. As far as he knew, the patient's symptoms had completely subsided afterward. "I actually know someone who's done a resection of one of these. I'll put her in contact with Lorenzo."

Again.

Lorenzo Giorgino—the good-looking man who'd held Anna in his office—was one of the top neurosurgeons in Italy. And he actually welcomed outside advice, unlike some specialists. Hopefully Elyse would be willing to help. She could even consult over the phone if she didn't want to actually come in to the clinic.

A little whisper at the back of his brain questioned whether that was a good idea. He'd had a visceral reaction when he'd found out the baby in Lorenzo's arms was actually his own daughter.

But they were all grown-ups. He could handle it.

Luca let the team know they'd found the problem and didn't need to put the patient through another round in the MRI machine. It would be up to Lorenzo and some other specialists to recommend treatment to control her symptoms until a surgery date could be set. The sooner the better.

As soon as that was resolved, he moved on to see the rest of his patients, putting Elyse, Lorenzo and everyone else out of his mind.

"Of course I'll help. I'd love to look at the scans."

Elyse was surprised that Luca had asked her to consult on a case after what had happened in Atlanta.

But this was Italy, not Atlanta. She was no longer the one in charge of his department. She was on Luca's turf now.

"I remembered the cavernoma case you had. The patient had a really good outcome, if I remember right."

"Yes, she's had no more problems since. It was in the right lateral ventricle rather than the left, but the procedure would be the same. You have a neurosurgeon who can perform it?"

She and Peg had moved into the house that afternoon. Her aunt loved it. She'd taken Annalisa into the garden to explore while Elyse had curled up on the couch with a magazine, which was where Luca had found her.

Even his housekeeper had left for the day. And meeting her had turned out to be a lot less awkward than Elyse had expected it to be. She wasn't sure if the woman knew the exact circumstances surrounding her sudden arrival, but it had to be pretty obvious. A woman shows up at her boss's door with a baby in tow…it didn't take a genius to figure it out. Emilia had eyed her daughter with interest, but the kindness behind the glance had prevented Elyse from bristling.

"We do. It's actually the doctor who brought you up to my office yesterday. I don't know how many, if any, of these he's done, but he's an excellent surgeon. One of the best."

"If he's careful and really pays attention to where he is at any given second, he should be fine."

"Which is why I wondered if you'd speak with him and compare notes. He's a good guy, I'm sure he'd be amenable."

"He seemed nice. I'll need to talk to Peg and see if she's okay with me going, but it sounds fascinating. And much better than lying around your pool all day, nice though that is."

He smiled, coming over to sit on one of the chairs flanking the couch. "You could always treat this like a vacation. Where's Annalisa, anyway?"

"She's in the garden with Peg. She should be in any moment. Whatever your housekeeper left in the oven smells divine, by the way. I could get a little too used to this."

Then realizing he could take that as agreement to his marriage proposal, she added, "At least for this month. I haven't decided on moving to Italy, though, Luca. I'm not sure I'm ready to leave my job. I don't even know what I would do here."

"It wouldn't be forever. Could you at least ask for your leave of absence to be extended? Just long enough for us to think things through properly. I don't want either of us to feel rushed and then later be unhappy with the decisions made."

He'd done that exact thing once. Only there was no hint that he was unhappy with that decision.

He was right. A month was a very short time to come up with a plan for a lifetime.

"I don't know if they'll let me. I have a contract that spells things out." What if they decided to let her go just like they had Luca and the rest of them?

Well, her former colleagues had all bounced back, from what she'd heard from various sources. Surely she would too, if it came to that. She was pretty sure any of the larger hospitals in Atlanta would welcome her on board. She just wasn't sure she would welcome them. She'd been at Atlanta Central Medical Center ever since she'd graduated from med school. She didn't know anyplace else.

That fact may have led her to make her own rash decisions. Like staying on at the hospital instead of walking out with her team in protest at the firings. Everything had happened so fast she'd had no time to digest what it really meant to her.

She set aside the magazine she had been looking through when Luca leaned forward. "Will you at least try? Ask them and see if it's a possibility? If it's not, and you're not willing to quit, then we have some things that need to be done quickly. Like getting my name added to her birth certificate."

A zip of shock went through her. Oh, Lord, she hadn't even thought about that. Hadn't thought about much other than informing him that he had a daughter. And now when she thought about it, that had been a pretty cold-blooded way to go about it. This was his child and yet in her head she'd made it into a mere formality, like a business letter: *We would like to inform you that...*

Annalisa was anything but business-oriented. She was a living, breathing human being who had a mother...*and* a father. To make it about anything else would be criminal. Maybe marrying him wouldn't have been as big a stretch as she'd made it out to be. It would make officially naming him as Anna's father easier.

Her heart cramped. But to marry him for anything other than love... She couldn't do it.

She wasn't sure how to add him to Annalisa's birth certificate, or if they could even do it from Italy. He was right. She needed to at least ask the hospital for more time off. If they said no, her decision was made. But if they said yes...then she had some decisions of her own to make. And quickly.

"I'll call the hospital tomorrow morning and get the lay of the land."

"The lay of...?"

"Sorry. It means see if they're agreeable to an extension."

His English was so good it was easy to forget that it wasn't his native tongue. Some of the expressions didn't make much sense when you dissected them. That was another thing. He spoke excellent English, but her Italian was limited to what she'd learned from Luca and some of that made her blush. Not exactly the kind of talk that occurred around the dinner table. In fact, she could feel her face heat at the memory of some of those desperate phrases muttered in the heat of passion.

She hurried to ask, "Lorenzo speaks English pretty well, if I remember right."

"Yes. Most of the staff have some understanding of English. Anything you or they don't understand, I can translate."

"Thank you. If Atlanta does give me additional time off, I think I'd like to take a language course, if I can have Annalisa there with me."

"If you can't, I'm sure Emilia would love to watch her. Or I could set up a portable crib at the clinic and have her there. With me."

She opened her mouth to argue with him, but then snapped it shut when she remembered she'd already had four months to get to know her daughter. He'd had under a day to adjust to the fact that he was a father. Guilt pressed hard against her chest, making it difficult to breathe.

She uncurled her legs and leaned forward to take one of his hands.

"I'm really sorry, Luca. I should have found a way to get word to you. I just didn't know if she was even going to—"

"You're here now. Let's just leave it at that." Something in his eyes flashed, though, making her wonder if he was really that quick to forgive her.

She let go of his hand, stung by the coolness of his voice. Especially after the way the slide of her palm against his had awakened nerve endings that had gone into hibernation. It had been a long, cold season and there was no end in sight.

Who could blame him if he hated her? She hadn't been that quick to forgive herself. But how much worse would it have been if Anna had gone looking for her father once she reached adulthood and he'd found out about it then? Now, that would have been unforgivable. And both Annalisa and Luca would have missed out on some precious memories.

In the end, she'd done the right thing. Even if it wasn't the easy thing.

"Okay." The whispered word took a while to get out. "I don't know what else to say."

"I know this has been hard on you as well." His gaze softened. "I'm glad you came. Really glad."

With his black hair and dark eyes, he'd been the epitome of tall, dark and mysterious. And with the difference in cultures, his body language wasn't as easy to pick up on as American men's were. Maybe that's why she'd been so drawn to him, even as she'd tried so hard to keep her distance. Unlike her, though, he'd let his feelings come through loud and clear from the very beginning, making her sizzle inside.

That had been wildly attractive. Looking back, it had only been a matter of time before she gave in. Only she'd never expected to be the one doing the asking. But she had. It had seemed inevitable at the time, though.

Luca knew what he wanted and set out to get it. Not something she was used to in the men she'd known. Not even Kyle had been so driven. Getting swept off her feet had been a heady experience.

She just had to be careful that she didn't let his charm affect her all over again or influence her in certain areas of her life. Like talking her into a sham marriage. For a second or two, the word "yes" had teetered on the tip of her tongue. But down that road lay craziness. Even if it had been for *their* daughter. A fact she had to remind herself of several times a day. She was no longer calling all the shots when it came to making decisions about Anna.

Before she could think of anything else to say, he stood

and reached down his hand. "You must be hungry. And tired."

From her position her eyes had to skim up his body to get to his face. Heat flared as her glance swept over parts she'd once known in all their glory.

If it had been anyone else, she might have thought he was standing over her to intimidate her, to make himself look bigger and stronger, but she knew that wasn't how he operated. And other countries didn't have the same bubble of personal space that Americans did. At least, that's what she'd learned from Luca. He tended to stand close. To kiss close. To love close.

Elyse closed her eyes for a second before forcing herself to nod in the hope that he'd take a step backward, so she could stand as well. He must have read her mind, because he did just that, the hand he'd held down toward her dragged through his hair instead. He took a second step back. She climbed to her feet, only to discover that he was still well within her personal space. And with the couch behind her, she had nowhere to go.

His finger lifted to touch her cheek in a way that sent a shiver over her. "We're going to figure this out, Elyse. I promise."

Figure what out? How to kill the emotions swirling inside her that just would not die? Because his touch and the low rasp of his voice were doing just the opposite.

"I hope so."

Just then she heard the back door open and Peg's voice as she chattered to Annalisa.

"Perfect timing all around," he said, moving away from her.

"Yes, it is." Elyse smoothed her shirt down over her skirt with trembling hands, anxious to hide the turmoil whipping through her. She'd hoped all of those odd pangs of need for him would go away with time. And they had faded somewhat, but his presence had evidently popped a trapped bubble of longing, because a stream of it was hitting her system hard. So hard it was difficult to concentrate on anything but the way he looked, his scent, the way she'd once felt in his arms.

Staying at his house, for a week much less a month, was such a big mistake. She hurried over to Peg and lifted Annalisa out of her arms, hugging the baby to her.

Luca came over and chose that moment to kiss his daughter on the cheek, and when he looked up, they were inches apart, his lips heartbreakingly close. And there it was again. That quivery sensation she'd had a minute ago. Then he pulled back, with a smile that was full of hidden knowledge.

He knew exactly what he did to her.

"I'll go get check on dinner," he murmured, and then he was gone.

Her aunt glanced at her, eyes wide. Elyse wasn't the only one who'd noticed the disruption in the space/time continuum.

"Oh, my," she said, "I think I'll go help him. Annalisa is probably hungry for her dinner as well. She was getting a little fussy outside. Looks like I picked the wrong moment to come in."

"Oh, no, Peg. You picked the perfect time, believe me."

"I'm not so sure…"

But Anna *was* fussy again, starting to shift and snort. The precursor to a complete meltdown. The baby wasn't the only one close to a meltdown. She could feel one coming on herself. She threw her aunt a grateful smile. "Thanks, I'll feed her and put her down for a nap, so we can eat in peace."

Peace? Ha! Not much hope of that. Not as long as Luca was around.

Well, she was going to have to figure out how to deal with him before she did something completely stupid.

Like fall for him all over again.

CHAPTER FOUR

"I DON'T KNOW, Elyse, we were counting on having you back on time. Isn't there any way you can keep to your original schedule?"

Not the words Elyse was hoping to hear this early in the morning. She'd dragged herself out of bed, nursed the baby, stuffed her feet into flip-flops and made her way out of the bedroom. Annalisa had gone back to sleep as soon as she was full.

As it was so early, she'd decided to get the thing she dreaded most out of the way. She called the hospital and reached the administrator. He was not overly accommodating, which was normal. She should be happy he was being difficult, that she would have an excuse to leave when her month was over but, oddly enough, she wasn't.

She couldn't blame him. It had been several months already. Her complicated pregnancy had meant not working as many hours as she'd used to. And then she'd been put on complete bed rest. No more patients, no more going into work. At all.

"I'll do my best. I'll let you know in a few days what I've decided." She thanked him and hung up the phone.

The longer she was here, the more complicated things promised to get with Luca. Surely whatever they had to work out could be done in a month. And he'd talked about maybe moving back to the States once his patient load was redistributed, in about six months' time.

Elyse swallowed. In six months Annalisa would be crawling and doing all kinds of other things. And Luca would miss all of it.

How was that fair? But how was staying here for six months fair to her? She would probably have to quit her job, put her career on hold in order to stay. And then there was her mom. Where would she be in six months? Yes, she had her younger sister Peg, her husband and a multitude of friends she could call on. But she only had one daughter: Elyse. And she would only ever have one grandchild.

There was no good solution. Something she'd told herself all day yesterday. They were going to have to come up with some kind of plan, though. And she knew that "plan" needed to include having Anna's father in her life.

That little act of fertilizing an egg had bound them together for life in some way, shape or form. That had been the easy part. The fun part. She shivered; yes, it had been a lot of fun.

Oh, there was fun in raising a child too, but it was definitely life-altering, in more ways than one. Luca would find out the reality of that soon enough. Like giving up months of a career that had taken years to build. He'd told her he couldn't move back to the States because of his patient load and had asked her to move to Italy instead. The problem was, he'd already practiced medicine in Atlanta, so he could take up where he'd left off with his career, whereas she…

She would have to give up everything she'd worked for. Scrabble up the ladder all over again.

Wasn't Anna worth it? Absolutely. But if there was a better solution, she wanted to find it. And that meant some give-and-take on both their parts.

That would be something else they'd have to talk about. She didn't want to scare him, but she also didn't want him to just sit back and be content with coming over and kissing his daughter's cheek periodically. Annalisa's view of men was being formed with each interaction. It was up to both of them to make sure those interactions were meaningful and healthy.

She glanced down the hallway. Peggy was awake, evidently. Her bedroom door was open and when she made her way over there, there was no sign of her. Anna was still sound asleep. She padded to the kitchen, where she found her aunt chatting with Emilia, who was poised to crack an egg on the edge of a bowl.

"Good, you're awake. We were just talking about how you like your eggs." Peggy turned her head and mouthed, Oh, my God.

Elyse forced back a laugh. Her aunt wasn't used to having things done for her. She preferred to wait on people, not the other way around. "You don't have to cook for us, Emilia. We know how to make eggs." She said the words in rapid English before pulling herself up short and slowing way down. "I'm sorry. Did you understand?"

"Yes. I like cook," Emilia replied with a smile.

Hoping Peggy wouldn't jump in and try to take over, she pronounced each word carefully. "Thank you. And I like eggs…scrambled?" She made a stirring motion with her hand, hoping to get across the meaning.

"Why are you talking like that?" Peg asked.

"What do you mean?"

She laughed. "One of Emilia's kids is studying English in the States. She understands quite a bit, she just doesn't like to speak it because she's afraid of making mistakes."

The housekeeper nodded as if in agreement.

Well, Emilia wasn't the only one afraid of making mistakes. Elyse was too. And not just with regard to the language. She was afraid of making a terrible mistake with her daughter or with Luca. One she'd have a hard time recovering from.

Don't hurt either one of them, Elyse.

The thought came unbidden and was unwelcome. She wouldn't if she could help it. Right now she was doing the best she could with what she had.

While Emilia cooked their breakfast, Peg motioned her into the other room. "You're going to the hospital to consult on a case this morning?"

Luca must have told her.

"Exactly how long have you been up?"

"Long enough to sit and have a chat with him." She squeezed her niece's hand. "He wants a relationship with her, honey. You need to give him a chance."

She frowned. "That's why we came here. To tell him about her."

"That's not what I mean, and you know it. He told me he asked you to stay in Italy, but that you weren't sure."

"Did he also tell you he asked me to marry him?"

"He what?" Her eyes went round with surprise. "What did you say?"

Elyse grimaced. "What do you think I said? No, of course. It was an impulsive suggestion. He didn't mean it."

"Are you sure?"

"Very sure. And as for staying, I just don't know how that would work. My administrator basically said he wants me back at the end of a month."

"Are you going to go? This is Anna's future we're talking about."

Elyse looked off into the distance for a moment. "I know. He hurt me, Peg."

"Are you so sure that was a one-way street? He lost his

job, and you were the one who told him. You don't think that hurt *him*?"

"I had no choice about him losing his job. And I felt it was better coming from me than from a hospital bureaucrat."

"I'm not saying what you did was wrong. But it still had to sting."

She shrugged. "He left. Packed up his bags and was gone soon after the announcement."

"And you're afraid he'll do the same to Annalisa? He won't, you know he won't." Peg tilted her head. "Anna is a part of him. They'll always have that connection, no matter what his relationship with you is like."

Something burned behind her eyes. What Peggy said was true. That even if Elyse meant nothing to him, he would always love their daughter.

"You're right as usual."

"I'm going to go back to the hotel, if it's all right with you. It'll be harder for you two to work things out, if I'm hanging around. Unless you need my help with Annalisa. And my vacation is only for a week."

Elyse's eyes widened. "Please don't abandon me."

"I'm not. But you and Luca need this time together— even if it's only related to your daughter. I'm going back to do some sightseeing." She held up a hand. "Don't worry, I'll text you if I run into problems. And if you need a babysitter during the week, I'll be around. After that, you're on your own. And you'll be fine. You all will."

Elyse wasn't so sure about that.

She slung her arm around her aunt's shoulder and squeezed. "I wish I had your certainty, but I do understand." Of course Peggy wouldn't want to be in the room if she and Luca ended up having a huge argument about arrangements. They did need to hammer this out. Without an audience. Even though she hated the thought of being in the house alone with him.

Because of him? Or because she didn't trust herself?

She didn't dare answer that question.

"Thanks for coming with me to Italy. Are you sure you don't want company on your sightseeing tour?"

"I'm positive. I hear there's a romantic gondola tour down the Arno River. Maybe I'll meet a hunky Italian and get lucky."

"Aunt Peggy!"

"Don't you 'Aunt Peggy' me. You're no stranger to the birds and bees or you wouldn't have that sweet little thing in the other room."

She couldn't argue with that.

"You don't even speak Italian."

"Some things you don't need words for. Don't worry. I'll check on you every night until I'm back home in the States."

Elyse smiled. Her aunt was only ten years older than she was, so she was more like a sister than a parental figure. Peggy's husband had been much older than his bride and had died almost five years ago, leaving Peggy a fortune. But it hadn't changed her in the least. She was still the same fun-loving person she'd always been. She'd even insisted on paying for the trip to Italy.

"Make sure you do. Do I need to set a curfew?"

Her aunt laughed. "I'd only break it." She kissed her niece on the cheek. "It's not every day I get to see Italy."

Emilia peered around the corner and motioned to them. Judging from the luscious smell coming from the kitchen, breakfast must be ready.

She guessed Anna would be coming with her to the hospital this morning. She smiled. Well, Luca might as well have his first official reality check about having a baby. He was going to find out it wasn't always convenient.

But Elyse wouldn't change it for the world.

Going into the kitchen, she found two plates already set with eggs, ham, thick slices of what looked like home-made toasted bread, and small pots of jam. "This looks delicious. Thank you so much, but aren't you going to eat?"

"Eat…no…" The woman frowned. "Ate six o'clock."

She must have eaten with Luca, then. Glancing at Peg, she said, "Were you here when Luca was eating?"

Peggy sat and dug into her eggs with gusto. "I came after he was done. Emilia offered to make me something then, but I wanted to wait for you."

"I'm sorry. You should have knocked on the door."

"I knew Annalisa would wake you soon enough. I wanted you to get as much sleep as you could."

"Well, I slept great, thank you."

"I'll pack while you're at the hospital so leave the baby with me."

So much for Luca getting his first taste of real fatherhood. "I can take her with me."

"You'll have her to yourself soon enough. I need a few more snuggles before I go, since it looks like I won't be seeing her for a month. That's going to be hard on everyone back home. Especially your mom."

"I know, but it'll fly by."

And if she decided to stay longer than a month?

There was no easy answer. Luca was Anna's father. Nothing was going to change that. And she realized she wouldn't want to, even if she could.

Luca saw her coming down the hall, those hips swinging to an internal tune that he used to know so well. He'd half wondered if she would skip out on him once she found out that Peggy was going back to the hotel.

Her aunt had told him this morning that she wanted to give them time and space to talk things through. He'd tried to insist that she wouldn't be in the way, but she'd turned out to be almost as stubborn as her niece was.

It must run in the family.

Well, it ran in his family too, so he couldn't fault her there.

And he needed to be realistic in his expectations. Elyse had made concessions in coming here, so he needed to make some too. He was going to turn some of his patients over to another neurologist, so he could spend time with his daughter. They could sightsee, or picnic…or whatever the hell Elyse wanted to do. He wasn't courting her, he insisted to himself. He was courting his daughter, hoping to make up for lost time.

At least he hoped that was all it was. Because every time he saw the woman…

He forced that thought back as she reached where he was standing. "Thanks for coming. I have the patient workup waiting in my office. Lorenzo will meet us there in about fifteen minutes to go over everything. Surgery is scheduled for tomorrow."

"I was surprised that you had your own office."

"Yes, didn't you in Atlanta?"

She smiled. "*Touché*. Yes, I did. Sorry."

"It's fine. Anyway, I thought we could discuss the procedure and then see the patient herself. She's American and will probably be happy to see someone from her homeland besides her husband."

"I'm good with that." She sighed. "This is one of those times that I wished I'd paid more attention in Spanish class."

"Spanish?"

"It might help me at least a little bit. I mean, I know I won't need it with this patient, but what if you want me to weigh in on others?"

"Spanish is closer to Portuguese than Italian, although there are some similarities." He smiled. "I can teach you some. I'd really like Annalisa to learn Italian."

Elyse frowned, and he cocked his head. "Is that a problem?"

"No... I just..." The tip of her tongue scrubbed at her upper lip for a second before retreating, but not before the act made something in his gut tighten. He remembered that gesture and a thousand other ones. They were all there in his memory as fresh as the day he'd put them there.

Dio. Would they ever fade?

He hoped not.

Licking her lips normally meant she was going to say something she thought he wouldn't want to hear.

"What is it?"

"My administrator really wants me back at the end of my leave, so I only have this month. Unless I quit my job."

He wanted his parents and sister to meet the baby, but they lived in Rome, almost three hundred kilometers from Florence. They could make the trip there and back by train in a day, but he'd hoped to be able to spend a week or so in Rome to make proper introductions. They still could. It would just have to be carefully arranged.

He needed to call his parents first and let them know they had their first granddaughter. They would be thrilled, even though his folks were a bit old-fashioned about some things.

"We'll figure something out."

"I hope so."

"Is Peggy at the house with Anna?"

"Yes. Did she tell you, she's going back to the hotel and will be returning to Atlanta as planned?"

"Yes. She told me she was going to talk to you about it."

"She did. I'm not sure how I feel about it, but she doesn't want to be in the way. I guess in case we have bitter arguments about Annalisa."

"And will we?"

She looked at him as if needing to consider something. "I really don't want to fight over her. We're both adults, Luca. I'm assuming we both have our daughter's best interests at heart."

Said as if she wasn't sure that he did. That stung. Made him wonder if she'd ever completely trusted him. With anything. Including her heart.

The end of their relationship said she probably hadn't.

"You assumed correctly. Don't ever doubt it." His answer was sharper than he'd intended it to be and made him realize they were still standing in the middle of the hallway. "Why don't we talk more about Anna after our meeting with Lorenzo?"

"Yes, of course." She looked relieved.

"Elevator or stairs?"

"Stairs, if we can. Especially after that huge breakfast Emilia insisted on fixing us."

He smiled. Emilia had worked for his parents for years, helping them throw elaborate parties, so she did tend to go overboard where guests were concerned. Not that he entertained much outside work. He'd never actually brought a woman to the apartment. Hopefully Emilia wouldn't get any funny ideas. "She thinks everything can be solved by a good meal."

If only it were that simple.

They took the stairs to the third floor, where all of the offices were. Coming out into the main foyer, where leather chairs sat in a large circle on the marble floor, he headed to the far corner, where his office was.

"Why are there so many pictures on the walls? I noticed them downstairs in the entryway as well."

As he saw them every day, they had become so much background noise, but looking at the long line of images he could see how it might look to an outsider. The hospital in Atlanta had been sterile and efficient. But Florence was a city with a rich cultural history as far as art went. "Hospitals have started putting up pictures of nature as a way of enhancing the healing process."

Arched brows went up and she scanned the wall, the bottom half of which was painted blue, whereas a buttery cream covered the upper half. A handrail had been placed along the break in colors, the artwork providing another visual delineation between the two. "Interesting. Do all hospitals in Italy do this?"

"Probably not all of them. It's a relatively new concept. The Clinica Neurologica di Firenze adopted it about five years ago."

"Firenze?"

It was easy to forget, even with all the tourists, that the name of the hospital meant nothing to a non-Italian speaker. "Sorry, it's the way we say Florence."

He smiled, remembering the way she would puzzle through an Italian phrase, trying to make sense of it, when they had been together. She'd loved him speaking Italian while they made love, the little sounds she'd made sending him spinning into space more than once. Long before he'd been ready.

He swallowed. Not something he wanted to remember.

Unlocking his office, he motioned her inside. "What time do you need to get back to relieve Peggy?"

"I think I have a few hours. I'm still nursing, but more

in the morning and at night, since I was getting ready to go back to work. I've been supplementing with bottles for the last couple of weeks."

"Okay, sounds good."

There was a knock on the door and Lorenzo opened the door a crack and said, *"C'è stato um cambiamento di piani."*

Luca motioned him inside, answering him in English. "A change of plans? What kind of change?" He inserted, "Sorry. Lorenzo, you remember Elyse?"

"Yes. Of course." He took her hand and smiled at her. "But you must call me Enzo."

Her cheeks flushed a deep red. "Okay."

What the hell? Luca's eyes narrowed, centering squarely on his friend. "You mentioned that something had changed."

"Yes, Mary Landers has had two seizures in the last two hours. I've moved surgery up from tomorrow to today. In two hours, to be exact. I have to prepare in a few minutes, but I would like to run by you the method I'm planning on using, Elyse, if you don't mind."

"Of course not. Can we go over the chart together?"

Luca pulled the chart he had and handed it to Lorenzo. Soon the pair were going over things, heads bent close as they studied and discussed the findings. He didn't like the way they looked together, her blond locks contrasting with Lorenzo's close-cut black hair. Elyse spoke in quick, concise statements, explaining her case and how it was similar to and different from the one at hand. "My patient didn't have back-to-back seizures like this one, but they're similar. And going in with a ventriculoscopy followed by microsurgery is the same method I would choose if she were my patient."

Lorenzo looked at her and said, "Perfect. *Grazie*. Will you be observing?"

"If possible."

"Yes. There's a microphone in the observation room. If something strikes you during the surgery, feel free to mention it. Also, it might help the patient if you went in and spoke with her beforehand."

"I will. Thanks."

He took her hand again and gave it a squeeze. "See you soon."

Luca frowned. What was with his friend? And since when did he ask anyone to call him Enzo?

But before he could even formulate a response, Lorenzo was out the door.

"Are you sure you have time to observe? It will probably last several hours."

"Peggy has enough supplies for quite a while. I'll give her a quick call though and check." She glanced at him. "Are you scrubbing in as well?"

"They have another neurophysiologist who will be monitoring the patient's readings, but I'll be available to interpret a scan if they need it during the ventriculoscopy."

He remembered the first time he'd heard mention of a burr hole and realized that drilling through the skull was a practice that hadn't entirely faded out with time. It still had its place, and this was one of them.

"I wish embolization techniques worked for these types of malformations, but they don't."

He'd always liked talking about work with her. She was intelligent and thoughtful. Not hurried, not intimidated, even though neurology was still a male-dominated field. She wasn't in it to show anyone up. But she wasn't afraid to push back over a diagnosis either, which he'd witnessed firsthand. The death of a patient had changed things between them. She'd stopped discussing cases with him, had become distant and moody. It had continued until the layoff occurred.

He'd never been able to figure out exactly what had happened between them.

"No, it would be wonderful if it was a relatively easy fix, but with the type of procedure Lorenzo is going to do, he'll have to enlarge the burr hole to double its size and go in manually."

"Hopefully the seizures are caused by the cavernoma and not something else," she said.

"Testing has pretty much ruled out anything else." He paused. "Are you ready to go see her?"

"Yes. And thank you for asking me to come."

"You're welcome."

He put the computer to sleep and they both stood, trying to exit the same side of the desk. They bumped shoulders and she gave a husky laugh as they tried to maneuver and ended up doing a little dance that still put them in each other's path.

"Well, this isn't working." He tried to wait for her to move away first, but she didn't. When he looked at her, her glance was on his face. There was an intensity there that made his head swim.

Suddenly he was on a different plane—transported back through time and space.

Her teeth went to her bottom lip and clamped down, eyes shifting to his chest.

A blaze of heat went through him. Was she checking him out? His brain thought she was and that was enough for certain parts of his body to stir.

"Elyse?"

She didn't answer, but her brows went up, so he knew she'd heard him. She looked like she was waiting for him

to do something. He had no idea what, because the only
thing he could think of doing right now was kissing her.

Unless…that's exactly what she was waiting for.

That was enough for him.

His hands went to her shoulders and he stood there for
several long seconds.

Then he kissed her.

CHAPTER FIVE

THE SECOND HIS lips touched hers, her eyes slammed shut, and she was trapped in a warm sea of familiarity. One she'd blocked from her thoughts until this very moment. His mouth was firm, just like it had been, his taste exactly the same: dark roasted coffee and everything that went along with being Luca.

"*Dio.*" He came up long enough to mutter that single oath before kissing her again.

The word made her whole body liquefy. She could remember long strings of Italian that would help drive her to the very brink of ecstasy and then hold her there until he was ready to send her over the edge. And then he would start all over. A slow, wonderful torture that she never wanted to end.

Her arms went around his neck, and she pressed herself against him, needing to get closer even as he edged her back until her bottom was against the back of the chair. She struggled to balance herself on it, even as she wanted to turn and lean over it, inviting an exploration of a different type.

Lord, she was in trouble. Big trouble, but she didn't want to stop. Didn't want to do anything that would change the course of where this might be headed.

She'd missed him so very much.

His hand went to her breast, palm pressing against her tight nipple with a caress that sent a shock wave through her. And something else.

A warning tingle. Oh, no!

It was the signal that her body had felt the stimulation and completely mistaken the reason for it.

Her hands went to his shoulders and pushed, terrified she would end up with two wet circles on the front of her blue blouse.

As soon as his mouth came off hers, and he took a step back, she crossed her arms over her chest and applied pressure, hoping it didn't look as obvious as it felt. It worked. The tide began to recede.

In the meantime, Luca dragged a hand through his hair that she could swear shook a little. "*Dio*, Elyse. Sorry. I didn't call you to my office for that." His accent was suddenly thicker than normal.

She knew he hadn't. If he'd been interested in sex, there was always the house.

A house they would now be spending a lot of time in… largely alone.

She almost groaned aloud. If something like this happened when they accidentally bumped into each other, what would happen when it wasn't an accident?

Ha! She wasn't about to find out. She would have to keep their daughter between them as much as possible. Surely he wouldn't kiss her while she was holding Anna.

If she was embarrassed now, what would she be like if there were no clothes, no way to hide what was happening?

It was a natural process. Nothing to be ashamed of. She used her breasts to nourish her baby.

But they were also sexual. And right now it was hard to separate one from the other. She wasn't sure she even wanted to. She'd just assumed she wouldn't have sex again until after Anna was weaned, since there were no prospects hovering on the horizon. Not even a blip on the radar.

The breakup between her and Luca had been too traumatic. And with the shared reality of a baby, it was still too raw. Anna connected Luca to her in a very tangible way. That connection was now permanent, like it or not.

He was looking at her, waiting for some kind of response to his apology.

"It was both of us, not just you. I think our emotions—you finding out you have a child and me finding out that you want to be a part of her life—got the better of us."

Did she really believe that? Not for one second. It had been the past coming back to haunt her that had caused it.

"Yes, that must be it." The words were half muttered as if he hadn't really meant her to hear them.

He was staring at her chest, and she realized her arms were still tightly crossed over it. Now that the tingling had stopped she could let the pressure off. She unfolded them and allowed them drop to her sides. There was no way she was going to tell him why she'd been doing that, but hopefully he hadn't seen it as a self-protective gesture. It had been, but not in the way he might think.

She smiled. "Florence is a very romantic city. I'll have to watch my step from here on out."

"No. No, you won't."

The way he said it gave her pause. Was he saying he wasn't going to have a problem staying away from her? Well, that was good. Wasn't it?

Yes, it was. "Well, now that we've settled that, shall we actually go see the patient? Preferably before they prep her for surgery? I'd like to see how she is."

"Of course. The surgical unit is on the first floor, so it's back down the stairs for us. Or would you rather—?"

"The stairs are fine." She needed to keep moving. At

least for now. The hope was that it would keep her from thinking too much.

A few minutes later, they were in Mrs. Landers's room, and she chatted with Elyse in English. The woman seemed relieved to have another native speaker, although she had her husband, and most of the staff spoke English. Maybe it was just knowing that Elyse was in the medical profession that made her feel more at ease. "The procedure should help you feel a lot better."

"Will it clear up my double vision?"

"That's the hope. As well as the seizures and your other problems." She glanced back at Luca for confirmation.

He inclined his head. "You might not notice a huge difference right away, but once the inflammation from the malformation is gone, things should settle down."

"I hope so. Todd wanted me to go back to the States to have the procedure, but I just wanted to get it over with. And we read that this center is one of the best in Europe." She reached for her husband's hand.

"We do quite a few procedures on blood vessel problems. Cavernomas are fairly rare but, even so, they're well studied."

A nurse came in. "It is almost time. Are you ready?" Her English wasn't quite as fluent as some of the others', but it was enough to elicit a smile from their patient.

"More than ready." She squeezed her husband's hand and he leaned down to kiss her on the forehead.

"Love you."

"You'll be here when I get out?"

"I'm not going anywhere, sweetheart. Ever."

The words brought a lump to Elyse's throat. She resisted the urge to look over her shoulder to see what Luca's expression was—or if there was even any reaction at all.

Would he have been like this in the delivery room as she'd had Anna?

It was too late now. She'd never know. The lump turned to an ache that wouldn't go away.

Mary was wheeled from the room and Todd followed her, giving them a nod of his head.

She forced herself to speak. "Do we need to help him find the waiting room?"

"One of the nurses will show him where to go. He can walk with Mary as far as the doors of the surgical suite. It's kind of a ritual. Most loved ones accompany their family members."

"I don't blame them. I would too." She'd had no one but her mom and dad when they'd had to do the C-section for Annalisa. Luca had been long gone.

Not a helpful thought.

She was curious, though. "Did you come to Florence as soon as you left the States?"

She wasn't sure why she asked that, but once the words were out, there was no way to retract them.

"No, I spent some time in Rome with my folks first." He motioned for her to walk down a corridor. "By the way, I would like them to meet Annalisa, if you'd be willing."

That caught her up short for a second or two. She hadn't even thought about that.

"Yes. Of course. I can't imagine there *not* being time, even if I'm only here for a month."

They came to a set of double doors with red lettering that she took to mean authorized personnel only beyond that point. "Do I need a visitor's pass or anything?"

"As long as you're with me, you'll be fine."

Would she? She could remember a time when that hadn't been the case, when being with him had been anything but fine. That had been right before he'd left for parts unknown, and she'd never seen him again.

Until now.

She swallowed. He wanted his parents to meet Annalisa. Of course he did. She was their granddaughter. "How far is Rome?"

"It's about an hour and a half by train. Double that by car."

She remembered his patient load. "You'll be able to get time off work?"

"I should be able to move things around."

Luca led the way to a set of doors each with a number and the words "Sala Operatoria." Operating Suite, maybe? It was amazing how she could kind of decipher certain terms. But that was only if she was standing there studying them. Hearing someone speak was an entirely different matter. Even the word for Florence sounded nothing like the English word. It looked like the word for fire or something.

"In here."

He motioned to a room marked "Sala di Osservazione."

She went through and saw a tiered bank of about fifteen seats. There were already three people in there on the far side of the room chatting in low voices. Judging by their white lab coats, she assumed they were either still in medical school or were first-year residents. It didn't look like an entire class, since none of them had that "professor" look to them.

There was also a microphone hanging front and center, just as Enzo had told her there would be.

Luca found them seats in the front row toward the middle, and she sat, looking at the room below with interest. "Will they pipe sound in here? I know Enzo said we could make comments."

"Yes, *Enzo* did."

Why had he emphasized his colleague's name like that?

Before she could attempt to figure it out, he went on, "There's a microphone hanging above the operating table, just like in the States, and everything in the room is recorded. Surgeons are encouraged to relay what they are doing. All of it will go on record, unless there's an emergency, then everyone focuses on the patient's welfare above all else."

She had turned her head toward him to focus on what he was saying, only she kept finding her gaze dropping to the movement of his lips. Lips that had been on hers a few moments earlier. Not good. That kiss had done a number on her. She needed to forget it. Chalk it up to the rekindling of old emotions.

Only she'd thought those were all dead.

She jerked her attention back to the front, hoping he hadn't noticed. Maybe it was the lack of closure that was messing with her equilibrium. There'd been no time for closure. She'd received word that his job as well as several others were being done away with. She'd announced the news. They'd had frantic sex. And he'd left. Just like that. It had been a whirlwind breakup.

Nothing clean about it.

Her thoughts were interrupted when they wheeled the patient into the room. Enzo entered already scrubbed and ready and was bent over the patient.

"He's talking to her about what's going to happen. He likes to look his patients in the eye before beginning and asking if they have any questions."

"That's a little different than how I do it, but I like it." Elyse normally didn't come in until the patient was already sedated and surgery was ready to begin. But she did stay with them until they came out from under anesthesia and also visited them in Recovery—when they were more likely to remember her.

The surgeon then moved away, and his team gathered around him, except for one of the nurses and the anesthesiologist, who began administering the sedation drugs.

"It looks kind of like a football huddle."

"That is basically what it is. They're getting any last-minute information, and Lorenzo is making sure they know which instruments he plans to use and the order he'll need them." He glanced at her. "They're surgical nurses so they tend to be intuitive, and most of them know what to expect, but it still helps to be reminded."

Yes, it did. Just like she'd reminded herself a few minutes ago that their relationship wasn't just under general anesthesia. It had flatlined and was gone, not surviving what life had thrown at it. She shouldn't go looking for it to wake up and recover, like Mrs. Landers would hopefully do.

Soon the patient was sedated, and the area of her head where the surgery would take place was clipped, shaved and had a sterile drape placed over it.

"He'll do the trepanning first." It's what they had talked about. It would result in the burr hole being drilled to a larger diameter, but the smaller hole gave the endoscope a solid surface on which to rest as it was guided through the delicate tissue.

"Yes. He'll want a precise location and size before actually going in to remove it," Luca replied.

Even though there would be a record of those things on the MRI scans, nothing replaced having a physical look at it.

"I'm surprised you're not down there in the mix." She looked over at the monitor and saw a man to the left of the patient, checking the tracings. A neurophysiologist.

Just like Luca. He would be monitoring the patient's brain function during surgery.

"It was a last-minute change in plans, remember? The surgery was supposed to be tomorrow. I told him I'd be available for a second opinion, if needed."

"You were supposed to be in the operating room tomorrow? What happened? Why aren't you in there now?"

He looked at her, eyes meeting hers. "You happened. Anna happened. I need to free up my time. I'll be doing more of that in the coming weeks."

She swallowed then laid her hand on his arm, squeezing lightly. "I'm so sorry, Luca. Our coming here has totally disrupted your life."

Anna had disrupted hers as well, but she wouldn't trade it for the world.

"Not disrupted. I would call it more...*deviare*."

Her head cocked to the side, trying to figure out what the word meant. Devi...something. Deviate, maybe? From what?

"I think the word in English is to re-road?"

"Ah, reroute?" Okay, that was much better than deviated. Because to deviate from one's planned path was...

Exactly what she'd done. But it wasn't horrible. She'd adapted, and she was happy. Happier than she'd ever been, in fact. The only part that made her truly sad was knowing she couldn't have any more children like her daughter.

"Yes, reroute. But I am glad you came. Glad you told me the truth."

Even though she was more than four months late. More than that, if you counted the pregnancy itself. And she hadn't told him the entire truth, but the rest of her story didn't matter. It didn't affect him. Just her.

She glanced down when the sound of the cranial drill engaged. She remembered practicing how to stop precisely when the skull wall was breached so as not to damage the grey matter below. Newer technology was arriving and there were now drills that came with measured stops that took some of the thinking out of it.

Within seconds, they'd reached their goal, the hole swabbed, and the endoscope fed through. A screen on the far wall went live—she was pretty sure that was for the benefit of those in the observation room. Enzo looked through the overhead surgical microscope as the tube made its way toward the ventricle in question. With each step, he relayed to the listening device what he was doing and what he saw, with Luca translating close to her ear so as not to disturb the others in the room.

The tickle of his warm breath hitting her skin was intimate. Almost unbearably so. But she didn't want him to stop. In fact, she propped her chin on the back of her hand and let herself enjoy listening to the sound of his voice.

"Approaching lateral ventricle. Entering space." There was a pause while Enzo readjusted his instruments and probably took stock of what was appearing on the screen. "Malformation is approximately three centimeters in diameter, causing a slight deformity of the left side."

The voice in her ear stopped when the voice on the loudspeaker halted, but the reactions happening inside her head kept right on going, setting up a weird tingle that made her shiver. She'd told herself to enjoy it, but she was starting to like it a little too much.

There was a period of silence that went on for about thirty seconds. It was almost as if the room had gone into a state of suspended animation, with everyone waiting for Dr. Giorgino's verdict.

As much as she wanted Luca to continue, maybe she'd be better off wishing the surgery ended quickly. Before she did something stupid. Like she had during that kiss.

Enzo lifted his head and spoke. And so did Luca.

"We should be able to dissect it with minimal damage."

The words made her swallow, but it engendered a very different reaction from others in the room. Muscles that were tense went slack with relief.

The surgeon then called out orders as the burr hole was enlarged enough for the instruments he would use. She understood none of it.

"Do you want me to keep translating?"

"If something important happens, I'd like to know, but I'm familiar enough with the surgery to understand what's happening on the screen. Thank you, though. I did want to know what his verdict was."

She forced a smile, telling herself she was relieved that his lips were no longer at her ear. But there was also a sense of loss that she was no longer allowed those kinds of privileges.

He sat back in his chair, and Elyse thought she saw a hint of relief in his own eyes. Maybe she wasn't the only one affected by their proximity.

They'd been very good together in bed. He had taken her places she'd never been before. Her relationship with Kyle had paled beside him. She somehow doubted anyone else would move her the way Luca had, even though their time together hadn't been all that long. Just four months.

She'd never met his parents, although he'd met hers. Then again, her parents lived within an hour's drive of the hospital, while his lived on a different continent.

And yet he wanted them to meet Annalisa. He'd never said whether or not he'd told them about living with her in the States. She'd never asked, because she'd thought they had plenty of time for all of that.

Only they hadn't.

Elyse forced herself to settle in to watch the rest of the

procedure, noting the similarities and differences between what was done in this center compared to what she would have done back home. She made a mental note to herself to research a couple of items to see if anyone was using the techniques she was seeing here. Maybe she could learn a thing or two.

Had Luca carried any techniques back from the States with him? She was curious.

"Did you change the way you do things at all after you came back? Or is neurophysiology basically the same here as it is in Atlanta?"

"Why do you ask?" The look on his face was of genuine puzzlement.

"I don't know. I'm just curious. I've seen a couple of things that I'm going to look into. The order in which Enzo clamped off those blood vessels is a little different. Not in a bad way. I liked what I saw on the screen."

"Ahh, I see. Yes, I think there are things that I probably changed. Things I learned or saw during my time at your hospital that I have applied here."

Your hospital. A sting of pain went through her.

It had been his at one time too. Until she'd severed his connection to it.

Actually, she hadn't severed it. The administration had, and there'd been nothing she could do about it.

You could have quit too. It might have saved your relationship with Luca.

Doubtful. He'd asked her if she had put his name on the list of people to be fired. She hadn't. But at the time she'd been glad it was there, thinking that if she was no longer his boss, maybe some of her conflicted emotions about dating someone she worked so closely with would dissipate. Her reaction had probably been a knee-jerk one, and not entirely rational, but it had been very real. To her, anyway.

He was extremely talented, she'd thought. He could have worked anywhere in Atlanta.

He hadn't wanted to do that, though. Neither had he seemed interested in salvaging what they'd had.

How much of that had been her doing? Probably a lot. And she owed him an apology.

Keeping her voice low, she said, "Luca, I'm sorry for the way things at the hospital unfolded. I know it wasn't easy. For any of you." She hesitated, but needed to get the rest of it out. "I didn't put your name on that list. I had no idea who was on it until it was handed to me. But I should have found a way to warn you before I told everyone else. At the time, though, I was worried about that being seen as playing favorites."

"Playing favorites. We were living together at the time, no?" His jaw tightened. "It doesn't matter. It's...how do you say it? Water under the bridge. It's over."

Yes, it was. And so were they. The anguish of that day still washed over her at times. Except now they had a baby. Someone who could make her smile, make her glad that that period of her life had happened, despite the way it had ended.

Needing to pull herself together, she took her phone out of her pocket and checked it for text messages. There were none. Peggy knew her well enough to call or text if anything happened, even if it wasn't a big deal.

"Everything okay?" he murmured.

"Yes, just making sure Peggy wasn't trying to get a hold of me for anything."

"What time do you want to get home?"

The words confused her for a second, then she realized he was talking about his house, not her place back in Atlanta. "If the surgery won't run too long, I'm fine staying until the end."

They were still speaking in hushed tones, but Luca hadn't tried to lean in close to her again, for which she was thankful.

Ears were now off-limits.

Although she wasn't sure how she was going to break that to him if he decided to translate for her again, or if she even wanted him to.

Because she had a strange feeling that if he leaned in and started whispering again, she would sit there and pay rapt attention. Not to the words. But to the way he made her feel.

Not good, Elyse.

But how exactly was she going to stop her reaction? It was almost as elemental as the tingling in her breasts had been during that kiss.

The man coaxed feelings from her that she neither wanted nor needed.

No, scratch that. She didn't need them, but she did want them.

Wanted them enough to kiss him, as she'd already proved.

So how was she going to fix that and prevent it from happening again?

Simple, she needed to avoid situations where her self-control was at risk.

Ha! You mean something like living under the same roof as the man? A stone's throw from his bedroom?

She sighed. Yes. Exactly like that.

Only now that she'd gotten herself into that situation, she had no idea how to get herself back out of it.

CHAPTER SIX

ANNA CHORTLED WHEN Luca bit into his toast.

He cocked his head, trying to figure out what was so funny about it.

"She laughs at odd things. It's like she's trying to figure out her world."

Elyse had evidently noted his confusion and tried to explain what was behind it.

Watching the baby on her lap, he forked up a bite of egg, giving an exaggerated *"mmm..."* of pleasure, and the laugh got louder, turned infectious enough that Elyse started giggling along with her.

"Who knew eating could be so amusing?"

"She's only doing it to you."

To prove her point, Elyse picked up her toast and bit off a piece of it, chewing with exaggerated movements of her jaw. Anna didn't even spare her mom a glance. She just kept staring at Luca.

He tapped his finger on the very end of the baby's nose. "Glad you find your...father...so funny."

Why had he hesitated over saying that? Was it because he still didn't quite believe a child so perfect and beautiful could possibly be his? Elyse had already offered to have a DNA test done but, like he'd told her, he didn't need one. The baby was his. He felt it in his bones. There were things about her coloring, how different her hair was from her mother's, that made him sure that Annalisa was from his family.

Except for the dimple in the baby's cheek, which she definitely got from her *mamma*. Elyse had a dimple on the very same side of her face. He could remember touching it when she smiled, fascinated by the way it puckered inward. It was hellishly attractive. And when he saw Elyse in his dreams, she always had that secret dimple.

He dreamed about her.

He could finally admit it to himself, if not to her. But he hadn't quite figured out how to deal with those dreams. And when he had been translating for Lorenzo a couple of days ago, it had come back to him that he'd muttered in her ear in one such dream, saying all the things he wanted to do to her. He'd woken up hard, needing her so badly. Only she hadn't been there. It had all been in his head.

Well, not all of it. It had been elsewhere too.

When his body had begun to react to those memories as he'd translated for the surgeon, he'd decided he needed to stop it. He'd backed off, needing to get himself under control. He'd thanked his lucky stars when she'd told him she didn't need him to translate for her anymore.

"I called my parents yesterday."

She stopped playing with Anna's fingers. "You did? What did they say?"

There was a nervousness to her voice that he didn't like. "I didn't exactly tell them. Not yet. I thought maybe it would be better just to let them see her and then explain it."

"I don't know… It was easier with my parents. Although they were upset that you'd left. I told them it was my fault, but they didn't quite believe me, I don't think."

"I was hurt. And angry. And things hadn't been going

well between us for a while. I thought this was maybe your way of pushing me out of the picture."

She frowned. "I would have told you, if that were the case."

"So you think things were actually good?"

"I didn't say that."

He set down his fork. "You don't have to. We were over before you ever read out that list of names, and you know it."

"I guess we were."

She didn't look happy about that. Then again, she hadn't looked happy at the time either. She'd just looked…guilty.

He'd caught that same expression on her face a couple of times since she'd arrived in Italy, but he wasn't sure what that was about. At first he'd thought it was about her possible involvement in getting him fired. But she'd already made her big confession about that.

And yet even this morning she'd glanced at him and then looked away quickly.

Was she hiding something? Something other than her part in the layoffs?

He couldn't imagine what it might be. Or how it would even have anything to do with him, at this point. If Anna was his, that was the only thing that was important.

"You're okay with Mamma and Papà meeting her? And you, of course."

"I guess so. It's bound to be a shock, though. What if they hate me? I had convinced myself that because you didn't want children, you wouldn't want her either. I decided I'd come, do what I thought was right and then turn around and go home. I didn't stop to think who else might be impacted by the delay."

"I love her. How could I not? What I said back then about not wanting kids was…a moment of stupidity." She wasn't the only one who hadn't stopped to think about the impact of his behavior—or his words. He could see why she'd been afraid to tell him about Anna. "I'll just accentuate the positives when I tell them."

Her brows went up, and she shifted Anna to the other side of her lap. "Which are?"

"The fact that they have a healthy, happy grandchild. And..." What were the positives other than that? It was hard to list them when she said it in that tone of voice. "And they will fall in love with Anna as soon as they meet her."

"I hope so." She took another bite of her toast, chewing for a long time.

She was worried. So was he, for that matter. But what he'd said was true. Once they got over their surprise, they would welcome both Elyse and Annalisa with open arms. His mom would probably even try her hand at matchmaking—which he needed to shoot down right away and firmly explain that he and Elyse were no longer together, neither would they change their minds.

Was he so sure about that? He'd been positive that Elyse would forever reject his requests for a date. Then one day—out of the blue—she'd taken his hand and asked him instead. But that didn't mean she was suddenly going turn the tables and ask him to marry her.

If she'd accepted his proposal, would they be making an engagement announcement to his parents instead of just a birth announcement?

But she hadn't. And they weren't.

"It will be fine." He wasn't sure if he was trying to convince himself or her. "How is Peggy doing?"

Elyse smiled. "She's doing great, from what her texts and social media accounts say. She is taking full advantage of her newfound freedom. She's even been out on a date, which I did not approve of, by the way."

"You don't want her falling for an Italian?"

She laughed. "Since I fell for one once, that's not the issue. It's the fact that she's not going to be here long enough to start up anything meaningful."

"And encounters must always be meaningful?" He wondered if she would remember the first time they'd slept together. He had waited for that first date for so very long and when it had happened…it had been impulsive and wild, and she'd hooked him from the moment he'd caught his breath.

She looked away, those cheeks of hers turning a shade of pink that made his insides shift.

She did remember.

"At least we were living in the same country at the time," she said.

"So you wouldn't have given me the time of day if I'd been a tourist in your country?"

She wrinkled her nose at him. "Probably not. And since I was department head, I really shouldn't have done so even then." Her face went serious. "Those dynamics are never a good idea. I think we proved that."

He touched Annalisa's hand, the thought bothering him somehow. "And yet if we hadn't gotten together, Annalisa wouldn't exist. Wasn't she worth it?"

Her teeth came down on her lip. There was a pause. One that was long enough to turn uncomfortable. Then she said huskily, "Yes. She was worth it. I'd do it all over again, even knowing what I know now."

"So would I."

She gave a sigh. "Hopefully your parents will feel the same way. That having a grandchild is okay even without having daughter-in-law attached. Someday, I'm sure you'll meet a wonderful Italian girl and settle down. Maybe you'll even change your mind about wanting kids sooner rather than later."

"I think I already have. Quite some time ago, actually. Things just didn't work out quite the way I thought they would."

"You did? I—I didn't realize."

Why had she said it that way? Was she hoping he already had someone so that she was free to pursue whoever she wanted? Would she get married and allow his daughter to become someone else's?

"I already have a child. Don't ever forget that."

She caught his hand. "I didn't mean it like that, Luca. I just meant that Annalisa isn't the only grandchild they're likely to have. And you're probably not going to be single the rest of your life."

He didn't see himself getting involved with anyone else for the foreseeable future, and he wasn't sure why. He'd immersed himself in work for so long, he wasn't sure he knew how to stop. At least he'd thought that until Elyse had come back into his life. And now suddenly he was rearranging everything in his life for her.

No, not everything. And it was for Anna, not for Elyse.

Only the hand holding his said that wasn't entirely true.

"For now, I'll leave it to my sisters to give them grandchildren. If they ever meet someone, that is."

He hadn't thought about what might happen if Elyse met someone else and they had a baby together. Would her husband or boyfriend insist she cut off contact with him? Deny him access to Anna?

That thought made him feel physically ill.

"I know we talked about it before, but I'd still like to draw up an agreement."

As soon as he saw her face, he realized it was the wrong

thing to say. She let go of him and drew Annalisa closer to her. "What kind of agreement?"

He could have said a custody agreement, but he knew that would be met with swift resistance. Besides, she'd come to Italy in good faith, trying to do the right thing. She'd said so herself. And if he thought about it, Elyse was not the type of person to let herself be railroaded into anything.

He chose his words carefully. "About visitation."

The wariness didn't fade from her eyes. If anything, it grew. "You think we need something formal in writing? I wasn't planning on keeping her from you."

His intent hadn't been to make her angry, but something was going on with her that he really didn't understand.

"You talked about me meeting someone else, and it made me think about the reverse. That you might meet someone who wouldn't want me involved in your life or Annalisa's."

Her grip on the baby loosened. "Would *you* do that, if you had a child and started dating someone else: prevent the other parent from seeing him or her?"

"No. I wouldn't." There was no hesitation in his answer because it was the truth.

"Well, I wouldn't let someone do that to you either, Luca. I would never keep her from you unless I thought it was for her own good."

Her own good? How would that ever be the case?

It wouldn't. So stop being so sensitive to every little thing.

That was going to be hard. Because, like it or not, Elyse was only here for a little while. A month was nothing, in the greater scheme of things. And where Elyse went, Annalisa went.

"When you say 'for her own good' I'm not sure what that means."

She raised her brows and then grinned. "Well, let's see… If you were in an Italian prison on a life sentence for murder, I might hesitate before bringing her to see you."

He laughed. "Since I don't see that happening, I would have to have been wrongly convicted."

He'd been trying to lighten the mood, just like she had, but it must have fallen short because her smile faded. "What if you married someone who was unkind to Anna?"

Another hint that she had no intention of getting back together with him? It shouldn't sting, but it did.

"I will make sure that never happens." Not only because there were no current prospects but because he would never do anything to harm his daughter.

"How can you be so sure? Sometimes people aren't exactly who they seem on the surface."

He leaned closer, making sure she heard every word he said. "You seem determined to set me up with some unknown—but evidently unhinged—person. Why is that?"

"What? I'm not. I'm just setting up a hypothetical situation."

"Let's turn it around. What if you date a series of commitment-phobes and make Anna think relationships never last?" Lorenzo's knowing smile popped into his head. That man wouldn't know a serious relationship if it bit him on the ass. What if Elyse decided she liked that kind of man? After all, she seemed to have moved on with her life without a backward glance at him.

"I wouldn't. I won't. But I understand what you're saying. Let's just agree that we'll both try to do whatever's in her best interests."

The tense muscles along his shoulders eased their grip. "Agreed. Speaking of things that are in Annalisa's best interests, we've already talked about going to see my parents. Would you be okay with it being in the next couple of days? I know it's short notice, but I've checked my work schedule, and I think I can spare three or four days to spend with them."

"This soon?"

"Is that a problem?"

"No, I think I just expected us to have time to figure things out before jumping in at the deep end."

"If we wait until we iron out every tiny detail, Anna will be eighteen."

He'd decided that waiting for a break in his schedule wasn't going to happen if he didn't make it happen. This was the first step in doing that.

"You're right, of course. Let me check with Peggy, so she doesn't think I just abandoned her."

He'd forgotten about her aunt. "Does she need you to stay close by?"

"Are you kidding? She's pretty independent. I just meant that if she got into some kind of difficult situation, I'd want her to know how to reach me and that I'd be a few hours away. Oh! What should I take for a gift?"

"For my parents? No need to get them anything."

Annalisa started to squirm, a cry rising from her tiny chest. "I want to take something. I know they'd get a gift for me, wouldn't they?"

He held out his arms for the fussing baby. "Annalisa will be the only gift they need. They'll be thrilled to meet her and spend some time with her."

"I'm going to be stubborn on this one. Can you point me in the direction of a store that might have something they would like?"

He sighed. She wasn't going to take no for an answer. "Here in Italy flowers and wine are traditional gifts for a hostess, although I hope you'll think of my mother as more than just a hostess. She's Annalisa's grandmother."

"I know that. Really, I do. Any particular type of flowers?"

"Just not carnations. I know you use a lot of those in the States, but here they are primarily used for mourning and funerals."

"Okay." Her eyes widened. "Thanks for telling me that, because I almost certainly would have brought the wrong thing."

"I'll leave a couple of hours early on Friday and we can get something before boarding the train. There are shops not far from the station."

Annalisa wiggled and gave another—angrier-sounding—cry. At which point Luca smelled something that wasn't quite right. In fact, it smelled a little bit like...

Poop.

No wonder she was fussy.

"Do you have a diaper bag nearby?"

"Why?" She glanced at the baby and then up at him. "Oh...she..."

"I do believe she's filled her diaper."

"I'll take her." She stood and reached her arms out for the baby, waiting until she was back in her possession before continuing. "I need to feed her, anyway, so I might as well change her too. We can go over Diapering for Beginners at another time."

He smiled, liking the fact that she was willing to let him take on some of Anna's care. Elyse had talked about her aunt being independent. Well, it must be a family trait, because that independent streak reached to the furthest branches on that particular family tree. "I'll look forward to it."

"Hmm." She rocked the baby back and forth. "Wait

until you have one that shoots halfway up her back. You may change your mind."

"I won't. I promise." He nodded at his phone, which was on the counter. "I'll get the dishes cleaned up and then go to the hospital for a couple of hours. Maybe afterward we can do a little bit of sightseeing in town, if you and Anna are up for it."

"We will be, if you're sure you have the time."

"I'm learning to make time for what's important."

The smile she gave him reached her eyes, crinkling them at the corners. "Thank you, Luca. For everything."

She showed him how to strap the baby into the car seat she'd brought, unexpectedly nervous about spending time with him. Which was ridiculous. She'd spent loads of time with him when he'd lived in Atlanta. But this was different. That had been on her turf. And now she wasn't. She also had Annalisa to worry about as well. What if the baby was so fussy that she got on his nerves?

No, Luca was one of the most patient men she'd ever known. The only time she'd seen him truly irritated was when an insurance agency had tried to tell him that the procedure he'd wanted to do on a patient was experimental and wouldn't be covered. He'd hit the roof, going to the hospital administrator and demanding he help the company change their minds. Instead, the administrator had needed to sit Luca down and explain the way things worked in their health care system.

After a series of appeals and a peer-to-peer call between the insurance agency's doctor and Luca, they'd gotten it ironed out and the patient had gotten the surgery, which had ended up saving her life. From then on he'd been firm and insistent, but had followed the rules. In fact, Luca had been able to finagle more insurance coverage for patients than her, and she always tried her hardest.

It was in his voice. That deep mellow baritone that still made her knees go weak. It worked its magic on everyone. Except for hospital bean counters who were only worried about the profit margins and sometimes didn't see the faces behind their decisions. Like when they downsized her department. Now she was seriously overworked. So was everyone who was left in Neurology. In fact, Elyse wasn't taking new patients at all. She didn't have the time.

"There—is that right?" He fiddled with the straps to the car seat even after she'd assured him it was perfect.

"You're a careful driver, Luca, which helps."

He said maybe he'd changed his mind about having kids. When had that happened? When he'd seen his daughter for the first time? Her eyes closed, a lump forming in her throat. She was glad that he might want more. Wasn't she?

Thank God she hadn't accepted his marriage proposal only to find out he did indeed want more children.

He leaned over and kissed Annalisa's forehead, turning the lump in Elyse's throat into a boulder. "I will be even more careful than usual."

They got in, and he waited for her to buckle in as well. She gave an inward eye roll, swallowing down her earlier emotions and moving to a neutral subject. "How is Mrs. Landers?"

"I checked in on her yesterday. She's recovering nicely. They're hoping she can go home in a few more days. They want to make sure there's no more seizure activity first."

"Will they do physical therapy with her to help strengthen some of the affected muscles?"

"Yes, there is a rehab facility right next to the neural science clinic. And she'll be followed up by Lorenzo for a couple of months. Any scans will come through me, so I'll be able to see how she's doing as well."

In a couple of months Elyse would be long gone. She wasn't sure how she felt about that anymore.

Then they were on their way into the center of the city, where the famous Florence Cathedral could be seen.

"Why do you call the cathedral the *Duomo*?"

"It means dome, which is why most of the residents just use that, rather than its formal name, which is Cattedrale di Santa Maria del Fiore."

"Wow that's a mouthful. I can see how the Dome would be easier." Not only was it a mouthful but hearing Luca speak his native tongue still turned her insides to mush.

How was that even possible?

Within fifteen minutes they had found a paid parking area for the car. "Most of these are done with tour guides. We can join one of the groups, or we can do our own thing, whichever you prefer."

"I'm sure you know just about as much as the guides, so could we do it on our own, just in case Annalisa decides to give us trouble." She got out of the car and unstrapped the baby from the seat.

"I'll carry her."

"Are you sure? She gets heavy pretty quickly. I have a sling."

"She's as light as a feather. And, yes, I'm sure. Just show me how to put it on."

She helped Luca get fitted with the sling, surprised he would let himself be seen with something like that. But she had to admit he looked beyond sexy whenever he held Anna. Women were going to envy her. Little did they know they had nothing to fear.

He was available. But not today. Her chin went up. Today he was all hers.

She snugged Anna into the curve of the carrier. The poor thing blinked up at them as if trying to figure out what kind of trick this was.

It wasn't a trick, and Elyse had to admit she felt a trickle of jealousy. She used to love lying against the man's chest when they were in bed. And now they had a baby.

Before she could stop herself, she took her phone and snapped a picture of him.

"What are you doing?"

She had no idea. Just knew she wanted something to remember this moment by when she got back to the States. "She'll want pictures of you together."

It was a lie, but there was no way she was going to tell him the true reason. That there was something heartbreakingly beautiful about seeing him and Anna together.

He smiled. "As long as you don't plan to use it as blackmail material."

"Ha! No."

He settled the baby a little closer to his midsection, curving his left arm around her body. "We'll have to walk quite a bit as the streets near the center don't allow cars."

Another pang went through her. They'd done a lot of walking when they had been together in Atlanta. Only then they'd held hands as they'd strolled, having eyes only for each other. Sometimes those walks had even been cut short by a single look from him that had had them both hurrying back to her apartment.

There would be no holding hands today. Or hurrying home. Elyse gripped her hands together as if her life depended on it.

Maybe it did. Or at the very least her sanity.

She hadn't been able to get that kiss in his office out of her mind. It replayed itself time and time again, ending in that moment when her body had mistaken the signals for something else.

She hadn't explained it to him then, and she wasn't about to attempt an explanation now. Besides, it was better just to let him think that she'd come to her senses. And she had. Just not for the reasons he'd thought.

Despite all of that, it was exhilarating being with him, especially since there'd been a time when she'd thought she'd never lay eyes on him again.

It probably would have been better if she hadn't. His presence threatened to rip apart her defenses, leaving her wondering exactly what lay behind them. She had a feeling she knew. She just didn't want to face it.

She could get through a month, surely.

And meeting his parents? Would she get through that too? What if they tried to send little hints her way that she should marry their son? No. He wouldn't have told them about the proposal, surely.

"You doing okay?" He moved next to her, shoulder brushing over hers as he walked beside her. The brief contact and the concern in his voice left her with a longing that made her ache. He sounded like a concerned husband.

Only he wasn't.

And the sight of him carrying their child?

Oh, God. It looked natural, earthy, his white shirt rolled up over tanned forearms. Italians didn't dress down as much as Americans did, and seeing him in his own environment helped her understand so much about him. Like the fact that he hadn't been trying to impress people with his clothing choices when he'd been in Atlanta. It was just the way he was. His khaki slacks had a fresh-pressed look to them. Probably Emilia's doing, or maybe he took his clothes to a cleaner. But he was lean and devastatingly handsome with his sunglasses pushed on top of his head.

Elyse had opted to slide hers down onto her nose, not so much to protect herself from the sun as to provide an additional barrier between them. Or maybe it was to keep him from reading her thoughts.

Evidently, Luca needed no such protection. He was confident and completely unmoved by her. Or was he? There had been moments when she'd been sure that—

"All roads lead to the Duomo."

"Excuse me?"

He grinned at her. "No. I mean literally. All the streets in this area empty out at the cathedral."

"Oh." She hadn't been so much confused by his words as that they'd echoed her thoughts. Because at the time they'd been together all her roads had led to Luca.

And he likely knew it. He had women throwing themselves at him all the time. There were several at the hospital who had given him sideways glances, probably wondering how someone like her had landed someone like Luca.

She couldn't have given them an answer, because she had no idea why he'd chosen her.

And their last act as a couple had been to make Annalisa.

The huge cathedral suddenly loomed in front of them, jerking her thoughts to a standstill.

It was huge. Magnificent.

She touched his arm, wishing she could loop hers through it, just like in days past. "I can't believe I'm standing here looking at something so incredibly gorgeous."

"Neither can I." The low words made her glance over at him. Then she swallowed. And swallowed again, unable to figure out how to keep breathing in and out.

Luca wasn't looking at the church. Or Anna. Or the surrounding area. His gaze was fixed wholly on her.

CHAPTER SEVEN

LUCA'S ARMS CRADLED the baby's body in an effort to keep
from reaching out to Elyse. He'd dreamed of bringing her
to his home country one day, of showing her the sights, and
here they were. But it wasn't quite the way he'd envisioned
it. Because in his fantasies they'd had a huge Italian wedding first, with all his family in attendance. And all hers.

Only life and egos and what he'd seen as deception on
Elyse's part had changed everything.

But it hadn't been.

She'd said she hadn't been a part of the decision-making
process regarding the layoffs. So this whole time he'd been
operating under a faulty assumption. He suddenly looked
at her through eyes that weren't quite so cynical—weren't
quite so unforgiving.

But did it change anything, really? The events leading
up to the firing hadn't changed. And at the time they hadn't
been able to see their way through them.

And now?

"Scusami. Una foto?"

He jerked back to reality, realizing someone was trying
to take a picture and he and Elyse were in the way. Staring at each other like star-crossed lovers.

"Mi dispiace."

They moved out of the line of fire and headed toward

the cathedral itself. He could try to say he'd been looking at something in the distance and not at her, but it would be a lie. And he couldn't bring himself to force out the words. So he just kept walking.

Annalisa chose that moment to wake up, blinking eyes coming up to meet his.

Elyse was there immediately, leaning over to look at her. "I'm here, sweetheart."

His chest contracted. For the last four months, Elyse's face had been the first and last thing his daughter had seen each day. It was as if he hadn't existed.

And whose fault was that? If he hadn't stormed off after they'd had sex that last time—if he'd swallowed his damned Latin pride and come back and demanded she answer his questions about the layoffs and why she was pushing him away—he might have been able to experience his daughter's birth. Her first smile. And she might see him as a parent figure instead of just some random face in the crowd.

Elyse unbuckled their daughter and swung her up into her arms.

She glanced at him, as if realizing something was wrong. "I'm sorry. Why don't you hold her without the sling? She needs to get to know you."

It was as if she'd read his mind. And if the baby started crying?

Well, it was something they would have to work through if he wanted to be a part of her life. And he did. Objectively, it might be easier just to turn away and pretend none of this had ever happened, but he couldn't. Not only because he wanted to do the right thing but also because he already loved her.

In only four days.

It was unreal, but it was true.

He held his arms out and Elyse placed the baby in them for the umpteenth time. And it was magic. All over again. This was his child. His daughter.

He talked to her in Italian, just muttering things in a long stream of consciousness way that probably wouldn't make any sense to anyone. But he didn't care. There were emotions bottled up inside him that needed an outlet and it was better if Elyse didn't understand the words.

He bounced Anna gently, moving a little distance away. She was listening.

Whether it was five minutes or fifteen, he wasn't sure, but he finally walked back to Elyse, just as Anna started to squirm. "It's okay. Mamma is right here."

"And so is Daddy."

He wished she would stop smiling. Stop seeming soft and approachable again, unlike those last days when her demeanor had been cool and sharp.

There was a part of him that said he wasn't as over her as he'd thought he was. As he'd hoped he was.

He shut those thoughts down as the line started to move, and they had to put Annalisa back in the sling. Then they were finally inside the famed Florence Cathedral.

He wasn't disappointed by her reaction. Elyse gasped when she caught sight of the mosaic floors that were laid out in a grid, each section boasting a new pattern. He tried to see them through her eyes, although it was hard, since patterned streets, sidewalks and the like were such an ordinary part of life in Europe.

These were magnificent, however. And they were spotless.

He rocked Annalisa so Elyse could enjoy the sights without interruption. And she did, even as they moved along with the crowds. The tour groups were instructed not to linger so that everyone got a chance to see it. And even though their party was small enough that they weren't required to join one of the groups, he could tell Elyse was trying to be considerate of those behind them. Keeping his voice hushed as was the custom inside, he said, "It's beautiful at night with the lights. Maybe after our meal we can come back and look."

"I'd love that."

"Do you want to climb to the cupola?"

She glanced at Annalisa. "I don't think so. Not with her. I'm just happy to have been able to see the inside. The floors and ceilings are beyond anything I could have imagined."

The wave of tourists washed them back toward the exit, the crowd pinching together as it neared the doorway.

There was a sudden staccato burst of sound up ahead and then a scream of pain. Everyone froze for a second, then someone behind Luca shoved his shoulder and forced his way past. Someone else did the same. The crowd came to life, and what had been a steady procession became a frenzied rush as more and more people struggled to get to the exit.

Luca hadn't thought it sounded like gunfire, although in this day and age he couldn't rule it out.

He grabbed Elyse's hand when it looked like they might be separated, keeping his arm curled around Anna to keep her from being crushed against those in front of him. "Stay close!"

She did, letting go of his hand and wrapping one arm around his waist and gripping his sleeve with the other. They got to the doorway and Luca got a glimpse of something he recognized. A walker. Flattened as if it had been folded and lying on the floor. And next to it...

Oh, hell. He braced himself and stopped, using his body

to force those behind him to flow around. Elyse saw it at the same time he did.

Blood. And gray hair.

"God! We have to help her."

"Take Anna and go. I'll see if I can at least keep them off her until help comes. Tell anyone you see who looks official what's happened."

It wasn't easy, but they managed to get the baby out of the sling, and Elyse took her, doing her best to maintain her footing as she was swept through the doors along with the stream of tourists. He didn't dare kneel to check the victim; instead, he turned to face those still coming toward him, making himself as big as possible and shouting at those who would have shoved him aside, first in Italian and then in English. "Go around! There's an injured woman."

It worked. He kept shouting for what seemed like an hour, but was probably five minutes before the crowd thinned, slowed and then dissipated. He saw a set of barricades about twenty yards away, holding the people back.

He swiftly knelt to tend to the woman, a nun, her head covering pulled away. Blood came from a split lip and there was also a large gash on her forehead, the blood from which had formed a small puddle on the mosaic. She'd probably lost her footing and been trampled. A security guard hurried over and with him was Elyse.

"Thank you," he said to her. "Are you and the baby okay?"

"We're fine. They've called for a rescue squad."

She must have found someone who spoke English.

He felt for a pulse. It was strong but quicker than he'd like. "She's breathing, but probably has a concussion at the very least."

"Pupils?"

He smiled up at her. "You read my mind." He opened

the woman's eyes one at a time and checked the pupillary reflexes as Elyse knelt on the mosaic floor next to him, still holding the baby.

"They're both reactive. A very good sign." He then ran his hands over her arms and legs, palpating for breaks.

"There."

"What is it?"

The bone in her left leg was pressed against the skin but hadn't pushed through.

He didn't pull away the clothing, just said, "Her femur is broken. It won't take much to become an open fracture. We can't move her until the squad gets here."

"I agree."

Switching to Italian, he explained the situation to the guard. Not to mention there was no way of knowing if there were spinal or internal injuries.

Two other nuns approached. One of them put a hand over her mouth, turning her face toward the other in shock.

"It's Sister Maria. She fell behind our group. We're visiting from Rome. We had no idea she was hurt."

Elyse stood, putting her hand on the stricken nun's shoulder. "Help is coming."

The guard asked how many were in their party.

The one who'd spoken up answered. "There are two more sisters outside. They're waiting to see if we could find Maria. Will she be all right?"

Maria's eyes flickered and then opened, and she moaned, even as she tried to shift, one hand trying to reach her leg.

Luca pressed gently against her shoulder. "Lie still. You've been hurt. I'm Dr. Venezio and this is Dr. Tenner. We're going to stay with you until help arrives. Does anything hurt besides your leg?"

The woman closed her eyes for a minute, maybe taking stock of the different parts of her body. "My head. The fingers of my hand." She raised it to show digits that were swollen and purple.

He winced. How many shoes had trodden on that frail hand? Thank God Elyse had made it out with the baby. The same thing might have happened to her. Gently taking the nun's hand, he felt it, stopping when she gasped. He reassured her and then turned to Elyse.

"They'll need to get an X-ray to be sure, I can't feel past the edema."

Elyse nodded. "Could be crush injuries. They'll need to watch for compartment syndrome."

"I agree."

He'd forgotten how well they worked together. Most times, anyway. He glanced at Anna, surprised to see she was silently taking it all in.

A team pushing a stretcher hurried toward them. Luca quickly went through who they were and what they knew about the patient. "Trampling incident. She has a fractured left femur, which needs to be splinted. She'll probably also need her spine stabilized and a neck brace. Vitals are good, but she's complaining of pain in her head and her hand is pretty swollen, there may be a bleeder in there."

One of the techs was trying to get everything down while the other one gathered the necessary equipment from his bag. With Luca guiding the process with some input from Elyse, they soon had Maria loaded while someone went to find the other nuns, who were waiting outside, to let them know what had happened.

And then they were gone, leaving Luca to stand and reach down a hand to help Elyse up, as she was still holding Anna. They went outside before the barricades were taken down and watched to make sure there were no other incidents.

"Well, that wasn't how I expected the tour to end," he said.

"I'm just glad no one else was hurt. Trampling incidents can be horrific. She's lucky she's alive."

"Yes, she is." Something made him drape his arm around her shoulders and give her a quick squeeze. Maybe just thankfulness that it hadn't been her or Anna who'd been injured, even though he was sorry that anyone had been caught in that. All he could assume was that the walker had toppled over, hitting the hard floor a couple of times. The sound of it could have made people jump to the worst possible conclusion and panic, especially when combined with the screaming. As a result, an innocent woman had been badly hurt.

Elyse laid her head on his shoulder, sending warmth washing through his chest. He tightened his grip. Never in his wildest dreams about her had he pictured this scenario.

But he liked it. A little too much.

"You're still wearing Anna's baby sling, you know. I think you got a couple of sideways looks from those guards."

"Let them look. I'm proud to wear it."

"Are you?" She glanced up at him for a moment and there was something in those big eyes of hers that made him wish for impossible things.

He didn't think she'd want to know what he'd really like to do. What being with her right now was making him think. And adding that smile *à la* Elyse? It was deadlier than any aphrodisiac known to man. No little blue pills needed.

"I am."

Standing outside the cathedral once more, he glanced at his watch. Five thirty. It was still early by Italian standards, but maybe they could get into a restaurant without the normal crush of people. He actually knew of a place closer to the clinic that a lot of the staff went to. It would also give them a chance to swing by the house before they ate and change their clothes. He let go of her and held his arms out for the baby. "Are you hungry? I thought we might go out to eat early."

"That sounds wonderful."

When they got back to the house, Emilia was still there and insisted on staying to watch the baby while they went out and had an uninterrupted meal.

"Do not hurry back. I not hold baby since…my babies…" She held her hands to show how little they'd been, then reached out for Anna.

It was hard to say no when she so obviously enjoyed cuddling Annalisa in her arms. She dropped into one of Luca's recliners, which had a rocking feature.

He pulled Elyse aside. "She'll be fine, I promise. And Emilia will call my cell if there are any problems."

"I trust her. And I need to buy more diapers, since I'm close to running out of the supply I brought with me. Can we stop by a grocery store?"

"Yes. Of course. I should have thought of that."

"Some things don't cross your mind until it becomes a necessity."

He puzzled through the words. Was she only talking about diapers? Or was there another meaning behind the words.

Regardless, it was true. He'd just instituted a new rule of no touching when it came to Elyse, born out of necessity. Having his arm around her outside the Duomo had made him realize how dangerous it was to touch her, even when it started out innocently enough.

They said goodbye to Emilia and headed out in the car.

"Should we bring something back for her?"

"She'll have already prepared a meal and put it in the fridge. There is usually a lot of leftover food. I normally send some of it home with her, so she knows to eat what she wants."

"Oh, no. I didn't realize she was cooking something for us tonight."

"We'll eat it tomorrow. It's fine."

"If you're sure. How long has she been with you?"

"She is actually one of my parents' housekeepers. She's been with them for more years than I can remember. When I came back to Italy, she volunteered to come and make sure I didn't starve—my mom's words."

"I guarantee you won't. Not with the way she cooks." She paused, then added, "What happens if you leave again?"

Was she talking about her suggestion that he move back to the States? He loved his work at the clinic—felt like he was doing a lot of good where he was.

But he also loved his daughter. Wouldn't he move heaven and earth for the chance to be with her?

Yes, he would.

"If I left, she would probably opt to go back to my parents." His mother and father were wealthy, his father managing his own shipping company. "She's part of the family. They love her."

She laughed. "Your parents sound like great people. I'm still a little nervous about meeting them, though. Especially under these circumstances."

He could understand that. He was still a little worried

about their reaction himself. But probably not for the same reasons she was.

"You'll like them. And they'll love you."

"As much as they love Emilia?" She smiled as she said it.

"More."

She blew out a breath. "Did you tell them after we talked last time?"

He knew she was referring to Anna. "Not yet. I've been thinking through my approach."

"If we just show up with her in tow, that conversation might prove to be a little more difficult."

She was right. He couldn't just spring it on them and pray for the best. Especially not if Elyse was in the room. His parents needed time to digest the information and plan how they were going to approach it before they got there. "I'll do it tonight."

"Good." She looked relieved, getting out of the car and surveying their surroundings. "This is lovely."

"It's close to the clinic and pretty popular."

"I can see why."

They went in and the scents of garlic and mozzarella tickled his nose, making his mouth water. The hum of voices and laughter only added to it. He'd been right to come to Florence. He'd loved the city from the moment he'd set foot into it. There were complaints about the tourists from some quarters, but having lived in another country for over a year he felt a kinship with them that killed a little of the homesickness he'd felt for Atlanta. Even now when he heard a Southern accent from the States, it brought back memories. Good memories of warm food and even warmer people, even if he never had gotten the hang of drinking iced tea.

And if he moved back to the States, he would have to leave his new city behind.

"Luca! *Qui!*" He turned his head and saw Lorenzo motioning them over.

"Dammit." He groaned aloud. "Did I say this was a good idea?"

"Embarrassed to be seen with me?"

There was something in her face that said she really believed he might be.

"What? *Dio*, no. I'd hoped to have a little time alone with you after sharing you with the clinic." He hurried to add, "To discuss our future. With Annalisa." He was making a mess out of this whole thing.

Then again, he'd made a mess out of his relationship with her as well. They might as well join Lorenzo and the other two surgeons at the table. What happened to this being an early time to eat for Italians?

A waitress came up to them, and he motioned to the trio at the table. "Could we get another chair?"

She brought one and everyone adjusted their places to accommodate them. Even with the moves, Luca found himself squeezed in next to Elyse, knees touching. There was no way to avoid it. When he glanced at Lorenzo, who was on the other side of her, he wondered if her knees were touching his as well. The idea made him subconsciously press a bit closer, an impulse he neither liked nor welcomed.

Giorgino introduced her to the other two doctors, not waiting for Luca to translate. Drs. Fasone and Bergamini each stood to shake her hand.

He told the other two in Italian that Elyse was a surgeon in the US.

Dr. Fasone cocked his head. "What do you specialize in?"

"I'm a neurosurgeon."

Fasone smiled. "Working at a neuro-clinic, you can be fairly sure that many of us are as well."

Coming here had been a huge mistake. The only married man in the party was Dr. Bergamini.

Why did he even care? He and Elyse were no longer together. It shouldn't matter if she set her sights on someone else.

Well, Lorenzo was a serial dater, out with a new woman almost every week. And Fasone was…well, he was just a nice guy. Someone exactly like Elyse might fall for. He'd certainly be a stable influence on Anna. But that didn't make Luca like it any better.

He was suddenly conscious that his knee was clamped to hers. Unconsciously claiming her for his own?

Dannazione. He needed to get himself together.

He did that by remaining silent while they exchanged stories, with Lorenzo telling the other two doctors about the cavernoma surgery and Elyse's part in it. "It is sometimes good to have an outside perspective, yes?"

Lorenzo smiled at her in a way that made Luca tense.

The server came over and took his and Elyse's orders.

"I'll have whatever you're having," she murmured to Luca. The urge to shoot the other surgeon a look of triumph came and went. He was being childish. She wasn't going to fall for Lorenzo's charm.

He ordered two plates of ravioli with salads on the side, then paused for a second, turning to her. "Salads here come with anchovies. Do you want yours without?"

She blinked. "I've never tried them, but if that's how the salad comes, that's how I'd like mine."

A sliver of pride went through him. Not so much for his homeland but for the fact that Elyse was willing to eat what was common in his culture. "I hope you like it more than I did your sweet tea."

"Didn't I tell you? That's what I'd like to drink with my meal."

This time he laughed. "We have enough tourists that some of the restaurants do serve it. This one, I'm not so sure."

"I was joking. I'll have a sparkling mineral water."

He frowned. "No wine?" In the States she drank wine and Italy was known for its wide array of good ones.

"Not tonight." She gave him a pointed look, and then he realized she couldn't, because of Anna. How stupid could he be? It was too bad. He'd hoped to introduce her to Chianti—produced in the town that bore its name—which was only around fifty miles from here.

"Do they have sparkling water?"

"Yes." He turned to the server. *"Acqua frizzante e un chiante."*

Once the server left, he glanced at the men. "You've already ordered?"

"Right before you came in," Lorenzo responded, turning to Elyse once more. "You like the food *dall'Italia*?"

"I love it." This time her knee nudged Luca's twice. She'd sensed the hint of flirtation in Lorenzo's manner and was reassuring him. It was an old game they'd played many times before. If another man so much as looked at her, or if he thought someone was trying to come on to her, she would touch him. Or nudge his knee under the table. Or lay her hand on his thigh to reassure him that she wanted to be there with him. Only him.

That wasn't the case here, but it still helped his muscles release some of their tension. She was telling him she wasn't going to respond to the other man's subtle advances.

Luca had never been outwardly jealous, but she'd always been able to sense when he became uneasy.

Drinks were soon poured, and Lorenzo gave a toast in Italian, which Luca translated. "To interesting cases and even more interesting conversation." This time, though, Luca sent the other man a slight frown, which resulted in raised brows on Lorenzo's part. But he helped steer the conversation back to neutral territory, with the other surgeons asking about procedures in the States and comparing them to Italian medicine.

"What was your most disappointing case?" Fasone asked.

This time Luca did tense. He was pretty sure that would be the case that he and Elyse had disagreed on so vehemently and in which they had both been wrong. A simple blood test had ruled it to be something else entirely, but the diagnosis had come too late.

"Well, we had a patient who came in suffering from massive headaches that weren't responding to over-the-counter pain meds. The symptoms led me to suspect a tumor and Luca disagreed, thinking she had a blood clot. An MRI showed we were both wrong. But almost as soon as we wheeled her out of the imaging room, she threw a clot and had a massive stroke. She had polycythemia vera."

Luca added. "Her bone marrow was producing too many blood cells. But they were platelets, not the red blood cells normally found in the condition. It was a rarer form of the disease."

Fasone grimaced. "That's tough. It doesn't sound like you had much hope of saving the patient even if you had diagnosed it from the beginning, though."

"No, she waited too long to come in. She'd been experiencing symptoms for several years and there was already evidence of a couple of previous transient ischemic attacks."

"I'm surprised you two are still talking," Giorgino said with a smile. "Those are the kinds of disagreements that can ruin friendships."

He didn't know the half of it, but Luca forced a shrug. "We were both wrong. So I guess there was no gloating to be done."

Elyse added in a soft voice, "No, there wasn't."

But the disruption of a staff meeting followed by a two-hour argument over whose hypothesis they should follow had damaged their relationship. Not long afterward, the ax had fallen in the form of jobs disappearing.

She'd said she was sorry for that. And he believed her. But did it change anything? In some ways, maybe it did.

Their salads and antipasto came, and the conversation turned to food without him having to force the issue, which he was more than ready to do. If the subject of their breakup was going to be rehashed, he certainly didn't want it to be in front of an audience.

Elyse speared a piece of lettuce and added one of the slivers of anchovies. He waited while she put the bite in her mouth. Her eyes widened.

"Verdict?"

"It's salty. And quite strong. But I like it." She tilted her head and looked at the other surgeons. "So your turn. What were your most disappointing cases?"

They each shared a case that had turned out badly. One had been human error, but the others had all been just the difficulty of coming up with a speedy diagnosis when things were already heading south. So he and Elyse weren't the only ones who'd lost patients. And the PV case wasn't his only difficult one, but it had been the most dramatic. And the one with the most personal repercussions.

Was there anything he could have done differently?

He wasn't sure. If Elyse hadn't already started to subtly withdraw from him, it might not have become the volcano it had. But she had. In tiny increments he hadn't understood but which had become pronounced after the death of the patient.

Maybe it had been the fact that he and Elyse had worked too closely together. The emotions of their relationship had gotten in the way of how they'd dealt with that patient— he could see that now. It had also got in the way of how they'd responded to each other in the midst of that crisis. Sharp words had cut more deeply. Anger had seemed ten times more significant than it should have.

Her knee had shifted away from his when talking about the PV patient, but as the others had shared their defeats, she'd relaxed once again.

Her blond hair shimmered in the dimly lit restaurant. And with her expressive face, hands moving as she discussed disease processes, he could see why Lorenzo—or any man, for that matter—would be attracted to her. She had it all. Brains, beauty and an innate kindness that was rare. A man would be a fool not to be drawn to her.

Luca found himself staring at her, loving the way she smiled. And frowned. The sound of her voice. The way she listened intently as she tried to find her way around accents and unfamiliar words.

He pushed his plate away, just as she turned to him. "Do we need to check in with Emilia?"

"Maybe. I'm finished if you are."

"I am."

Luca motioned for the check and paid their bill.

She smiled at the table as they stood. "Thank you for entertaining me. I'm sure there are things you would have preferred to talk about other than medicine."

Bergamini, who'd been the quietest of the bunch, said, "It's always interesting to observe how we deal with difficult diagnoses." He fixed Luca with a stare. "Sometimes we get it right. And sometimes we don't. When that happens, we need to learn from our mistakes. And try not to repeat them."

The man wasn't talking about their cases. No wonder he hadn't said much. He'd been "observing" but it had had nothing to do with medicine and everything to do with relationships. It stood to reason. He'd been married a long time, so he'd obviously figured out how to get it right.

Well, contrary to the man's opinion, Luca *had* learned from his mistakes. He may not have gotten everything right, but he'd come out on the other side with some new ways of dealing with issues.

Mostly that meant not getting involved with the opposite sex. But was that because of the breakup? Or because he was still hung up on the mother of his child?

Soon they were out of the restaurant, the cool air showing the first hints of autumn. By the time Elyse left Italy, temperatures would be dropping at night and staying cooler during the day.

She glanced at him. "Hey. That case we had. It was a hard call. I'm sorry I was so hateful during that."

"You weren't hateful. Just…passionate." He hesitated. "And just so you know, I wasn't aware there was a possibility of a pregnancy that last night or I wouldn't have left, I hope you know that."

He tried to figure out how to express himself. "Our relationship had become like the PV patient: producing an unhealthy amount of tension with no way to drain it off."

Treating polycythemia vera often meant drawing off excess blood in a phlebotomy session. It lowered the red blood cell count, lowering the risk of a heart attack or stroke.

She sighed. "Maybe it's true what they say about business and pleasure. They need to be kept separate."

"With us, there was no way of doing that. We were already involved and both in the same line of work." He smiled. "And that's what drew us together in the first place."

"Really? That's funny, because I was only interested in your...looks."

That made him laugh, since that word had always been her euphemism for something else. "You were, were you?"

She tossed her hair over her shoulder and glanced back at him. "You were always pretty damned good in...the looks department."

The joking faded away, at least on his part. She still thought that? Even after all that had happened? Well, hadn't he just thought about how gorgeous she was a few minutes ago?

The attraction was still there on both sides. "I was staring at you back in the restaurant, thinking about how heartbreakingly beautiful you are and how I didn't want Lorenzo Giorgino anywhere near you."

She stopped in her tracks and turned to look at him. "Enzo doesn't appeal to me at all. Oh, he's nice enough, and he's certainly good-looking, but I have a feeling he has a serial case of wandering eyes."

Ah, so she had seen through him. "He tends to date a lot of different women. And I don't like it that he has you calling him Enzo."

"You don't?" She smiled. "Well, you don't have to worry. My sights were always set on a completely different Italian."

Those words hung between them, and Luca moved

a few steps closer, stopping right in front of her. "They were?"

"Yes." The whispered word slid through his senses like silk, winding around them and holding them hostage.

He swallowed. "Do I know this Italian?"

"I would hope so." Her palm went to the back of his head, fingers sliding beneath the hair at his nape, sending a shudder through him.

"Because…it's you, Luca."

CHAPTER EIGHT

HIS KISS TOOK her by storm, the awareness that had been bubbling just beneath the surface finally blowing the lid from the pan.

She loved the feel of his mouth on hers.

She always had. She'd ached for him since the day she'd landed in Italy. Long before that, actually.

She wanted him.

Desperately.

She was no longer his boss; there was no need to worry about consequences or what would happen tomorrow. They'd be dealing with each other for the rest of their lives. Wouldn't it be better if they were on good terms?

She shut down the center of her brain that sent out a warning that good terms and sex were not necessarily one and the same.

The kiss deepened, his tongue playing with the seam of her mouth.

God, she wanted to let him in. She pulled back, glancing pointedly at the door to the restaurant. They were still within twenty yards of it. She didn't want Lorenzo or any of the others seeing them. If this was going to happen, she wanted it to be in a place where it was just her…and him. "Let's go somewhere else."

"We can't go home."

Home. Did he even realize he'd said that as if it were her home too? She forced herself not to analyze that too closely. Especially since the word had been said against her lips in a way that pushed her closer to a line she recognized all too well.

"Hotel?"

"They'll be filled with tourists." He stared into her eyes. "How adventurous are you?"

"If you mean sex on a zip line, probably not that adventurous." She smiled. "We could always go back to your office."

"Mmm…" He smiled. "We've done the office bit once before. I was thinking of somewhere a little more intimate. Where we're guaranteed our privacy."

"Sounds promising." She slid her thumb over his lips. "So where is this mysterious place?"

"My car."

A ripple of excitement went through her. Luca always had brought a hint of danger to his lovemaking, going as far as sliding his hand under her dress once in an empty elevator. He hadn't taken her over the edge but had gotten her so desperate that she'd attacked him as soon as they were back in her apartment.

"And I know the perfect parking place. Are you up for it?"

"Yes." She trusted him not to put her in a position where she would be embarrassed.

He drove a few miles, his hand high on her thigh, reminding her of that encounter in the elevator. But this time he didn't venture any farther. Somehow that heightened her anticipation. Made her want him that much more. Fifteen minutes later, they pulled up in front of a gated house. No lights were on. "Are they home?"

"No, but it doesn't matter. We're not going inside. Reach into the glove box. There's a remote."

She quickly handed it over and watched as he pushed the button, sending the gates sliding in opposite directions.

"It's a friend's," he said. "I'm watching it for him."

"No cameras?"

"No."

"Ah...so this is what you meant."

"Yes. No one's around." He followed the driveway around to the side, where they were concealed from the nearby houses by a natural screen of vegetation. "The neighbors all know my car, and that I'll be popping in periodically to check on things."

"This probably isn't what your friend had in mind."

He turned off the engine and leaned over to kiss her. "Oh, I plan to check on things."

Lord, those "things" were starting to heat up. The thought of having sex in a car was suddenly the only thing she wanted to do. It was a first. One of many she'd had with this man.

But... She needed to do something before they reached the point of no return. Give him time to back out. Placing her hands on either side of his face, she held him a few inches away from her. "I have to tell you something. The last time we kissed, well... Something happened. Something you need to know about."

He gave her a wolfish grin. "Don't worry. It made some things happen to me as well."

"No, this was...embarrassing. My...um, breasts started tingling. Like when I get ready to nurse Anna."

His eyes widened. "That's why you pulled away?"

She nodded.

"*Dio.* I thought..." He closed his eyes and pressed his forehead to hers. "Never mind. It doesn't matter."

"Are you sure?"

Instead of answering, he leaned over and undid her seat belt, hands going to the bottom of her T-shirt and tugging it over her head. Her bra soon followed. "All I want to think about right now is you. And me. And what we're about to do."

Then he let himself out of the car.

"What are you doing?"

He opened her door and took her hand.

"I thought you said we weren't going inside."

"We're not, but it's a beautiful night. And I want to see you in the moonlight."

She stepped out of the car, trusting him when he closed the door and turned her around. He gathered her hair in his hand and leaned over to kiss her neck. "We're not going any farther than the hood of the car, where we're not cramped, and I can do this." His arms came around her and palmed her breasts, the sweet friction on her nipples making her moan.

"*Dio.* I love the sounds you make. Love what they do to me."

His hands slid over her torso and rounded her hips. Then his fingers walked down the backs of her thighs, the flow of cool air hitting her legs as he scrunched the fabric of her long gauzy skirt in his hands, his teeth still skimming the sides of her neck. It was heady and naughty, and she was frantic with need.

He'd always been good at this.

How she'd missed it. Missed him.

She gasped when he bent her over the hood of the car, which was still warm from the drive over. He braced his hands on either side of her, his hips pressed tight against her bottom.

Giving a shaky laugh, she said, "I don't think the nuns would approve of my attire right now."

"Maybe not, but I approve *con tutto il mio cuore*."

He played with the elastic of her boy-shorts. "I have missed your ridiculous choice of undergarments."

But it was said in a way that was the opposite of ridiculous. Evidently she wasn't the only one who'd missed things. She loved it when he mixed Italian with English. The more caught up he got, the more he reverted to the language of his heart. And it tugged at hers, turning her insides to mush.

Then those shorts were being pushed down. "Step out of them."

Gladly. And when his leg came between hers and urged them apart, she swallowed, spreading for him.

She would be lucky if she lasted until he was inside her. His wallet landed on the car next to her. Just when she was trying to figure out what he was doing, she heard the ripping of foil packaging.

Oh, God, she was so desperate for him, she hadn't even thought of protection—or the fact that she no longer needed it. An arrow ripped through her heart and came out the other side. The pain was short-lived, though, because right now nothing was more important than being with him.

The slow snick of a zipper made her heart pound.

So close.

There was a momentary pause as she imagined him rolling the condom down his length. Then he was back, and one hand slid under her rib cage, finding her nipple without hesitation, pulling hard and strong in rhythmic strokes.

"Ahh…" The sound came out as a long breath of air.

"You make my loins want to explode."

The odd wording would have made her giggle under

normal circumstances, but right now she had never felt less like laughing in her life. Her body wound hard and tight with the continued stimulation. She'd never felt anything like this in her life.

She should ask him to slow down, but she didn't want to. Wasn't even sure she was capable of speech right now.

And that spring inside her was slowly twisting, getting closer and closer to the breaking point. She pushed her hips back, finding him briefly only to have him slide back out of reach.

"No!"

"What do you want, *cara*?" he squeezed her nipple and held it tight.

She pressed her lips together to keep from crying out, but the words spilled past the barrier. "I want you inside me. Please."

"Yes! *Dio*." His initial thrust was hard and fast, filling her completely.

A second later, she went off, her body contracting crazily around him.

He grabbed her hips and stabbed into her with an intensity that made her breathless and weak.

Then he gave a hoarse shout, before going completely still, straining inside her for several long seconds.

Then he slowly relaxed, curving his body over hers and staying right where he was.

He was still for what seemed like an eternity but was probably only minutes.

"Hell, Ellie, that was…"

"I know." His use of that pet name brought tears to her eyes. Ever since she'd arrived, he'd called her Elyse.

Until now.

What had happened to them? How had life become such

a damned struggle? But that was then. This was now. So what was holding them back from being together?

He eased out of her and turned her around to face him. He leaned down and gently kissed her, even as he crumpled the empty foil from the condom. That act made the tears that had been teetering on the edge of her lashes overflow their banks.

That. That's what was holding her back.

Stopping, he looked at her. "What's wrong?"

She gave him a shaky smile. "Hormones." It was a lie. But it was all she had.

"You're sure?"

"It's just been a while. I'm good. Just weepy in general." About the fact that they would never again produce a beautiful baby like Anna. That suddenly seemed like the biggest tragedy imaginable.

He nodded as if knowing he needed to give her a little space. Handing her the discarded pieces of clothing, he turned to give her privacy, zipping himself back into his khakis. Hurrying to get dressed, she dried her eyes, grateful to him. And very glad that this had happened here rather than at his place or, worse, at his parents' house. If it had to happen, better for it to be on neutral ground. Ground that she would never see again.

"Thank you," she said.

"For what?"

She wasn't sure. The gift of being with him one more time, maybe? "For not being weirded out by my crazy emotions."

"I have never been, how did you say…'weirded out' by anything to do with you." He tipped her chin up. "We are good?"

"Yes. We are." Good, but still not back together. There were no words of undying love. Which she was glad of, right? That would only create complications further down the road that neither of them wanted. His life was here now. And hers was back in the States. Anna was the only thing linking them.

At least for now.

Once their daughter was old enough to travel on her own, they wouldn't need to ever see each other again.

No. She'd already thought this through. There was always Anna's wedding and, later, hopefully grandchildren.

She frowned. Why was she trying to find excuses to see him?

Probably because there was still a part of her that cared about him. That probably always would.

Not a good thing.

Because she was discovering that looking at something through the eyes of passion was a whole lot different than seeing it in the cold light of satiation. And as reality crept up over the horizon and shone down on them, Elyse wondered what this would look like to her tomorrow. The next day. And on the day she actually left Italy—and returned home to Atlanta.

Luca threw a bucket of water over the hood of his car, removing any evidence of what had happened last night. Not that they'd left any marks that he could find. Only the ones burned into his skull.

What the hell had he been thinking?

He didn't know.

They'd wanted each other, there was no doubt about that. But he'd wanted women long before he'd known Elyse and had not acted on that desire. He'd never been one for casual sex that went nowhere. And as it stood right now, his relationship with Elyse would do just that: go nowhere. And tomorrow they were to leave for their trip to Rome.

Elyse had brought Annalisa out for breakfast, but would barely look at him, which was why he'd gone out to wash his vehicle down, thinking maybe the physical act would help him erase the thoughts clogging up his head. He rubbed the hood dry, trying to blot out the heady memories of having her in his arms.

Impossible. They were engraved on his nerve endings and written on his heart. But he was going to have to figure out how to live with those memories or find a way to bury them.

Elyse came into the garage unexpectedly and glanced at the car before looking back at him. "Could I talk to you for a minute?"

He threw the rag into the bucket and faced her. "Okay."

"I'm not quite sure how to say this."

His sense of foreboding grew. "I find the best way is to just say it."

"About the trip tomorrow…"

"Yes?" Was she going to back out?

"I don't want to share a bedroom with you when we get there."

He sagged against the fender of the car, laughing. "Is that all?"

"I'm not sure why that's funny, but yes."

He glanced up to see a hint of anger in her face.

"No need to worry. My mother wouldn't let us share a room, even if we wanted to. She's *multo* old-school about things. In fact, she attends Mass every Saturday."

Her eyes widened. "Is that what that whole marriage thing was about?"

"Marriage thing?"

"When you asked if it would be easier if we were married?"

This time the anger was on his side. "You think I'd ask

you to marry me as a way to appease Mamma? I would never do such a thing."

"I'm sorry, I just thought—"

"Listen. She would be disappointed if we married for anything other than love. I was wrong to have suggested it."

Her shoulders relaxed. "I'm glad. Because I would be disappointed in myself if I let myself be talked into marriage just to give my child a mother and a father."

He stiffened. "She has a mother and a father. Even without the piece of paper."

And that had not been at all why he'd asked her. Although for the life of him he still wasn't sure what his reasons had been.

"That's not what I meant."

"Then what did you mean?" The words came out sounding stilted and formal, which wasn't how he'd meant them to, but her words stung. She didn't have to convince him that she no longer loved him. It had been obvious that day in the hospital staffroom, when she'd read that list of names and tossed him from her life. And it was obvious now.

"I was talking about sharing the same last name. Anna doesn't care about any of that."

"No. You're probably right." He went on so that she didn't think he was overly bothered by the conversation. "I'm going to be heading to the clinic in about a half hour. Do you want to come with me, or would you rather stay here?"

She didn't answer for a few seconds. Then she said, "Could I come and bring Anna with me? I can put a cot in your office and lay her down for a nap. I really would like to see more of what the clinic does."

He smiled, a few of his muscles uncoiling. At least she hadn't come out here to say that she'd booked a flight out of Italy. He'd call his parents and make his explanations seeing as he'd been too distracted by Elyse to phone them last night. Everything was still on track.

At least he hoped it was. Time would tell if it would stay that way.

"How soon do you need me to be ready?"

"I have rounds in around an hour, so...thirty minutes?"

"Sounds good, I'll gather Anna's things."

His gaze skimmed her figure against his volition. If she noticed she gave no indication of it. "If you just put everything in the living room, I'll load it into the car."

"Thanks. Are you sure you don't mind us coming with you?"

"I'd be disappointed if you didn't."

Keep your enemies close, wasn't that how the saying went?

Only he really hoped Elyse was no longer his enemy. Because by the end of her time here he hoped they could at least be friends.

She was ready in thirty minutes, just as she'd said. But unlike the mountain of things he expected to see on the living-room floor, there was only a collapsible crib and a diaper bag packed with supplies. He glanced at it. "Are you sure you don't want to leave her with Emilia again for a few hours?"

She gave him a sideways glance and said, "No, I think I'd like her with me this time."

Was she afraid he'd try to sweep everything off his desk and take her there like he had on her desk in Atlanta? Or the hood of his car?

He'd learned his lesson and wasn't likely to repeat either of those mistakes. Only he wasn't sure the latter *had* been a mistake. There was such a thing as closure. Something he hadn't quite gotten before he'd left Atlanta. Maybe their encounter had been the formal goodbye he'd needed.

He didn't like that idea. At all.

"We can set up the baby cam in my office or use the camera on my laptop to observe her."

"I thought the same thing, so I have the baby monitor in the diaper bag."

"Great. My office door can be locked, but I'd rather be able to check on her from time to time."

"It's just like leaving her to sleep in her room at home. The monitor will alert us to any peeps she might make."

With that settled, he picked up the portable crib and the diaper bag and loaded them into the car while she picked Anna up from the baby blanket she'd spread on the floor.

Emilia came over to kiss the baby on the cheek. "You leave?"

"I'm taking them to the clinic with me. But don't forget that Elyse and I are going to Rome in the morning," Luca said.

"I no forget. But I miss Annalisa."

He smiled. He was sure his housekeeper would probably miss the baby more than she would him.

"We'll only be there a week."

Elyse shifted and looked away. Maybe "only a week" to her seemed like an eternity. But, for his parents, it would fly by, and he wouldn't be able to tell them when they'd be able to see their granddaughter again.

No, he was sure Elyse would want to work out some kind of schedule. But if he only saw Annalisa once a year, that added up to just eighteen times before she was an adult. The pain that idea caused him was so deep he wasn't sure it would ever go away.

That brought him back to the question he'd asked himself over and over again. If he'd known Elyse was pregnant, would he have still left America?

His response was the same as it had been last time. No. He wouldn't have left.

But she hadn't known at the time, and he *had* left, so asking those types of questions caused nothing but torment.

He needed to concentrate on the here and now and figure out a plan for the future. Or he would be left with nothing to look forward to, except recriminations—aimed solely at himself.

CHAPTER NINE

Mary Landers had had no seizures in the last two days. Elyse gave her hand a quick squeeze. "I'm so glad you're doing well. I hear they're releasing you today."

"Yes, they are. We're going to wait a couple of weeks and then we'll head back to the States. School starts soon, and we don't want our daughter to miss any of it."

Annalisa was sound asleep back in Luca's office. In fact, he'd stayed behind to watch her, not quite comfortable with leaving her alone, despite the baby monitor. She wondered if that was the real explanation or if he simply couldn't get his fill of his daughter.

If so, she knew the feeling.

She couldn't quite get her fill of him. And she was pretty sure she never would. She'd proved that by having sex with him on his car.

Her heart had cracked in two over him once before, and the way she was going, it could very well break all over again.

"What grade is your daughter going to be in?"

"Fifth. Bella starts at a new school, so we want to make sure we're back."

The couple only had the one child. Mary had shared that they'd tried to get pregnant again but couldn't. And adoption took so long they'd opted not to go in that route, especially since her husband was in the military, and they might change locations before the process could be completed.

She understood completely. It was something she hadn't told Luca, even after he'd used a condom the other day. In the beginning, she'd kept it to herself because she hadn't thought it was any of his business.

And now?

She wasn't so sure. When she'd gone out to the garage and looked at the car, it had been on the tip of her tongue to tell him. But she'd chickened out.

What would be accomplished by telling him?

"Is she excited?"

"She misses her friends, but since we moved locations and not just schools, it makes it easier. Military kids learn early to cultivate relationships where you find them, because you never know when life will drag you somewhere else entirely."

"I can certainly understand that."

Elyse had a lot in common with those families. Life had changed drastically for her in the space of thirteen months. Her relationship with Luca had ended. Then had come the pregnancy and the resulting hysterectomy.

That was about as drastic as it got without someone dying.

On the positive side, she still had her ovaries, so she hadn't been thrown into premature menopause in the midst of everything else.

A hot flash might be a little difficult to explain, and since Luca hadn't taken her skirt off he hadn't even seen her hysterectomy scar, not that he would have surmised that she'd had her uterus removed from that scar alone.

Didn't she owe it to him to tell him? She didn't know. Everything was just a tangle of confusion right now.

"Elyse, could I see you for a moment?"

She whirled around, expecting Luca to be standing in the doorway, leaning sexily against the doorjamb, but no one was there.

"I think it came out of your pocket," Mary said in response to her obvious confusion.

"My…oh, the baby monitor." Luckily it had a two-way speaker feature. She pulled the receiver from her pocket and used it like a walkie-talkie. "What's up, Luca?"

"Anna's hungry. Or something." She suddenly heard the sound of Annalisa crying over the speaker. Luca must have aimed it at the baby, or maybe he was holding her.

"I'll be there in just a minute. Thanks." She dropped the device back in her pocket, a sense of amusement going through her at the tinge of panic that had colored Luca's voice. She remembered feeling that very same fear the first time Anna had cried, when all of the doubts she'd repressed during her pregnancy had come roaring back. What if she wasn't enough for her baby? What if she couldn't get her to stop crying? Or, worse, what if she couldn't tell the difference between something simple and something serious?

So far, she'd dealt with each crying session as it came and had learned the difference between distress and simple hunger. Despite her difficult pregnancy, Anna had become a relatively healthy baby.

So far, anyway.

She went over and gave Mary's arm a gentle squeeze. "If I'm not here when they release you, take it easy and have a safe flight back."

"Thank you for everything."

She actually hadn't done anything, except to consult with Enzo and give the family some encouragement. But she could imagine how grateful she'd be for a visitor from her homeland if the situation was reversed.

"You and your doctors did all the work. I was only here

in case they needed translation work, but Luca could have done that on his own, anyway."

"Luca?"

Ugh, she'd used his first name rather than his title. "Dr. Venezio."

"Oh, yes, of course. He did speak great English. Is Anna your baby?"

"Yes, she is."

"With Dr. Venezio?"

Suddenly she realized that the patient had added everything up and come to the right conclusion.

Mary was leaving soon, though, so it didn't really matter if she knew.

"Yes, he's her father."

"I thought so. There was something there between you. A couple of looks…"

Her brows went up in surprise. "You were a pretty sick lady when you came in here. I'm surprised you had time to notice anything besides what you were going through."

"I think there was a need to know everything I could about my doctors before I underwent surgery."

"Dr. Giorgino performed your surgery."

"Yes, but Dr. Venezio played a pretty big role in diagnosing it."

"That's true." She paused, then finished the story for her. "Luca and I broke up before I realized I was pregnant."

Mary blinked. "That must be hard, especially working with him." She reached out a hand and Elyse took it. "I hope everything turns out for the best for both of us. This is my husband's last tour of duty and then he plans to use his engineering degree to go into architecture. So let me know if you want a house designed. He's pretty good."

"I will. And thank you." She leaned down and gave the woman a quick hug. "Take care of yourself."

"You too."

And then Elyse left and walked toward the elevators to see what was going on with Luca and her daughter.

When she entered the office, it looked like a tornado had hit. There were three diapers strewn on the floor and Luca was standing in the middle of the room with a big wet mark running down his shirt. "I thought you said she was hungry."

"I thought she was too, but I tried to change her diaper first, like you told me."

"And?"

"We never exactly finished Diapering for Beginners."

Her eyes widened as she realized what the wet spot was. Annalisa had peed on him. She hurried to take the baby. "Oh, Luca, I'm so sorry. I was saying goodbye to Mrs. Landers and lost track of time. I thought the diapers were self-explanatory."

"They are. But trying to hold her and get the diaper situated were harder than I expected."

"It's okay. I remember how hard it was that first time." She dragged the baby blanket over to the discarded diaper, laid her daughter down on top of the barrier and quickly strapped her into it. She glanced around. "Where are her shorts?"

"In the crib. That's where I tried to change her first, then when I couldn't figure it out, I put her on the desk to see if I could get it right."

He hadn't. "At least you tried." She picked up the shorts and stuck one of Annalisa's legs into it and then the other.

The baby stopped crying. Immediately.

Luca dropped into his office chair looking like he'd just been through a particularly difficult surgery. "I'm sorry. I wouldn't have interrupted you if I'd realized."

"It's okay. We were done, anyway." She hesitated, but

then decided to come clean just in case Mary let it slip before she left. "Mary guessed that Annalisa was ours."

He frowned. "So?"

"I wasn't sure if you'd want anyone here to know."

"Since Lorenzo was holding her when you two walked into my office, I'm pretty sure someone already does. Besides, I'm not ashamed of her. Or of you. Better to admit everything than to have some twisted version of events travel down the gossip chain."

Admit everything. Something she hadn't exactly done.

Maybe she should take his advice and admit everything.

She touched his hand. "Hey, I think I should—"

There was a knock at the door, and Lorenzo stuck his head in, eyes taking in the scene. "Sorry, am I interrupting something?"

"No." Luca stepped closer to the door. "Did you need something?"

The other man frowned but only hesitated a fraction of a second. "I sent a note asking for a read on a patient this morning, did you get a chance to do it?"

"What time did you send it?"

"Eight this morning."

That would have been around the time she had gone out to the garage and seen him wiping down his car.

The memory of him bending her over that hood sent heat scorching through her.

Luca glanced at her, head tilting before saying, "I can look now, if you're okay with waiting."

"Yes. I have a consult in about fifteen minutes. The patient is adult. Worsening symptoms since yesterday."

Luca went to his computer, the keys clicking as he looked for whatever it was the surgeon wanted him to see. "Elyse? Care to throw your opinion in as well?"

She went around the desk to find him looking at a series of MRI slides. "Oh, wow."

The images showed a series of lesions in different parts of the brain. "MS?" she asked.

Giorgino nodded. "This is what I thought too."

It looked like a typical case, but there was something…

Luca shook his head. "I don't think so. They're on the basal ganglia. Nothing on the brain stem, like you'd expect with MS." He stared at the images. "Maybe acute disseminated encephalomyelitis?"

"ADEM?" she said. "Yes, it could be."

Similar in many aspects to MS, ADEM often came on after an illness. But it was seen mostly in children, not adults. "How old is she?"

"Fifty-four," said Lorenzo.

"Was she sick recently? Have any type of vaccine?"

The surgeon came around to look at the screen as Luca scrolled back through the medical history. "Nothing."

"Is there someone here with her? A relative, maybe?"

"Suo marito."

Giorgino explained that her very worried husband was down in the waiting area. Calling down to the lobby and asking them to relay the question, they soon had their answer.

"She came down with the shingles virus about a month ago."

Elyse bit her tongue to keep from playing devil's advocate. She hated to be wrong, but in this case she had to admit that Luca probably was correct in his diagnosis. Plus the fact that looking at the scans a little closer, the lesions were more perivenous as opposed to the way multiple sclerosis normally presented. At least this time they hadn't argued about it. Although she might have presented her theory more vehemently if they had been on her home turf, which made her wonder why she hadn't here. Maybe because they weren't as close as they once had been.

Or maybe she'd learned a thing or two since then. If that was the case, something good had come of their last few arguments. Something besides Annalisa.

"Standard treatment, then," she said, "consists of high doses of dexamethasone or methylprednisone to lower inflammation, wouldn't you say?"

Luca and Giorgino suddenly began speaking in rapid Italian that she couldn't keep up with. The surgeon's glance went to her once then back to Luca.

Did they disagree with her treatment plan? Or was the surgeon asking about what she meant to Luca?

No, of course he wasn't. She was being paranoid. They had to be talking about treatment options.

Then Giorgino was gone with a wave and a quick word of thanks.

"Everything okay?"

Luca clicked off the computer screen. "Yes, he went to initiate treatment. He said to tell you thank you."

"That was a pretty long thank you. Besides, you came up with the diagnosis first."

He grinned. "Yes, but I'm not nearly as cute as you are."

"You're a funny guy."

Through it all, Anna had remained quiet as if she knew that they were doing something important. Now that they were done, though, she gurgled, then jammed her hands into her mouth.

"I thought you said she wasn't hungry."

"She shouldn't be. Not yet. And now that the Great Diaper Crisis is over, she should be fine."

"Diaper crisis?"

"Um, you still have a little wet stain on your shirt." A sudden thought made her laugh. "No wonder Enzo looked at us kind of weird. Probably thought something kinky was going on in here."

"Good thing he didn't see us yesterday, then." The sardonic note in his voice stopped her in her tracks.

She guessed what they'd done was a little beyond what they'd experimented with in the past. But it had been incredibly exciting, and she was finding she didn't regret it nearly as much as she should have. "Yes. Good thing."

The moment of telling him she couldn't have kids had come and gone.

"Is the department in Atlanta still downsized?"

The question came out of the blue, taking her by surprise. Was he thinking about her suggestion of moving back to the States? "Yes, unfortunately."

"Why did you stay, then? Afterward?"

"I couldn't leave the patients without anyone there. I know they would have replaced me, but I felt an obligation to them. I still do."

"Even if the hospital works you to death in the process? With those kinds of cutbacks, there's no way you can do justice to the patients that come in."

He was voicing exactly what she'd been thinking. Her voice went very soft. "I know that. But I have to try, while attempting to turn the boat back in the other direction. Sooner or later, they're either going to have to close our trauma center or hire more staff. Because lots of times those trauma cases involve neurological issues."

"Agreed." He touched her hair. "Anna needs you healthy and well. Not a...a wrung-out towel that has nothing left for herself."

"A wrung-out towel?" Is that how he saw her? Not very flattering.

"It doesn't quite come across the same way in English."

"I think I understand what you're trying to say. But

since I haven't worked since I had her, I don't know how it's going to be yet. The hospital is using a borrowed surgeon from a sister hospital until I come back online."

"Online. Like a computer program?"

She knew he was trying to help, and she shouldn't be offended, but she didn't like the inference that she would give Annalisa any less than all she had.

And if she really did become a wrung-out towel, like he'd said?

"You have your life together, no bumps in the road, I suppose."

His brows went up. "There have been some very big bumps, especially recently, but as you can see I am making time for both of you."

"As will I when I go back to work."

He nodded. "Very good, then. Let's talk about something else. Like our trip to Rome."

They spent the next twenty minutes discussing their game plan for that first actual meeting. And when they were done, Elyse wasn't sure whether tomorrow was going to be a celebration. Or a wake.

But they would all find out, very soon.

CHAPTER TEN

His mother's greeting over the phone was filled with warm excitement. "Everything is ready here. I have the ingredients for your favorite meal, ready to prepare. Are you bringing Emilia with you?"

"Not this time, Mamma, but I am bringing someone with me."

"Una fidanzata?"

He cringed at the word fiancée. How exactly did one explain that someone was the mother of your child but not attached to you in any way, shape or form? You didn't.

"Are you sitting down?"

"Don't tell me. You really have chosen someone?"

His mother had been on his case to find a wife for the last several years. Even in medical school she'd asked about girls, despite the fact that the last thing he'd had time for was finding that special someone.

Until he'd met Elyse.

"No. But there was a girl. For a while. In Atlanta. We broke up, but I've since found out that there was…is…a…" He cleared his throat. "A baby involved."

"I don't understand, Lucan. A baby involved in what?"

"She has a child, and that baby is mine."

There was silence over the phone, then he heard her shrieking for his father to come into the room.

Luca held the phone away from his ear to avoid hearing loss.

Dio. He'd known she'd be shocked. Dismayed, maybe. But ultimately he'd thought she'd be happy.

His father must have arrived because he heard rapid-fire voices, but he couldn't make out what they were saying. Then his father came on.

"Luca, what the hell is going on? Mamma says you have a child?"

"Is she okay?"

"She's sobbing."

Damn. She was taking this a lot harder than he'd thought she would. He was glad now that he'd gone into his bedroom to make the call and doubly glad he hadn't waited to tell her upon their arrival in Rome. "I'm sorry, Papà. I only found out myself recently."

"Sorry?" He paused and shouted something to someone, evidently his mother. "I can't hear over her wailing. Why are you sorry?"

"Well… Mamma is crying."

A gust of laughter blew through the line. "She's not crying because she's sad. She's happy. Ecstatic. She was sure this day would never come."

"I'm not married to the baby's mother—and I don't plan on ever getting married to her." That sent a shaft of pain right through his chest. Because at one time he had fantasized about Elyse walking down that aisle. He'd had the ring in a little box in his drawer for a month. He'd held on to it, waiting for the right moment to come. It never had. And now it was stuffed in his sock drawer somewhere, since he'd never had time to return the ring before he'd left for Italy.

"Is she a good girl?"

He blinked at that. "She's a grown woman, Papà, and

if you mean is she nice, then, yes, she's very nice. It just didn't work out between us. She flew to Florence to tell me a week ago."

"How old is the baby?"

"Four months, and she's a girl. Annalisa Marie Tenner."

He waited while his dad relayed the information. "Why doesn't she have your last name?"

"Because I wasn't there when she was born. And maybe Elyse wasn't sure what to do about that fact."

He'd assumed she hadn't wanted to give Annalisa his last name because she hadn't been sure how he would react to the news. Or maybe there had been a period of time when she wasn't sure if she would even tell him.

But that was something he could do nothing about at the moment. Maybe later, once they'd come to some sort of understanding and things weren't quite so emotional.

Strike two for having sex with her on the hood of his car. It had muddied the waters and made it hard for him to do anything but think about those last memorable seconds. Because he badly wanted to do it all over again.

And there was no way he could. He needed to keep his head about him, especially now that his parents knew. He didn't want to give them false hope.

Again, his dad stopped to relay the information. "Papà, just put Mamma back on the phone, please."

A minute later, she came on the line, speaking so fast that he could barely understand her. Something about wanting to have a huge party to introduce the baby to the extended family.

Dio! That hadn't been on his radar at all. "Let me talk to Elyse first. She might not want that kind of attention."

"Elyse? This is the mother?"

"Yes. And I'm not sure she's up to one of your parties."

"Of course she is. This is our first grandchild. Everyone must know."

He was pretty sure everyone already did with the way she'd carried on a few moments earlier. "We're only going to be at the house for a week. There won't be time to put anything together."

"Yes, there will. I'll make it work. It can be on your last day at the house." She paused her tirade. "But only a week? How will we get to know either of them in that time?"

He hadn't talked to Elyse about spending more time than that, although she was slated to be in Italy for a month. But he'd been hoping to get to know his daughter a little bit better without his mother hovering over his every move. "She won't be here that long. She's only in Italy for a month and she's been here nearly a week already."

"A month? Spend the rest of the time with us, then."

"No, Mamma, I can't. I have to work. I've already taken a week off as it is."

"We barely see you." The complaint was one his mother always made.

"That's not true. You saw me less than six weeks ago."

"Why don't you come back to Rome and work?"

They'd been over this same argument time and time again. Priscilla believed all her children should be gathered around her. And his sisters were. They had both settled less than ten kilometers from their birthplace. After his breakup, though, Luca hadn't been able to bear the thought of moving back to Rome. His mom was far too intuitive. Between her and his sisters, they would have yanked every last detail from him.

It looked like they might get that chance after all.

"I told you. This clinic specializes in neurology. They're doing great work."

"There are clinics here in Rome as well."

"I'm already here, Mamma. I can't just uproot myself." He paused, not letting his voice run ahead of his mind. He decided to steer her back to one of her original subjects just to save himself. "About the party. Nothing too big. Promise me."

Elyse was going to kill him for throwing her to the sharks, so to speak.

"It will just be family. Maybe fifty people."

"No. That's too big."

"But your aunts, uncles and cousins will be offended if they're not all invited."

"I don't think I even have that many cousins and aunts."

"Oh, at least that many. I can think of a hundred off the top of my head."

Okay, so now fifty was sounding a whole lot better. "Let's not invite all of Rome, Mamma. And I really need to ask Elyse if it's okay. If she says no, we'll have to skip it."

"Ask, then. I'll wait."

"She's probably already asleep. I'll ask her in the morning before we leave and call you then."

He doubted that Elyse was asleep at nine o'clock, but the last thing he wanted to do was knock on her bedroom door and have her answer in pajamas. Or worse.

"Do you promise? Call me early. I have a lot of work to do as far as planning goes."

This time he gave an audible sigh. "Nothing too extravagant. Please, Mamma."

"Of course not. You know me."

Yes, he did, which was why he'd said it. But it really didn't matter. She was going to do whatever she wanted to, and his sisters were probably going to be cheering her on the whole way. Not the way he'd wanted to introduce Elyse to his family. Priscilla had a kind of frenetic energy that others tended to feed off. Either that or they were horrified by it.

She was in her element when planning *festas*. He could remember all the huge Christmas and Easter bashes that she'd hosted. "Just a few family members" quickly became "the" place to be on holidays. Distant relatives finagled invitations just to come and see what his mother had cooked up for that particular celebration. Time to hammer his point home.

"Keep the guest list small. Elyse doesn't speak Italian, so she's going to feel totally out of place as it is."

"I will enlist your father's help. I will tell him to rein me in if I'm getting too...what was the word? *Stravagante*."

She said it with such a flourish he had to laugh. "You're impossible, but *ti amo*, Mamma. Don't do anything until I call you in the morning."

"I won't, I promise. I love you too, *mio figlio*."

He hung up the phone and sat on his bed for a minute. Should he ask Elyse tonight?

No, because, again, that would entail him knocking on her bedroom door. Which was probably why his subconscious was pushing for him to do just that.

Well, it could keep pushing all it wanted. This time he wasn't listening.

"She wants to do what?"

Elyse was horrified. Luca's mother wanted to throw a party—for Annalisa—and she knew nobody. Suddenly she wondered if coming to Italy had been a mistake, if everything she was doing here was just going to make things worse. She glanced in the back seat, where Annalisa was sleeping, hoping beyond hope she was doing the right thing.

"It will keep her busy and stop her from asking too many personal questions."

She could just imagine what some of those questions might be. A party didn't sound too bad when you looked at the other possibility. She relaxed in her seat. "I don't even speak Italian."

"I'll translate for you. It's only for relatives, and she's excited about meeting Annalisa. That's what you were worried about, right?"

True. Luca had said his mother was old-fashioned. It would have been worse if she'd wanted to hide Annalisa away and never speak of her to anyone outside Luca's immediate family. But the last time he'd translated for her, she'd been a royal wreck. She'd have to be careful about letting that happen again.

"Yes. Tell her okay. I just don't want to embarrass anyone."

"Elyse, you could never embarrass a soul."

She shivered the way she always did when he said her name. His accent combined with that low graveled voice gave the word an exotic sound that got to her. Every single time.

"Oh, believe me, I could. I embarrass myself all the time. In lots of different ways."

He took his hand off the stick shift and touched her knee. "You're an excellent surgeon. And caring and compassionate with your patients."

A smile came up from deep inside her. "Right back at you."

He tilted his head, and she realized he wasn't sure what she meant. His English vocabulary was so extensive that she sometimes forgot there were still things that confused him. "It means that I think you're also an excellent doctor and caring and compassionate with your patients."

He grinned. "In that case, I thank you."

"Your mom knows we're not together?"

His hand went back to the gear stick and she immediately regretted voicing the words. He'd already said he would let his mom know that they had broken up. "Yes, she does."

"Sorry. I just wanted to make sure I wasn't supposed to play your doting wife."

He laughed. "Would you? Play a doting wife, if I asked you to?"

He's joking, Elyse. He doesn't mean anything by it.

"Of course I would." She batted her eyelashes at him in a theatrical sort of way. "Think your mother would believe us?"

"Probably not." He took a turn that put them on the ramp to a highway. "She always knew when I was lying before I even opened my mouth."

"Well, I guess we shouldn't lie about our relationship then, should we?" Which made Elyse a little nervous, since she was no longer certain what was truth and what wasn't. She'd told herself she was over him for so long that she'd come to believe it. But was it the truth? There were moments when the past came blazing through in all its glory and she was sure she'd been wrong about everything. Like after they made love the other day. It had taken everything she had to reason herself out of it.

If Luca asked her today to stay in Italy, stay with him, would she?

He didn't love her.

But what if he did? something inside her whispered. What if he did?

"So no lies, right?"

The words made her jerk around to look at him. "What?"

"Where were you?"

"Oh, sorry, I was thinking about what to wear to the party."

One of his brows went up and stayed up, but he didn't challenge her words.

No lies? Ha! She was starting out on the right foot with that one.

If his mom was as intuitive as Luca said she was, she was going to have to watch her step before the woman decided she and her son were actually meant for each other. "Go ahead and call her."

"Thank you. She promised it would be a small affair." He pushed a button on his dashboard and she heard a woman's voice answer in Italian. Luca answered in kind and a rapid-fire conversation took place, none of which Elyse understood. But she heard Luca placing emphasis on certain words and his mother answering.

Priscilla—wasn't that her name?—had a melodic voice that Elyse instinctively liked. There was a strength to it, but not the kind that forced its will on anyone.

Within five minutes it was over, and Luca pushed another button. "She said to say thank you and tell you that she loves you already."

Her heart clenched.

"She sounded sweet on the phone, even if I couldn't understand her."

"My sisters are a lot like her."

"Tell me about them." That seemed like a safe enough topic.

"Well, Isabella is a lawyer. She's very smart and intuitive about people."

Another person who would be able to see right through her. She was starting to get this horrible sense of foreboding about this whole visit. "And the other one?"

"Sarita is the baby. She is studying to be a psychologist. She's in her final year of studies."

A lawyer and a psychologist walk into a bar…and try to figure out the biggest lie of them all: that she no longer loved their brother.

Because she suddenly realized she did. She still loved him, after all this time.

God. How had this happened?

So much for thinking her feelings for him were dead. Obviously that wasn't the case.

Fake it. Fake it good, Elyse.

"So do Sarita and Isabella live in Rome?" Maybe they would only arrive for the party and then head right back out.

"They both do, so you'll get to spend some time with them."

Well, at least he'd mistaken the reason she'd asked. "That will be great. Do they speak English?" Maybe if they couldn't understand her, they wouldn't read between the lines.

"Yes, they both are pretty fluent, unlike my parents, so they can help translate as well."

That was the last thing she wanted. Would her body language immediately give her away?

"Great." Time to switch her thoughts to the road in front of them to keep herself from keeling over in shock. Or start to worry that every little thing she said would make him guess the truth. She swallowed, trying to shake the fear away.

"The signs on the highway look so bizarre to me. Did the ones in the States seem strange to you when you were there?" Thank heavens her voice didn't come out as shaky as she felt inside.

"What?"

"Everything being in another language."

He glanced at her. "A little. The worst was getting used to miles instead of kilometers and Fahrenheit instead of Celsius."

"I can see how that would be strange." She licked her lips and reached for another neutral topic. "Italy is gorgeous. I love everything about it."

There was a pause. "Everything?"

Had he seen through her already? If she kept on like this, she was doomed.

She tried to deflect one question with another. "Did you love everything about Atlanta?"

"Pretty much. Maybe not the traffic, even though we have that here as well."

She ran out of questions, so she sat there and leaned her head against the headrest. Anna was sound asleep in the back, so she focused on the sound of the tires against the roadway, instead of the realization that had shaken her to the core.

Random bits of thought swirled around like the leaves caught in a stiff breeze. She might be able to reach out and catch one of them, but she was too afraid of what she might find written on it. So she let them go on their way, closing her eyes and blocking out everything except for that constant background hum, her limbs slowly relaxing. Gradually getting heavier and heavier.

The swirling stopped, and one leaf drifted downward, settling in the corner of her mind. And on it was a single terrifying word.

Love.

Elyse had seemed distracted ever since they'd arrived at his parents' house. It was understandable, but he was sure there was something else underneath it. That feeling that she'd kept something hidden from him ever since her arrival in Italy.

Well, he hadn't spilled his every thought to her either.

He'd translated the introductions, and she'd responded politely when they made small talk, but he couldn't shake the feeling that something was wrong.

So far the only genuine smile he'd seen on her face had happened when his mother had lifted Anna into her arms and squeezed the baby to her chest, eyes closed, tears pouring down her cheeks. At that moment Elyse had glanced his way and smiled, putting her hand over her trembling lips.

That had been genuine. But it had also been short-lived.

Priscilla, who'd installed herself in an ornate rocking chair, looked up. "Would you show Elyse to her room and carry her bags up? I'll hold the baby."

She wasn't likely to let go of Anna anytime soon. And that was fine with him. It was better than the alternative, which was for her to have given Elyse a much cooler reception.

But she had been warm…effusively warm. His dad had beamed as well. He hadn't had a chance to hold Annalisa yet, but he'd only left his wife's side long enough to bring a pitcher of water and some fruit juice, setting the offerings on a sideboard with some glasses. He wasn't as openly emotional as his wife, but he too was deeply moved by seeing his grandchild for the first time.

He glanced at Elyse. "Are you okay with that?" He wasn't going to assume anything. Not anymore. Especially with the mood she was in.

"I am. But I can get my bags."

He picked them up before she could make a move. "I've got them. Care to follow me?"

Leading the way up the stairwell, he glanced back and saw her hand reach for the banister and grip it tight.

Hell, she was shaking.

"They love her." If that's what she was worried about, he wanted to set her mind at ease. "I told you they would. She's their granddaughter. Even if she wasn't, they would still love her."

"She's yours. I swear."

He reached the landing and turned around quickly, which made her pause a couple of steps from the top. "Have I ever implied that I thought she wasn't mine?"

"No, but I could understand how—"

"I know she's mine. I don't need a test to tell me that. I never did. I *know* you. Know I was the only one you were involved with, even if we weren't always getting along very well." He set the bags down and went to her, cupping her elbows. "She has your eyes, but I definitely see a melding of the two of us when I look at her."

"So do I." She wrapped her arms around his midsection and laid her head on his chest. The move left him glued in his spot.

"I wish…" She sighed. "I guess it doesn't matter what I wish. It is what it is, and we just have to do the best we can."

He rested his chin on her hair, closing his eyes. He'd missed these moments.

Suddenly her arms dropped back to her sides and he felt that slow withdrawal that had happened so many times toward the end of their relationship, when he'd been left wondering what had gone wrong.

Dammit. Turning, he started back up the stairs.

They stopped at the end of a long hall of closed doors. This door in front of them was also shut tight. "This is yours. Mine is right across the hallway."

She gave a quick laugh. "I would have thought they'd have put us as far apart as possible. Maybe even on different floors."

"No, it would have been you who did that." He couldn't resist throwing out a reference to a distance that was so much more than physical.

"What do you mean?"

He wasn't touching that question, because he might say something he regretted. "You're the one who insisted on separate bedrooms."

"I know." She muttered something under her breath before pushing open the door. Her breath came out in a whoosh of sound. "Luca, it's beautiful."

The room was big, as were all the bedrooms. And directly across from them was a huge four-poster bed carved from mahogany.

"I'm glad you like it."

He set her bags on the floor just inside the door. He nodded over at a matching tall dresser. "The drawers will be empty. Feel free to unpack."

"Will your mom be okay with Annalisa for a while?"

"Of course. I'm sure she's hoping we'll be a while."

He realized how that sounded when something flashed in her eyes, and she was suddenly back from wherever she'd gone, wholly present, wholly accessible.

Unsure how long this reprieve was going to last, his gaze trailed over her features before settling on her lips.

She'd fallen for him at one time.

And what about now?

If he kissed her, would she kiss him back?

Would they slam the door and fall onto that tall bed and make love?

If he stood here much longer, he was going to do exactly that. So it was time to leave. And fast.

Before he put his thoughts to the test and gave his mother a false sense of hope. Because even if he would have liked another chance to work things out, it was doubtful that Elyse would. Despite that one episode on the hood of his car.

"Do you want anything before I go?" His lips tightened when those words were as blundered as the last ones.

"No. Nothing, thanks. I'll be down in a few minutes."

He took that as a dismissal and was through the door in an instant, closing it behind him before he said something he'd regret. Something that could never be erased.

Heading back the way he had come, he threw one last glance at the dark wooden surface of the door and wondered if she knew.

Wondered if she realized that as he'd stood there wishing he could kiss her, he'd almost muttered the phrase he'd held back that night in Atlanta.

He loved her. Had never stopped loving her.

And, hell, if it wasn't going to be his undoing.

Because there was nothing he could do—no deity he could implore—that could erase what was now burned onto his very soul.

CHAPTER ELEVEN

THE PARTY HAD been organized for tonight, the penultimate night of their stay, which was both good and bad. It was good in that she'd barely seen Luca the evening before except for dinner. Elyse wondered if he was making himself scarce on purpose, which would be good for her. Except she didn't seem to feel that way.

This morning, though, he'd met her for breakfast and said he'd show her around the grounds. "If you need some privacy, there's a small *terrazza* a little way from the house, which is where I used to go as a kid. I built a fort there for just that reason, in fact."

"Wow, is it still there?" Somehow she couldn't imagine Luca needing to get away from anyone. He was self-assured and confident. She was pretty sure he hadn't suddenly gained those characteristics the second he'd become an adult.

"The *terrazza*. Yes, it's still there. The fort? No, it's long gone. It was made out of a collection of cardboard boxes. It even had different rooms."

"I somehow can't imagine you making a play fort."

He tilted his head. "Why not? Don't most kids?"

"Yes, I made my share in the house. Blankets over the dining-room table. I didn't quite get as ambitious as you did. I just wanted to have a secret place to read."

"So did I."

That was another thing that surprised her. She'd pictured him playing soccer and doing sports, not being a kid with his nose stuck in a book. "You liked to read?"

"Loved it. Especially adventure stories. I loved danger."

Now, *that* she could see. Maybe the danger in those books had infused itself into his being, because she couldn't imagine a man more dangerous to her senses than Luca was.

Before she could think of an answer that was as far from that thought as she could get, Priscilla swept into the room and said something, which Luca translated as a greeting. Then she and her son had a quick argument, and his mom gave him a frown and looked at Elyse and said something in Italian. When Luca didn't explain, she said in broken English. "Please say her."

Luca sighed. "She wants to know if she can take Annalisa into town and get her a new dress. I told her she has all the clothes she can possibly use, but Mamma wants her to have something that's from her. For the party." He looked in her eyes. "If you don't want her to, I'll explain that."

"Heavens. Of course she wants Annalisa to have something new for the party. It's fine. I have a bottle ready in the fridge for her."

When he relayed that back to Priscilla, she smiled, setting off a dizzying array of crinkles beside her eyes that really brought out the beauty in her face. Luca looked like her. So did Annalisa, if she was honest.

An hour later the two were out the door, leaving Elyse almost alone in the house with Luca, since his father had gone to work for the day.

The housekeeper was there, but she was busy with the caterers and other professionals who were getting things ready for the party that night. Luca had promised her it would be a small affair but, seeing the crew in action, somehow she didn't believe him. Who hired caterers for dinner with the family? And something about the way Luca had said "party" when he'd first talked to her about it made her think it wasn't going to be as simple as he made it out to be. All she could do was smile and hope for the best.

"Do you want to go for a walk? I can show you the actual garden where treasures were smuggled and dragons were slain."

That made her laugh. "Well, when you put it that way, how could I refuse?"

He led her down a mown path, the splash of flowers on either side of them looking wild and free. The funny thing was, those flowers had probably been carefully tended to do exactly what the gardener wanted.

"So where was this magnificent fort?"

"Right here."

The flowers had given way to an open cobblestoned area that had a couple of benches. Off to the side was a crystal clear pond that bubbled with fish and water plants. "Your parents let you have a cardboard village in the middle of all of this beauty? How long was it here?"

"A couple of years on and off. My sisters tended to tear it down almost as fast as I could build it. This is where they brought their friends, and they certainly didn't want their brother messing things up for them."

She could picture that scene happening. Since she was an only child, she hadn't had any of the competition that faced siblings. "They probably brought their boyfriends here later. It's the perfect place."

"Yes. It is. And they did."

She didn't want to ask, but she couldn't help it. "And you. Did you bring your girlfriends here?"

"Hmm... I can remember a time or two."

"A time or two? I bet you had them swarming over you."

He motioned her to a bench and then sat next to her. "No. No swarming. I've never been one to play around."

"No. You never were." Memories of them colored so many parts of her brain that she was pretty sure he'd traveled along most of her synapses.

He turned toward her. "Thank you."

"For what?"

"I don't know, exactly. Annalisa. The crazy times we had. Something beautiful came from what I'd always seen as scorched earth."

"Oh, Luca. I feel the same way. If we'd never gotten together...never had that fight in my office...she wouldn't be here."

His fingers touched her face. "We built our own fort and hid away in it for a while, didn't we?"

"Yes, we did."

Dark eyes stared into hers. "Is it completely gone?"

She could lie. Or she could tell the truth.

Hadn't they agreed not to lie to each other?

"No," she whispered. "It's not."

He exhaled heavily. "I so needed to hear that." His palms skimmed her jawline. "Because I don't think it is either."

Then his mouth was on hers in a kiss that tested the whole scorched-earth theory, because it was still as beautiful and wild as those flowers they'd passed on their way here.

He stood and held his hand out to her, and there was no hesitation when she answered his invitation. Two minutes later they were in her room in that big bed, where he undressed her. Slowly. Carefully.

So different from the car experience, where things had

been removed in frantic haste, but this was no less fulfilling. They explored each other, relearning curves and planes, seeking out subtle changes that had taken place over those lost months. He found her scar, but even as she stiffened, he shushed her.

"It's beautiful. This is where my Anna came into the world."

He made her feel cherished and cared about. And maybe even…loved?

Did he love her?

She swallowed. *Did he?*

Ask. Do it.

She couldn't make the words form on her lips, so she decided to show him instead, in the hope that he would whisper the words she longed to hear.

Instead, he climbed off the bed and pulled his wallet from his trousers and laid it on the bed. She closed her eyes, knowing exactly what that represented.

It didn't matter. She could tell him later. Once she knew for sure how he felt. Maybe he wouldn't need more kids. Maybe he'd be okay with just one. Just their Anna.

He went into the attached bathroom and when he returned he didn't have a stitch of clothes on. But he did have a small towel.

The question was almost lost when he climbed on the bed and straddled her. Then she found it. "What is the towel for?"

"I'm glad you asked." His smile was wicked. "Because I'm about to show you."

He draped the towel over her chest, covering both breasts. At first she thought he was worried about her modesty, until he gripped either end of the towel and slowly drew it back and forth over her. The thick terry teased the nipples underneath, creating a kaleidoscope of sensation that soon had her writhing on the bed.

"Ah… Luca, I'm not sure…" The words ended on a moan when he increased the downward pressure as he continued to seesaw the towel, over her, driving her wild.

Her hips bucked under him, but his weight on her upper thighs kept her from getting any kind of satisfaction. He leaned down next to her ear. *"Ti voglio così tanto bene."*

Was he saying he loved her?

Didn't know. Didn't care.

The towel stopped, making her eyes open.

"Don't worry, Ellie. I'm not done yet. Not by a long shot."

Picking up his wallet, he opened it, started to draw out a condom.

She stopped him with a hand on his. "We don't need one."

That was as close as she could get to the truth. She could explain it all later, but right now she just wanted to feel him. All of him.

"Dio. Cara. Yes. I want that too. You don't know how much." He leaned down and took her mouth in a kiss that sent pretty little lights spinning behind her eyes.

Then the weight came off her thighs, freeing her for a second or two, before he gripped her hips and turned them so that she was where he had been. On top. Positioned in the perfect spot.

She went still for several seconds, poised on the very edge of heaven and not quite sure how she'd gotten there, or what she'd done to deserve it.

"Do it." His hands tightened on her hips, but he didn't try to yank her down. "Please."

Instead of taking him in a hurry, she eased down, feeling each silky inch of him as she took him in.

He muttered those words that meant nothing and yet told her everything she wanted to hear as she rocked her hips, retracing her path up and then sliding back to the bottom.

There was something unhurried and yet desperately rushed in her movements, and she couldn't quite choose one or the other. Until one hand covered her breast and the other tangled in her hair, pulling her toward his mouth. The combination of the friction of his palm and his tongue over hers made the decision for her. Her movements quickened, and she suddenly didn't care about anything other than how he was making her feel.

Up and down. Empty and full. She couldn't get enough. And when his fingers slid out of her hair and worked their magic elsewhere, she lost it, pushing down hard and then pumping to an internal rhythm. She climaxed, crying out against his mouth, even as he flipped her onto her back and drove into her again and again until he lost himself inside her.

There were several moments when she felt suspended in space. Untethered. Floating free.

Loved.

He hadn't questioned her decision about the condom. Had seemed to embrace it.

That had to mean something. Didn't it?

A single worry reappeared, joined by a second. Then a third.

She opened her eyes to find him watching her. She searched for something to say. "How long before your mom gets back?"

Groaning, he kissed her cheek. "I have no idea, but…"

She laughed. "You don't want to be caught necking in the back seat?"

"But we're not in a back seat. We're in bed."

God, she loved him. Loved these little differences that

gave their world color and dimension. "It means we don't want to be caught together. In bed."

His nose nuzzled her ear. "I don't want to go."

"I don't want you to go either. But eventually someone is going to come looking for us. And when they do, I'd rather be fully clothed. And in our separate rooms."

He rolled off her, drawing her into his arms. "Okay. I'll go. But only because I don't want Mamma's party guests to go home with any salacious tales."

"Salacious?" That was suddenly her new favorite word.

"Yes. Of what we were making in this room." He got out of bed and leaned over her. "And just so you know, I do want more."

And then he was gone, leaving her with a tingle in her belly that wouldn't quit.

He wanted more.

Just the thought made her want to go find him and snatch him back to the room or to their fort or whatever they wanted to call it. As long as they were together.

With a joy she hadn't felt in a long time—one that was different from the day-to-day happiness that Anna gave her—she got up to shower and dress for the party.

CHAPTER TWELVE

HE HELD HER hand for most of the evening, trying to give her a boost of confidence while people spoke Italian all around them. Although he wasn't sure if the hand holding was for her...or for him. Those moments in the bedroom had been beyond anything he could have imagined, and they hadn't had a chance to talk about it.

She hadn't wanted to use a condom. Surely that meant she wanted a fresh start together? And more children. He'd made sure she knew he was in favor of that by whispering that he too wanted more.

She loved him, he was sure of it. Even if she hadn't said the words.

Then again, neither had he. But he would. Very soon.

He expected his mother to say something about all of this hand-holding, but she seemed oblivious. Everyone's attention was riveted on Annalisa, who was taking everything in her stride much better than she should have as she was passed from person to person.

"Are you okay?" Hell, he hoped he wasn't just imagining things.

She turned to him with a smile. "I am. For the first time in over a year." She nodded toward Anna. "She looks adorable in that dress your mom found."

"She has a knack for finding the perfect gift."

Anna was wearing a mint-green dress, complete with tulle around the full skirt and a satin bodice. She looked like a princess from a movie. She even had a tiny glittering tiara perched on her head. Luca had no idea how they'd kept her from knocking it off. But she hadn't. She was smiling and cooing and generally being the most beautiful thing he could imagine.

Other than Elyse.

While she wasn't wearing mint green to match her daughter, she did have on a black dress that ended just above the knee, her shoulders bare and tempting, her hair swept up into some kind of fancy knot with strands that wound their way down the sides of her face and tickled her nape. And she had on these high heels that made him think of things that were better off left unthought.

"Oh, I almost forgot! I brought that wine for your mom. We were going to get the flowers here, remember?"

"We can do that first thing tomorrow morning."

She licked her lips. "So your mom would definitely be scandalized if we shared a room?"

Two days ago he wouldn't have been able to envision a scenario where that kind of a question would come up. Or even thought. But he liked it…wanted things to keep moving in this direction.

"Ellie, I'm surprised at you." He gave her a grin. "In the best possible way. But yes. She probably would, although if I happen to have a nightmare involving the two of us kissing, and sneak into your room for comfort…"

She giggled. "A nightmare? Really? Should I be insulted?"

"Perhaps nightmare was a poor choice of word."

"I should think so." But she said it with a smile. And Elyse seemed…happy. He couldn't remember seeing her this way since…well, when there had still been some good in their relationship.

Her eyes trailed their daughter as she was handed over to yet another family member.

"Do you want me to bring her to you?"

"No, she looks happy."

"And how about you?"

Her brows went up and she leaned her head on his shoulder for a second. "What do you think?"

He noticed his mother was finally staring at them, and he had a fleeting thought that maybe they shouldn't be putting on a display of affection in front of everyone until they worked out the rest of their differences, but he wasn't about to push her away.

It was okay. Elyse was relaxed, and if she didn't care about his mother mentally putting rings on their fingers, then he shouldn't worry about it either. But he did have second thoughts about sneaking to her room tonight. If he was serious about doing this thing, then he wanted to do it right, not rush her into anything. His own prideful determination had messed up their relationship once before. He wasn't about to let that happen again.

Hopefully, if things went well, there would be many, many more moments like these. Slow, easy moments that led to something strong and lasting. And if it meant him moving back to America to get there, then so be it.

Elyse's arm flapped around on the bed beside her for a minute. Empty. A flicker of disappointment was quickly extinguished.

So what if he hadn't come to her room as he'd suggested he might? It had been a long evening. He had probably been exhausted. Just as she had been.

Cracking open her eyes and stretching, she couldn't

stop a smile from forming. She'd been hoping to talk to him about the reality of her situation and why they hadn't needed to use that condom, something she hadn't been able to say when they had been making love.

He cared about her. She'd felt it brewing under the surface yesterday. His words had seemed to confirm that fact, but she wanted him to go into this relationship—if he even wanted one—with his eyes wide open. This time there would be no holding back or letting things fester and foment.

He'd held her hand last night. In front of his mom, his relatives and everyone. That meant something.

She glanced at her watch. It was barely seven o'clock and it was their last full day here. Climbing out of bed, she jumped in the shower, lathering up in record time. Maybe she could still catch him and have that talk before breakfast, if he hadn't already gone downstairs. Or maybe when they went to buy those flowers he'd talked about as a thank-you present for his mom for hosting her. There was still time. She was sure of it.

With her hair damp, and her face washed clean, she found the bottle of Chianti and dropped it into the red silk wine bag they'd bought to go with the flowers and put it on the mahogany dresser. She ran her fingers over the ornate lines that looked so at home in this room. Her glance snagged on the crib, where Annalisa was still fast asleep. Last night had worn her out. Her daughter didn't normally stay awake that late, but it had been a special night, and she'd fallen asleep in her grandmother's arms, bringing a lump to Elyse's throat and an ache to her heart. Suddenly a week with them seemed like no time at all.

You need to find Luca. Maybe you can work something out.

She went across the hall and softly tapped on his door,

hoping that if the rest of the household was still asleep she wouldn't wake them. When there was no answer, she knocked a little louder. "Luca?"

Still no answer. She pursed her lips to the side. He could be in the shower. Or he could already be downstairs. She went back over and peeked in her room. Anna was still out. She'd nursed right before going to bed last night, so she could zip downstairs, find Luca and ask him if they could talk.

Tiptoeing down the treads, she stopped when she heard voices coming from the kitchen. One of them was Luca's. He was talking to a woman and sounded...concerned. Or something. Since he was speaking in rapid Italian she wasn't sure if she was reading him right. She started to turn and go back up the stairs but then the housekeeper appeared in the doorway and smiled at her, motioning her forward.

Ugh. But she was going to have to face him sometime. Except all the hopeful thoughts she'd had moments earlier were now faltering. Who was he talking to?

She forced herself to breeze through the door with a smile, hoping it didn't look like she'd been skulking in the doorway. Luca and his mother saw her at the same time, and the conversation immediately went silent.

They'd been talking about her. She swallowed. Maybe his mother had seen them last night and decided she didn't want her son taking up with someone from a different culture.

No. Things like that didn't happen anymore, did they?

She forced herself to speak, even though her throat felt packed with sawdust. "Good morning. How is everyone?"

Luca came over to her with a smile, throwing another glance toward his mom. He gave a quick shake of his head.

He didn't want her telling Elyse what they'd been discussing.

The sawdust turned to glass. Was it about Annalisa? Were they plotting how they were going to get her to spend more time in Italy?

You're being ridiculous. And paranoid.

His mom came over and took her hands, holding them up and kissing one. She winked at her son then turned her attention back to Elyse.

"Mamma…" Luca's voice was full of warning.

"Pssht."

Her response made Elyse's eyebrows go up. When they came back down they were contracted into a frown. "What's going on?"

Priscilla gave her hands a gentle squeeze. "You give Luca more babies?"

Babies?

The pain that stabbed her insides was sudden and intense, like the scars from her surgery when they had been new and raw. "Wh-what?"

Suddenly Luca's words from last night took on a whole new meaning.

Just so you know, I do want more.

Was that what he'd meant? He hadn't just been talking about making love?

God. Hadn't he mentioned changing his mind about having children? She could have sworn the word "maybe" had been in there, though.

Had he talked to his mother about it before discussing it properly with her?

Luca came over and touched his mom's arm, saying something that made her let go of Elyse's hands and turn toward him. "She love…" the woman tilted her head as if trying to find the right words. "She love you."

His mom's gaze swung back to her.

She expected Elyse to respond? What could she say, when this went to the very heart of her fears?

Of course Luca would want more children. And she'd fostered that expectation by saying they didn't need to use a condom. No wonder he'd seemed so happy about it. He'd thought they were on the same page.

Oh, how wrong he was.

He and his mom had been talking about children and families. And they had left her completely out of the conversation.

What would happen if he knew she couldn't have any more?

That wasn't something she was going to discuss in front of anyone else. And suddenly she didn't want to discuss it with Luca either. Not now. Maybe not ever.

Hurt and regret streamed through her system. If he hadn't left and had been beside her during her pregnancy, he would have known exactly what she'd gone through. The heartbreak of finding out she could never have another child.

But he knew none of it. And she hadn't told him when she'd had the chance, allowing things to become twisted beyond repair. Just like they had in Atlanta.

"Ellie, are you okay?"

The room was blinking in and out of focus, and she realized tears were very near. She could answer his mom's questions truthfully, if she chose to: Yes, she loved her son. And, no, she wouldn't be having any more of his babies.

"I'm fine." She forced a smile, desperately needing to escape. "We'll have to sit down and talk about that. But I think Annalisa is about ready to get up."

"I'll come up with you," Luca said.

"No." She snatched a quick breath. "I'll bring her down in a few minutes, once I've fed her."

His mom came over, her smile gone. "You cross…" she pointed at herself "…me?"

Elyse's heart did the very thing she'd feared. It snapped in a few more places.

She leaned over and kissed her cheek. "No, I'm not cross. I love you." She hoped the woman would understand those simple words, because she did. She loved Priscilla, Carlos, Isabella and Sarita and most of all, Luca. She'd fallen in love with his whole family while getting to know them this week. But she couldn't stay here any longer.

The smile came back even as Elyse's tears floated closer to the surface. She was going to leave. She had to. The thought of telling Luca the truth was suddenly the last thing she wanted to do. He deserved to have those babies. Italian babies. Babies that were part of a large and happy family. She'd seen evidence of that wider family last night. They loved each other, had laughed and conversed. Even if he loved her, she didn't want to keep him from what someone else could give him.

He would get over her. He had once before. Quite easily, in fact.

She knew exactly what she was going to do. She was going to make sure Priscilla had some quality time with Annalisa today, and then her aunt was suddenly going to call her and ask her to return to the States. Her ticket back home wasn't for a couple more weeks, but surely she could find a flight out of Italy sooner?

And then she was going to try to forget this trip had ever happened. She would make sure Luca and his family were able to see Annalisa, but as far as rekindling a dead romance, she was going to let those smoldering ashes grow cold, once and for all.

CHAPTER THIRTEEN

SHE MADE IT to the airport.

God, she couldn't believe she'd gotten out of the house without Luca cornering her. Sporting dark glasses to keep anyone from seeing the state of her eyes, she went to the desk to ask about getting on the first flight she could find. Anywhere in the United States would work. She could worry about getting back to Atlanta once she was there.

She should have told him about the hysterectomy from the very beginning, but her stupid pride had kept telling her it was none of his business.

Well, she'd made it his business when she'd had sex with him. But to try to clear it up now?

No way. He'd said he wanted more children. He might be able to unsay it, but he couldn't un-want it.

"I need a flight to the United States. The first one you have available, please." Peg, who'd never intended on staying for the entire month, had flown home almost three weeks ago, and Elyse missed her desperately right now. Anna was in her baby sling and Elyse had one suitcase with her. She'd left everything else behind. Not that he'd try to come after her.

Except he might. She had his daughter. This wasn't like last time, when he had been the one who'd left.

The woman behind the desk leaned closer. "Are you okay? Do you need help?"

Yes. She needed a ticket. Then she realized the agent thought she was in some kind of trouble.

Of course, you dummy. You didn't give her a destination other than the whole country.

She was eventually going to have to get back in touch with Luca and work out arrangements for visitation. But she could do that with a long-distance phone call—the longer the distance the better.

"I'm fine, sorry." She reached in the front pocket of the diaper bag and pulled out her original ticket and handed it to the woman. "I need to get home sooner than I expected, that's all. Are there any flights to somewhere in Georgia or, if not, one of the neighboring states?"

The ticket agent looked relieved. "Let me see what I can do." She did some clicking of keys, her mouth twisting one way and then another as she seemed to mentally shoot down each option. "Wait. I think I can get you to Atlanta, actually. The flight leaves in two hours. You'll have a few hours' layover in Miami, if that's okay."

"Yes, that's perfect. Thank you so much." She tried to smile but was well aware that it didn't quite come out the way she'd hoped. "How much for the ticket?"

The price was steep. Very steep. But it was worth it.

"I'll take it."

She took out her wallet, only to have a voice behind her say in English, "The lady isn't going anywhere."

Elyse froze. No. It couldn't be.

She whirled around.

Luca! How had he...?

How had he gotten here so fast? Unless he'd left Rome at around the same time she had.

She could hear the ticket agent asking her again if she

was okay. She wasn't. Not at all. But unless she wanted the authorities called and Luca hauled away for something he didn't do, she needed to allay the woman's fears. She took a deep breath and faced her once again. This time there was a phone in the agent's hand. "Would you like me to call someone?"

"No, I'm sorry. He's the baby's father." Then realizing that sounded off as well, she explained. "We're both her parents. Everything is okay."

She got out of line, hoping that she hadn't just sunk their chances of talking this through without getting arrested.

Walking a few feet away, she half hoped he wouldn't follow her. But of course he did.

He stared down at her, then his hand went to his baby's dark head, sifting through the wispy strands. Anna looked up at him, her face breaking into a toothless grin.

Guilt clawed at the edges of her heart. This was wrong. She shouldn't have left without talking to him first, should have realized he would figure out where she was.

This time when the tears came she didn't try to stop them. "You shouldn't have come."

"Yes. I should have. I'm prepared to go back to the States with you if necessary until you tell me why we can't be together." He removed her sunglasses and lifted her chin. "Don't shut me out, Ellie. You did it in Atlanta too, and it tore me apart. Talk to me. Is it something I did or said?"

"No, you didn't do anything. I— It's…" She swallowed hard. "Why are you here, Luca?"

"Isn't it obvious? I love you."

Oh, God, she was right. But it was too late.

She shook her head, the tears coming faster. "It's not going to be enough."

"Why? If you're talking about the layoff, it doesn't matter anymore. We'll work at different hospitals." He used his thumbs to brush away her tears.

"It…" She closed her eyes and tried again. "You want more children, and I can't have them."

He frowned. "What?"

This was where he would hear what she had to say and walk away.

Or would he?

There was only one way to find out.

"The reason I didn't come to Italy with Anna before now was that when she was born there were complications. I had to have a hysterectomy. I can't carry any more children." Ever.

"But the condom… *Dio*. You said we didn't *need* it, not that you didn't want me to use one."

"You misunderstood. And I misunderstood when you said you wanted more. I thought you were talking about more…" she lowered her voice "…sex. But you actually meant you wanted more children."

She sucked down a breath. "And then your mom told me to have more of your babies and—"

"One minute." He appeared to be working through something. "First of all—how do you say it? My *madre* isn't the boss of me. Not since I turned eighteen."

"I know, but—"

"I am not finished." He pressed his forehead to hers. "I did say I wanted more children, but it was in response to what I thought you wanted when we were in bed. Would I like more children? Yes, maybe in the future. But there are other ways of expanding our family and plenty of time to work it out. For now, you and Anna are enough. You will *always* be enough."

It couldn't be this easy. Could it?

"It's not fair to you."

"No." He plucked her old ticket from her hand. "This is what isn't fair. You leaving without telling me."

"You did it to me once."

His eyes closed. "And I was wrong. What I felt when I realized you were gone... *Dio*. I put you through hell, didn't I?"

"I think we put each other through hell."

"No more. The only question I have is this. Do you love me?"

She licked her lips. One last hurdle. *Do it, Elyse.*

"Yes, I love you. But what about your job? My job?"

"Those are things we can work out. Together." He slid his arm behind her nape and pulled her cheek to his. "When I realized you weren't in your room and that most of your belongings were gone, I couldn't believe it. My hands shook, and my gut twisted inside me.

"I made a mistake by leaving Atlanta last year. I told myself a hundred times I should go back and talk things out with you, but my pride wouldn't let me. And the longer it went on, the less likely it seemed that you would want me back. But this time—this time—I wasn't going to repeat that mistake. I am ready to move heaven and earth to make this work." He took a deep breath. "I just needed that 'yes' to my question about you loving me."

He kissed her forehead and then his daughter's. "Whether we're here or in the States, the only thing that matters is that we're together. Our little family."

"I want that too."

His finger traced down the side of her face. "Anna is going to need both of us. And when the time comes, we'll add more."

Before she could react, he smiled. "I've always wanted to help children who are in difficult situations. What do you think?"

"Adopt?" She said the word softly, not quite believing that he was saying the very thing she had thought of doing.

"Yes. Would you like that?"

She closed her eyes and sucked down a deep breath, believing at last. "Yes. I would love that."

"So...there's only one more question. Will you marry me? My *mamma*, she's old-fashioned, remember? And she's very good at throwing big parties. Or a big wedding."

Somehow she didn't think this had anything to do with his mom's prowess as a hostess.

"Well, we wouldn't want to disappoint your mom, would we?"

"So your answer is yes?"

"It's definitely yes."

With that, his lips came down on hers with a promise of things to come. Of promises kept. Of futures realized.

And this time she was not going to second-guess herself. Or him. She was just going to love him. And let herself be loved.

There was nothing more important than that.

EPILOGUE

THEY'D TIED THE KNOT. Not because of Annalisa or anyone's parents, but for them. And true to form, Priscilla had put on the wedding of the century, even though they would have been just as happy standing before a justice of the peace. Elyse had talked Luca into letting his mom have her way. It made her happy.

And Luca had chosen Enzo as his best man, despite those earlier fears. It gave Elyse confidence that he trusted their love was strong enough to withstand any storm.

Her parents and Peggy had flown in from the States to celebrate, and Peggy had pulled her aside to whisper, "I knew it wasn't finished between you two. If Anna hadn't pulled you together again, he would have come back for you."

Luca had admitted as much in the breathless moments after the ceremony was over and they were ensconced in their swanky hotel room. "I already knew I'd messed up. My conscience wasn't going to leave me alone. It might have taken as much as another year, but I would have flown back to Atlanta and confronted you."

She'd shivered at the confirmation of her aunt's words. For her part, Elyse told him why she'd withdrawn back then as he held her tight and kissed her on the temple. "I'd had a bad office romance, and I was determined not to do it again. But then you came along, and I felt like I was making some of the same old mistakes."

"But we won't. I promise you that."

Promises were made and kept. She'd promised to talk to him instead of withdrawing emotionally, and he'd promised to call her on it if she didn't.

She'd torn her plane ticket up and called the hospital administrator and officially resigned, deciding to spend six months in Italy immersing herself in the language and culture. How could she not? Hadn't Luca done the same in America? Her Italian still wasn't the best, but she'd learned what some of those naughty words meant, and they made her blush even harder. She still had another month of language school, and then they would decide where to go from there.

Right now, none of that mattered.

Luca came up behind her on the veranda and looped his arms around her waist. "Everything okay?"

Turning to face him, she leaned back on the railing. "Just counting my blessings."

"You were up late last night and early this morning too."

"Thanks to you." She tipped her face up to look into those dark eyes she loved so much. "You know you're very sexy in the morning." She reached up to run her fingers along the stubble lining his jaw. He had on an old faded T-shirt and pajama bottoms and his tanned feet were bare. Sexy didn't begin to describe her husband.

"And you're evading my question."

She laughed. "You didn't ask a question. But I heard what you were asking. No regrets. I'm happy. Anna loves you desperately. I love you desperately. I'm just enjoying the moments we have to ourselves. Now that she's older, we don't get many of them."

So far they hadn't talked any more about expanding their little family. Adoptions in Italy had stringent requirements and they'd need to be married for three years before going through the process. And there was always surrogacy, if they decided to harvest her eggs. They had time. For once, Elyse was in no hurry to get things done.

"Emilia likes eating with her. You should give yourself a break every once in a while."

"I've had a long break. And I appreciate all her help. I just don't want to miss anything," she said.

"I know what you mean."

She wrapped her arms around his neck. "I'm so grateful for second chances."

"So am I." He leaned down and brushed his cheek against hers, before murmuring. "I love *second* chances. And maybe even third chances. Very, very much."

Since they'd made love only an hour earlier, he surely couldn't mean…

Something stirred against her. A sensation she knew all too well. "You're kidding."

"Does it feel like I'm kidding?"

The man was insatiable. And she loved it. They had a lot of time to make up for.

"Well, then, what are you waiting for?"

He swung her up in his arms. "Is that an invitation, *Dottore Venezio*?"

Dr. Venezio.

Oh, how she loved hearing him call her that. And, yes, she loved second chances. Would never tire of them.

"It is indeed, *Dottore Venezio*."

Then he was striding back through the French doors

that led to their bedroom. Their own private sanctuary, where nothing was taken for granted, and where every kiss, every touch, every sigh centered around the most powerful word of all time: love.

* * * * *

SURGEON IN A
WEDDING DRESS

SUE MacKAY

To Tania
For all the moments we have shared, and the
moments to come.

And
Kate David: the newest and very supportive member
of the Blenheim Writers' Group.

CHAPTER ONE

NEW YEAR'S DAY. Resolutions and new beginnings.

'Huh.' Sarah Livingston scowled. As if anything new, or interesting, was likely to be found down here in the South Island, so far from the cities. Thanks to her fiancé—very *ex*-fiancé—coming to this godforsaken place had more to do with excising the pain and hurt he'd caused, and nothing at all to do with anything new.

But there was a resolution hiding somewhere in her thinking. It went something like '*Get a new life*'. One that didn't involve getting serious with a man and being expected to trust him. Surely that was possible. There had to be plenty of men out there willing to date a well-groomed surgeon with a penchant for fine dining; who didn't want anything other than a good time with no strings.

So why couldn't she raise some enthusiasm for that idea? Because she hadn't got over her last debacle yet. Six months since she'd been dumped, let down badly by the one man who'd told her repeatedly he'd loved and cherished her. Her heart still hadn't recovered from those lies. Or from the humiliation that rankled every time someone at work spoke of how sorry they were to hear about her broken engagement. Of course they were. Sorry they'd missed out on going to her big, fancy wedding, more like.

After learning of the baby *her* fiancé was expecting

with that sweet little nurse working in Recovery, Sarah had started putting in horrendous hours at the private hospital where she was a partner. It had been a useless attempt to numb the agony his infidelity caused her. Not to mention how she'd exhausted herself so she fell into bed at the end of each day instead of drumming up painful and nasty things to do to the man she'd loved.

And it was that man's fault her father had decided, actually insisted, she get away for a few months. What had really tipped the scales for her in favour of time away from Auckland was that her ex was due back shortly from his honeymoon in Paris.

Swiping at the annoying moisture in her eyes, Sarah pushed aside the image of *her* beautiful French-styled wedding gown still hanging in its cover in the wardrobe of her spare bedroom.

Why couldn't she forget those damning words her fiancé had uttered as he'd left her apartment for the last time. *You should never have children. You'd be taking a risk of screwing up their lives for ever.*

It had been depressingly easy to replace her at work with an eager young surgeon thrilled to get an opportunity to work in the prestigious surgical hospital her father had created. And who could blame the guy? Not her. Even being a little jaded with the endless parade of patients she saw daily, she still fully understood the power of her father's reputation.

'So here I am.' She sighed. 'Stuck on a narrow strip of sodden grass beside the coastal highway that leads from nowhere to nowhere.'

Her Jaguar was copping a pounding from a deluge so heavy the metalwork would probably be dented when the rain stopped. If it ever stopped.

Using her forearm to wipe the condensation from the

inside of her window, she peered through the murk. The end of the Jag's bonnet was barely visible, let alone the road she'd crept off to park on the verge. Following the tortuous route along the coast where numerous cliffs fell away to the wild ocean, she'd been terrified of driving over the edge to a watery grave. But staying on the road when she couldn't see a thing had been equally dangerous.

So much for new beginnings. A totally inauspicious start to the year. And she still had to front up to the surgical job she'd agreed to take. Sarah's hands clenched, as they were prone to do these days whenever she wondered what her future held for her. These coming months in Port Weston were an interim measure. This wasn't a place she'd be stopping in for long. Fancy leaving a balmy Auckland to come and spend the summer in one of New Zealand's wettest regions. Yep. A really clever move.

Her father's none-too-gentle arguments aside, the CEO of Port Weston Hospital had been very persuasive, if not a little desperate. He'd needed a general surgeon so that Dr Daniel Reilly could take a long overdue break. A *forced* break, apparently. What sort of man did that make this Reilly character? A workaholic? She shuddered. She knew what they were like, having grown up with one. Or was she an arrogant surgeon who believed no one could replace him? Her ex-fiancé came to mind.

Sharp wind gusts buffeted the heavy car, shaking it alarmingly. Was she destined to spend her three-month contract perched on the top of a cliff face? On the passenger seat lay one half-full bottle of glacial water, a mottled banana and two day-old fruit muffins that had looked dubious when she'd bought them back at some one-store town with a forgettable name. Not a lot of food to survive on if this storm didn't hurry up and pass through.

Sarah returned to staring out the window. Was it raining

in Paris? She hoped so. Then she blinked. And craned her neck forward. There was the road she'd abandoned half an hour ago. And the edge of the precipice she'd parked on—less than two metres from the nose of her car. A chill slid down her spine, her mouth dried. Her eyes bulged in disbelief at how close she'd come to plummeting down to the sea.

With the rain easing, she could hear the wild crash of waves on the rocks below. Reaching for the ignition, she suddenly hesitated. It might be wise to check her situation before backing onto the road.

Outside the car she shivered and tugged her jacket closer to her body. A quick lap around the vehicle showed no difficulties with returning to the road. Then voices reached her. Shouts, cries, words—snatched away by the wind.

Pushing one foot forward cautiously, then the other, she moved ever closer to the cliff edge. As she slowly leaned forward and peered gingerly over the side, her heart thumped against her ribs. The bank dropped directly down to the ocean-licked rocks.

More shouts. From the left. Sarah steeled herself for another look. Fifty metres away, on a rock-strewn beach, people clustered at the water's edge, dicing with the treacherous waves crashing around their feet and tugging them off balance. Her survey of the scene stopped at one dark-haired man standing further into the sea, hands on hips. From this angle it was impossible to guess his height, but his shoulders were impressive. Her interest quickened. He seemed focused on one particular spot in the water.

Trying to follow the direction of his gaze, she saw a boat bouncing against the waves as it pushed out to sea at an achingly slow pace. She gasped. Beyond the waves floated a person—face down.

Happy New Year.

* * *

Daniel Reilly stood knee-deep in the roiling water, his heart in his throat as the rescuers tried to navigate the charging waves. Aboard their boat lay an injured person. Alive or dead, Dan didn't know, but *he'd* have a cardiac arrest soon if these incredibly brave—and foolhardy—men didn't get back on land before someone else was lost.

The whole situation infuriated him. If only people would read the wretched signs and take heed. They weren't put there for fun. It was bad enough having two people missing in the sea, a father and son according to the police. It would be totally stupid if one of the volunteer rescuers drowned while searching for them.

'Doc, get back up the beach. We'll bring him to you,' a rescuer yelled at him. 'It's the lad, Anders Starne.'

'He doesn't look too good,' Pat O'Connor, the local constable, called over the din.

Like the middle-aged cop, Dan had seen similar tragedies all too often around here. It wasn't known as a wild, unforgiving coastline for nothing. But most calamities could be avoided if people used their brains. His hands gripped his hips as he cursed under his breath.

The kid had better be alive. Though Dan didn't like the chances, it was inherent in him to believe there was life still beating in a body until proven otherwise.

Waterlogged men laid Anders on the sand, a teenager with his life ahead of him. Dan's gut clenched as he thought of his own daughter. Even at four she pushed all the boundaries, and Dan couldn't begin to imagine how he'd cope with a scenario like this. He totally understood why the father had leapt off the rocks in a vain attempt to save his son. *He* would do anything if Leah's life was in jeopardy.

'Except take a long break to spend time with her.' The annoying voice of one of his closest friends, and boss, resonated in his head.

Yeah, well, he was doing his best. And because of interference from the board's chairman, Charlie Drummond, he *was* taking time off, starting tomorrow. Pity Charlie couldn't tell him how he was supposed to entertain his daughter, because he sure didn't have a clue. Hopscotch and finger puppets were all very well, but for twelve weeks? What if he got it all wrong again? He'd be back at the beginning with Leah an emotional mess and he distraught from not knowing how to look after his girl. That scared him witless. He focused on the boy lying on the beach. Far easier.

Dropping to his knees, he tore at the boy's clothing, his fingers touching cold skin in their search for a carotid pulse. A light, yet steady, throbbing under his fingers lifted his mood. He smiled up at the silent crowd of locals surrounding him. 'He's alive.'

'Excuse me. Let me through. I'm a doctor.' A lilting, female voice intruded on Dan's concentration.

Annoyed at the disturbance, he flicked a look up at the interloper. 'That makes two of us,' he snapped, and returned his attention to his patient. But not before he saw a vision of a shapely female frame looming over him. *Very* shapely.

'Where'd you come from?' he demanded as he explored Anders's head with his fingers.

'Does that matter at this moment?' she retorted.

'Not really.' He was local and therefore in charge.

'What have you found so far?' She, whoever she was, knelt on the other side of the boy.

He was aware of her scrutinising him. 'His pulse is steady.' He was abrupt with her as he straightened and looked her in the eye. Her gaze slammed into him, shocking the air out of his lungs. Eyes as green as the bush-clad hills behind them. And as compelling.

'Then he's one very lucky boy.' Her tone so reasonable it was irritating.

And intriguing. Who was she? He'd never seen her before, and she wasn't someone he'd easily forget with that elegant stance and striking face. He shook his head. Right now he didn't need to know anything about her.

Jerking his gaze away, he spoke to the crowd again, 'Someone get my bag from my truck. Fast.' To the doctor—how did she distract him so easily?—he said, 'I'll wrap him in a survival blanket to prevent any more loss of body heat.'

The kid coughed. Spewed salt water. Together they rolled him onto his side, water oozing out the corner of his mouth as he continued coughing. His eyelids dragged open, then drooped shut.

'Here, Dan.' Malcolm, his brother and the head of the local search and rescue crew, pushed through the crowd to drop a bag in the sand. Dan snapped open the catches and delved into the bag for tissues and the foil blanket.

'Thanks.' The other doctor flicked the tissues from his grasp. Dan squashed his admiration for her efficiency watching her cleaning the boy's mouth and chin as she tenderly checked his bruised face simultaneously. Her long, slim fingers tipped with pale rose-coloured polish were thorough in their survey.

'I don't think the cheek bones are fractured.' Her face tilted up, and her eyes met his.

Again her gaze slammed into him, taking his breath away. The same relief he felt for the boy was reflected in her eyes. Facial bones were delicate and required the kind of surgical procedures he wasn't trained to perform. He gave her a thumbs-up. 'Thank goodness.'

The rain returned, adding to the boy's discomfort. Dan began rolling Anders gently one way, then the other, tucking him into the blanket, at the same time checking for injuries. He found deep gashes on Anders's back and one arm lay at an odd angle, undoubtedly fractured. For now the wounds weren't bleeding, no doubt due to the low body temperature, but as that rose the haemorrhaging would start. The deep gash above one eyebrow would be the worst.

'Where's the ambulance?' Dan asked Pat.

'On its way. About three minutes out. It was held up by a slip at Black's Corner.'

Anger shook Dan once more. This boy's life could've indirectly been jeopardised because of some officious idiot's unsound reasoning. For years now the locals had been petitioning to get Black's Corner straightened and the unstable hillside bulldozed away, but the council didn't have a lot of funds and small towns like Port Weston missed out all the time. He'd be making a phone call to the mayor later.

Looking down at the boy, Dan asked, 'Anders, can you hear me?' Eyelids flickered, which Dan took for a yes. 'You've been in an accident. A wave swept you off the rocks. I'm checking for broken bones. Okay?'

Dan didn't expect an answer. He didn't get one. He wasn't sure if the boy could hear clearly or was just responding to any vocal sounds, so he kept talking. It must be hellishly frightening for Anders to be surrounded by strangers while in pain and freezing cold.

Beneath the thermal blanket Dan felt the boy's abdomen. No hard swelling to indicate internal bleeding. The spleen felt normal. So far so good. But the sooner this boy was in hospital the better.

'That left arm doesn't look right,' a knowledgeable, and sensual, feminine voice spoke across the boy.

Dan's fingers worked at the point where the arm twisted

under Anders's body. His nod was terse. 'Compound fracture, and dislocated shoulder.'

'Are we going to pop that shoulder back in place now?'

'We should. Otherwise the time frame will be too long and he might require surgery.'

'I'll hold him for you.' No questions, no time wasting. She trusted him to get on with it.

Daniel appreciated anyone who trusted his judgement, or anything about him, come to that. His mouth twisted sideways as he slid the boy's tattered shirt away from his shoulder. 'A shot of morphine will make him more comfortable.'

The drug quickly took effect. Dan raised the arm and, using all his strength, rotated the head of the humerus, popping the ball joint back into its socket. Sweat beaded on his forehead.

The woman lifted Anders's upper body while Dan wound a crepe bandage around the shoulder to hold it in place temporarily. As they worked, a whiff of her exotic perfume tantalised him, brought memories of another fragrance, another woman. His wife. She'd always worn perfume, even when mucking out the horses.

'Where's that ambulance?' He was brusque, annoyed at the painful images conjured up in his mind by a darned scent.

Warmth touched his face, and so distracted had he been that it took a moment to realise that it was the sun. A quick look around showed the clouds had rolled back and once again the beach was sparkling as it bathed in the yellow light. Things were looking up.

As though reading his mind, Pat said, 'Now that the rain has moved up the coast, the helicopter will be on its way. That'll make our search a little easier.'

The boy's father. Dan's stomach clenched as he looked

up at Pat, saw the imperceptible shake of the cop's head in answer to his unspoken question. Deep sadness gripped him. Time was running out to find the man alive.

'It was sheer chance the men found the lad when they did.' Even as Pat talked they heard the deep sound of rotors beating in the air.

'Hey, Daniel,' a familiar voice called. Kerry was a local volunteer ambulance officer. 'What've we got?'

Dan quickly filled him in and within moments Anders was being ferried on a stretcher to the ambulance. There went one very lucky boy. Dan watched the vehicle pull away, thinking about the waves throwing a body onto the sharp jags of the rocks. He shivered abruptly.

'What happened out there?' The woman stood beside him, nodding towards the sea.

Dan shook the image from his head and turned to face this other distraction. His world tilted as he once more looked into those fathomless eyes. It was hard to focus on answering her question. 'Anders and his father were fishing off the rocks—'

'In this weather? That's crazy,' she interrupted.

'Of course it's crazy.' His jaw tightened. 'But it happens. Anders slipped and his father leapt in after him.'

'And the father's still missing.' It was a soft statement of fact. Her eyes were directed to the sea, scanning the horizon.

'I'm afraid so.' He lightened his tone. 'Thank you for your help. You happened along at exactly the right moment.' He wouldn't thank her for the unwelcome hollow feeling in his gut that had started when this perturbing woman had arrived. Or the sensation of something missing from his life that he hadn't been aware of until now. Soon she'd be on her way and then he'd forget this silly, unwelcome impression she'd made.

'You can thank the appalling weather for that. I'd pulled off the road, and when the rain cleared I saw you all down here.'

His eyes scanned the close horizon. Already the sun was disappearing behind a veil of clouds. 'Looks like we're in for more.'

'When doesn't it rain?' Exasperation tightened her face.

'If it's not raining around here that's because it either just stopped or is about to start.' In reality it wasn't all that bad, but why destroy the coast's reputation for bad weather? Especially with someone just passing through. Weird how that notion suddenly saddened him. Odd that a complete stranger had rocked him, reminding him of things he'd deliberately forgotten for years.

A sudden, unexpected thought slammed into his brain. Maybe it was time to start dating again. Like when? If he didn't have time for his daughter, how would he manage fitting another person into his life? He couldn't. End of story. End of stupid ideas.

The woman's tight smile was still in place as her hands wiped at her damp jacket. 'Guess we just had a fine spell, then.'

'At least you got to see it.' He mustered a joke, and was rewarded with a light laugh. A carefree tinkle that hovered in the air between them, drew him closer to her, wound an invisible thread around them both.

Then she glanced down at her feet and grimaced with disgust as she noticed the sloppy, glue-like mud that coated her pretty sandals. He'd swear she shuddered. Definitely a city dweller. Nothing like the women he knew and loved: wholesome, country women like his sisters and his late wife.

Trying to sound sympathetic, he said, 'You should've worn gumboots.'

'Gumboots?' Those carefully crafted eyebrows rose with indignation.

'Yes. Rubber boots that reach the tops of your shins.'

'I know what gumboots are.'

Bet she'd never worn them. 'Sure you do.'

'Do you suppose I might be able to get a designer pair?'

'Possum fur around the tops?' Keep it light, then send her on her way before he did something dumb, like offer her coffee.

She tilted her head to one side. 'How about crochet daisies? Yellow, to contrast with the black rubber.'

'Hey, Dan, you heading to the hospital?' Pat called across the sand.

Thankful for the interruption, Dan shook his head. 'No, Alison can take care of the lad. I'll hang around in case the guys find Starne senior.' He patted his belt, checking for his pager.

'Who's Alison?' the woman beside him asked.

'She's in charge of the emergency department and has a surgical background. She'd call if she needs me.' *What does this have to do with you? You're an outsider.*

'Do you mind if I wait a while with you?'

Yes, I do. Inexplicably he wanted her gone. As though a safety mechanism was warning him to get away from her before it was too late.

Yet he couldn't prevent his head turning towards her. Blonde strands of hair whipped across her cheeks in the skittish wind. He let his gaze wander over her. She was designer from head to foot. Her jacket was soft suede. Her well-fitted trousers had not come off a rack, at least not any ordinary shop rack. But what really caught his interest were the long, shapely legs those wet trousers clung to. They went on for ever.

'Pardon? Oh, sorry. You want to stay? It's not necessary.' Flustered at having been sidetracked, he tripped over his words. First she had him joking with her, then she addled his brain. He struggled to focus on the important issues, not her. 'If the searchers find anything now, it's more likely to be a body. No one can survive in that icy water for very long.'

'True, but it's hard to give up hope, isn't it?' Her eyes were enormous in her pale face.

'Very hard.' His stomach tightened, because of the sad and pointless waste of a life. Not because of the empathy in her eyes.

'I'd still like to wait.' She wasn't asking him, she was telling him, quietly but firmly.

Then from left field he felt a stirring in a region of his body he'd thought long dead. For two despair-filled years, he'd been unintentionally celibate. Now he couldn't help himself—he glanced down at his groin. Relief poured through him. His reaction had been small. Tipping his head back, he laughed. Another long-forgotten act.

Definitely time to get out and about. That new nurse in the neonatal unit had dropped enough hints, and she obviously liked babies if she worked with them, which had to be a plus. Leah needed siblings. He'd never wanted her to be an only child.

He rubbed his arms. Wanting more children had led to a load of stress and difficulties in his otherwise wonderful marriage. Family was so important. Look how his sisters and brother had rallied round when Celine had died. But Leah would miss out on so much if he didn't rectify the situation soon. Dating meant getting involved with another person. Was he ready? Would he ever be ready? Not while his guilt over letting down Celine hung over him like a dirty cloud.

Their marriage had been cut short by an aneurysm.

Cut short before they could resolve their problems. The shock of finding Celine's lifeless body in the bathroom, with Leah sitting beside her singing as though nothing was wrong, still rocked Dan when he thought about it.

Which was why he didn't think about it.

That's also why dating was a bad idea. The whole concept of having someone else he might care about taken away from him so abruptly sent him into a cold sweat.

Suddenly the unknown woman thrust a hand out. 'By the way, I'm Sarah Livingston, your replacement surgeon.'

'Stone the crows.' Shock barrelled through him.

It hadn't occurred to him she might be the locum they expected to arrive tomorrow. The idea was absurd. She was too citified to be stopping here. Too...different. She wouldn't fit in at all. His stomach tightened another notch. So she wasn't passing through.

She was moving in.

Into his hospital, his clinic. Into his house.

Sarah tensed. What did the guy mean? *Stone the crows.* Hadn't she just performed in a capable and professional manner? 'You've got a problem with me?'

'Ahh, no.' The man sounded flummoxed. 'Not at all.'

'I didn't try to take control of your accident scene.' Which was unusual. She hated playing second fiddle to anyone. But in this circumstance she'd gone along with him without any concerns. Odd. Was she coming down with something?

So far her impressions of him were straightforward. Strong hands. Sopping-wet, longish hair that appeared black. Eyes that held a load of caution and a quick anger. Then there were those wide shoulders that V'd down to narrow hips. He totally lacked style—his jeans and the baggy, woollen overshirt under his jacket were way past their use-by date. On a professional note, which was far more important, he'd performed very competently with the boy.

'You certainly made things easier for me.' His voice was deep, gruff, reminding her of a thistle—rough and prickly exterior, soft inside.

'You are Dr Daniel Reilly? I heard someone call you Dan so I presumed so. If I'm mistaken, I'm sorry.'

His handshake was firm but brief, as though glad to get the niceties over. But not so fast that she didn't notice the electricity flaring between them at his touch. Heat sizzled across her palm. Deep in her tummy warmth unfurled, reached throughout her body, reddened her cheeks.

'It's my practice you'll be looking after.' His tone hardened.

So that was it. He wasn't happy about leaving his practice in someone else's hands. The reluctance came through loud and clear. So why had he been told to take a break?

'I thought you'd be pleased to see me, eager to get on with your holiday.' She swallowed her disappointment at his lack of welcome. At least with him going on leave she mightn't see much of him. She hoped.

Really? Truly? You don't want to follow up on this attraction for him that's gripping you? Absolutely not. Too soon after Oliver's betrayal. Who said anything about getting close? What about a fling? A sigh slipped across her bottom lip as she studied Dr Reilly. She doubted her ability to have an affair and not get a little bit close to him. What a shame.

He ignored her jibe, instead turning his back to the pounding surf and nodding at an old, weatherboard building on the other side of the road. 'We'll wait in the Gold Miners' Pub. Can't have you catching a chill.'

As if. Sarah looked around at the sodden beach, the

black, churning waters of the Tasman Sea, the heavy, leaden clouds racing in. Everything was wet, wet, wet. How could she have thought leaving home would help put the last few months behind her? She could've decided about her future in an environment she was used to, not on an alien planet.

How stupid to think doing a complete flip-over of her life would change anything. She shoved her fists into her jacket pockets, already knowing she should've stayed at home for these months, should've told her father no. Right now she'd be in her gorgeous apartment overlooking Auckland's inner harbour, the vibrant City of Sails, where money talked. Where gorgeous, chic sandals stayed gorgeous, not getting ruined the moment she hopped out of her car.

The months in Port Weston stretched out before her like an endless road. But she wasn't quitting. Port Weston might be like nothing she was used to, but she had to stay. She'd given her word.

Then her eyes focused on Daniel Reilly, and for some unknown reason she wondered if she'd be wise to leave right away, while she still could.

CHAPTER TWO

DR REILLY made Sarah, at five feet six, feel almost short. Following him into the dark, wood-panelled interior of the Gold Miners' Pub, she admired his easy, smooth gait, his natural grace that belied his big build. The latent strength she'd glimpsed when he'd popped Anders's joint back was evident in the set of his shoulders, in the loose swing of his hands. Her tongue licked her lips. Gorgeous.

He turned to her. 'A shot of something strong will warm you through and stop your teeth chattering.'

'I'd prefer Earl Grey tea.'

He winced. 'Earl Grey? On the Coast?' His eyes rolled. 'That fancy city stuff won't win you many friends around here.'

'As that's not why I'm here, it doesn't matter.'

'I'd like a practice to return to.'

'Not a problem.' The man's looks might take her breath away but his prickly disposition annoyed her. Was she the only one he treated that way? Probably not, if he had to be forced to take leave. The intensity with which he studied her sent a blush right down to her toes. Did he like what he saw? Did she care? Uh, hello? Unbelievable how quickly her awareness of him had reached the point where she wondered how his touch on her skin would affect her. It would burn her up, she suspected. Her overreaction must

be due to the contrast between the overly hot room and
the chilly dampness outside. What else could it be?

Try lust or physical attraction; forget the weather.
Really? Then her stomach growled. That's what this was
all about. Lack of food. Not Dr Yummy.

'I heard that grumbling,' the man dominating her
thoughts said, amusement briefly lightening those cool,
assessing eyes.

'I'm starving.' Hardly surprising. Unable to bring herself to eat those woeful muffins, her last meal had been
breakfast. A glance at her watch showed it was now after
five.

Behind the long bar a pretty woman with wild red hair
called across the room. 'Dan, the hospital phoned to say
everything's under control.' The woman looked pointedly
at Sarah. 'Can I get you both a drink? I'm sure your friend
might like something.'

Shock registered on Dan's face. 'This is Sarah Livingston.
My locum.'

Not his friend. Probably never would be. What a pity.

'Are you really?' the woman asked Sarah, her face lighting up with a speculative gleam as her gaze moved to Dan
and back. 'Wonderful.'

Sarah gulped. Don't get any bright ideas about matchmaking. If Oliver's defection had taught her anything it
was not to trust as easily as she had last time. Besides, Dan
Reilly was far too unsophisticated for her liking. Except
that sculpted body did fascinate her. Maybe she could cope
with unsophisticated—as an interlude. Hadn't she thought
about having fun with men who didn't want anything more
demanding? But an affair with this man? Not likely. That
could complicate things when she had to step into his shoes
at the local hospital.

Dan continued the introductions. 'Jill's our head theatre nurse, and a barmaid in her spare time. She'll get you whatever you want, though a slug of brandy would do you a sight more good than tea.'

Sarah retorted, 'Suggestion noted.' Forget the interlude. If she ever progressed to having an affair it would be with someone personable and fun, not grumpy and domineering.

Jill leaned across the counter. 'Welcome to Port Weston. Since we'll be working together, give me a call if you have any questions about work or anything else. Or if you're ever hankering for a coffee, I'm available.'

'Thanks for that.' At least someone was pleased to see her here. 'You must be busy, with two jobs.'

'Malcolm, my husband and Dan's brother, runs the pub except when he's out rescuing fools who don't read warning signs.' Jill banged two glasses on the counter. 'What'll it be?'

'Two brandies.' Dan didn't consult Sarah, instead told her, 'Malcolm's the search and rescue coordinator.'

'He was one of the men who'd carried Anders in?' No wonder Jill looked worried.

'Yep.' Dan sipped his drink appreciatively.

'I'll bet he went straight back out to sea after handing his charge over to you.' Jill glared at Dan.

'Hey, steady up. You know there's no way I could've stopped him. A team of Clydesdale horses couldn't have.' Dan reached across and covered Jill's hand with his.

There were tears in the other woman's eyes. 'I know, but he worries me silly. One day he won't come back from a rescue mission.'

Sarah found herself wanting to hug Jill. And she didn't do hugs. Not very often anyway. Certainly not with people she'd only just met. But, then, she wasn't normally rattled by a man like Dan either. Or any man, come to think of it. Must be something in the West Coast air.

Dan said to Jill, 'Don't think like that. You know you wouldn't change him for anything.' Then he turned his attention back to Sarah. 'We'd better get out of our wet clothes. You're shivering non-stop.'

'I'll get some dry things from my car in a moment.' Sarah took a large swallow of brandy, gasping as it burned a track down her throat. 'Wow.'

'Wait till the warmth spreads through you, then you won't be twisting your nose sideways like that.' Dan actually smiled. A long, slow smile that at last went all the way to his eyes.

Blue eyes. So what? It was a common colour. But other blue eyes didn't remind her of hot, lazy days at the beach. Or make her toes curl up in anticipation of exciting things to come. Like what? Who cared? Anything with this man would be exhilarating. Was it possible to become drunk in thirty seconds? Because that's how she felt.

'Where're your keys? I'll get your bag, save you getting another drenching.'

So he could do 'nice'. She dug into her jacket pocket, handed her keyring to him. 'My car's out the front.'

His fingers were warm against hers as he took the keys. 'I know. It's the odd one out amongst the dirty four–wheel-drives and family wagons.'

'It fits in where I come from.'

'I'm sure it does.' Dan hauled the heavy front door open with a jerk. 'Malcolm still hasn't shaved this blasted door, Jill.'

'Tell him, not me.' Jill topped up Sarah's glass even though it wasn't empty. 'Here, a bit more won't hurt you. There's no colour in your cheeks.'

'Thanks, but I'd better go easy on it.' What she really needed was food.

'A hot shower will do you wonders. You can use our bathroom.'

A blast of cold air hit her as Dan poked his head around the door, looking bemused. 'Which bag?'

'The small one.' Hopefully that contained everything she needed.

'You didn't bring a small one,' Dan retorted. 'Why do some women have to cart their whole wardrobe everywhere they go?'

'Guess that's a rhetorical question.' Sarah stared at the closing door.

'Guess he's exaggerating?' Jill's smile warmed her.

'Definitely not *all* my clothes.' Already she liked Jill enough to relax with her. Could she be making a new friend? What was the point? She'd be gone in three months. There again, a friend would be good. She missed the three women she'd known since high school and done all her growing up with.

They'd gone to university together, coming out well versed in life and clutching degrees to their proud chests. Two doctors, one architect and an advertising guru. Three marriages, three mothers; and then there was her. Sometimes she knew she didn't quite belong to the quartet any more. Conversations over dinners and coffee seemed to revolve around children and school timetables, husbands and schedules—things Sarah didn't have a clue about.

Jill was still talking. 'Dan's okay behind that rugged exterior. A pussy cat really. You'll get along fine.'

Sarah knew pussycats, even those in disguise. Dan didn't fit the bill. Tiger was a more apt description. Stealthy when he had to be. Fast when he went for the kill. There was a mix of strength and stubbornness in the set of his chin. His classic handsome features were made interesting by a too-wide mouth and a ragged scar on the point of his chin.

'Here you go, the small one,' Dan said from behind her, causing her to jump. Definitely stealthy.

Jill asked Dan, 'Can you show Sarah to my bedroom? The rescue crew can't be far away and they'll be wanting food.'

At the mention of food Sarah's stomach turned over. 'I'll be as quick as I can, and then I'll give you a hand,' she told Jill. Whoa, back up. She'd help? In a pub? She'd get messy and greasy.

New year, new life, remember?

'Along here.' Dan led the way out to the back and into the private quarters. He opened a door and let her precede him into a double bedroom. 'The bathroom's through there.'

He smelt of damp wool and warm male as she brushed past him. No trace of expensive aftershave or hair product. A clean, uninhibited masculine scent. Sarah hesitated, looked back over her shoulder at him, a sudden longing for something she couldn't put her finger on gripping her.

'What about you?' She was suddenly, oddly, nervous.

Placing her case in the middle of the floor, he turned to leave. His look was cool, his mouth a straight line. 'There's another bathroom next door.'

As she poked through her case for suitable clothes she could hear Dan moving about in that other bathroom, presumably preparing for his shower. An image of a well-muscled body filled her mind. And of a rare but endearing, smile tinged with sadness. What caused that sadness? Of course, she could be wrong about the muscles. She hoped not. A thrill of pleasure warmed her body—and shook her carefully formulated concept of her time in Port Weston.

The jets of water were piping hot against her skin and she gave herself up to them, putting aside thoughts of Daniel Reilly, good and otherwise. Especially those about his body. But how could a bad-tempered man wearing such shapeless clothes ooze so much sex appeal?

The bar was crowded and the mood sombre when Sarah returned. Dan was perched on a stool at the end of the long counter. He waved her over. 'Do you want another drink?'

Schooling her face into a smile, Sarah looked him over as she replied, 'No, thanks.'

His clean shirt fitted snugly across his chest while his dry, worn jeans were tight. Her mouth dried. Beneath the faded denim his thighs were every bit as muscular as she'd imagined.

'Anders's father still hasn't been found.'

'That's not good.' She pulled her shoulders back, focusing on what Dan said, not what he wore.

'That lad needs his father alive and well, not dead and washed up on a beach,' Dan snapped.

'Some people will always take chances.' But not her. She'd focused on her career, foregoing a relationship until she'd specialised, at the same time working on making her father proud.

'They shouldn't, not when they've got a family to consider.'

Sarah totally agreed with him, but diplomatically changed the subject. 'Does Port Weston have a GP? I didn't see one on the beach.'

'Tony Blowers. He's up a valley, delivering a baby, at the moment.'

'Lucky for Anders you were here, then.' She looked around, spied Jill busy pulling beers, and remembered her promise. 'I said I'd help with the food so I'd better find out what's to be done.'

'You did?' He didn't bother disguising his surprise. Those intense cobalt eyes measured her up and down, making her very aware of the snug black slacks and black figure-hugging cotton sweater she'd pulled on.

Dan drawled, 'You might just fit in here yet.'

Pity he didn't sound like he meant it. 'You don't want me here, do you?'

'No, I don't.'

'Thank you for your honesty.' *That* she could deal with. It was a little harder to ignore the fact he wouldn't give her a chance.

'It's nothing personal,' Dan added quietly.

'That's a relief,' she muttered, hoping he meant it and wasn't trying to placate her.

The door crashed back against the wall and drenched men, carrying a stretcher, pressed into the pub. Pat told Dan, 'We've found Starne. He washed up further along and tried to climb the cliff. Fell, and broke his arm, by the look of it.'

'Put him on the couch. It's warmer in here than in a bedroom.' Dan removed cushions and the men lowered the stretcher.

Kneeling down beside the man, Sarah told him, 'I'm Sarah Livingston, a doctor. Can you hear me?'

The man's eyes flew open. 'Where's my son? Is he all right?' He tried sitting up, pushing on his elbows, only to flop back down, groaning with pain.

Dan laid a hand on the man's chest. 'Take it easy.'

Starne tried to knock Dan's hand away with his good arm. 'Is my boy all right? Tell me what happened to him.' The distressed man looked ready to leap up off the couch.

'I'm Dan Reilly, a surgeon. I saw Anders when the rescuers brought him onto the beach.' Dan continued giving Starne the details about his boy, finishing with, 'He's in hospital and doing well.'

Jill helped Sarah tuck blankets around the man. 'I'll have hot-water bottles ready very soon.'

Tears streamed down the man's face. 'The waves banged Anders against the rocks so many times. I couldn't reach him. I thought he was gone.'

'You're both very lucky.' Sarah noted his pulse rate as she talked.

Dan nudged her, spoke softly. 'You're doing great with him, calming him down better than I managed. I'll do the secondary survey.'

She nodded, pleased with the compliment, however small, and silently counted the rise and fall of their patient's chest. 'I'm onto the resps.'

As his fingers felt for contusions Dan told their patient, 'I'll check you over, starting with your head.'

Those firm, gently probing fingers on Starnes's scalp tantalised her. What would they be like on her skin, stroking, teasing, racking up the tension? 'Damn.' She started counting again.

Dan glanced at Sarah as he worked. 'The sooner we get this man to hospital where he can see his boy, the better. I know that's what I'd want if I'd been thinking the worst.'

Sarah's heart squeezed. No parent wanted to outlive their child. As hers had done. 'The downside of being a parent.'

She hadn't realised she'd spoken aloud until Dan said, 'Children cause a lot of worry and heartache, that's for sure. Have you got any?'

'No.'

'I guess now's not the time to ask why not.'

There'd never be a right time. 'Resps slightly slow.'

'Temperature?' Dan asked. At least he could take a hint.

Sarah looked around for Jill. 'You wouldn't have a thermometer?'

'Coming up.' Jill was already halfway out the room.

'Finding anything?' Dan asked Sarah as she palpated Starnes's stomach and liver.

She shook her head. 'These two should buy a lottery ticket.'

'We're certainly not giving you time to settle in quietly, are we?' Dan looked at her for a moment.

No, and being so close to him, breathing his very maleness, added to the sense of walking a swaying tightrope. 'Guess I'll manage,' she muttered, not sure whether she meant the patients or Dan.

Someone handed them hot-water bottles, Sarah reaching for them at the same moment as Dan. Their hands touched, fingers curled around each other's before they could untwine themselves. 'S-sorry.' Sarah snatched her hand back.

'No problem,' snapped Dan, his eyes wide and his face still.

Sarah cringed. Did he think she'd done that on purpose? Surely not? She couldn't deny her attraction for him, but to deliberately grab his hand when she hardly knew him was not her style. Knowing that to say anything in her defence would only make the situation worse, she kept quiet, and again reached for the bottles, making sure to keep well away from Dan.

She placed the bottles in Starnes's armpits and around his groin to maximise his potential for absorbing the warmth.

'The left ankle is swollen, possibly sprained,' Sarah pointed.

'My thoughts exactly.'

'Will we—I—be required to go into theatre if surgery's needed?' Sarah almost hoped not. She was tired and hungry, not in good shape to be operating.

Dan sat back on his haunches and those piercing eyes clashed with hers. 'You don't officially start until tomorrow so if someone's needed I'll do it.'

Why? She'd come for one reason only, and he was holding her back. As her blood started heating up and her tongue forming a sharp reply, he continued, 'You'll want to unpack and settle in at the house. Alison should manage unless she's got another emergency.'

Sarah eased off on her annoyance. How could she stay mad when those eyes bored into her like hot summer rays? 'As long as you know I'm happy to assist if needed.'

A blast of cold air announced the arrival of the ambulance crew. 'Hi, there, again.' Kerry hunkered down beside Dan. 'What've we got this time?'

While Dan relayed the details Sarah stood and stretched her calf muscles, arching her back and pulling her shoulders taut. Dan's gaze followed her movements as he talked to the paramedic, sending a thrill through her. Those eyes seemed to cruise over her, as though they could see right through her to things she never told anyone. Which was plain crazy. How could this man, a stranger really, see through her façade? See beyond the clothes to her soul? He couldn't. Could he?

'Here...' Jill waved across the punters' heads. 'Sandwiches and a coffee. Or would you like something stronger?'

'Coffee's fine.' Grateful for the food, Sarah swallowed her disappointment at the mug of murky instant coffee being slid across the counter towards her. 'Do you still need a hand in the kitchen?'

'I've got it covered. Bea arrived while you were in the

shower, and she's happy as a kid in a sandpit out there cooking up fries.'

'Bea?'

'Dan's sister.'

'Is everyone around here related to him?' Biting into a thick sandwich filled with ham and tomato, Sarah told her stomach to be patient, sustenance was on the way down.

'Not quite.' Dan sent Jill a silent message before turning to Sarah. 'You want to share those?' He nodded at the sandwiches.

Not really. She could eat the lot. 'Sure.' Sarah prodded the plate along the counter towards him, wondering what he hadn't wanted Jill to mention in front of her. 'So you come from a big family.'

'Yep, and they're quite useful at times.'

'What he means is we all run round after him most of the time.' Jill winked at Sarah.

They needn't think she'd play that game. She'd come to run his clinic, nothing else. 'How far from here is the house I'm staying in? I've got some directions but it's probably quicker if you tell me.'

Wariness filtered into Dan's eyes. 'You can follow me shortly.'

'I'd really like to go now.'

'Soon.' Then suddenly his eyes twinkled and he waved at someone behind her. 'Sweetheart, there you are.'

Disappointment jolted Sarah. Of course Dan would have a wife. No man as good looking as this one would be single. Turning to see who he was smiling at, her heart slowed and a lump blocked her throat. The most gorgeous little girl bounded past her, her arms flung high and wide as she reached Dan.

'Daddy, there you are. Auntie Bea brought me here. She made me some fries.'

'Hi, sweetheart. Guess you won't be needing dinner now.' Dan scooped the pink and yellow bundle up and sat her on his knee.

'You're late, Daddy.'

'Sorry, sweetheart.' The man looked unhappy, as though he'd slipped up somehow. 'I had to help Uncle Malcolm.'

Sarah stared at father and daughter. Their eyes were the same shade of blue. They had identical wide, full mouths, the only difference being the little girl's was one big smile while Dan's rarely got past a scowl. Except now, with his daughter in his arms. The lump blocking Sarah's throat slowly evaporated, her heart resumed its normal rhythm. But she melted inside, watching the child.

Since when did children do that to her? Since her wrecked marriage plans had stolen her dream of having a family. Why hadn't Oliver taken that test for the cystic fibrosis gene as he'd promised to do when she'd first told him she was a carrier? Had he been afraid he might find he was imperfect? Did the idea that they might have to decide whether to have children or not if he'd tested positive prove too hard to face? Whatever the answers, he could've talked to her, not gone off and played around behind her back.

'Hello.'

Sarah blinked, looked around, caught the eye of Dan, and, remembering where she was, immediately shoved the past aside. 'Hi.'

The child wriggled around on Dan's knee until she was staring at Sarah. 'Are you the lady who's coming to stay with us?'

Definitely not. 'No, I'm Sarah, a doctor like your father.'

'Sarah…' Dan eased a breath through his teeth. 'Leah's right. You are staying with us.'

'What?' Absolutely not. No one had ever mentioned such a notion. Perspiration broke out on her forehead. Had she missed something? No, she couldn't have. Staying with the local surgeon would've been one detail she'd definitely not overlook. 'The board arranged a hospital house for me.'

'That's right. The one and only hospital house. Where I live with my daughter.'

Her shoulders sagged. He meant it. She was staying at Dan's house. With Dan. And his daughter. 'Your wife?'

'There's just the two of us.' His mouth tightened. 'You'll be comfortable enough.'

No way. She couldn't, wouldn't. What about her un-precedented attraction to him? How could she handle that when they were squeezed into the same place? Then there was the job. He'd always be asking how she was doing. Who had she seen? How was she treating them? Her voice sounded shrill even to her. 'There must be somewhere else. I don't mind a small flat or apartment.'

'This is Port Weston, not Auckland. Rental properties are few and far between. When I say there's nothing else then there's nothing. Believe me, I've checked.' Dan stood up. 'I'm not happy about it either. Unfortunately we're going to have to bump along together—somehow.'

Of course Dan didn't want her staying with him. He didn't want her here, full stop. Tiredness dragged her shoulders down as she stood up from the stool she'd been perched on. 'I'll get my case.'

Bump along together, indeed. Her eyes widened and her face heated up. In a fantasy world, bumping up against Dan might be a whole heap of fun. There were definitely some very intriguing ways. But not in the ho-hum kind of way he was suggesting. Right now she wanted to bang him over the head for letting this happen.

* * *

Swinging Leah down to the floor, Dan watched Sarah striding across the room in a second, clean pair of silly sandals. Her cheeks had coloured up, and her shoulders were stiff. Those amazing eyes were giving off sparks. Passion ran through her veins, he'd bet his job on it.

'Sarah's unhappy, Daddy.' Leah wriggled down to the floor and grabbed his hand.

So was he. He didn't need a sex siren in his home. Not when his body suddenly seemed to be waking up. But he couldn't be blamed for the board crying off outlaying money for separate accommodation for her. It was part of his tenancy agreement that visiting doctors stayed with him. Of course, none of them came for more than a week at a time.

Charlie had also stressed the importance of keeping Dr Livingston happy during her time here. *And then they put her in with me?* Dan bit off an expletive.

Everyone in the district knew that Dr Livingston had to be looked out for. There'd be a concerted effort to make sure she wanted for nothing. The board had a plan. One where the locum would fall in love with Port Weston and its hospital and want to stay on when the contract was up. The plan was doomed from the start. By all appearances Sarah would not stay one minute longer than her contract stated. But the relief that knowledge should engender within him wasn't forthcoming.

Did he want her to stay? No.

Did he want to cut back his working hours permanently? Maybe. If it all worked out with Leah. If he learned how to give her what she needed and didn't fail her like he had last time he'd tried to be a hands-on solo dad. If. If. If.

Then he had to think about those little mistakes he'd begun making at work because he'd become exhausted. Thankfully none of them had been serious. Yet. He'd been doing horrendously long hours and Charlie had been right to start looking for another surgeon to share the load. Those long days had been an excuse to avoid going home and facing the truth that Celine was never coming back. He'd worked until he was so tired he could fall into bed and sleep.

He should be grateful to Sarah. She hadn't forced this holiday on him, he had. By all accounts, she appeared to be the perfect locum, despite being an arrogant 'suit' from Auckland. Okay, not totally arrogant, but she was going to have difficulty fitting in here with those city mannerisms.

His eyes were riveted on the way her legs moved as she negotiated the crowd. Long, long legs that he imagined going— *Get a grip.* She was a colleague, not some female to be drooled over as though he was a sex-starved teenager. He winced. He was sex-starved. And only now beginning to notice. It had been so long he could barely remember what making love was like.

Now was not the time to find out. Which was another reason to wish Sarah on the other side of the planet.

Reaching her, he leaned down for her case at the same moment that she grabbed the handle.

'Let me,' he said quietly. And tried to breathe normally. The skin on the back on her hand was soft, smooth. Strands of blonde hair settled on her cheek. His heart stuttered. Such a mundane and delightful thing.

'I can manage,' she retorted.

'I know, but let me.'

Her mouth fashioned a fleeting smile. 'Thank you.'

This close he could see the dark shadows staining her upper cheeks. 'Do you feel up to driving, or would you rather come back for your car in the morning?'

'What, and have you hauling all those cases between

vehicles?' She managed another almost-smile. 'I'll follow you. Is it far?'

'About five kilometres, on the other side of town.' Thinking of the short street of shops, mostly farming and fishing suppliers, he knew Sarah would be shocked. There was one, surprisingly good, café run by a couple who'd opted for the quiet life after many years of running a business in Christchurch. Hopefully their coffee would be up to this woman's expectations.

Sarah pulled the outside door open. 'Allow me.'

'Oh, no. After you.' Dan gripped the edge of the door above her head.

She shrugged and ducked under his arm, out the doorway, bang into a throng of people crowding the steps. Leah danced along behind her. Fishermen crowded the porch, gathering to celebrate the rescue operation's success.

'Careful, lady!' someone exclaimed. 'Those steps are slippery.'

Sarah teetered at the edge of the top step. She put a hand out for balance but there was no railing to grab. Tripping, she made a desperate attempt to regain her footing. The heel of her sandal twisted, tipped her sideways and she went down hard, crying out as she thumped onto the concrete.

'Sarah.' Dan dropped her case, pushed through the men to crouch down beside her. 'Don't move. Let me look.'

She was on her backside, one leg twisted under her. 'I'm fine. Just help me up, please.' She put a hand out to him.

'Wait until I've checked your leg.'

'There's nothing wrong with it. It's my foot that hurts. Probably bruised.' Putting her hands down on either side of her hips, she tried to stand, but couldn't. 'Are you going to give me a hand, or do I ask someone else?'

'Sit still.' Those sandals weren't helping. 'How do you

expect to be able to stand up on that narrow spike you call a heel?'

'Typical male. Women are born to walk on heels,' she retorted through clenched teeth. Leaning to one side, she straightened her leg out from under her bottom, and bit down on her lip.

He gently felt her ankle, then her foot. The tissue was soft, already swelling, and her sharp intake of breath confirmed his suspicions. 'I think you've broken at least one bone. An X-ray will verify that.'

He'd call the radiology technician on the way to A and E. Technically a fracture in the foot could wait until the morning, but he didn't want this particular patient finding their small hospital lacking.

'That easily? That's crazy.' Sarah shook her head at her foot as though it was responsible for her predicament, and not those ridiculous shoes.

So much for Sarah taking over his practice this week. He should be pleased he'd be going to work. But even he understood his promise to Leah was meant to be kept. It didn't matter he was terrified he wouldn't measure up as a full-time dad for three months, and that Leah might revert to the disconsolate little girl he'd finally handed over to his family to help. He'd promised to try. Now, before he'd even started, their time together had to be postponed. He might've resented Sarah coming here, but right now he'd give anything to have her back on both feet and eager to get started.

CHAPTER THREE

SARAH hobbled after Dan as he carried a sleepy bundle of arms and legs into the weatherboard house. Leah had been tucked up in Jill's bed when Dan had finally had time to pick up his little girl on the way home from hospital.

Guilt for keeping this tot out late swamped Sarah. Due to her clumsiness Leah hadn't been with her dad when she should've been.

'Make yourself comfortable while I tuck Leah into bed,' Dan snapped over his shoulder, not easing Sarah's heavy heart.

He had every right to be annoyed with her. As had the other people whose time she'd intruded upon. Jill had driven her car here and someone had followed to pick her up. The radiology technician had gone into the hospital especially for her. And then there was Dan, who hadn't bothered to hide how he felt about this development.

Injuring her foot was a pain in the butt for her, too. If she hadn't been so intent on putting some space between her and Dan, it wouldn't have happened. The X-ray showed two broken bones. Her foot was twice its normal size and hurt like crazy. Thank goodness for painkillers.

Ignoring his order, Sarah followed Dan down the hall. Was he a good dad? Inexplicably she wanted to watch him tuck the child into bed, wanted another peep of Leah looking so cute with a blanket hitched under her chin and a bedraggled teddy bear squashed against her face. 'She's gorgeous,' she whispered, afraid of waking the girl, worried Dan might tell her to go away.

'Especially when she's asleep.' Dan's soft smile made Sarah's heart lurch. His big hand smoothed dark curls away from Leah's forehead. 'Actually, she's gorgeous all the time but, then, I'm biased.'

'So you should be.'

Dan placed feather-light kisses on his daughter's cheeks and forehead. 'Goodnight, sweetheart.'

From deep inside, in the place she hid unwanted emotions, something tugged at Sarah. A reminder of how much she'd been looking forward to having a family of her own when she and Oliver were married. That man had taken a lot from her.

'Are you all right?' Dan stood in front of her.

'Yes, of course.' Or could these emotions come from something else? An image of her own father tucking her into bed floated across her mind. As if. That was a fantasy. Dad had always been at work at her bedtime. No, she was overtired and getting confused.

'Your room is at the end of the hall. You've got an en suite bathroom so you won't have plastic toys to trip over.' Dan turned back towards the kitchen. 'I'll bring your cases in.'

'Thank you. I'll put the kettle on. Do you want a hot drink?'

'If you wait a few minutes, I'll get that. Go and put your foot up.'

'Dan, I am not incapable of boiling water.'

Loud knocking prevented Dan from answering, which by the tightening of his mouth and the narrowing of his eyes had saved her a blasting. Sarah trudged after him, her gait awkward because of the clunky moonboot clipped around her injured foot.

Dan growled at the visitor, 'Charlie, come in. I take it you've heard the news.'

'Three times since I got home from the river.' A dapper man in his sixties stepped into the kitchen. 'How is Dr Livingston?'

'I'm fine.' Sarah made it through the kitchen door and went towards the visitor with her hand out. 'Sarah Livingston.'

'Charlie Drummond. I'm sorry about your accident, lass.' Warmth emanated from his twinkling eyes.

She shrugged. 'Bit of a nuisance but nothing I can't deal with.'

'It changes everything.' Dan frowned. 'I've already told the nanny I'll need her for at least a week.'

Charlie shook his head. 'Oh, no, you don't. You're on leave. That's non-negotiable.'

'For goodness' sake, Charlie. There is no one else.' Dan's voice rose a few decibels. 'Until Sarah's back on her feet I'm your surgeon.'

'I'll ring around, see who I can find. Might don some scrubs myself.'

'It took months to find Sarah. You haven't got a chance in Hades of finding someone quickly, if at all.'

Sarah winced. 'Excuse me, but there's nothing wrong with my hearing.' She'd made a mess of things so she'd sort it. 'Or my brain. I'll be at work tomorrow.'

'Don't be ridiculous,' Dan snapped.

No one talked to her like that. 'Maybe late in the morning but I will be there. Trust me.' Sarah braced as a glare sliced at her, but when Dan said nothing she turned to the other man. 'I'm really sorry this has happened but it won't affect the board's plans too much.'

'Sarah, get real.' Dan dragged a hand through his damp

hair, making the thick curls stand up. Cute. Mouthwatering. Totally out of bounds.

Parking her bottom against the edge of the table, Sarah repeated, 'I'll be at work tomorrow.' She had to take control of the situation before Dan took over completely. 'Is there any surgery scheduled?'

Charlie smiled. 'It's a public holiday, remember? You've got a light week, emergencies not withstanding.'

'I'd planned on taking you in to meet any staff on duty, check out the theatre, and go over patient notes.' Dan shook his head in despair.

'Then there's no problem. We'll decide how to deal with emergencies if and when they arise.' Dan would be the last person she'd call for help. Having caused him enough trouble already, she was unusually contrite. 'If I have to, I can operate sitting down. It won't be easy but it's possible. Let's leave tomorrow's plans as they stand.'

And she could spend the night hoping she'd be fighting fit in the morning.

There was a speculative look in Dan's eyes as he regarded her, his arms folded over his thought-diverting chest.

'What?' How would it feel to curl up with him, her head lying against that chest? Protected and comforted? Huh! The last thing Dan Reilly was was comforting.

He shrugged. 'We'll see.'

'Sarah, I appreciate you coming down here at such short notice. I'm sure we can make this work until you're fully recovered,' Charlie said.

Dan grunted.

Sarah gripped the edge of the table tight as she sucked back a sharp retort. No need to aggravate Dan more than she already had. But hell if it wasn't tempting.

* * *

Dan was dog-tired. Every muscle ached. His head throbbed. He'd performed urgent surgery for a punctured lung following a car-versus-tree accident at three that morning. When he'd crawled into bed afterwards Leah had been grizzly so he'd had a squirming child to keep him awake for the remainder of the night. Then the nanny had been grumpy when he'd woken her for breakfast. Throw in a near-drowning, Sarah's arrival and accident, and he was almost comatose.

He peeped in on Leah. Lucky kid, dead to the world, unaware of the drama that had been going on and how it would affect the holiday he'd promised her.

Sarah's assumption that she'd be able to take over tomorrow wouldn't work, but he was fed up with arguing. Women. When they were in the mood they knew how to be difficult. It came naturally, like curves and bumps.

He sucked a breath. What was happening to him? He didn't usually give women more than cursory glances. Truth, with most of them he wouldn't even notice that they were female. But Sarah had woken him up in a hurry. He didn't know how. He just knew she had. Why her, of all people? Because she was one damned desirable lady.

She was one pain in the neck.

They were opposites: syrup and vinegar.

Opposites attracted.

He shouldn't be thinking about her except in her professional role. Not possible when they were going to be sharing such close living quarters. So how was a man to cope? How could he ignore what was right in front of him? Even with one foot strapped in that ugly moon boot she was more distracting than was good for him.

'Daddy?' Leah murmured in her sleep.

Gorgeous, that's what Sarah had called his little girl, and she was right. Beautiful, innocent, and in need of a mother figure. Someone special she could call hers; not all the aunts and cousins who were there for her. Someone to call Mummy. Someone he wasn't ready to bring into their lives.

'Go back to sleep, little one.' He tucked the blanket over her tiny shoulder. When she was like this he believed himself capable of being a good dad. It was the bad times when she hurt or cried that undermined his confidence. He loved how Leah trusted and loved him without question. He certainly didn't deserve it. Not when she spent most of her time in day care or with various other people while he ran around being busy and avoiding the issues that threatened to swamp him.

'You're so beautiful, my girl. Just like your mother. She'd be proud of you just for being so special and funny and adorable.' *But would Celine be pleased with the way her sister and mine are bringing you up for me? More like she'd be disappointed in the way I've ducked for cover every time the going's got tough.* He kissed Leah's soft cheek, his throat tightening at the feel of her soft skin. 'I love you.'

He stood gazing down at his child, the most important person in the world, and his heart swelled to the point it hurt. He mightn't have done much of a job of it yet but being a dad was so different from anything else he'd ever tried. Now he had to work hard to make up for lost time, learn to be there for Leah all the time. Where to start? What to do? Ask Bea and Jill. They wouldn't hold back in telling him, or coming to his rescue. He shuddered. No, it was time to stand on his own two feet.

Back in the lounge he dropped into a large armchair and studied the other female in his house. The enigmatic one. The more he saw of Sarah, the more she piqued his curiosity. Why had she been available to come here at such short notice? He'd read her CV, knew she held a partnership in some fancy, private surgical hospital with her father and some other dude. So why'd she been available?

'Does Leah sleep right through the night?' Sarah spoke in her lilting voice, now tinged with exhaustion.

'Like a log.' Usually. When she wasn't crying for Mummy. Which happened less and less these days, he realised with a start.

Sarah didn't have children and her résumé hadn't mentioned a husband. Why, considering she was thirty-five? Divorced? What if she hated kids? His heart thumped. He wouldn't accept that. 'Are you used to being around children?'

'Not a lot.'

'Got any nieces or nephews?' This wasn't looking good. How would she cope with Leah?

'No.'

'Siblings?'

'My brother died when he was eighteen. I was sixteen at the time.' Her voice was flat, but there was pain in her eyes, in her fists on her knees.

Her words sent shivers down his spine, made him gasp. 'Sarah, I'm truly sorry. I can be too nosey at times.' There'd been a stoplight in her eyes, but he'd pressed on with his questions regardless, too concerned about his own problems.

What to say now? A tragedy like that stayed with a person for ever. What had happened to her brother? Was there more to her story? For sure he wasn't about to ask. Not with that massive chunk of hurt radiating out from those eyes. But he understood firsthand how death changed things. Everything crashed to a halt. You didn't even notice life was still going on around you. Only after months of agony did you slowly begin to move again, begin to function semi-normally. It took even longer to recover from the guilt. 'How awful.' How inadequate.

She jerked her head affirmatively. 'It certainly is.'

Is. Not was. Hadn't she got over it a tiny bit? Her fingers were twisted and interlaced in her lap, her eyes downcast. Dan fought the impulse to reach for her, hold her safe. A friendly gesture that she definitely wouldn't appreciate. When she finally raised her head he saw sadness and loneliness lurking in those compelling eyes.

Then he surprised himself. 'Leah was two when her mother died.' Which was too much information. He didn't want to share personal details with Sarah, not even one. It was enough that they were sharing his practice, and his home.

Celine slipped into his mind again. For the past two years he'd taken the approach of ignoring the gaping hole left by her passing, hoping that one day he'd find it filled in with life's trivia. In reality he should've been facing up to things, like looking after his daughter instead of leaving that to everyone else. Like accepting he couldn't wind back the clock and pack Celine up to take her home to the city she'd loved and missed. Back to her interfering mother who'd put those ideas of distrust in Celine's head.

'That's really tough. For both of you.' Sarah's tone was compassionate. 'How does Leah cope?'

'She's very resilient.' More so than him. 'Most of the time. She has her moments. We manage.' Sort of. With a lot of help. 'I hope you'll get on with her.'

'I doubt I'll see much of her.' Then she changed the subject. 'Tell me how your local health board operates. It seems to be very successful when others in remote areas have failed.'

'It wasn't always like this but with a bit of lateral thinking the board members came up with a scheme to employ a full-time surgeon. Instead of sending patients out of the area, they contracted for the overflow from Christchurch public hospitals. It was a perfect solution for my wife and me as we wanted to be near my family once Leah was born.' Yes, *we* wanted to make the move. Celine had been as much for it as he had. She'd loved her horses; enjoyed getting to know Jill, the sister she hadn't grown up with. When had he forgotten that? Had he been so immersed in self-pity that he hadn't looked at all sides of the problem? Celine had had a part to play in her welfare too. Because the other side of the story was that he fitted in here, loved giving back to his community through his work.

'So you grew up in Port Weston?' An alien female voice intruded.

He blinked. Sarah sat opposite him, an expression of polite interest on her beautiful face. 'Yes, I did.' What had they been talking about? Of course, the hospital. What else? That's all Sarah would be interested in. 'There's been a flow-on effect for the town from having the surgical unit here. Most patients coming for elective surgery bring friends or relatives with them. Those people need entertaining, feeding, housing.'

'So you've got a lively metropolis out there somewhere?' Her sweet, tired smile pulled at his heart.

How could that be when he'd known her less than twelve hours? Something to think about—later.

Back to her question. 'Not quite what you're used to.' The understatement of the year. 'But the shops are improving, and you'll be glad to know our café is first rate.'

'Can't go past a great coffee shop.'

He saw her stifled yawn in her tightened mouth and clenched jaw, and leapt up. 'Here I am blathering on and you're half-asleep. I'll help you get ready for bed.' And gain some freedom from those all-seeing eyes.

Taking her elbow, he helped her up onto her good foot, then without warning swung her into his arms and carried her down to her room. She felt wonderful. Soft. Warm. Desirable.

He croaked, 'Stop wriggling. You're making it difficult for me to hold you.' *And causing certain soft feminine parts of your anatomy to rub against my chest. Very nice.* Shocked described how he felt. And hot. Hard. Stunned.

'Then put me down,' she responded, instantly tense and remaining that way until he sat her on the bed and bent down to remove the moon boot.

'I'll do that.' She yanked her leg away from him, groaning when pain jagged her.

'Let's be reasonable about this. You're all-out tired and with my help you'll be in bed a lot quicker. Probably with much less pain. I am a doctor, remember?' Great logic that.

'I'm sure you're right, but I'll manage,' she wheezed through gritted teeth. 'I have to get used to this boot as soon as possible.'

So she was concerned she wouldn't be functioning properly tomorrow.

'Take it easy and leave worrying about how you're going to get around till the morning.' He stared at the three cases he'd hauled in earlier. Gucci, of course. 'Which bag has your night things?'

Sarah took the negligee he finally found and pointed to the door. 'I'll do this.'

Plastering his best bedside manner on his face, he put a hand under her arm and, trying to ignore his increasing pulse, said, 'There's the easy way, and the hard way. Let's go for easy.'

She tipped her head back to stare up at him and he saw the exhaustion in her eyes, in her loose shoulders, in the slack hands lying in her lap.

'You're right.' And then she lifted her top up over her head.

Dan's mouth dried, and it was a lifetime before he moved to help her. Her creamy skin was like warm satin. The swell of her breasts in their frothy, black lace cups caused him to bite painfully into his bottom lip. His hands shook when he took the garment from her and tossed it onto a chair in the corner. It missed.

Her fingers fumbled at the button on her waistband. He tried to help but she pushed his hands away. Lifting his eyes to her face, he saw the faint pink colour rising in her cheeks. Had he embarrassed her with his quickening interest? *Daniel Reilly, you need your head read. You have to live with this woman for twelve whole weeks. Keep everything above board.*

'Here, I'll lift you so you can slide your trousers down,' he muttered, and placing his hands on her elbows focused on being practical. As if. But he tried.

Next he knelt to remove the moon boot, taking care not to jar her foot. Under his fingers her satin skin reminded him of sultry summer nights. He ached to caress it. Common sense prevailed. Just.

'Thanks.' Sarah flopped back against the pillow, pulling the covers over herself. Then she closed her eyes. The determination and fierce independence she'd displayed all evening disappeared, leaving her looking defenceless. Any pain from her foot was hidden behind her eyelids.

Without thinking, he reached out to brush a strand of hair off her cheek, hesitated, withdrew. How would he explain such impulsiveness? She was one tough lady, and he suspected that sassy attitude hid a lot of things from the world. Things he'd like to learn more about. But right now it was way past time to get out of her room. 'See you in the morning.'

He'd made her door when he heard her whisper. 'Is it safe to open a window? It's very stuffy in here.'

'That's because we're between rain spells again.' He crossed to the windows. 'And of course it's safe. You're not in the city now.'

'I suppose you leave your doors unlocked.' She rolled onto her side and the covers slid off her shoulders.

Again Dan's gaze was drawn to her flawless skin and her negligee highlighting the swell of her breasts. He mightn't have had a sex life for a very long time but suddenly that didn't seem to mean a thing. It was as though he'd—she'd—flicked a switch and, whammo!

'Just one window open?' he said breathlessly, his throat as tight as a clamped artery.

'I think so. Is that the surf I can hear?'

'Yes. We're quite close to the sea.' He made for the door again, this time with no intention of stopping, regardless of what she said. *Keep talking so she can't get a word in.* 'The high fence surrounding the property is to stop Leah from wandering down to the water. Even with the main road and a stretch of grassed land between us, I don't take any chances.'

Of course he wouldn't. That much Sarah had figured out already. A yawn stretched her mouth. Despite the exhaustion gripping her, she doubted she was about to get much sleep. If the pain didn't keep her awake then a load of other concerns would. For starters, she'd let Dan down big time. He needed her here, whether he accepted it or not.

Already she sensed her time in Port Weston wasn't just about sorting out her own life. She may have come to free up Dan's life, but now she wanted to do more for him. And for his daughter. But what? Her experience of children and happy families was non-existent.

An image of a darling little girl floated across her mind. Leah. How to remain aloof when the child had already touched her heart? She had to. That's all there was to it. Getting attached to Dan's daughter had no place in her life. And she must not listen to the increasingly loud ticking of her biological clock.

What about Dan himself? His wife had died. No wonder he was running solo here with Leah. It wouldn't be easy to put his loss behind him with a child to care for.

So she had to get a grip on her unprecedented attraction to him. But what would his kisses be like? Hungry? Soft? Demanding? *Hello, Sarah, back to earth, please.*

The man crashing through her head placed a glass by her bed. 'Thought you might like some water.'

'Thanks.' She clenched her fists. How long had he been standing there? 'I don't usually make such a hash of things. I'm truly sorry.' But she felt even more regretful she wouldn't taste his kisses. Kisses had to be avoided if she was to keep her relationship with Dan strictly professional.

'It was an accident, okay?'

'You're not putting off doing all those dad things Leah's hankering for.' She pulled the bedcover back up to her neck. He could stop peeking at her negligee. He'd already had more than an eyeful. Admittedly she'd enjoyed the appreciative glint in his eyes. Enjoyed? Get real. When he looked at her so intently she became a very desirable woman. What a salve for her battered self-esteem. By having an affair, Oliver had made her feel unwanted, undesirable.

Dan hesitated, his hand on the light switch. 'Why don't

you wear oversized T-shirts to bed, like most women I know?'

'They didn't have any in my colour.'

How many women did he see in their night attire?

CHAPTER FOUR

'HURRY up, Daddy. We'll be late,' Leah shrieked the next morning, bouncing between Dan's knees as he brushed her hair.

'Stand still, young lady,' Dan answered at a much lower decibel, his eyes narrowed as he fought the hair into submission.

'Flicker's waiting for me.' Leah bit into her bottom lip as she struggled to keep from jiggling.

Sarah grinned at Dan. 'You need to speed up, man.'

'I'm never fast enough for Leah. She was born in a hurry.'

'Flicker doesn't go very fast. Auntie Bea won't let him cos I could fall off.' Leah twisted around to stare at her father. 'You're riding Jumbo.'

'I was afraid of that.' Dan smiled at his daughter, love shining out of his eyes. 'Of course, if you don't stand quietly while I do these ponytails, neither of us will be riding any horse today.'

'Daddy, we must. Flicker will miss me.'

'Is Flicker your horse?' Sarah asked the little girl.

Big blue eyes peeped back at her from under an overlong fringe. 'He's Auntie Bea's but I'm the only person allowed to ride him. Can you ride a horse?'

'Me? No way. I don't like being so far off the ground.' Anything higher than a short stool was too high.

Dan wrapped an elastic tie around a ponytail, his gaze firmly on the wayward curls he was struggling to contain. The part between the ponytails was well to the side of the middle of Leah's head. 'Have you ever tried?'

'Once, when I was about Leah's age. The horse took exception to having me on its back and tossed me off. No amount of bribery got me back on.'

'I haven't been throwed off.' Leah's eyes glowed with pride.

Dan put the brush down and reached for the ribbons lying on the table. 'Nearly there, missy. Flicker will think you're looking cool today.' His mouth curved with a smile just for his daughter. Pride and love mingled across his face, his big hands gentle as he tried to fashion the blue ribbons into bows.

Leah stood absolutely still for the first time, her elbows resting on Dan's thighs, her little freckle-covered face puckered up in thought.

Sarah caught her breath. They belonged together. Father and daughter. If only she had a camera to take a picture showing the love between these two. The air was warm with it. There was a vulnerability in Dan's eyes she'd never expected from the gruff man she'd known so far.

Her stomach tightened. What these two had was special, something she'd like to share. What? She wanted to be with Dan and his daughter? Only for the time she was in Port Weston, of course. Of course. Because she still loved Oliver, hard as that was to admit after everything he'd done to her.

'Sarah, do I look pretty?' Leah bounced in front of her, unwittingly dragging Sarah's attention onto her and away from the desperate thoughts that threatened to ruin her day. Leah had pulled away from Dan's hands, effectively ruining the bow he was working on.

'Very pretty. Now, hand me those bows and I'll help your dad make you even prettier.' Her throat closed over as she quickly tied two big bows, trying hard not to feel as though she was missing out on something very important. She reached over and flicked one of the ponytails, making Leah giggle. 'If he hasn't already, then Flicker's going to fall in love with you.'

Who wouldn't fall in love with the child? Panic seized Sarah. What if she did? She mustn't. There were too many complications for all of them otherwise. And the child must be protected first and foremost.

Dan shook his head in disgust. 'That easy, huh?' He stood and stretched. 'If you're not careful, the job's yours while you're here.'

She might get to like that. 'Guess you've never had long hair.'

'You think I should've put my hair in ponytails? What sort of guys did you mix with as a teenager?' He blinked at her, but she obviously wasn't meant to answer. 'We'd better get going before my sister sends out a search party.' He ran his knuckles over his bristly chin, worry clouding his eyes. 'I hope I survive the morning.'

'You can't keep up with Leah?' Sarah challenged with a laugh, trying to lift his spirits.

'Sometimes I wonder if she's really only four, she's so confident.'

'Four to your, what? Thirty-two,-three?'

'Flattery is supposed to get you everything. Try thirty-five.' His lips widened from tight to relaxed.

The same age as her. 'Where'd you go to med school?' They'd have been training around the same time.

'Dunedin, then Christchurch to specialise. You?'

'Auckland and London.' Where she'd met Oliver. At first they'd been friends. Liar. She'd thought he was hot from the moment she'd set eyes on him, and he'd known it. But she'd finished her specialist training before succumbing to his charm and going out with him.

'Daddy, come on.' Leah grabbed his hand and began tugging him towards the back door.

'Sure you'll be all right? Nothing you need, like a sandwich, another cup of tea?' Reluctance shadowed his voice. Was it the horse riding he worried he couldn't cope with? Or Leah? 'You could come with us.'

'I don't think so. I don't know much about entertaining children.'

'Sure you don't want to start this morning?'

'Stop procrastinating. Apart from getting a sore backside, you'll be fine. Look how excited Leah is about this.'

'Yeah, that's the problem. And the fact I've forgotten which end of a horse is which.'

'You're not expected to be an expert. Dan, go, now.' Sarah deliberately stood up and turned her back on him, reaching for the kettle to show she could manage. She didn't turn around until the door closed quietly behind her.

Then she stared out the window, watching Dan's vehicle bouncing down the drive, rolling along the highway until it disappeared out of sight around a bend. The tightness in her shoulders eased. This was the first time she'd been alone, without Dan in reach, since she'd charged down the beach yesterday. She should be pleased not to have his disturbing eyes watching her, his acerbic tongue ready to refute everything she said.

Instead loneliness threatened to swamp her. In Auckland she never felt lonely, despite not having a wide circle of friends. There were shops or the hospital to keep her occupied. Here—here there wasn't a lot in the way of distractions now that Dan had gone out.

Beyond the road the sea kept rolling onto the shore. Wind whipped spume off the hypnotic wave-tops. A long, wild coastline with no one in sight. 'What a godforsaken place.' She kept staring at it until a kind of peace stole over her. 'But it's sort of beautiful.'

The strident tones of the phone awoke Sarah from a deep sleep. Confused, she stared around at the unfamiliar room. Her vision filled with soft, warm colours: blues, a dash of yellow, a hint of green. A complete contrast to the clean, white walls and terracotta furnishings of her Auckland apartment. Then she remembered. Port Weston. Bad-tempered Dr Reilly. Her broken bones.

Pushing off the couch, she hopped to the table where she'd unwisely left the phone. Her moon boot bumped against a chair. Pain snatched her breath away. Gripping the back of the chair, she fumbled with the phone, anxious not to miss the call and give Dan another reason to believe she was incompetent.

'Hello, Dr Reilly's residence.'

'This is the hospital A and E department. Is Dan there?'

Apprehension made Sarah straighten up. Please, not an emergency. 'Dan's gone horse riding at his sister's.'

'No wonder I can't reach him on his cellphone.' The caller sounded harassed. 'No coverage up there.'

'Can I do anything? I'm Sarah Livingston, a doctor.'

'Thank goodness.' The relief was obvious. 'I'm Alison Fulton, A and E specialist. We've got a six-year-old girl with appendicitis and, if I'm not mistaken, we need to hurry. Apparently the child's been complaining of stomach pains for hours.'

'I'll come straight away.' This wouldn't be so bad. She'd be able to handle an appendectomy sitting down.

'Thank you so much.'

'You're aware I can't drive at the moment?' Sarah knew how well hospital grapevines worked.

'Dan mentioned it. I'll get someone to pick you up.' Then the specialist's voice changed, became concerned. 'You do feel up to this? I don't want you to think you have to come in. I haven't tried Charlie's phone yet. He's my last resort, though I know he's gone after another trout.'

So Dan had been warning people about her situation. Looking out for her? Or indicating he'd prefer he was called in so he had an excuse to return to work? Putting all the confidence she could muster into her voice, Sarah reassured Alison. 'Operating will be fine. Just send that car.'

She crossed her fingers. Just the one op, please.

Wee Emma Duncan's face was contorted with a mix of fear and pain as she lay on the bed, tucked into her father's side. Her eyes were enormous in her pale face. Neither of her parents looked much better.

'Emma, I'm Dr Sarah, and I'm going to make your tummy better.' Sarah winked at the frightened girl. Then she introduced herself to the parents, trying to ignore their obvious glances at her crutches. 'Mr and Mrs Duncan, Theatre's ready so we'll be getting started very shortly.'

'Where's Dan?' Emma's father asked.

'I'm his replacement while he's on leave.' Sarah forced a smile at their obvious distrust of a stranger. 'Please don't be worried about the fact that I've broken a couple of bones in my foot. I assure you my operating skills are still intact.'

'It's just we know Dan,' Mr Duncan explained.

Not used to being questioned about her role, Sarah tried

to imagine what these parents must be going through. They'd be terrified for their beautiful girl. 'I do understand, but the real concern's whether I'm good at what I do. Dan and Charlie must believe I am, or they wouldn't have taken me on.'

'Never mind the fact that there wasn't a queue of applicants for the job,' Sarah muttered to herself. That wasn't the point. She was a good surgeon.

Emma's mother gazed at her daughter with such love Sarah's heart expanded. To be a parent had to be one of the most wondrous privileges on earth. For the second time that day deep regret at her childlessness gripped Sarah. Within twenty-four hours Port Weston had got to her in ways she'd never have expected. Or was it Dr Dan sneaking in under her skin that had her emotions rocking all over the place? Because something sure was.

Back to Emma. 'Do you want to tell me how long you've had this tummyache?' Sarah asked.

'Em started complaining first thing this morning, Doctor.' Her father still looked uncertain but thankfully he answered all Sarah's questions thoroughly and quickly.

Sarah read the lab results and Alison Fulton's notes. Emma's high white-cell count backed the diagnosis of appendicitis. But it worried Sarah that there were indications of a burst appendix.

An orderly appeared at the doorway. 'Hey, Emma. How's my favourite niece? I'm going to take you for a short ride on the bed.'

Was everyone related in this town? How weird was that? Sarah's living relatives numbered two, her mother and father. She couldn't begin to imagine what it would be like to have cousins, uncles, grandparents, all those extra people in her life. Certainly had no idea how different growing up might have been. If she ever fell in love again, maybe she should find a man with relatives she could come to know and love. Her ex had only one sister who lived in London and they weren't close.

Sarah spoke to Emma's mother. 'It's Gayle, isn't it?'

The woman nodded. 'Sorry if we seem silly but—'

'It's okay. I know I'm asking the impossible but please try not to worry too much. I'll come and see you the moment I've finished,' Sarah tried to reassure her.

Then a nurse helped Sarah to scrub up. Surrounded by people she didn't know, about to operate at a hospital she'd never worked in before, it all seemed a little surreal. But theatres were theatres wherever she went. Nurses and anaesthetists did the same job everywhere. She just had to get over herself and concentrate on Emma's operation.

Jill popped her head around the corner. 'Heard you got called in and thought you might like a friendly face.'

'Yes, definitely.' Warmth washed through Sarah as she raised a thumb in acknowledgment, thrilled that Jill had been so considerate.

'We've found you a stool if you need it,' Jill told her.

In Theatre Hamish, the anaesthetist Sarah had met moments earlier, administered the drug that would keep Emma unconscious throughout the operation.

Sarah shuffled awkwardly on her injured foot, trying to find the most comfortable position without having to use the stool. Taking a deep breath, she lifted a scalpel and looked around at the attending staff. 'Ready?'

She concentrated on finding the infected appendix and assessing the situation. 'We're in luck. It hasn't perforated.'

Jill held out a clamp in a gloved hand. 'Poor kid. She still must've been hurting bad.'

Sarah clamped off all circulation to the appendix. 'Wonder what took her family so long to bring her in?'

'They live about a hundred and fifty kilometres from

here, up a valley in very difficult terrain,' Jill explained. 'It's no easy ride out of those hills.'

Sarah moved abruptly to one side to get a better view of the incision. Pain shot through her foot, diverting her attention briefly.

'You okay?' Hamish was watching her closely. 'Use the stool.'

'Thanks, but I prefer standing.' The stool might be too clumsy. Hamish's concern for her was nice. So far, working with this team was going well: no tension, everyone confident in their role yet also believing in each other's competence. Very different from the surgical hospital back home where everyone seemed to be trying to outdo each other on a regular basis. Today, here, she was beginning to understand how jaded she'd become and that her father might've been right to nudge her out of town. Working in this theatre was like a breath of fresh air.

Finally Sarah began tying off internally. The appendix stump. The blood vessels she'd had to cut. Her hands were heavy, like bricks. More thread required. Her back ached from the lopsided stance she'd maintained to counterbalance her boot-encased foot.

There was a soft whooshing sound as the door swung open, then closed. Sarah didn't have to be told Dan had arrived. With every nerve ending in her body she sensed his presence. She tried to concentrate on her work and not glance up, but her eyes lifted anyway. She looked directly at him. Warmth spread through her tired muscles and momentarily she felt recharged and capable of going on for ever.

He was fully scrubbed up, looking at Emma carefully. Checking up on his replacement? Sarah tried to read his eyes, saw a reprimand.

'Want a hand?' His voice was muffled behind his mask,

but there was no mistaking his anger. What exactly had she done wrong?

'I'm perfectly capable of finishing off.' She didn't need his help. Except that moments ago she'd noted how tired she'd become. Emma was her priority, not her pride. 'Could you close up for me?' she asked quietly.

Admiration filtered through his eyes, toning down the anger. Relief relaxed Sarah. She'd done the right thing. Gingerly shuffling sideways, she made room for Dan. Despite his unnecessary disapproval, it felt so right standing beside him here in Theatre, two professionals working to help Emma.

'Alison's message came through as we got to the bottom of the valley so I dropped Leah off at her nanny's and came straight over in case I was required. Obviously I wasn't.' Dan deftly pressed the suture needle through the flesh to pull another section of the wound together. 'You still should've got someone in to assist you, under the circumstances.'

'I'm glad it wasn't anything difficult,' Sarah admitted. But when Dan raised one eyebrow at her in an 'I told you so' fashion she retorted, 'There wasn't anyone else. Alison checked, and she was too busy to help.'

'I can see Emma was in excellent hands.' The grudging admittance in his voice confused her. Why did he find it hard to accept she knew what she was doing?

As Sarah swabbed away a speck of blood Jill reached across from the other side of the operating table to do it. Lifting her gaze to meet the other woman's, Sarah nearly choked. Jill was winking at her, her eyes holding a knowing glint. It could be interpreted in a trillion ways, but Sarah bet Jill still had ideas of matchmaking. A scheme that was doomed to crash and burn. Sarah had to go back to Auckland, if not at the end of her contract then some time in the next six months. Her father didn't mean for her to walk away from her partnership, just recoup her energy. Neither did she want to. She liked her comfortable lifestyle and the predictability of her job in Auckland.

Get real. You were bored. Exhausted. Fed up. Burying yourself in work to get over a broken heart. Why would you want to go back to that? Because it was the only life she knew and understood.

So, learn a new one. This is the perfect opportunity. A trickle of excitement seeped into her veins, lifted her spirits. Could she do that? Did she want to? She grinned. Possibly.

She headed for the scrub room, struggling to remove her gown. Her fingers fumbled with the knots on the ties.

'Let me do that.'

She hadn't heard Dan come in. 'Thanks.'

His fingers covered hers, took the cotton ties and tugged lightly to undo the impossible knots. 'You ready to go home?'

Home? 'Sure.'

Dan's fingers rested on the back of her neck. A simple touch, a very potent touch that made her feel good about herself. At the same time he disturbed her on a deeper level. Right now it was all too much to take in, she needed time to sift through the emotions pinging around her head.

She twisted around. 'I promised Emma's parents I'd see them as soon as I was finished.'

'No one expects you to. You must be exhausted.' His hand didn't shift.

'Maybe, but I do keep my word. And they must be fraught with worry by now.' With effort she shuffled away, forcing his arm to drop. She had no right to continue standing there enjoying his touch, no matter how innocently he gave it. She couldn't afford to surrender to wild needs. But, heaven knew, she wanted to. And, worse, it was hard to ignore those needs. But to give in to them with this man? After knowing him how long? One day. No, she must not. Hadn't she learnt anything from Oliver?

'You're right.' Daniel tugged his gown off. 'I'll come with you.'

All she was going to do was tell Emma's parents that their precious little girl was doing fine, but Dan accompanying her seemed right. Like they were a team. Scary. So she reacted with a verbal swipe. 'You're on holiday.'

'Coming from a large city, you can't be expected to appreciate how our patients are also our families, or our friends and neighbours. We treat the whole picture, not just the immediate illness.'

'I understand.' How mortifying that Dan thought so badly of her. He was totally wrong. She did care for her patients outside the operating theatre. *Huh? How often do you see any of your patients in any other capacity?* They come for consultation, surgery, a follow-up visit, then goodbye. She swallowed her chagrin. Dan had a point. But that didn't mean she wasn't as compassionate as he was. 'What are we waiting for?'

Jill poked her head around the door. 'Since you're both here, Anders and his father would love it if you dropped in on them when you're done with the Duncans.'

'Good idea.' The more time spent at the hospital meant less at home with only Dan and the conflicting emotions he stirred up. Sarah swung awkwardly on her crutches, hoping the ward wasn't too far away.

'Here, park your bottom in this.' Dan spun a wheelchair in her direction.

Great. 'I don't think so.' Where'd he found that so quickly?

'No one's going to think worse of you for conserving

your energy and protecting your foot.' Dan waited to push her. 'Sit,' he growled when she started to protest.

'Oh, all right.' Sarah eased into the wheelchair. Arguing took too much energy.

'Very gracious,' Dan muttered in her ear as he took the crutches from her.

Emma's parents were soon brought up to date and then a nurse took them to see their daughter. Dan whizzed Sarah along to the Starnes men, Jill going with them.

Anders and his father were sitting up in their respective beds, two dark heads turning at the sound of Sarah's chair wheels on the vinyl floor.

'Are you the doctors who saved me?' Anders raised his arm and winced.

'Don't move too much yet,' Dan advised in a friendly tone Sarah hadn't heard before. 'That shoulder will be tender for a while. This is Dr Livingston and I'm Dan Reilly.'

'We're very grateful for all you did for my boy,' the older man said, thrusting out his hand. 'Peter Starne.'

'You're both looking a lot better than the last time I saw you.' Sarah smiled as she took his hand.

'Unlike you, Doctor. What happened?'

'A slippery step got in my way.'

Dan's mood changed and he glared at the father. 'You're very fortunate, the pair of you. That's a wild coast out there.'

Peter looked sheepish. 'I know. I was an idiot to take Anders fishing off those rocks. Won't be doing that again in a hurry.'

'Glad you've learnt your lesson,' Dan snapped. 'A lot of people were involved in your rescue and any one of them could've been hurt. Or worse.'

Jill stepped closer, gripped Dan's elbow in warning. 'Pat

and Malcolm have been in to talk to Peter and Anders this morning. They've got the message loud and clear.'

'They'd...' Dan spluttered to a stop as Jill wrenched him away.

'Come on. You can show Sarah around the medical ward.' Out in the corridor Jill continued talking to Dan. 'Leave it. Pat gave them enough of a talking to about safety to last them a lifetime. They don't need the same lecture from you.'

'Why not? Did you see him? He looked embarrassed, not contrite.' Dan stared at Jill. 'He should be on his knees, thanking every last man who went out in that horrendous sea to save his butt.'

'Keep your voice down. This is a medical ward, not the sideline of a rugby field.' Jill cuffed him lightly. 'I understand how you feel, what with Malcolm being one of those men, but it's not our place to tell Peter Starne.'

Dan jerked a thumb over his shoulder. 'I haven't finished in there.'

Jill looked exasperated. 'Dan, leave it.'

'I need to check the boy's dislocated shoulder.'

Sarah looked up at Dan and asked gently, trying to keep reproof out of her voice so as not to antagonise him any more, 'Today's the first day of your holiday, remember? That means I'll take a look at Anders.'

He frowned. 'Don't you think you're being a little too keen to get off the mark, Doctor?'

'I suppose I could return to the house and put my foot up on pillows, demand pots of tea, and flick through magazines to while away the rest of the day.'

'What a good idea.' His frown lightened and he began pushing her. 'Let's go.'

'Dan.' Jill stepped in front of the wheelchair, effectively

stopping Dan's progress. Her eyes drilled into him. 'You're being obstructive'

'I'm trying to do the right thing for Sarah.' He began pushing the chair around Jill. 'Okay, she can go over next week's surgery schedule while I see to Anders.'

Sarah retorted, 'And then you will hand over the reins and go enjoy yourself.'

When the wheelchair moved off at speed she widened her smile. Men. Obstinate creatures.

'Why are women so difficult?' Dan asked Jill as he leaned against the nurses' station, reading Anders's case notes. 'Why aren't they more like men? What's wrong with accepting your limitations?'

Jill cocked her head on one side and looked at him, her earlier annoyance with him gone. 'You're talking about Sarah, I presume.'

Dan didn't like that all-knowing glimmer in his sister-in-law's eyes. 'Who else?'

'Sarah's being a real champ. She's certainly not bemoaning the fact she's been incapacitated, despite being in some pain. Nothing stopped her coming in when Alison called her for help.'

Dan's gaze rested on Sarah as she studied patient files at a desk at the other end of the ward. A little frown creased her brow as she concentrated. He'd noted that frown in Theatre when she'd focused on Emma, again when she'd explained everything about the operation to Gayle and John. He'd wanted to smooth the crease away then. He wanted to smooth it away now. What a distraction the woman was becoming. A very sexy distraction.

'Tell me.' Jill picked up the conversation again. 'What would you have done in the same circumstances? Stayed at home, grizzling? Or would you've got on with things, taking it on the chin like a man?'

'I am a man.'

'Yeah, and I don't think Sarah's a woman who spends a lot of time feeling sorry for herself.'

'You've got her all figured out already?'

'Call it woman's intuition, but I think our locum is one very self-contained lady who doesn't shirk her duties.'

'Huh,' Dan muttered. He had a sneaking suspicion Jill was right. 'That'll make Leah one happy kid. She's not sure of Sarah yet, gave her the fifth degree about her broken foot over breakfast.' Dan grinned. 'Then told Sarah she was naughty for going too fast and falling over. That child takes after her dad.'

Jill rolled her eyes. 'Poor little tyke.'

'Thanks very much. Glad to know who my friends are.' He covered a yawn. 'Having Sarah in the house might work out after all.' He'd get help with Leah and Sarah would learn to enjoy being around kids.

'Sleepless night?' Jill asked, her eyes widening and her mouth twitching.

'Sort of.' He'd taken hours to fall asleep, only to dream of creamy skin and a black lace bra filled to perfection. Not to mention a beautiful face and endearing smile. 'I think I'm already winding down into holiday mode.'

'Oh, sure. Nothing to do with your house guest, I presume.' Jill elbowed him. 'Go on, get out of here. It's time you had some fun. And I'm not just referring to Leah. Sarah could be the best thing to happen to you in a long time.'

It's time he had some sex, he knew that. But not with Dr Livingston. There again, why not? She was only here for a few months, long enough to have some fun with but not so long as to create problems. Like which side of the wardrobe she could hang her clothes. As if there'd ever be enough wardrobe space for all her outfits.

No, if he was getting back into the man-woman thing then it should be with a woman he could settle down and have more kids with. That job description did not suit Sarah. Except she'd been good with Leah that morning, and Gayle had said Sarah knew how to talk to Emma before her surgery.

On the other hand, she was too upmarket for Port Weston. For him. And he'd learned the hard way what happened when you tried to take the city out of a woman. It didn't work. She'd start blaming him for everything that went wrong, looking for problems that didn't exist.

In his pocket his phone vibrated as a text came through. He sighed as he read the message. Leah needed to change her top and Dan hadn't left the bag of clean clothes with the nanny.

One step forward, one back. Or was it sideways?

CHAPTER FIVE

'CAN we pull over for a moment?' Sarah asked Dan on the way to the hospital and her Saturday-morning patient round three days later.

'Something wrong?' He turned his four-wheel-drive into a lay-by on the ocean side of the road.

'Not at all.' As the vehicle stopped she pushed her door open and began to ease down on her feet, favouring the bad one. 'I want some wind and salt spray on my face.' The huge breakers that continuously rolled in fascinated her, drawing her into their rhythm. They lulled her to sleep at night, lifted her mood during the day. Very different from the sounds of downtown Auckland—dense traffic, sirens, people of every nationality calling out to each other.

'Can I sit in here, Daddy? I'm listening to the Singing Frogs.' Leah was belted into a back seat, twisting the cord of her small CD player.

'Sure can, kiddo.' Dan appeared at Sarah's side in double-quick time. 'This coastline is wild. Crazy and dangerous. It's very much a part of Coasters and who they are.'

'You're so right.' He could be referring to himself. Wild, crazy and dangerous. Definitely dangerous to her equilibrium. She breathed in the vibrant air, smelt salt and wet sand and seagulls. The thudding waves drowned out extraneous sounds except for the screeching gulls rising and falling on the air currents above them.

'Have you been to the Coast before?' Dan's hands rested on his slim hips, which drew her eye.

'Never.' She concentrated on the sea, trying to ignore the man. 'There weren't a lot of holidays when I was growing up, and none to the South Island.' Her brother, Bobby, might have got ill while they were away, which would have thrown her mother into a spin. 'And I confess that as an adult I've tended to head overseas for vacations. Not very patriotic of me, I guess, but the friends I used to go away with are more interested in the exotic and I've always gone along.' Even to her that sounded like a copout. 'Willingly,' she added.

Dan shook his head at her. 'Tourists say this is exotic. They pay to come here.'

'Tourists usually do pay.' Stop being difficult with him. 'You're right. I should've seen my own country by now. Maybe I'll have time to look around a bit while I'm here.' She could take a day trip on her day off. Shifting the conversation away from herself, she asked, 'Did I hear you've got a sister in Australia?'

'Pauline, our adopted sister. I'd like to take Leah over to get to know her extended family some time.'

'Adopted? Older or younger?' Family. Why did everything come back to that? Was she just being over-sensitive since Oliver had left her?

'She comes between Bea and me. Her mother and ours were sisters. Pauline's mother was a single mum and when she died in a house fire our parents naturally took Pauline in. No one ever knew who her father was.'

'What a wonderful thing for your parents to do.' Hers couldn't wait to see the back of each other after her brother had died. The stress and pressure of losing their son had taken a big toll. And no matter how hard she'd tried, she hadn't been able to make them understand she'd needed them to stay together as much as Bobby had.

Dan looked at her in disbelief. 'Not at all. That's what families are all about.'

Really? He didn't get how lucky he was. 'When did you last see Pauline?'

Dan turned to stare out over the waves. 'Two years ago. She came over for Celine's funeral and stayed on for two weeks, helping me get my head around what had happened. She was incredibly patient with me.'

'Had your wife been ill?' All these questions. Any minute he'd tell her to mind her own business, but she wanted to know what made him tick.

'Celine had never been ill in her life. She was struck down by an aneurysm.' His fingers dug into his hips, the knuckles turning white. His gaze went way beyond the waves to some place only he could see.

Wishing she hadn't caused him distress, Sarah said the first thing that came into her head. 'Do you want to take a hobble along the beach? There's time before my first patient.' She glanced down at the moon boot. 'It won't matter if I get this a bit wet.'

'Hang on, there're some plastic grocery bags in the Toyota I can put over it for protection. Sand inside that thing will be a pain.' Dan went to get a bag and Leah clambered out of the vehicle to join him, skipping in circles as Dan slipped the bag over Sarah's foot.

Looking down as he deftly knotted it at the top and tucked the ends inside her boot, the urge to run her fingers through his thick, dark hair was almost uncontainable. Almost. He'd think her whacky if she followed through. *She'd* think she was whacky. Touching another person unasked went totally against who she was. Having never had lots of hugs or kisses, no spontaneous touches, from her parents or Oliver, she usually struggled with reaching out to people like that. And yet right now she had to fight the urge to touch Dan.

She'd seen the bleakness in his eyes and touching him would be a way of saying she was sorry he had been so badly hurt, to show she understood. Instead she shoved her hands deep into her trouser pockets, distorting the perfect line of the soft fabric. And said nothing. What could she say that wouldn't sound trite? Her brother had died, having a terrible effect on her. But to lose the love of your life? The mother of your child? Much worse.

He stood up and his gaze clashed with hers, sending warmth spiralling through her despite her muddled feelings.

'Let's go.' He began striding down the hard sand, leaving her to follow at an uneven, slower pace.

His shoulders were hunched as he studied the ground in front of his feet, his hands clenched at his sides. A man hurting? Or angry at her again for intruding on his privacy? Keep this up and they were going to have many clashes over the coming months.

Then Leah ran up to her, pulled at Sarah's arm to free her hand. Warm, sticky fingers wrapped around Sarah's forefinger and she was tugged along the beach. Suddenly Sarah laughed. A completely unexpected laugh that relaxed the tension that had been dogging her for weeks. What was happening to her?

'Want to share the joke?' Dan stopped to wait for her. 'I could do with a good chuckle.'

'Nothing, really. It's good to be walking on the beach as though I've got nothing to worry about. I haven't done anything like this on a regular basis.' Face it, she didn't go for any sort of exercise, ever.

'Lucky you,' her companion grunted.

'Dan, give it a break.' She wouldn't let him drag her mood down, and as Leah ran off to study a dead gull she asked, 'What are you two doing today?'

'We've got a birthday party at twelve for one of Leah's preschool mates.'

'That sounds like fun.' What did adults do at those things? Play pass-the-parcel with the kids or hide in the kitchen, drinking wine? She knew which she'd be best at and it had nothing to do with parcels.

Dan jerked his head around to glare at her. 'Fun? Fun? Lady, what do you do for entertainment if you think spending hours with a bunch of four-year-olds is fun? Want to swap places?'

They were on the same wavelength—sort of. 'Okay, it's fun for Leah, but I'm sure you'll manage to raise a smile or two of your own.'

'Why would I want to do that?' But his eyes twinkled briefly. If only he knew how gorgeous and sexy and wonderful he looked when that twinkle appeared. 'At least I won't get a sore butt today.' He ran his hands down his thighs. 'Remind me again how great a time I had riding that bolshy horse. I'm sure Bea gave me Jumbo deliberately.'

'You need Deep Heat rubbed into your muscles.' Uh-oh.

The tip of his tongue appeared between his lips. His eyes widened, darkened. 'What are you suggesting? Massaging my thighs?'

She'd prefer his backside. Oh, great. Prize idiot. If he read her mind he'd think she was making a pass at him. Again. Charging along the beach as fast as her foot allowed, she said loudly, 'So no more riding?'

'We're going again tomorrow. I think Bea has a sadistic streak that I'm only just learning about.'

'You could say you're washing your hair.' Sarah grinned, thankful the subject of rubbing his muscles had been got past even if a very definite picture of her hands on that backside remained uppermost in her head.

'Can you see Leah letting me get away with that?' He kicked a small pebble into the froth surging at the water's edge. 'Seriously, do you think you're going to enjoy your time here? Yesterday, on my way to the supermarket, I tried to see Port Weston through your eyes and I must admit the town looks a little scruffy. The tired, weatherboard buildings, the shopfronts that belong to another generation. It's not flash.'

'I wasn't expecting a miniature Auckland. I'd have stayed at home otherwise.'

'So why did you take up the contract? I mean, you're a partner in a big, modern clinic. If you wanted a change, why not cruising somewhere like the Caribbean?'

'My father talked me into taking a break.' The words slipped out without thought.

'This is a break?' He shrugged his shoulders. 'Doing my job is a holiday?'

Damn, did he think she was mocking him? 'Not at all. It's just that it's so different working here. New people, total change of scenery. Hopefully not so competitive.' So much for self-control. Around Dan it was always disappearing. 'I'd been putting in extremely long hours.'

'Why? There must be enough surgeons lining up to work with your father to last his lifetime. His reputation is awesome. You could've backed off the hours.'

And then what would she have done? How would she have filled in the time and blocked out the pain caused by

Oliver? 'I wanted to do the hours. There were things going on in my life I was ignoring.'

'I can certainly sympathise with that sentiment.' Dan sighed. 'The exact same reasons I'm now on leave. I tended to spend time with my patients rather than deal with Leah and all her problems. Because she didn't react well to my way of dealing with her distress, hasn't ever since her mother died. Family kept stepping in and helping out, taking Leah home and making her happy for a while.' He shrugged. 'It all just became so much easier to leave them all to it and I could get on with building up the hospital's surgical unit.'

'Dan, you're great with Leah. She seems so happy and well adjusted.'

'I wish you hadn't said that.' Dan winced.

'Think I'm tempting fate? That now she'll be a little hellion? I can't see it. She's so sweet.'

'You can be quite supportive, did you know that? I could get used to having you around,' he growled, but his mouth lifted at the corners.

She stared at him. 'You'd better not. I don't intend staying on past the end of March.'

He shrugged. 'Fair enough. So what were you working so hard to avoid?'

'Not avoid,' Sarah grumbled, not wanting to go there. But Dan had shared some of his story with her. It seemed natural to return the favour. 'Actually, you're right. That's exactly what I was doing. I should be in Paris right now on my honeymoon.'

Dan's eyes widened. 'Really? It'd be very cold over there at this time of the year.'

Good, a spiteful little voice squeaked in her head. 'I was supposed to get married at the beginning of December but my fiancé called it off six months ago. He was having an affair with one of the clinic's nurses, which resulted in the baby they're expecting.'

'Whoever the guy is, he doesn't deserve you. That's a lousy thing for any man to do. Didn't he have the gumption to come to you from the moment he decided the nurse was the centre of his attention?' Dan looked hurt on her behalf. Which felt good, in an odd way.

'Oliver's also a partner in my father's surgical hospital, which kind of complicates things.' There was an understatement. 'Thankfully the nurse was more than happy to give up work once she learned she was pregnant.'

'Unlike you. You'd want to keep your career on track.' His eyes bored into hers.

'Yes, I would. But I believe I'd have managed to balance a family with work.' She'd have cut back her hours, certainly not spent evenings away lecturing or studying, as her father had done. 'Anyway, it doesn't matter now. I'm single and can remain focused entirely on my career.'

'What about love, Sarah? Surely you haven't cut yourself off from that happening. The kind of love that melts your heart, makes you jump out of burning buildings, brings you home every night? Don't you want to try for that again? And what about kids?'

Of course she wanted all that. Some time in the future. It was still too soon, although she already felt more at ease about her situation than she ever had.

'Time I went to work.' She spun back the way they'd come. Her foot jagged, the pain taking her breath away. What had happened to being careful?

Dan had happened. That's what. So distracting, so annoying, so endearing, that's what. He had her so mixed up emotionally it could take months to get back on an even keel. And now he'd taken her elbow to lead her slowly back to the car, ever mindful of her foot.

Emma was full of beans when Sarah hobbled into the ward, Dan beside her, his hand hovering on her elbow.

'I can manage from here,' Sarah muttered, desperate for a break from those sensual fingers on her skin. The tension she'd hoped to dispel while walking on the beach had increased beyond reason, tightening her tummy further. Instead of pushing Dan away with her revelations, they seemed to have drawn a little closer to each other. She had yet to work out if that was a good thing. 'I could've managed from the car park.'

'I've got half an hour to fill in.' Dan shrugged away her annoyance as if he didn't care what she thought. Which he probably didn't.

'You must have something else to do, something that has nothing to do with the hospital or patients.' She ground out the words through clenched teeth. Why had he come here? To check out her patient skills? Or did he just like being with her? If she had to choose a reason she hoped it was the second. Wishful thinking. Daniel Reilly was a control freak struggling to let go of his practice.

Jerking out of his grasp, Sarah waved to Emma across the room. Dressed in blue shorts and a T-shirt covered in bright pink daisies with flaming red centres, she looked a picture of happiness and health.

'Hi, Dr Sarah. I'm going home today.'

'Emma, sit still for a moment.' Gayle Duncan tried to grab hold of her daughter. Not a chance. 'Sorry, Sarah, but she's so happy to be getting out of here.'

'Who can blame her for that?' Sarah had got to know

Gayle quite well while she'd spent the days since Emma's appendectomy reading or playing games with her daughter.

Just as she would in the same situation. The thought slammed into Sarah's brain. Tick tock went the biological clock. She bit down on her bottom lip, desperately wanting this uncalled-for need to go away. Why now? Why here? Her gaze went straight to Dan standing on the other side of the bed, his thoughtful expression focused directly on her. Uh-oh. Did he have anything to do with this need? No way. He might be very attractive and distracting but what she felt for him was plain old lust. Certainly not grounds for considering having babies with the guy.

'Dr Dan, is your holiday finished?' Emma bobbed up and down before him.

He was slow to look away from Sarah to the girl trying to get his attention, and Sarah worried that she'd given away too much in those brief moments. He seemed able to see past all her defences right to her real wants and needs. Almost as though he knew her better than she did.

Which made him very dangerous to be around.

'Not yet. I brought Dr Livingston in and soon I'm going to pick up Leah from the library reading morning.'

So go. Get out of here. Give me space to gather my thoughts and put my head back in order. Sarah sent silent messages to him but he didn't move. *That's right, be obtuse. You were reading my mind fine before.*

'I'm going to play outside when I get home,' Emma told him.

Gayle asked Sarah, 'Do you want to check Emma before we go?'

Sarah scanned Emma's charts and notes. 'Everything looks absolutely fine. My main concern was Emma's temperature. As that's now completely normal you can take her home and spoil her.'

Sitting on the edge of the bed, Sarah patted the covers beside her. 'Emma, I want you to do something for me. Your tummy has been very sick so you have to look after it for a few more days. You mustn't do rough things that might hurt it. No climbing trees or riding the bike yet.'

Gayle chipped in before Sarah could say any more. 'Careful. This calls for reverse psychology. A certain young lady will immediately do anything you tell her not to.'

'I'll be very, very good. Won't I, Mummy?' Those enormous brown eyes were turned on Gayle.

Sarah chuckled. 'I don't know how you can say no to her.' She'd make a hopeless parent, spoiling any children she had. Children. Plural. Thinking of more than one child now? Unbidden, her longing swamped her, making her powerless to move. Then Emma leaned close to place a damp kiss on her chin, causing Sarah's eyes to mist over. Wordlessly she reached for Emma, gave her a quick hug.

She had to get out of here. She was making an idiot of herself. Getting all teary and giving spontaneous hugs. Next she'd be turning up to work in track pants and a T-shirt. This place sure had a way of playing havoc with everything as she knew it.

'Tell me again how I got to be at a child's birthday party?' Sarah asked Dan as they sat on the lawn, watching Leah leaping along in a sack trying to beat all the other kids to the finish line.

'You had nothing else to do.'

Sure, but a kid's party? 'I'd have found something.'

'Relax. No one's going to bite you.' Dan grinned at her discomfort, reminding her of the first morning when she'd been shocked awake by Leah crawling under the covers with her. Once the surprise had faded Sarah had enjoyed having a warm tot wriggling down beside her under the sheet.

She nudged Dan. 'Think you're needed. Leah's taken a tumble in her sack.'

'The tears will be because she hasn't won, not because she's hurt herself. Let's hope they don't last long.' He was quick to lift Leah up and set her on her feet again. 'Keep going. You've got to finish the race.'

Leah's heart wasn't in it. 'No, I'm going to sit with Sarah.'

'You've got to learn not to quit, my girl.' Dan's hands were on his hips.

'She's only four,' Sarah said. Sounding like a mother? Eek.

'Got to teach her these things right from the start.' Dan reached down to Leah as though to set her in the right direction but she ducked and slid past him, in her hurry tripping over the sack again and skidding on the rough grass.

The ensuing shrieks and cries were ear-piercing. Everyone turned to see what had happened. Two mothers rushed over to check on Leah. Dan scooped her up into his arms, holding her to his chest. 'She's all right,' he told everyone, and kissed Leah's forehead, at which point Leah squealed louder. 'Carry on with the race.'

One of the mothers remained with them while the other returned to the young partygoers and got them racing again. Leah cried louder. 'It hurts, Daddy.' And she snuggled in closer to his chest.

Panic filled Dan's eyes. He sat down on the ground, his big hand on Leah's head. 'Shh, little one. Take it easy. Where does it hurt?'

'Everywhere,' Leah answered between sobs.

Sarah was perplexed. A tumble in a sack shouldn't cause

this amount of distress. Unless… 'Does Leah suffer from any medical condition that would precipitate this reaction?'

Dan gulped. 'Ah, no. Here, can you hold her while I look her over?'

About to put her arms out to take the child, Sarah hesitated. Why the panic in Dan's eyes if there wasn't a condition to worry about? What upset him so much? Leah needed him more than anyone else. Light-bulb moment. That was the problem. He was afraid he couldn't comfort her. 'No, Dan, it's you Leah wants.' Sarah knelt down beside them. 'I'll look her over while you hold her.'

Dan's eyes darkened with disappointment and something like fear. He looked around, spied the mother still standing with them and began to lift Leah towards her. 'Would you?'

Sarah shook her head at the woman, silently asking her to say no. She sensed Dan had to get through this moment without letting his daughter go to someone else.

'Sarah's right, Dan. Leah needs her daddy right now.'

'But listen to her. She's not quietening down for me.'

'With some kids it takes a while.' The woman gave Sarah a knowing smile and strolled away.

'You're doing fine. I think the volume might be lowering a bit.' Sarah's heart squeezed for this big man totally out of his depth. She gently took one of Leah's arms and checked it over, then her legs. 'You've scrapped some skin off your knee, sweetheart.' And she bent to kiss it. 'There you go, all better.'

Sarah sat down beside Dan to wait while Leah slowly began to quieten down. The crying became soft sobs, then hiccups, and finally a large yawn as she settled further down into the comfort of her father's arms. And slowly the tension eased in Dan's muscles, relaxing away until he watched Leah in awe, his chest rising and falling as his breathing became settled.

Sarah swallowed around the lump in her throat. 'See, you're a great dad.'

'That's the first time I've managed to settle her when she gets that worked up.'

Leah's reaction had been out of proportion. 'Does she always do that? Get herself totally wound up?'

'Ever since her mother died and it's been up to me to comfort her.'

'I think there are two issues there, not one. It's not that you can't console her, it's that she just needs to work through her pain about her mum. You've made a habit of handing her over to others to comfort, haven't you?' *Don't do that, Dan. Your daughter loves you more than anyone else. You're her father.* There were a few things she'd like to point out to Dan but didn't want him thinking she was a know-all. And she wasn't about to tell him she had first-hand experience of a father who was never there when she really needed him.

Dan glanced across to Sarah. 'You're the first person to ever refuse to take her for me.' He gulped. 'Thank you. I think.'

Sarah forced a laugh. 'You were trying to palm her off on someone who hasn't a clue how to console an upset child. I had to do something to save her.' She leaned over and kissed the top of Leah's head, got a lungful of the heady male scent of Dan. Her eyes closed for a second before she lifted her head and placed a light kiss on Dan's cheek.

Shock rippled through her as her lips touched his freshly shaven cheek, as she inhaled the scent of him. What had she done? She jerked back, out of reach. She was crazy. Risking a glance, she saw surprise reflected in Dan's eyes.

'Daddy, what's a three-legged race?'

Thank you, Leah, now your father can concentrate on you and forget my little mistake. But Sarah rolled her lips together softly, thinking it didn't really feel like a mistake. If she wound back a few minutes to before she'd brushed her lips over Dan's cheek, would she have done it? Yes.

Dan's gaze dropped to his precious bundle. 'You tie one of your legs to someone else's and run to the finish line.'

'Can we do that? Will you run with me?' Leah asked, her eyes wide and puffy.

'This I can't wait to see.' Sarah tried for a laugh. Five minutes later the laughter was wiped off her face.

'The three-legged race is split between girls with their mothers, and boys with their fathers.' Dan studied Sarah with a big question in his eyes.

'Um, I'm not Leah's mother.' Why had she come to this party? Because Dan had talked her into doing something she didn't want to do. And now he wanted her to take part in a race with his daughter. 'Sorry, got a moon boot, remember?'

Leah's little face fell. 'We can tie the other leg to me. Please Sarah. There's chocolate for the winner.'

That face got to her. What a sucker she was turning into. How much would it hurt her foot to try? She held her hand up to Dan to be hauled off the ground. 'Go easy on me, okay?' She tickled Leah under the chin and tried to ignore Dan's fingers as they tied the ribbon around her leg.

Together with Leah she hobbled to the start line, Leah tripping over more than once. Gritting her teeth as her fractures protested, Sarah said, 'Okay, we need a plan.' And whispered in Leah's ear.

Leah wrapped her arms around Sarah's waist and put her free foot on top of the one joined to Sarah's leg. And at the blow of the whistle they were racing. Step, thump. Step, thump.

'Daddy, Sarah and me got chocolate,' Leah shrieked a few minutes later.

'Sarah and I,' Dan automatically corrected.

'Cos we were the most un-unusualist.'

'Unusual,' Dan corrected her again, before turning to Sarah. 'Thanks. You've made Leah's day.'

'It was kind of fun.' Despite her foot, and that people were looking at her funny, as though she and Dan were an item, she was enjoying herself. Quite a few women were glancing at Dan and her, questions written all over their faces. So she obviously wasn't his usual type. They needn't worry. He wasn't hers either.

'Looks like lunch is next.' Dan led them to the laden tables. 'Ready for jelly and chicken nuggets?'

'On the same plate?' Sarah shuddered.

'Live dangerously.' Dan winked.

'Sarah, do you like fairy bread?' Leah peered up at her, holding out a plate filled with bread smothered in the tiniest dots of coloured sugar.

Sarah, do you like fairy bread? she could hear her brother asking, pressing a plateful into her hand. Where had that come from? There hadn't been parties like this when she was little. Yes, there had. When she'd been about Leah's age Robbie had had a birthday party and her parents had taken them to the zoo, along with lots of other children. They'd fed the monkeys with leftover food. No way. She was in lala land. That had not happened. She'd never forget a party.

'Sarah? Are you okay?' Dan took her elbow as though he expected her to fall down in a heap.

She shook away the memory, if that's what it was, and said, 'I'm fine. And, yes, I love fairy bread.' She had thirty-something years ago anyway. *See, it's not a dream. It happened.* What else from her childhood had she forgotten? What other good, fun things had been lost in the need to impress her father and gain his attention?

CHAPTER SIX

DAN flicked the vegetable knife into the sink and snapped the cold tap on so fiercely water sprayed over the bench and across the front of his T-shirt. The walls closed in on him as he leaned back against the bench.

At the kitchen table Sarah and Leah were making cookies. Both of them had cute smudges of flour on their cheeks. Leah's eyes were enormous in her face as she followed Sarah's instructions on mixing the chocolate pieces into the dough.

'Oops!' Sarah chuckled and scooped up a handful of creamed mix from the table where it had flicked from the bowl due to Leah's over-enthusiastic stirring. 'Slow down a bit. Here.' She popped a chocolate button into Leah's grinning mouth.

'Look, Daddy, I'm mixing the biscuits.'

'You're doing a great job.' Warmth stole over him. His girl couldn't be happier. Sarah had done that for her. Antsy Sarah, who swore she knew nothing about children's needs. Sarah, who did three-legged races with a moon boot just to give a child a special moment. 'So are you, big girl.'

He got glared at with piercing green eyes. 'Big girl?'

'As in Leah's my little one.' The glare sharpened. 'Can I pour you a wine? It's that time of the day.' He opened the fridge and took out a bottle of white wine, waving it at her. Hopefully diverting her.

The green lightened, her mouth twitched. 'Yes, please.'

'Me too, Daddy.'

Dan shook his head as he poured one wine and a juice. What had happened to his plan to have dinner cooking and Leah bathed and in her PJs by now? Females, young and older, that's what had happened. Both distracting in their own way. Both taking over his kitchen and making the mother of all messes.

'Aren't you having anything?' Sarah asked as he put the bottles back in the fridge.

'Yes, actually, I am.' He'd forgotten to get himself a beer. His nice, orderly world seemed to be going all to hell. How could this woman cause so much mayhem just by being—being there? He was even starting to think that she'd make a good mother for his Leah, and that was a really, stupid idea. It would never work. He wasn't moving to Auckland with all its traffic and no green paddocks. And Sarah? Well, she'd never consider living permanently so far away from those spas and dress designers. Though those trousers she had on now weren't as posh as some of the outfits she'd worn so far. Slumming it? Snapping the tab on a can of lager, he grinned. Sarah was most definitely relaxing a bit.

'Good, I don't like drinking alone.' A smile curved her full lips. 'What are we having for dinner?' she asked.

'You're as bad as Leah. We've got fresh blue cod caught by a local fisherman.'

'Yum. How are you cooking it?'

'In the pan.' This wasn't one of her fancy restaurants where she'd get sauces and fresh herbs and other garnishes.

One corner of Sarah's delectable mouth curled upward before she asked Leah, 'Do you want to stir the nuts in now?'

'I don't like nuts.' Leah stopped poking the buttons into the mixture with her fingers. 'They're yukky.'

'Have you tried them?' Sarah looked a bit stunned.

'Not many kids Leah's age do. Could be because parents don't let them have nuts in case they choke.'

Sarah's face fell. 'I didn't think. How stupid of me. Chocolate hazelnut cookies are a favourite of mine.' She looked at Dan, lifted her shoulders in an eloquent gesture. 'I blew it, didn't I?'

'It's not a biggie, Sarah.'

'Yes, it is. I've gone and spoiled the whole thing of having fun with Leah and being able to eat the cookies together.' She leaned down and hugged Leah to her. 'I'm sorry, sweetheart.'

'Can I eat the rest of the chocolate?'

Dan shook his head at his daughter. 'You're never one to miss an opportunity, are you? I've got a suggestion.' He looked at Sarah. 'How about Leah stirs in the rest of the buttons and makes them double chocolate cookies?'

Gratitude shone back at him. 'Good thinking.'

As the mixing resumed, Dan added for Sarah's benefit, 'You didn't spoil anything. Even if a certain young lady hadn't been able to eat the biscuits, she's still having a blast. I've never cooked with her, but it is something I'd envisaged she'd do with her mother. You've started something that I might have to keep up.' When carefully sculpted eyebrows rose he added, 'Seriously, the fun is in the doing, not just the eating.'

'Thanks.' She took a big gulp of wine. 'I remember making biscuits with Gran when we stayed at her house.'

Why the surprise in her eyes? 'Didn't you enjoy it?'

'I loved it.' Another gulp. 'I'd forgotten we did that.' Then she murmured something like, 'Seems as though I've forgotten a lot of things.'

Dan wanted to ask her what her childhood had been like but twice already he'd put his size-eleven feet in his mouth when asking her personal things so he kept quiet.

Soon the cookies were in the oven and Sarah stared at the messy table. 'Guess I know what I'm doing next.'

'I'll take care of that.' It would keep him busy for half the night. He jerked a thumb at the door. 'Go and put that leg up. I bet it hurts like crazy.'

'That's to be expected.'

'I'll check it for swelling once I've finished here. You did spend a lot of time standing on it today. Not to mention the race.'

'I'm glad I opted for the moon boot. A cast would've been clunky.' She leaned her saucy hip against the kitchen table. A smattering of flour had somehow got onto her trousers, smeared over her butt.

Dan tried desperately to focus on filling a pot with spuds rather than on the mouthwatering sight at his table. The very feminine curves appealed to his male senses. More than that, his hormones were stirring up a storm. Again. Still.

'It isn't necessary for you to check my foot. I'm qualified to do my own check-ups.' Had her voice wobbled?

'Daddy check-ups my hurts.' Leah's eyes sparkled.

Dan smiled over his shoulder at Leah, warmth bubbling through him. He'd do anything to make his girl happy. Even clean up after the sex goddess. Only days into it, he seemed to be getting a handle on this full-time-dad lark. Though he'd nearly blown it when Leah had tripped in that silly sack race. The one scenario he'd been dreading since the day he'd learned he was going on leave had happened, but Sarah had forced him to face up to his insecurities. And, with no alternative, he had. And won.

He owed Sarah big time. For the first time one of Leah's crying episodes hadn't escalated into a full-blown meltdown that he couldn't manage. He'd consoled her, comforted her, and within a short time she'd been happily bouncing all over the place, not refusing to talk, and crying for hours as had happened so often in the past. *He'd* done it. Without Auntie Bea, or Jill, or the nanny. But with Sarah on the sidelines, encouraging him with her sweet smile. What about that sweet kiss she'd dropped on his cheek? It had taken his breath away.

'Daddy, can I take the plaster off my knee now? It's all better.'

'Of course you can.' He looked at his daughter, grateful of the interruption to where his thoughts were heading. 'You're a cracker kid.'

'A Christmas cracker.' Leah put one hand in Sarah's and the other in his. 'Pull me. See what's inside like a real cracker.'

'A paper hat and a plastic toy.' Sarah smiled at Leah before her gaze turned to him.

What was she thinking? She'd appeared to enjoy the baking session until she'd realised her mistake about the nuts. Did she wish she had her own family? Of course she would. Who didn't? Not anyone with a heart. Sarah might think she'd hidden hers but he'd watched her with Emma, with Anders. Sarah gave more of herself than was expected of a surgeon dealing with a young patient. She'd taken some knocks, which could explain why she tried so hard to remain aloof. She certainly coped with Leah's demands like a veteran.

'Pot's boiling over.' Sarah nodded at him.

'What?'

'Daddy, you're dreaming. The pot's too hot.'

He spun around, flicked the gas to low. Goddamn it. He *had* been daydreaming. Why wouldn't he? A beautiful woman stood in his kitchen and he hadn't had sex for a long time. What else would a bloke be doing? It had been for ever since he'd scratched that particular urge.

A town the size of Port Weston made it difficult to have a brief fling. The gossipmongers would have a field day. Mostly when he got randy as hell, he took to digging up the garden. Nothing like hard, physical work to douse the urge. The fact that his garden was extremely overgrown was testimony to how often that happened.

But it would be impossible to find any red-blooded male who wouldn't be interested in the stunning Dr Livingston. Except, maybe, this Oliver character.

He was going to have to take Leah away for some overnight trips. Living under the same roof as Sarah was akin to lighting a fire and leaping into it.

'Thought I'd give you a treat today.' Dan spoke from Sarah's office doorway.

She leaned back in her chair, shaking her head at him. Some time over the week since the baking fiasco Dan had finally managed to stop wanting to read all the patient files and going over cases with her. But occasionally he still turned up unannounced to see if she needed help with anything. 'You're going to whisk me off to a beauty clinic where I'll be pampered for hours on end.'

'I don't think so.' He looked stunned, as if that was an odd suggestion.

'Not my lucky day, then, is it?' She smiled to soften her words.

'What about a real coffee in a real café? If you're not busy, that is? It's time you met George and Robert.'

'Sounds wonderful.' She glanced at her day planner. 'As you know full well, I'm not exactly rushed off my feet.'

'Come Monday you will be. That's a heavy schedule you've got so let's make the most of today's opportunity while we can.' His mouth twisted in a sheepish manner when she raised an eyebrow at him. 'I happened to see the operating list when I stopped to say hello to Jill.'

'Left it lying around, did we?' The list had been in a drawer at Jill's desk half an hour ago.

'I was looking for a pen.' Then he shrugged and gave her a rare grin, one that hit her right in the belly and had her wanting to know more about him. 'All right. I can't help myself. I'm an interfering beaver, I know. But for the record, you're doing a brilliant job and I couldn't have asked for a better replacement.'

About to get out of her chair, Sarah found her arms didn't have the strength to push her up. 'You what?' *Close your mouth, you're looking like a fish out of water. I feel like one.*

Dan jerked a thumb over his shoulder. 'You want that coffee or not?'

'I guess,' she croaked. She'd been paid a compliment. By Daniel Reilly. What had brought that on? Mr Grumpy had more sides to him than a hexagonal block. Or else he wanted something from her.

The ride to Port Weston's main street was a silent one. Sarah dwelt on what Dan might want and as he pulled his Land Cruiser into a park outside the café she decided she'd been a bit harsh. As far as she'd noted, Dan didn't do devious so there probably wasn't any ulterior motive behind that statement. He'd meant it. And he was taking her out. Not on a date, as such, but they were going for coffee where they'd be seen by locals. So when he came around to open her door and help her down she gave him a full-beam smile. Which seemed to fluster him completely.

Inside the café he pulled out a chair for her, then waved to the two men working behind the counter. 'Robert, George, can we have some coffee please? And you'd better meet Sarah.'

Watching the men hurrying to the table, Sarah grinned. 'Seems you're popular.'

Dan twisted his mouth sideways in that wry way of his. 'It's you they want to meet. You're about to get a thorough going over.'

'Like a bag of coffee beans, you mean?'

Dan merely raised his dark eyebrows. 'Something like that.'

The shorter of the two men touched her lightly on the shoulder. 'I'm Robert, and this is my partner, George.'

George held out his hand. 'Pleased to meet you.'

She shook hands with both men.

'Your reputation has gone before you.' Robert took a long look at her.

'What am I reputed to have done?' Sarah asked, intrigued despite herself.

'It's nothing to do with what you've done, apart from falling down the pub's steps. Talk about making a grand entrance to our little community.' Robert paused, then, 'Everyone's talking about the new surgeon and her absolutely fabulous car, not to mention her exquisite clothes.'

Leaning sideways, Robert appraised her stylish mid-calf, café-au-lait-coloured trousers and peach sleeveless shirt. 'I'd have to agree. Very classy.'

Dan leaned back on his chair, arms folded across his chest, a well-worn black T-shirt stretched too tight across his muscular frame. 'Not like me at all.' And the damned man winked at her.

Sarah tried to ignore that wide chest and failed. Miserably. Her mouth dried. She itched to slip her hands between the fabric and his skin. As her stomach did a flip she wondered how she could think like this when the man annoyed the daylights out of her most of the time. Somehow, despite that, contemplating those muscles under his shirt kept her awake most nights until the sound of the sea worked its magic on her.

Wasn't she supposed to be grieving over a broken engagement? Yet here she was, drooling over the first man she'd spent any time with since Oliver. Looking up at his face, she was shocked to see him watching her. Heat pooled in the pit of her stomach as something dark and dangerous glittered back at her.

Finally Dan waved a hand. 'Hey, there, Robert, could we have some coffees? Today would be good.'

Robert rolled his eyes. 'This is what happens when you try keeping Sarah all to yourself. But we can't have her thinking we can't match it with the city types so excellent coffee coming up.'

Keeping her all to himself? Not likely. He'd taken her to that birthday party, hadn't he? Hardly the social event of the year, but there had been lots of mothers there. Not her scene at all and yet she'd had fun.

Sarah leaned her elbows on the table and dropped her chin into her hand. 'How long have George and Robert been living in Port Weston?' she asked, while her mind was still on Dan.

'About five years. Robert's a West Coaster, originally from further south in Hokitika.'

'He limps quite badly, and seems to be in some pain.' Sarah had noted the sideways drag and occasional grimace when he'd approached their table.

'He snapped a tendon and, despite surgery to reattach it,

he's had nothing but trouble since. Don't waste your breath suggesting a second operation. He's adamant he's not having one,' Dan explained. 'I've tried countless times to get him to see an orthopaedic surgeon I can recommend.'

'That's sad when he possibly could be walking around pain free.' Sarah wondered why Robert felt so strongly against a repeat op. 'Did something happen during surgery?'

Leaning his chin on his chest, Dan murmured, 'He's not saying. It was done in Christchurch but without his permission I can't request his file.'

'Has George said anything to you?'

Dan shook his head. 'He's promised Robert he won't, though I think he's bursting to discuss it. See if you can get anything out of him once you've been here a little while.'

If Dan couldn't convince Robert when he knew them so well, she didn't stand a chance. Sarah twisted around to look out the window onto the street and the people wandering past, all dressed very casually. Despite the summer temperature, many of the men wore gumboots or heavy work boots, and some people had caps on to keep the sun off their faces.

She couldn't get much further from the fashionable, bustling crowds of downtown Auckland. But if she'd been back there she'd have been tense, tapping the floor with the toe of her shoe, in a hurry to down her coffee and get back to work. Not a lot of enjoyment in that, while here she was happy to take her time, savouring the company, and hopefully the coffee when it came.

Robert placed their cups on the table, turned to Sarah. 'I hear there's a roster for driving you to the hospital.'

'There is. It astonishes me how total strangers are waiting outside the gate in the morning, ready to drive me to work. The same thing happens when it's time to go home.'

'That's what living on the Coast is all about, helping one another,' Robert said.

Even at three o'clock that morning someone had picked her up when she'd been called in to an emergency. She hoped it wasn't part of their 'keep Dr Sarah here' plan, which she'd heard about through the hospital grapevine.

She'd be disappointing the board about that. Although she'd begun appreciating the friendliness of everyone, and their genuine enquiries about how she was coping, the reality was that this place did frustrate her at times. Yesterday had been a prime example.

Turning to Dan, she said, 'I ordered a book from the local stationery shop, and they told me it would be a week before it arrived. A week!'

'So?' Dan drawled.

'So in Auckland it would arrive overnight. What are they doing? Writing the thing longhand?'

'Get used to it. That's how it is around here.'

'Be glad it's only a book you want.' Robert chuckled from the next table where he was wiping the surface. 'The bench top for our new kitchen took two months.'

Sarah pulled a face. And people seriously thought they could persuade her to stay? Apart from the fact that she had a partnership at the clinic to go back to, one she'd barely given a thought to since she'd arrived, she realised with a start, there was nothing in this sleepy hollow that attracted her. Not even its exceptionally up-to-date surgical unit.

What about a certain surgeon with the gentlest touch whenever he took her elbow to guide her around some obstacle? The man's startling blue eyes seemed to follow her every move. Was Dan a man who could possibly be trusted? Whoa. That was going too far. She didn't know him well enough to make that assumption. She'd known

Oliver a long time and still hadn't seen his infidelity coming.

She tapped her forehead in a feeble attempt to dash Dan from her thoughts. Impossible when he was sitting opposite her, those very blue eyes watching her.

'Sorry to gatecrash this cosy scene.' Jill loomed into Sarah's peripheral vision. 'But I've got to tell Dan my news.' Jill was bobbing up and down on her toes, grinning from ear to ear, her eyes glowing like coals on a fire.

'Jill? What is it?' Sarah looked from her new friend to Dan and saw a surprised kind of excitement lightening his face. 'Someone tell me what's going on.'

'I'm pregnant.'

'I'd say she's pregnant.'

They spoke in unison. Then Dan was out of his chair and swooping his sister-in-law into his arms and swinging her around in a circle, nearly colliding with the next table. 'Aren't you?'

'Yes, yes, yes.' Jill's eyes brimmed and fat tears spilled down her cheeks as Dan gently let her down again. 'Yes.' She squeezed her hands into fists and shook them with glee.

'That's wonderful. I'm thrilled for you.' Sarah got up to hug Jill. Oops, she didn't do hugs. Too late. And it felt good.

'We've been trying for well over a year. Malcolm and I were beginning to think we'd never be parents.' Jill danced on the spot. 'I intended keeping it a secret for a few weeks in case something went wrong.' She faltered for a moment. 'But we couldn't. So here I am, making sure you're one of the first to know, Dan.'

Dan wrapped his arms around her again, rested his chin on her head. 'Thank you, sis. I've been hoping for this news for so long, you've made my day. You really have.

And now I suppose I'd better give that brother of mine a call. He'll be busting a valve with excitement.' He tugged his phone out of his pocket.

'A call?' Jill laughed. 'He'll want a party.'

'That can be arranged.' Dan grinned. 'Yes, that's exactly what I'll do. Leave it all to me.'

Jill dropped into a chair beside Sarah, and a cup of coffee appeared at her elbow.

'Congratulations, Jill.' Robert hugged her too.

Sarah smiled as if it was the most wonderful news she'd ever heard. 'When did you actually find out?'

'First thing this morning I was banging on the door of the pharmacy before they opened. I'm late but at first I was afraid to do the test. I didn't want to find out it was a hiccup with my system. Malcolm and I agreed we'd wait until I was at least two weeks overdue.'

'How did you manage that?'

Jill hugged herself. 'We didn't. That's why I had to go get a test kit. Two weeks aren't up yet.'

Sarah grinned. 'That's better. I'd never be able to wait. I'm thrilled for you.' She really meant it. So why the gloomy sensation seeping through her? Everyone except her was having babies.

Thankfully her pager beeped. 'Guess that's the end of my break.' She read the message. 'Yep, I'm needed in A and E.' She drained her superb coffee and pushed away from the table.

Dan snapped his phone shut after a cheeky quip to Malcolm about being an old father, and said to Sarah, 'I'll drive you back and come in to see what's up. I've still got time to fill in before Leah's library session finishes.'

'Then go and see Malcolm.'

'Can't. He's got a beer tanker being unloaded, and the freight truck's due in any minute.'

There had to be something he could do rather than hang around with her. 'Then go shopping or something.'

His eyes rolled in that annoying manner. 'Shopping? Me? What for?'

'I don't know. How about some new clothes? Or groceries?' Anything, but get out of her hair, give her some breathing space. She was getting too used to him hanging around, found herself looking for him whenever he was away for very long.

Dan was still shaking his head at her suggestion as he pulled away from the café and turned back to the hospital. Then he lightly slapped the steering-wheel. 'Actually, you're right. I'll go to the shops and get something for Jill and Malcolm to celebrate their news.'

'Lovely idea.' Why hadn't she thought of that? She'd arrange for some flowers to be delivered to Jill at the pub. And she must remember to pick up a new platter from the gift shop to replace the chipped one at home.

'Malcolm's stoked.' He slowed for a truck pulling out of a side street. 'It's kind of neat we're having another child in the family. Leah's going to be so excited. A new cousin.'

'Isn't she just?' Sarah tried not to feel like even more of an outsider than she was. But it was hard to deny the twinge of envy. Dan's family had such strong bonds of love tying them all together. Unlike hers.

'I'd have loved more babies but Celine kept miscarrying.' Dan's smile dimmed briefly.

'It's not too late.' She swallowed. 'I mean, you could remarry and before you know it you'll have kids from here to Christmas.'

'Really? Now, there's a thought. Were you thinking of next Christmas?' He recovered quickly. Jill's news had made him happy. She'd have thought it would have made him sad, bringing back all those memories of Celine and the family they'd planned.

'That might take some fast work on your behalf. Unless you've already got a woman in mind.' Did he have a woman friend out there that she knew nothing about? Why wouldn't he? He was a very attractive man with a lot going for him.

'When have I had the time to date?'

'Where there's a will there's a way. Or so they say.' Relief trickled through Sarah, lifting her spirits. Something she shouldn't be feeling. She and Dan were never going to have a relationship, at least not one that led to babies. And if he was intent on having another family, he wouldn't want to be wasting time on a fling with her.

'What about you? You're not going to let that ex-fiancé spoil your chances, are you?' His eyes were fixed on the road ahead.

'Give me time to get over him before suggesting I find another man to have babies with. There's the little matter of falling in love with someone first.' But when had she last thought about Oliver? Certainly not at all today so far. He didn't keep her awake at nights any more either.

Dan did.

Dan said casually as he pulled up outside the hospital's main entrance, 'Don't take too long mending that broken heart of yours. It's holding you back from getting the most out of life.'

Her mouth fell open. 'Like what?' She shoved her door wide and snatched up her handbag. 'I've still got a lot: a fantastic apartment, my partnership in the clinic, a great job. More than enough to fill my days.' Even she found it hard to get excited about that picture.

'By the way,' he called out his window as she headed up the hospital steps, 'you'd make a wonderful mum.'

CHAPTER SEVEN

'I'M OUT in the spa,' Dan called out to Sarah as she came through the front door that evening.

And when she stepped out onto the deck he heard her faint gasp. 'That looks wonderful.'

'Come and join me.' Would she? Suddenly he was silently begging to whatever was out there that made these things happen. *Please make her want to soak in the hot water. Please.* 'The warmth works wonders on tense muscles.'

'I'm not tense.' Her teeth nibbled her lip.

Sure you're not. 'We can have dinner any time. It's all prepared.'

'Maybe I'll take a stroll along the beach instead. I've had a big day.'

Yep. I can see your tight shoulders, your tired eyes.

Just then a gust of wind blew through the trees, filling the air with the sound of rustling leaves. *Thank you.* Dan grinned. 'There's rain coming.'

Her eyebrows rose in that delightful way she had. 'I'll go change into my swimsuit.'

Thank goodness she'd packed a swimsuit. He'd have blown a gasket if she'd told him she was coming in naked. When she wandered out five minutes later he still nearly blew one. Her simple black costume fitted superbly, outlining those full breasts to perfection, accentuating the curves of her hips. Her flat stomach sent his into spasms. He could not take his eyes off her as she climbed into the bubbling water and sat beside him.

Beside him? Being in the spa with Sarah suddenly became a really, really bad idea. His blood pressure started rising. What was wrong with him? Of course. Blame Sarah for being so delectable.

Clearing his throat, he tried to sound nonchalant. 'Would you like a wine?'

She glanced at the low table beside the spa where two glasses and a bottle stood next to a plate of crackers and Brie. Again her eyebrows rose, and her mouth twitched. 'A very small one.'

Stupid, stupid. Dan berated himself as he poured her drink. She must think he was seducing her. That's how it looked from here. He'd wanted everything seeming effortless so she wouldn't think anything of it when he suggested she join him. Went to show how out of practice at entertaining women he'd become. He was more like the new kid at kindergarten with all the unfamiliar toys and too frightened to touch any of them than a confident man and father of one.

Right now he should be leaping out of the spa, putting distance between them. Then she'd think him a really hopeless case. He'd stay put, but for the life of him he didn't know how he was going to keep his hands to himself.

Sarah slid deep into the warm water, letting the bubbles roll up her back, around her neck. Her eyes closed and she smiled. 'This has to be the best invention ever.'

He passed over her glass. 'Keep an ear out for the oven timer. I've got some muffins baking for tomorrow.' Keep the conversation on normal, everyday things and he might

survive the next half-hour without making a complete fool
of himself.

'You and Leah going somewhere that you need muffins?'

'Depending on the weather we might head to the river
for a swim.' Dan studied her over the rim of his glass.
Something was bothering her. Occasionally over the last
few days he'd seen her wandering along the beach, hands
in her pockets, chin on her chest, deep in thought. And
when she'd come back those beautiful big eyes had been
dark with sadness, and he'd want to haul her into his arms
and hug her tight. Like he would for any of his family. That
look was there now.

*Sarah isn't family. Sarah's a hot woman whom you'd
like to bed. There is a difference, man.* Couldn't he bed
her and help her at the same time?

'You're enjoying your time off now, aren't you?' She
sounded wistful. 'Having a great time with Leah.'

'Absolutely. I wish I'd done it ages ago. Who knows
what I've missed out on with my girl? If I ever have any
more kids, I'll definitely be there all the time, not hiding
at work.'

'You said you wanted more children. Got a number in
mind?'

He tasted his wine and looked out beyond the end of
the lawn to where he could hear the waves pounding their
relentless rhythm. 'There was a time I wanted four.'

'Four?' She smiled. 'You're a devil for punishment.'

'I've always been surrounded by people. I can't imagine
life without siblings and I want the same for Leah. Celine
and I were trying but she kept miscarrying. Five times.
The doctors couldn't explain it. We saw everyone, and
I mean everyone. Specialists here and in Australia. The
more we were told there was no obvious reason, the more

Celine blamed herself. Nothing I said made the slightest bit of difference.'

'That must have been hard for you both.'

'Very.'

'How did Celine cope?'

'At first she was distraught, as any woman would be. I admit, so was I. But after each miscarriage she became moodier, filled with despair, spiralling into a black hole that no one could coax her out of.' He gulped at his drink. He recalled those dark nights and days, trying to make Celine understand that he was happy with their small family; that she and Leah were precious to him. She'd argued she wasn't good enough for him because she couldn't give him what he wanted. That had hurt. Badly. 'Not even me. Heaven knows, I tried.'

Movement in the water and Sarah leaned closer to lay her hand on his arm. She didn't say anything, just touched him.

He took her hand in his and sat there looking at the woman who was changing so much for him. Her determination to carry on even when her foot hurt, her cheerful manner, her sweet smile, the way she was always ready to listen, even her occasional crankiness—all these things and more were helping him get back a life he'd forgotten existed. A life that looked pretty darned good from where he sat. As did his companion. Her cheeks had coloured to a soft pink, and the tiredness staining her face had vanished.

When Sarah turned to place her glass on the table her gaze clashed with his. Without thought he caught her arms and tugged her gently towards him just as she leaned forward. They slid off their seats. Dan instinctively wrapped his arms around her, holding her to his chest, as they bobbed in the bubbling water.

Sarah slid her arms around his waist. Her hands spread out over his back. He could feel each fingertip where they pressed lightly on his skin. The swirling water and her touch were a sensual mix of satin and silk, of soft and firm. He'd arrived in heaven.

His lungs suspended all breathing while his mind assimilated the feel of Sarah's slick, warm skin under his palms. He moved closer, placed his lips on her throat. Her pulse thumped under his mouth, and he could feel her throbbing response in the fingers that were now pushing through his hair, beating a feverish massage on his scalp. Heard it in the hiss of her indrawn breath.

His tongue traced a line under her chin and up to the corner of her mouth, where he teased her lips gently with his teeth, warming the cooler flesh. He lost all sense of time, place, everything—except Sarah, and he couldn't get enough of her. Her mouth, when he tasted it, was sweet with wine. An outpouring of exquisite sensations overtook him.

Then she touched his face, held his head closer, and kissed him back with all the fierceness of a starved woman. He didn't, couldn't, stop to question what was behind her actions. Her need fired his own to an even deeper level and he leaned further into her, his bones melting.

On the periphery he thought he heard something. What? Ignoring it, his mind sank back into the pool of whirling sensations Sarah stirred up.

Beep. Beep. Beep.

He dragged his mouth away from those wondrous lips. Cocked his head to one side. Every swear word he could think of flicked through his mind as he tried to blink his eyes into focus.

'What?' Sarah croaked.

'The goddamned muffins are ready.'

'Let them burn.'

'You want the fire brigade turning up?'

Dan swore under his breath. The kitchen floor was slippery with water that had dripped from his shorts when he'd charged inside to save the wretched muffins. He fetched a mop and began cleaning up, at the same time trying to put that kiss into perspective. Yeah, right. Like how? When his body was in a state of expectation, turned on as quickly as a flick of a switch. Unfortunately it couldn't be turned off as swiftly.

Sarah walked through from outside, quietly, as though hoping he wouldn't notice her. She'd have to be invisible for that to happen. And not wear that special fragrance of hers.

'Sarah?' he couldn't resist calling in a low voice as she passed. He did not want her to ignore what had just happened between them. That kiss had been as real as the waves pounding the beach across the road. And as hard to hold onto. Especially if Sarah decided to pretend it had been a passing clashing of lips with nothing more to it.

'I'm going to have a shower and head to bed. It's been a long day.' The yellow of her towel highlighted the gold flecks in her eyes when she met his gaze.

He couldn't read her. 'You don't want tea and a muffin?' She always had a cup of tea and something sweet to eat before retiring. 'You haven't had dinner.'

'No, thanks.' She was rejecting him—after that heart-stopping kiss.

A chill lifted bumps on his arms. The depth of his yearning shocked him. Whatever they'd started must not stop. He wanted more from her, much more. So he should be grateful this was as far as it was going, should be glad one of them had the sense to put the brakes on before it got out of hand.

But he'd begun to enjoy having Sarah here, in his house, his hospital. In his life. He woke up in the mornings feeling happier than he had in years and he didn't believe that was only because he was on leave with his daughter. He grimaced. Even if making daisy chains had been a novel way of filling in an afternoon. No, he enjoyed having another adult at home to talk with, to share meals with.

Get real. You enjoy having a very hot woman under your roof and you're only biding your time until she's under your sheets.

He managed to say something sane and sensible. 'Goodnight.'

Her relief was almost palpable as she paused. 'Goodnight, Dan.' Her fragrance reminded him of the scent of lavender on a gentle breeze. 'I'm, um, sorry we were interrupted.'

'What?' Talk about mixed messages.

'But I think it's for the best. We've got to live together for quite a while and if we'd carried on it would only have made life very difficult for us.'

Okay, not mixed. Clear as day. He gripped his hips in an attempt to stop reaching out to touch her. To stop from running his fingers behind her ear and down beneath her chin, over the fair skin of her throat. He yearned to kiss away that frown, to make her mouth soft and pliant under his again.

'Yes, you're right.' Damn it. She was. An affair might solve the immediate problem of needing sex, but Sarah was still hurting from what that other character had done to her. She needed time, patience and care before she was ready for something as hot and casual as a fling with him. But now he'd tasted her it had become even harder to ignore the frisson of tension she whipped up in him.

The Jaguar crawled along, the big engine purring. Thankfully Sarah's foot had pretty much returned to normal, allowing her the luxury of driving again. As long as she didn't go jogging or anything equally mad.

What a busy week with long hours, though nothing like the pressure she worked under back home. She hadn't seen a lot of Dan since that kiss. As though he was staying well away from her.

Tonight, knowing she didn't have to be up at the crack of dawn, she'd relax with a glass of wine, cook a meal that did not involve satisfying a four-year-old palate, and watch a good crime programme on TV. Something that didn't involve a red-blooded male's idea of good television, meaning cricket or any other sport.

Turning into the drive, her foot lifted off the accelerator as disappointment enveloped her. Vehicles were parked haphazardly between the gate and the house. Worse, people, lots of them, were gathered on the lawn and the deck.

'There goes the poached salmon.' Sarah eased the Jag between Dan's Land Cruiser and a small truck. Gathering up her groceries, she eased open the door. Laughter and voices carried to her, Leah's shrieks outdoing them all. Reaching back into the car, she lifted up the bunch of roses and the twisted glass vase she'd purchased that afternoon at the florist next to the café. The house needed a sparkle put into it.

'Can I carry those for you?'

She jerked around at Dan's question. 'Sure. Are we having a party?'

Guilt clouded his eyes to almost black. 'Sorry. I

should've warned you.' He waved a hand towards the over-crowded deck.

'So all these people...' she nodded '...just turned up?'

'Not exactly. Remember I told Jill I'd give Malcolm a party to celebrate the pregnancy? Well, she decided tonight was the night.' His hand brushed hers as he took the grocery bags.

The familiar tug of heat stopped whatever she'd been about to say. No matter that they'd managed to avoid each other most of the week, the desire their kiss awakened had only been tamped down, not put out.

Obviously Dan wasn't affected in the same way because he was strolling up the drive, explaining what had happened. 'This is way bigger than I'd intended. Malcolm's to blame. He took it into his head to organise someone to run the pub tonight and then invited half the patrons here.' Dan didn't look at all repentant.

'Right.' With her body shivering and shimmying with desire it was difficult to concentrate on what Dan was saying as she walked beside him. 'You must've spent the whole day preparing food.' There'd been next to nothing in the fridge that morning when she'd got her breakfast and she could see a large table laden with containers of food.

'That's just it. They all know me enough to bring food with them. I've been working on the section all day—mowing, weeding, trimming trees. No time for the supermarket.'

Sarah looked around, for the first time noticing how cared for the property looked. 'You have been busy. The place looks wonderful.'

Dan growled, 'I probably shouldn't have started. Now I'll have to keep it looking like this. I'd forgotten how much effort it takes. It's years since I gave a hoot about gardens and lawns, but when today dawned sunny and calm I made the most of the opportunity to get stuck in.'

'Don't tell me you're a surfer from way back?' She pointed to a surfboard leaning against the shed. Her mouth dried as she pictured Dan in swimming shorts, his legs braced on the board as he rode a wave, balanced by those strong arms.

'Like the horse riding, it's been years. But I'm going to give it a crack over the next few days. More sore muscles coming up.' He smiled at her. 'And there's something else I'd obviously forgotten.'

'What's that?'

'How to have fun. I can thank you for my awakening.'

'How's that?' Leah made better conversation than she did.

He pointed to the flowers. 'You make our house feel like a home again.' Dan flicked out a second finger. 'I'm enjoying cooking for cooking's sake. It's no longer a chore to be done as quickly and effortlessly as possible. And I spend more time on the deck watching sunsets and sunrises than I've ever done. It's great.'

He was crediting her with that? He needed his head read. She'd contributed less than zilch to the way he got on with his life. 'You're on leave and finally relaxing.'

The third finger popped up. 'It dawned on me today when I began poking around in the shed that there's a lot more to do than work, work and work.'

'There's Leah.' Could she learn a thing or two from Dan? Find something else to do other than work? Like what? Sport? Knitting? Flower decorating? Nothing rang any bells of excitement. She'd never spent time playing.

'And there's me.' Dan spun around in front of her. 'No one is going to be me, do my things—except me. So let's get rid of these bags and party.'

Right. Sure. Surely his plans for living didn't include her?

'Sarah, there you are.' Jill approached to give her a hug. 'You're becoming a bit like Dan, all work and no play. Come and meet the rest of the mob.'

'I thought it was a family affair.' Not Dan's comingout party. 'Is there anyone left in town?'

Jill rolled her eyes. 'This is family, sort of. These Reillys are a prolific lot.'

Dan retorted, 'Especially since Malcolm has finally worked out how it's done. I'm looking forward to meeting the newest member of our clan.'

Jill laughed. 'You've got eight months to wait.'

Sarah grinned. 'Eight months. You're obviously counting the minutes.' Did she fear something happening to her as it had to her sister? Did she ever think her child might be left motherless like Leah? If the glow on her face and the happiness in her eyes were pointers then definitely not. Besides, it must be reassuring to know someone in the extended family would look out for the child if the unimaginable happened.

Sarah moved towards the house. 'I'll go and put my bag in my room and change into something more in keeping with a barbecue.'

'No, you don't. You'll hide away and I'll have to drag you out here.' Dan followed her.

She'd been going to sit down, try to pretend that a crowd of strangers weren't outside having a great time, and that she had to meet them all. 'Five minutes?'

'Two.'

Stifling an oath, she stomped through the house, threw her handbag on the bed and quickly divested herself of her suit, replacing it with shorts and a blouse. Port Weston had turned on a superb day, which was continuing into the evening. She could do with some sun on her skin. As long as it didn't bring out the freckles.

What could she talk about to everyone? They had nothing in common with her. Everyone she'd met since arriving here had been very friendly but she stood out like a bean in a fruit salad.

'Time's up.' Dan leaned against her bedroom door.

'You ever heard of knocking?' At least her blouse was buttoned up and her shorts zippered.

'No one's going to eat you, so you can take that worried expression off your face.' So why did he look like he wanted to indulge in a little nibbling? 'And here's a glass of your favourite bubbles.' He offered her the cold glass, and as she gratefully took it, he added, 'Relax, you'll be fine. They're mostly my family.'

Exactly.

Sarah parked herself on the steps leading from the deck to the lawn and very soon a tall, slim woman joined her. 'I'm Bea, Dan's older, and apparently bossier, sister. I hope we're not overwhelming you.'

'There are quite a few of you. Especially when Jill's relatives are added into the mix.' Could she ever get used to having so many people in her life, people who would want to know her business? Want to share the ups and downs of life? Why was she even wondering about it?

'When my brothers married the two sisters, our family seemed to expand rapidly. Jill and Celine have even more family than the Reillys.' Bea glanced across the lawn. 'Speaking of children, here comes Leah, heading directly for you.'

'Me?' Sarah blinked. 'I doubt it. I hardly see her during the week. She's usually in bed by the time I get home, and I'm gone again before anyone's up.' But her heart warmed as she watched Leah racing towards her.

'Yeah, and whenever I have her she talks nonstop about you. Sarah this, Sarah that. She adores you.'

'Sarah, you came home for the party.' A bundle of arms and legs hurtled into her, knocking her glass over and tipping her back against the railing post.

'Hey, kiddo, slow down.' Automatically Sarah wrapped her arms around Leah's body to protect her. And to hug her. She did a lot of hugs these days. Then Leah plonked a sloppy kiss on her chin. Tears threatened, and Sarah blinked rapidly. Leah adored her? Her? Surely not. So why was her heart dancing?

'What did I say?' Bea winked at her. 'Seems like you're having the same effect on our Dan, too.'

'Dan's talking nonstop about me?' Bea was crazy. First Leah adored her and now she was changing Dan too. Did insanity run in the family? She glanced at Leah, a perfectly normal child if ever there was one.

Bea shook her head at Sarah. 'No. He doesn't mention you at all, not a word.'

Now she was really confused. 'I'm not following you.'

'My brother's always talking about people, mostly how useless they are at this, how bad at that. But you, nothing. His lips are sealed. Which says to me you are getting to him.' Bea stood up, and added, 'For the record, I like it. I really do.'

'You don't know me.' With her arms still wound around Leah Sarah stared up at Bea. People didn't love her, not unconditionally as Bea had suggested Leah might. 'For the record, Dan definitely isn't interested in me.'

Bea only laughed. 'I'll get you another drink while you and Leah talk about your respective days.'

'I've been helping Daddy clean the shed.' Leah wriggled around on Sarah's knees. 'We found lots of his toys.' Her little hands picked up one of Sarah's and held it tight.

Warm and sticky hands. A small, bony bottom that bounced on Sarah's thighs. Leah chattered nonstop, her sweet, freckled face lit up with an enormous smile, a smile just like those rare ones of Dan's. A lump closed Sarah's throat. Her arms gently tugged Leah a little closer. Darn, she'd miss Leah when she went away.

'Here.' Dan handed down the refilled glass. An odd look filled his eyes as he looked from his daughter to Sarah and back. 'That was a big welcome home.'

Wasn't he happy Leah had raced to see her? Sarah gulped at the bubbly, studying his face and preparing to put Leah away from her. No, she'd read Dan wrong. He looked more…confused. As though he sensed a bond growing between Leah and herself that he was unsure about. His protective instincts kicking in? Very wise. Someone had to look out for Leah's heart and Dan was the man.

Sarah put down her glass and placed Leah on the step beside her, growing cold when the contact between them broke. *And I'll look after my own heart, keep it intact, avoid too much involvement with this gorgeous man and his child.* The lump in her throat expanded. Could be she was already too late.

Bea's conversation filtered into her mind. So Dan didn't say a word about her to his sister.

She needed to get away from his looming presence to make some sense of what Bea had said. She'd mix and mingle, meet some of these people. Meet the family. Okay, jump back in her car and head somewhere, anywhere. Reaching up to the railing to haul herself onto her feet, her hand encountered Dan's and he helped her up.

'Thanks,' she muttered, and leaned down to retrieve her glass.

'You're very good with Leah. Patient and fun.' Those blue eyes locked with hers. Searching for what?

'Patience is not my strong point.' Certainly not with children. What was with these people? Pushing Leah at her as though it was normal.

Dan ran a thumb across the edge of her chin. 'You underrate yourself.' Then he repeated Bea's words. 'Leah thinks you're the best, and I'm starting to think she may be a good judge of character.'

Before Sarah could think up an answer to that, they were thankfully interrupted.

'Hello, there, Dan. Sorry we're late but Brent's truck got stuck out at the mine.'

'Cathy, you're looking good.' Dan gave the very pregnant woman a hug before introducing her to Sarah. 'And here's Brent and their daughter, Cushla. Hey, cutey-pie.' Dan chucked the girl under her chin and received a shy smile in return.

'Hi.' Sarah shook Brent's hand and smiled at the toddler with the flat facial features suggestive of Down's syndrome. 'Hello, Cushla.'

The child peeked up at her from behind her father's legs. 'Wello.'

Sarah turned back to Cathy. 'When's your baby due?' The woman appeared to be in her late thirties, maybe early forties.

'Five weeks, and counting,' Cathy rubbed her extended tummy. 'Hot days like today are very uncomfortable.'

'And you can't wait for him to arrive so you can do all those things mums do with their newborns,' Brent hugged Cathy around the shoulders. 'Cathy's a wonderful mum.'

'I just love it,' Cathy agreed. 'Now I've got to see Jill. It's so exciting. Two babies being born into our family this year.'

Sarah raised an eyebrow. 'Don't tell me you're related to the Reillys too?'

'Dan and I are cousins.'

Sarah shook her head. This went way past her idea of a big family.

Dan glanced at her. 'Always room for new blood.' His gaze slid over her, hesitating at her mouth, before he turned away.

Surely he wasn't considering her for the role? They'd shared one kiss. That was all. He could not be getting ideas of having all those extra children he wanted with her. Lighten up. That look had been more about sex than babies. Hadn't it?

Did she want Dan's babies? As Dan wandered away she glanced from him to Leah and back, her teeth nibbling her lip. Leah was gorgeous. Dan made beautiful babies. But, then, he was gorgeous too. She smiled, despite herself. This was so out of left field. They'd shared one kiss and she was thinking happy families with him.

She needed to get to know him a whole lot better before she gave in to this need building in her. But already Dan had woven a spell around her, had her looking to the future with more hope than she had been on New Year's Day. Had her father been right, pushing her to come here?

Across the lawn Dan talked with two women who'd just arrived. He was completely at ease with them, and they were laughing at something he'd said.

Dan. A likeable, reliable man. A loveable man. An excellent parent despite the problems he had to sort out with Leah. He wasn't ready for anything more exciting than an affair either. So go for one. Could she? Dared she?

A sobering thought crashed into her head. Was he trustworthy? Women gravitated to him, here, at the hospital, in the street. Could he be trusted not to stray? She thought so, especially for the duration of an affair. But she was afraid to believe so. History had taught her to be very careful about that.

CHAPTER EIGHT

SARAH sat on the deck listening to the waves slapping onto the beach, hearing Dan in the kitchen as he rinsed the remaining few glasses. The last couple had finally left at about one o'clock. Leah had been sound asleep in her bed for hours. Apart from the rattle of the dishwasher being stacked, the quiet she'd been looking forward to all day had finally settled over the house.

Stars twinkled, so much brighter here on the coast without a huge city lighting up the sky. A full moon turned the sky black and made shadows on the lawn. She stretched her legs out and tipped her head back, studying the universe, looking for familiar constellations.

Instead an image of Dan's face floated across her vision. His deep-set eyes were unreadable, his lips inviting. Reminding her of their kiss. The kiss that stole into her dreams every night, that hovered in the air whenever they were in the same room together, that filled every other minute not filled with work.

That kiss had begun undoing all her defences. Dan had kissed her as though she was to be treasured and awakened, like she was hot. Some of her lost self-esteem had begun creeping back, still fragile but there nonetheless. Being desired by a sexy man like Dan did her good. She was coming alive, and suddenly wanted to reach for more.

She'd taken to staying late at the hospital, sometimes eating in the cafeteria, striving for normality. Or calm at least. Keeping her distance from temptation. She might be thinking about wanting to take this further with Dan but she'd never put herself out there, afraid he might turn her down.

'I've made you some tea.'

Sarah jerked her head around. 'Tea?'

When she was thinking about the effects of Dan's kiss, he was making tea. Suddenly she giggled, just like Leah. This whole scene was crazy.

'Earl Grey.' Dan's look was quizzical. 'What's so funny?'

Did he think she was laughing at him? 'Tea's great. Truly.' Then the words just popped out. 'A little tame.'

And was rewarded with the sound of his sharply indrawn breath. 'You don't like tame?'

Now it was her turn to be rendered speechless. She turned back to the stars. She should leave flirting alone. She wasn't up to speed, and now she'd backed herself into a corner. One she had to get out of in a hurry. Before temptation overrode common sense.

Dan would swear Sarah wanted him as much as he wanted her. Her gaze never left him for long. Then there was the way her tongue did that quick little flick at the corner of her mouth whenever he looked at her. So what was she afraid of? Not him, surely? Getting involved? Yeah, well, that scared the hell out of him too. Which was why a fling was the answer. But was Sarah ready for that? Did he nudge her along, or give her space to come to her own conclusion? The right one for him, of course.

His hands clenched at his sides. Go do something practical and get over her. For now, anyway. Nothing was happening tonight. Stomping inside, he headed for the laundry, his brain ignoring his warning, taunting him with sensations her lips had evoked. He wanted her. In his bed.

'You're not having her.' He bit down on an expletive. But... 'But nothing.' It would be the dumbest idea to sleep with her when they had to share his house for many more weeks. Flings were exactly that—flings. Throwaways. They invariably finished. How much more uncomfortable it would be for them then, sharing the same house. Even if she did find somewhere else to stay, it was a small town, and they'd inevitably bump into each other.

The way his relatives had taken to Sarah tonight, she'd be going to every family meal, picnic, celebration for the rest of her time here. There'd be no getting away from her. And now Bea and Jill seemed intent on helping a romance blossom for him with Sarah. As though it was the most natural thing in the whole wide world. Damn their meddling. He'd have to put a stop to that.

Except he kind of liked the idea, when he thought about it. So he shouldn't think about it. But what if he convinced Sarah to stay on come the end of March? They'd be able to pursue this thing going on between them. Because something sure as hell was. He couldn't rid his head of her. Look at the way his hormones ramped up whenever she was around. And sometimes when she wasn't.

The washing-machine lid slammed back against the wall. Dan made to toss in the wet kitchen towels, and noticed Sarah's clean washing still in the bottom of the machine. She must have forgotten it. Or been in such a hurry to get away in the morning that hanging it out was rendered unimportant.

Tugging out her clothes, he tossed them into the washing basket, before putting his wash on. When he had the machine running he took Sarah's clothes and headed out to the back porch, where there was a line under the roof. That was the norm, living on the Coast. Otherwise there'd be weeks when nothing dried.

Bending down for a handful of pegs and clothes, he groaned at the lacy white pieces of fabric in his hand. Bras and a thong. He dropped them. Blew a breath up over his face. She wore thongs. His erection was back with a vengeance.

Cool sand pushed between Sarah's toes, covered her feet, as she strolled along, easily avoiding stones and driftwood in the moonlight. Down here the waves were louder. Foam spread out, pushed towards her, rolling shells over and over. Beautiful. This coastline drew her in, gave her a sense of peace when her mind was flip-flopping all over the place. She wanted Dan. She wasn't going to have him.

'You're restless tonight.' Dan spoke from behind her.

She jerked her head up, dragging her mind with her. The tension she'd been trying to ease cranked tighter. 'Why are you here?'

'I saw you wander down and thought I'd join you.'

'What about Leah? Shouldn't you be with her?'

'She's sound asleep, with Toby guarding her. If she even tries to roll over, that dog will make such a racket I'll hear.'

'Why's Toby at your place?' She still couldn't call it her house. If she did she'd be admitting that she liked sharing a home with Dan and his daughter.

'Sometimes Bea leaves him with us. Leah adores him and wants her own puppy, which I don't have the time for. It would be left on its own too much with me at work and Leah going to kindergarten.' Dan reached for her hand, began walking again.

'Oh.' Why had he taken her hand? *Why* wasn't she tugging it away? 'Dan?' she whispered.

He stopped, turned to her and gently pulled her in against him. His chest was hard and firm under her cheek, his thighs strong against her legs. His hands held her head, each fingertip a touch of magic.

'Sarah.' His voice was low, commanding. Tipping her head back, her breath caught in her throat as Dan's mouth came down to cover hers. Those lips she'd dreamed about for a week now a reality. Only better. Firm, demanding. Was this wise? She pulled away from him. Dan tugged her close again. This time her body folded in against his and she lost herself in the sweet longing his kiss stirred up. His tongue gently probed her mouth, exploring, tasting.

Her arms wound around his back, pulled him even closer. She wanted more of him. She craved all of him.

Lights from a car travelling along the road lit up his face. Toot, toot.

Sarah leapt back, feeling like a guilty schoolgirl. Dan chuckled. 'Takes you back, doesn't it?' He reached for her again. 'But I don't remember kisses being like this.'

Neither did she. Under his mouth her lips curved into a wide smile. Kissing was rapidly becoming her favourite pastime. Her fingers touched the light stubble on his jaw, traced over his bristly cheeks. That quintessential maleness sent shivers of desire down her spine, spreading through her body.

The sea air brushed her arms as Dan's hands slid under her blouse. Goose-bumps lifted on her skin. From the air? Or from the excitement of fingers teasing her nerve endings by tracing circles over her back? Her muscles felt languid. Any moment she'd drop to the sand, her legs unable to hold her up. Dragging her hands down his cheeks, over his chin, throat, she touched his chest, the muscles hard through his shirt.

Dan pulled his mouth from hers, stared into her eyes.

'Sarah Livingston, you're going to the undoing of me.' His voice cracked, his mouth took on a wry expression. 'But I am enjoying the experience.'

'Then hush and kiss me some more.' Sarah took a handful of shirtfront and pulled him closer. Her mouth stifled his laugh.

Hungry lips melded with hungry lips. Hot tongues danced around each other. Dan's hands gripped her buttocks, hugged her against him. Heat roared through her, over her. Desire wound between them, joined them. Sarah had no doubt how this would end if she let it. Which was why she pulled back, tearing her mouth away from Dan's, putting space between their bodies. 'I'm not sure we should be doing this. I'm sorry, I got a bit carried away.'

He didn't say a word, just shoved his hands deep into his jeans pockets, staring at her all the while.

How to tell him she wanted him so much but daren't? Her heart wouldn't take another pounding. *But he's not asking for your heart.* Dan might be thinking about having an affair, and she'd thought that's what she wanted too. But some time over the last week or two, somewhere between the hospital and this house, she'd started feeling strongly for this man. And if she went further then she was going to get very hurt when it all crashed to an end when she headed north again.

Turning back towards the house, she glanced over her shoulder. He was skimming pebbles across the wave tops, his shoulders slouched, his chin on his chest.

Her heart rolled over. She wanted him so much it burned, but she was behaving sensibly by walking away.

Dan heaved another pebble, watched it sink into the cold, black water. Why couldn't he keep his hands to himself? His blasted hormones would be the death of him if he wasn't careful. He should be grateful Sarah had had more self control than him. From the moment her mouth had met his he'd had absolutely none.

The next pebble bit the dust, bouncing along the sand. Sarah had been hurt, was still grappling with getting her life back together. She didn't need to add some randy man with his own problems to the mix. She may have wanted him, and he'd swear she did, but she certainly didn't need him. He was bad for her. She had trust issues.

So did he. He needed to be trusted one hundred and ten per cent. Something Celine had found impossible to do once the miscarriages began taking their toll on her. Being accused of infractions where there hadn't been any had hurt him deep inside. No, Sarah was wise to have walked off.

None of which made him feel any happier with himself. Bending down, he tugged his sandals off his feet, tossed them up the beach. Then he started running along the sand, heading away from the house, going faster and faster, trying to outrun the need for Sarah Livingston that gripped him hard.

'Wake up. Now.' Leah tugged at the pillow, disrupting Sarah's sleep and jerking her head. 'Daddy's taking us to the Pancake Rocks.'

Sarah cracked one eye open. 'Hello, lovely.' Who let little girls out of bed before midday in the weekend?

Leah giggled. 'Hello, sleepy.' Then she began pulling back the sheet. 'Get up. We're having pancakes for breakfast.'

Breakfast? It was far too early. The bedside clock showed eight-thirty. Definitely too early. She tried to retrieve the sheet and a tug of war ensured. Leah won.

'Why pancakes?' Sarah flopped back against her pillow, her stomach groaning at the thought of something so heavy this early.

'Cos we're going to the Pancake Rocks. Get it?'

'Leah, I'm not going there.'

'Daddy said you were.' Leah's bottom lip pushed into a pout, turning Sarah into a spoilsport.

'Sorry, Leah. I'm going to the library today.' She'd decided to join up and get back into reading for pleasure, something she hadn't done for years.

'Daddy will make you come.'

Daddy, whose fault it was she'd been awake for a substantial part of the remainder of the night. 'Your father,' she ground out, 'is making assumptions.'

'Not at all.' A deep, gravelly voice cut across the room from the doorway.

Instinctively Sarah reached for the sheet, pulling it from Leah's grasp, tucking it around her throat. When she looked at Dan he had a glazed look. Because he'd seen her in a negligee? Surely not. Looking around the room, checking out Leah, she couldn't see what else might've put that look on his face.

Dan's tongue slid across his bottom lip. 'Have you ever been to Punakaiki?'

He knew very well she hadn't. 'I must've driven past it on my way here but didn't see anything through the driving rain.'

'Then you're in for an experience.' Dan finally dragged his gaze away from her and looked to his daughter. 'You'd better get dressed, my girl. No one eats pancakes in their pyjamas.'

'Hello? Dan? Which part of "I'm not going" don't you understand? I'm on call, remember? I've also got a patient round to do. There are people expecting to go home today.'

'All taken care of.'

That was it? All taken care of? She rolled one hand through the air, finishing palm up pointing at him. 'How? Who? Since when did you think you can organise my life? My work?'

'By phone, Charlie, this morning.' His smile was slow and cheeky, and devastating to her heart. 'You are entitled to weekends off, you know.'

Dan whisked the pancake batter fast. He wanted sex so badly he hurt. Not just any old sex either. Only the kind that involved Sarah Livingston.

She looked beautiful in that black negligee thing, the front scooping down over the swell of her breasts. He didn't get why she wore those things when she went to bed alone. What a waste. But she had come out of a relationship so maybe she had drawers full of the stuff. His teeth were grinding hard.

'Look, Daddy, Sarah helped me get dressed.'

Dan peered down at his daughter, the familiar tug of love tightening his gut. 'You look pretty, little one.' How had Sarah managed to cajole Leah into wearing that particular T-shirt with those cute shorts? He'd never been able to persuade Leah that the elephant on the shirt was not going to squash the puppies on the shorts. A tick for Sarah.

'Are the pancakes ready?' Leah dragged a chair over to the bench and hopped up to take the bowl from his hands. 'Can I stir them? You didn't put blueberries in them. How many are you making? I don't know if Sarah likes pancakes. She didn't say.' Leah turned towards the door. 'Sarah. Do you like pancakes?' she yelled at the top of her lungs.

Dan covered his ears and grinned at his girl. 'You'll wake the seagulls with that racket.'

Leah giggled. 'Daddy, they are already up. There're lots of them. Look out the window.'

He did, and noted the birds circling a spot on the beach. A dead fish or bird must've washed up on the morning tide. 'We'll go and take a look while we wait for slowcoach.'

'Who's a slowcoach?' Sarah stood in the doorway, dressed in perfectly fitting, white knee-length shorts and a crimson, thin-strapped top that hugged her curves.

And sent his pulse rate into orbit. He turned away to break the connection he felt with her. Otherwise he'd reach out to take her into his arms and kiss her senseless. Despite the talking to he'd given himself on the beach last night. 'Why don't you two go and see what the gulls are squawking about while I make these pancakes? But don't take too long.' Just long enough for him collect his scattered emotions.

Idiot. That would take for ever. He tapped his forehead. You invited, actually insisted, that Sarah come with us today. Now you're going to spend the whole day noticing how sexy she is every time you look at her. Idiot, he repeated.

Through the window he saw Sarah take Leah's hand as they got close to the road. Sarah had the right instincts with his child, for sure. And Leah liked her.

So did he. A lot. This wasn't about lust. Some time while he'd been trying to keep her at bay she'd sneaked in under his skin anyway. Touched his heart and had him wanting to share so much more with her. Truth? From the moment he'd set eyes on her he'd felt a connection that would take more than a tumble in the sheets to fix.

But last night had shown she wasn't ready. And neither was he.

He dropped a large knob of butter into the hot pan and poured in some batter. The smell of melted butter teased his senses, overlaying the scent of Sarah that permeated the house these days. She'd made her presence felt in a lot of little ways. Like those stinky lilies on the dining table. At least the roses she'd bought yesterday smelt sweet. Even if she'd only put something back in its place at a different angle, he felt her aura. In every room except his bedroom.

He hadn't felt this much in need of intimacy in for ever. If this was what stopping work for a while did then he should be getting back to the job. Except that his former life, that one prior to the arrival of Sarah, now seemed dull and uninteresting.

He flipped the first pancake. He needed a hobby. Tomorrow was supposed to be fine. He'd put the surfboard in the water, try riding a wave or two, and likely make a fool of himself. Anything would be better then hanging around Sarah like a lovelorn teen.

'Those pancakes were fabulous.' Sarah stacked dishes in the sink and began wiping down the table. 'Now, off you go and enjoy the rocky version.'

Dan put his hand over hers, effectively stopping the wiping. 'Please come with us. I'd really like you to.'

Spending a day in Dan's company without the benefit of staff or his family to break the friction between them would only increase the tension. 'Leah needs more time with you, just you.'

'She doesn't need my attention every single minute of the day. Now, I…' he tapped his muscular chest '…need some adult company.' His finger under her chin tilted her head back. His eyes met hers, pleading with her. 'Please say you'll come.'

'I shouldn't.'

'Why ever not?' He turned them both to look out the

window. 'How many stunning, clear days like this one have you seen since you arrived?'

'We had one yesterday.' A trip out would be fun, a day away from patients and staff and decisions. She'd been here nearly a month and because of Dan she now had her first full day off. The library was never going to compete.

'I've packed lunch for when we're watching the water spouts and the seals. I used your salmon steak to make a quiche and there're plenty of salads left over from last night.'

'Okay,' she submitted, and felt surprisingly relaxed about it. Suddenly it seemed like time to go and play.

'Daddy, what are those animals? The ones on the pancakes?'

Dan sat Leah on the rail of the safety fence circling the top of the viewing platform and held her firmly. 'Those are seals. They're sunbathing after hunting fish in the sea.'

'I want to pat one.'

'Definitely not, my girl. Seals give big, nasty bites.' Loud grunts could be heard over the waves crashing against the edge of the Punakaiki Rocks. 'Listen to them talking. They sound like you with a tummyache.'

'Do not.'

Sarah studied the cumbersome brown bodies sprawled across the sun-warmed rocks. 'Hard to believe how fast they can move, isn't it?'

'I've seen a grown man running pretty quick with a seal snapping at his heels.' Dan grinned. 'It was funny once the guy made it to safety. We ribbed him about it for weeks.'

'Charming.' Sarah heard the tide roaring in. 'Look at the pancakes, Leah. You might see the water fountain coming out the top.'

'Where? I can't see, Sarah. Show me.'

Sarah leaned on the railing, putting her head close to Leah's, and pointed. 'See that rock that looks a bit like Dad's stack of pancakes? They're a lot bigger than your father's and not as lopsided.' Sweet little-girl smell teased her, made her want to cuddle Leah. 'The rocks on the other side of the seal that's staring at you?'

She stood up straight again. Warm masculine smell tantalised her. Since when did men smell so divine? Or was Dan the only one who did?

'I can't see the fountain.'

'Patience, my girl.' Dan jiggled Leah, smiling over the top of her head at Sarah, sending Sarah's heart rate into overdrive. 'Lopsided, huh?'

'The maple syrup only ran one way.' She grinned at him, her heart turning over. 'Your way.' He looked magnificent in his navy chinos and white shirt so new she'd had to cut the label off the collar as they'd made their way out of the house earlier.

He looked so relaxed and comfortable that Sarah wondered why she'd argued about coming. She couldn't remember the last time she'd enjoyed herself so much. And there wasn't a spa or upmarket wine bar in sight. Three people happy to be together doing something as simple as having a picnic and staring at blowholes in the rocks. Like a real family. Everything seemed easy here with Dan. All the usual worries and fears that haunted her had disappeared in the magic of the day.

She said, 'You never mention your parents.' Neither did she, come to think of it.

Dan looked at her over the top of Leah's head. Sadness tinged the piercing blue of his eyes. 'Mum died of cancer six years ago. Dad missed her so much he died of a broken heart a year later.'

'I'm sorry, that must've hurt.'

'It did. We all felt we might've let Dad down. But at the same time they'd had such a strong marriage I can see why one couldn't live without the other.'

'That's lovely, I think,' Sarah sighed. 'You know, I sometimes wonder about my parents. When Bobby died they separated, but neither of them has remarried, or even had a deep and meaningful relationship.' Her father had found solace in his work.

'You're wondering if they still love each other?'

'I'm being silly. They can't, not after the horrible things they said to each other back then.' But stress did funny things to people. 'I know Dad still supports my mother in a very lavish way, bought her a beautiful house in an up-market suburb, makes sure she has support in anything she does.'

Dan turned to her. 'You always say Dad and my mother, not Mum. Are you not close to your mother?'

Her lips pressed together for a moment. 'I guess not. We never seemed to have anything in common.'

'I'm hungry.' Leah twisted around in her father's arms. 'Can we have our picnic?'

Dan laughed. 'You've only just had breakfast. We'll go for a walk first.'

An hour later Sarah spread a blanket on a patch of grass where they could overlook the rocks and Dan unpacked the lunch he'd put together. Leah sipped a juice and leapt around laughing and talking nonstop.

'I wish I had as much energy.' Sarah leaned on an elbow, her legs stretched out over the grass.

Dan's gaze landed on Sarah. 'Glad you came?'

'Actually, yes. It's ages since I've been on a picnic.' When had the last time been? 'I remember Gran taking my brother and me to the beach once.'

'Only once?' Dan didn't bother to hide his surprise.

'Now I think about it, she took me a few times.' How had she forgotten those happier times? Well, whatever was in the water down here it had given her memory a tickle.

'Did she always take your brother as well?'

Behind her eyes she could see Bobby sitting on the red plaid blanket. She could feel the childish jealousy that used to flare up within her. She'd wanted Gran all to herself. 'Gran was the only adult in our family who gave equal attention to both of us. I latched onto that as my parents were so busy I missed out on a fair bit.'

'Because you were the youngest? Or because they were too busy with their careers?'

'Mum gave up work when she married and had Bobby. Dad was definitely into establishing himself in the surgical field. Add in conferences, studying and teaching. All those things kept him very busy.' But he did come home for Bobby. It wasn't until later that he'd stopped coming home at night.

Dan touched the back of her hand with a finger. 'And you missed him?'

Sarah bit the inside of her cheek. Turned her hand over and wound her fingers through Dan's, drawing warmth from his touch. 'All the time. I tried everything to get his attention, from being super-good to being a teenage brat. I'm not proud of that.' That hadn't got her anywhere either. By then her brother had become severely ill, and he'd got most of their parents' time.

'I imagine you were only doing what any kid would do in the circumstances. I don't know what you did but I'm sure I'd have been ten times worse.' He paused, staring over Punakaiki. 'I wonder.'

'Yes?'

'Is that what I've done to Leah? I know I haven't been

there very much for her, always busy at work. What if she doesn't even know how much I love her?'

'Dan, your love shows in everything you do.' Had her own dad always loved her? Did he now? He'd sent her here, hadn't he? He'd seen she wasn't coping after Oliver had dumped her. Wasn't that love? She wasn't sure. Her father equally could've been putting the clinic first as an overworked surgeon could become a liability.

Beside her Dan said, 'I hope you're right.'

'You've taken three months off for her. I'd have given anything for my father to do that.' She nibbled her lip. 'I followed him into surgery partly so I could work with him.'

'Daddy, I want a biscuit.'

'Can I have a biscuit, please,' Dan gently admonished his daughter. 'And, no, not until you've had a sandwich.' Then he squeezed Sarah's hand and dropped a light kiss on her cheek. 'Ready for some food?'

She stared into his eyes, looking for pity, found only understanding. Her shoulders lifted, her mouth curved into a smile. 'I'm starving.'

Dan drove carefully, his two passengers sound asleep after their day out. They'd all had so much fun. Once Sarah had got over her hesitation about joining them she'd made the day really work, giving a sparkle to everything they'd done.

Leah clearly adored her. Today she'd seemed even happier than usual, getting all the attention she needed from him and Sarah. Like they were a real family. Unlike what Sarah had grown up with. She wouldn't know a lot about children, and yet she always seemed to get it right with Leah. Did Sarah want kids?

His hands tightened on the steering-wheel. Why did any of this concern him? His feelings for Sarah had little to do with families, more to do with raging hormones and hot sex. Didn't it? Even if he had started developing deeper feelings for her he wasn't ready to contemplate going down the relationship track. He'd believed he'd had the perfect marriage with Celine and that had gone pear-shaped when the depression had come into their lives.

'What's that grim look for?' Sarah's voice was sleepy. She stretched her legs as much as the cramped confines of the vehicle allowed. 'I thought you'd enjoyed your day.'

'I've had a wonderful day, thanks to you.' Dan's eyes slid sideways to gawp at her knees. He quickly turned his attention back to the road. But his tongue cleaved to the roof of his mouth. See? This whole Sarah thing was about sex, and only sex. If they didn't make it into bed soon he would explode, and if they did hit the sack they'd open up a whole new can of problems.

And then his mouth got the better of him. 'Since it's your day off, let's make the most of it and go out for dinner tonight. I'm sure Jill or Bea will take Leah for the evening.'

He shot a quick glance over at his disturbing passenger, saw her tongue do a fast circuit of her lips. Should've kept his eyes on the road. Too late. Even now that he'd refocused on the tarmac unfolding before his vehicle he couldn't get the sight of her tongue out of his befuddled brain. What was happening to him? He'd agreed with himself that he had to put space between them, give her time, and then he'd gone and asked her out. On a date. Dinner for two. No child involved.

It's all right. She'll say no, for sure.

'I'd like that.'

So, he knew absolutely nothing about women. Especially this one.

CHAPTER NINE

DAN placed his elbows on the table and laid his chin on his interlaced fingers, his gaze fixed on Sarah. 'How was your venison?'

'Divine.' Instantly she wished she hadn't licked her lips as Dan's eyes followed her tongue. Pushing her plate aside, she struggled to come up with a conversation starter that would divert his attention. 'Leah had a great time today.' How lame was that?

'She'll drive Jill mad talking about it until she goes to bed.'

Bed. Dan. Funny how the two words seemed to combine in her head. She really had it bad for him. 'Today was wonderfully exciting for her.' *And me.*

Mischief twinkled in Dan's eyes. 'I'm discovering I like doing exciting things. Coming out for dinner falls into that category. It's been so long since I did anything remotely like it.'

Was it the dinner that was exciting? Not her company? She'd had a lot of dinners, and most of them at far more sophisticated restaurants than this one, but she couldn't remember feeling quite so relaxed and tense at the same time in any of them. 'You should make a regular thing of eating out.'

Dan nodded, then asked, 'What's it like, working with

the famous Dr David Livingston? I remember hearing a lot about him when I was training.'

Sarah sank down into her chair. 'He's a hard taskmaster. You give your absolute best and it's never good enough. And that's not just with me, he treats all his staff the same.'

'Bet he gets the results, though.'

'Yes, everyone strives to impress him.' They all wanted his attention in one way or another. That could be hard on her father at times.

'But you haven't followed his penchant for research.'

'I considered it, but no.' Her fingers fidgeted with the dessert spoon lying on the table.

'Not interested?' Dan's question seemed innocuous enough, but would he understand how much pain was behind her reply?

'Not really.'

'I'd have thought that would've been the way to get the attention you craved.' His fingers lightly brushed the back of her hand.

So he did understand. 'So did I, but I quickly found it didn't suit me. I enjoyed fixing people, using tried and true techniques.'

Dan was studying her closely. 'Enjoyed? As in the past? Not any more?' He didn't miss a thing.

'I had begun losing interest in surgery. For every operation we did, two more people popped up on the list and I began to feel I was working by rote.' She glanced into those blue eyes, saw understanding. 'I always did the absolute best I could. But before I came down here I'd reached the stage where there seemed to be so many patients that if one walked up to me in the street the day after I'd operated on them I'd not have known who they were. That doesn't seem right to me, doesn't seem to be the reason I started on this career in the first place. I felt I'd lost my compassion, my need to heal.'

'Sounds familiar,' Dan drawled. 'We have something in common. We were both sent away from our jobs to get some perspective.'

A small smile tugged at her mouth. 'And it is working for both of us. You're getting your life back, discovering the joys of those big toys you'd hidden away in your shed, having fun with your daughter. I'm finding the fun in surgery again. It's great to work with other professionals who are there for the good of the locals and the hospital, not arguing amongst themselves over who's the best. I'm finding I enjoy operating on people that I'm likely to bump into again.' Her smile widened. 'Two days ago I walked into the supermarket and little Emma Duncan came charging down one of the aisles calling out to Dr Sarah and landing a big kiss on my chin. At least it would have been my chin if she'd been a metre taller.' It had felt so good.

Dan laughed. 'There you go. You're fitting right in here.'

Which reminded her... 'Charlie talked to me yesterday. About staying on at the end of my contract.'

Blue eyes bored into hers, the smile hovering on Dan's lips frozen. 'What did you say?'

'That I'd think about it.' Which was a giant step forward considering she'd arrived here intent on getting through the three months and hightailing it back to Auckland quick smart. 'There are a lot of things to consider, not least my father and his clinic.'

'How will he feel if you sell your partnership?'

Once she'd have said he'd be disappointed, angry even, but now she could see how he'd been trying to help her by sending her away. 'Maybe he'd be happy for me.' Sarah leaned forward, watching Dan closely as she asked, 'But how would you feel if I did stay on? It is your clinic. You've built it up from scratch. Do you want someone working alongside you? Specifically, do you want me in that role?'

Caution filtered through the blue, making his eyes dark and brooding. 'If I say I don't know the answer to any of those questions, you've got to understand I'm not trying to hurt you.'

She dipped her head in acknowledgment, hoping he didn't see the spurt of disappointment she'd felt. 'Sure.'

'I'm surprised Charlie has approached you so soon. I thought he'd wait until the end of March, and I admit I was putting off making up my mind about the hours I want to work until then, too. But one thing's certain, I'm not going back to working those long hours I did before I got kicked off the roster. Not when I'm finally straightening out things at home.'

'You were hardly kicked off.'

'Of course I was, and fair enough. I needed to be.' Dan glanced out the window, back to her. 'I guess the only question I can't really give you an answer to is do I want you to stay on? There's a lot more to that question than hospital hours. It's early days to be contemplating that.'

Her stomach tightened uncomfortably. Her heart squeezed and slowed. 'I shouldn't have asked.'

'Always tell me what's on your mind. That's being honest.' His hand touched hers again, covered it, holding her fingers in his. A caress that quickly went from warm to heated.

She certainly wasn't telling him what was on her mind right this instant. It had nothing to do with clinics and hours and staying or going. All to do with desire and hunger and need. All to do with learning more about each other, taking this thing between them to another level, admitting what she'd been denying since the day she'd arrived in town. Daniel Reilly was hot and she wanted him. Come what may.

Tugging her hand away, she swallowed around the heat blocking her throat. 'Can we order some coffee?'

'In a hurry to get home?'

She'd ride a speeding bullet to get there. 'No, definitely not.'

His eyes now sparkling with heat, Dan said, slowly teasing out the words, 'We've got the whole night to enjoy.' Sexual tension ricocheted between them.

Was that a promise? Her blood cranked up its pace, racing through her veins. Was she finally going to touch those muscles, feel all that hard body, kiss that suntanned skin? What had happened to her usual arguments for keeping distant from Dan? He wanted her to be honest with him. Right now she was being honest with herself. She wanted him.

'Let's have dessert.' Dan leaned over the table, his mouth barely moving, the tip of his tongue slipping across his bottom lip.

She'd never manage to swallow a dot. Her stomach was wound so tight it would repel food like a tennis racquet hitting a ball. She squeaked, 'I'll have the cheesecake.'

He smiled, a long, lazy smile that curled her toes and tightened her belly. 'How do you know they've got cheesecake?'

Thankfully their waitress appeared. 'Would you like to see the dessert menu?'

Dan leaned back and looked up at the girl. 'Have you got cheesecake?'

'Boysenberry or lemon,' she replied.

Dan lifted an eyebrow at Sarah in a quirky fashion, making her incapable of deciding which flavour to have. Not that it mattered, if eating was beyond her.

'Lemon,' she croaked.

'Make mine berry,' Dan told the girl as he reached for his glass of water and took a long drink.

The desserts seemed to arrive in super-quick time as though the staff were working at keeping her wound tight.

Dan picked up his spoon and dipped into the cheese-cake. His mouth closed over the spoon, and he slowly slid it out over those lips she ached to kiss. 'Divine,' he whispered. 'You should try it.'

Just like that the delicious tension rippled through her body, sending out tingles of desire so sharp her fingers shook. She pushed her plate aside. Her appetite had totally disappeared. For dessert, that was. Not for Dan. Dan she wanted to kiss and taste and—

He stood up abruptly and came around the table. 'Let's get out of here.'

'Did you pay the bill?' she asked ten minutes later as Dan swung into their drive.

'I think so.' Dan slammed to a stop at the back door. He was out of the Land Cruiser and around at her door so fast he had to be dizzy.

She practically fell out, into his arms. His hands gripping her shoulders were hot on her suddenly hyper-sensitive skin.

His eyes locked with hers. The baby blue caution was gone, replaced with such carnal intensity that she rocked back on her heels. Her lungs stalled. Without any order from her mind her hands gripped the front of his shirt, tugged him closer. Then her lips sought his, found them, covered them. She gave herself up to kissing him. Heady kisses that he returned enthusiastically.

His tongue pushed between her lips, tangled with hers. He tasted wonderful. Hot male. From deep inside a groan crawled up her throat, giving sound to a primitive longing. A need to make love, a hungry urge to be with this man intimately.

Then his hands were pressing her shoulders away from him. 'Sarah, I've wanted to touch you all day.' His voice caught in his throat. 'If we take this any further, I won't guarantee I can stop.'

Leaning back, she looked into those beguiling eyes again. 'I won't ask you to. I don't want you to.'

'You're sure?' His hands held her face, his thumbs rubbing exquisitely tender circles across her cheek bones.

Sarah nodded, unable to speak around the need blocking her throat. She was past being able to hold out. Past rationalising. She wanted him.

'Then why are we standing out here?' Dan took her hand in his and together they raced for the house.

Inside he leaned back against the door and pulled her close again. His mouth found hers, his tongue slid between her lips. Pent-up desire exploded through her taut body. Heat, molten fire, spread through her muscles, her stomach. Her bones liquefied, no longer able to hold her up. Dan alone did that. He wound her tight against him. His response pressed hard against her belly.

Her tongue explored his mouth. Tasted him. She fell against him, needing to touch the whole length of his body with hers. It wasn't enough. Her hands ran over his back, down to his buttocks, over the curves. She was touching those muscles she'd been sneaking looks at for days. Weeks.

Clothing lay between her and his skin. She tried to slide her hands under the waist of his trousers. They were a tight fit. Frustration made her groan, and her mouth temporarily slid away from his.

Dan pulled his mouth well clear. 'This dress...' he slid the thin straps off her shoulders and down to her elbows

'…is stunning but it has to go.' His head ducked and he ran feather-light kisses down her neck, further down between her breasts. His hands gently pushed her dress further and further down, over her breasts, past her stomach, the hemline lowering from mid-thigh to her knees, pooling at her ankles. The silk fabric light and sensual against her skin, Dan's lips hot and demanding as they trailed a line of kisses from her breasts to her stomach. And lower.

She ached to touch him. Everywhere. Her hands touched here, there. Hard to concentrate while he stroked her. Would Dan be shocked if he knew how desperate she was to take him inside her? Her eyes flew open, met his delirious gaze. No, he wouldn't. The bite she gave her bottom lip stung, sharpening all her senses. Who was this woman acting wantonly?

Dan smiled, a quick curling of those full lips that made her heart flip. 'Bedroom. Now.'

She'd never remember how they got from the back door to Dan's bedroom. She only remembered falling onto the soft, cool bed, Dan sprawling on top of her. His tongue traced a hot, slick path over her taut nipple, moving around, over, beneath, until she believed her skin would split wide with desire. He was merciless, and she cried out for more. The only reprieve came when he swapped one nipple for the other and began again. Between her legs the heat built into a hot, moist pool, reaching an intensity she'd never experienced, never believed possible. How much more could she take? How long would this last before she fell apart in his hands?

'Dan, I can't wait. Can we…?' Then she blushed.

He grinned, a wicked, heated grin that did nothing to slow the rapid pounding of her heart. 'We need some protection, if I've got any.' Horror showed in his eyes.

She managed a chuckle. 'All sorted.' Pregnancy was one thing she'd never risk.

'Thank goodness. For a moment there I thought I'd have to do the impossible and stop.'

Her hands hooked at the back of his head, caught at his hair. 'Oh—my—Dan.' She didn't recognise her voice. It was raspy, fragmented.

And then at last they were together as one. Sarah's world exploded into a trillion beautiful fragments as Dan tipped her over the edge into that place where there was no beginning and no end, only pleasure and fulfilment. And so much more.

'You can remove the padding from Toby's throat.' Sarah nodded at Jill over the prostate body of their patient.

Jill used surgical tongs to lift the blood-soaked cotton padding that had been used to prevent blood pouring down the boy's throat during the tonsillectomy. While Sarah waited she arched her back, turned her head left then right, freeing the tight muscles of her neck.

'It's been a long day,' Hamish stood up from his seat at Toby's head, leaned over his monitors to begin bringing his patient round.

Sarah swallowed a yawn. 'It sure has, and we're not finished.' They'd started the day with a breast lumpectomy, followed by a torn Achilles' tendon.

'Anyone for coffee before the next one?' Jill asked.

'Most definitely. An extra-strong one for me.' She needed a caffeine fix. Too much late-night activity at home had left her happily tired. Since dinner on Saturday her relationship with Dan had ramped up big time. It had begun raining on Sunday, continued through Monday, Tuesday, Wednesday, making him restless. Until night-time after

Leah was sound asleep and then he came to life. They'd fall into his bed, making love as though they'd just invented it.

She was astonished at her appetite for Dan. Occasionally she'd lie awake beside his warm body and wonder where they went from there. It frightened her to think that she wanted more, was beginning to seriously considering staying on in Port Weston—if Dan agreed to the idea. During the early evenings when Sarah couldn't go for her usual after-work walk they'd talked and talked about just about everything. But not about what would happen come the end of March.

Neither had Sarah told him about the CF gene she carried. If they were going to take their relationship any further, she had to tell him. The day would arrive when she had to ask him to take the test to see if he was a carrier too. If he was, there'd be some huge decisions to make about taking the chance on having a baby that might have cystic fibrosis. One thing at a time, she told herself.

'What was that noise?' Hamish asked the room in general.

'Sarah's stomach,' Jill replied.

'A chocolate biscuit wouldn't go amiss,' Sarah agreed.

'We didn't have chocolate biscuits until you arrived.' Hamish grinned.

'I'm not that bad.' They didn't have them at the clinic back home either. Everyone there watched waistlines more carefully than the six-o'clock news.

'Yes, you are,' Jill and Hamish answered in unison.

A girl had to keep her energy levels up. Sarah's vinyl gloves snapped as she tugged them off, and she idly wondered what Dan had been doing during the day. He'd hoped to go fishing with mates but while the rain had lightened a strong wind had picked up. Just thinking about the man made her warm.

'What's that smile about?' Jill murmured quietly as she cleared away dirty instruments and blood soaked cotton. 'Or should I say who?'

'Nosey, nosey.' Sarah elbowed her way through the doors and began to change out of her theatre scrubs.

'You've had a permanent grin on your face for the last three days. What have you two been up to?' Jill was right behind her.

'I'm a smiley person.' Especially after mind-blowing sex before coming to work.

Jill rolled her eyes. 'Whatever you say.'

Familiar male laughter came from the other side of the door. Sarah gaped as Dan sauntered through dressed in scrubs and talking with the house surgeon. Her heart rate raced, her fingers itched to touch him.

'Anyone want one?' He said.

'Where's Leah?' Sarah asked.

'Hello to you, too.' Dan shot her a quick, secret look. 'She's gone to the movies with Bea and the girls.'

'But why have you come in here?' She leaned closer and whispered, 'I haven't got time to sneak into the linen cupboard with you.'

A huge sigh crossed his lips. 'Damn. I had such high hopes.' He suddenly looked serious. 'There was an accident on one of the fishing boats a couple of hours ago. A winch handle snapped and smashed into one of the men, rupturing his liver. Since you were already busy with a big schedule, I put my hand up to help out.'

She'd have liked to watch Dan at work. As opposed to watching him in the kitchen, the garden, the bedroom. 'I hope you don't think this excuses you from cooking dinner. It's your turn.'

'On my way to the supermarket as soon as I've finished this.' He waved his mug through the air. 'Bossy woman.'

Sarah chuckled. 'Someone's got to be.'

Jill's jaw dropped, and she looked from Sarah to Dan and back again.

'What?' Sarah asked.

Jill shook her head. 'He's laughing and joking. Whatever you've done to him, keep it up.'

Sarah spluttered into her coffee. 'Time we went back to work. Mabel Carpenter's hernia is next, isn't it?'

Sarah watched Robert closely as he brought across the coffee she'd ordered. His limp was very pronounced, putting his posture out of alignment and no doubt making his hips ache. Fatigue darkened his eyes and lined his mouth. Why did he put up with it?

George caught her eye and shrugged. 'I keep trying,' he said quietly.

But not quietly enough.

'What do you keep trying?' Robert asked, placing the large cups on the table.

'To get you to see another doctor about that leg,' George said.

Robert scowled at him. 'Don't waste your breath. I'm never going through all that again.'

George ignored the outburst, turning instead to Sarah. 'See what I have to put up with, cupcakes?'

Sarah was torn between smiling at her new name and taking Robert's fear seriously. Cupcakes won—for a moment. And then it was too late to talk to Robert as a customer came in, demanding coffee strong enough to take the soles off his shoes.

George raised an eyebrow. 'We sure get them.' Then he leaned closer to Sarah. 'Could you talk to him? He's in a bad way. He thinks I don't know how often he gets up at night because of the pain, but I'm aware the instant he gets out of bed.'

'I'll do my best.' But Sarah knew that would be woefully little unless Robert wanted to talk with her.

Then a familiar voice called across the room, 'Morning, guys. Is that my coffee? Or are you having two, Sarah?'

'I don't want coffee, Daddy.' Leah bounded over to George. 'Can I have a juice?'

'Please,' Dan told her.

'Please, George, can I?'

'Come with me, young lady. I'm sure there's a special treat somewhere for you to go with that juice.'

Watching Leah slip her hand into George's and skip along beside him Sarah felt the now familiar tug at her heart. So much for not getting involved with the child. Or her father. She was more than halfway in love with the guy. Leaving was rapidly becoming the last thing she wanted to do.

'Sarah?' Dan grinned down at her. 'I've bought you a present.'

She studied the large plastic bag with a local farmer's supply shop logo that he placed in front of her. Squinting up at him, she asked, 'What have you done?'

'Just a little number for your shoe collection.'

'Gumboots?' She dug into the bag and pulled out bright red boots painted with sunflowers. 'Heck, I don't think I've seen anything quite like them.' She jumped up and kissed Dan's cheek. 'They're gorgeous.'

He looked smug. 'Thought they'd come in handy now that you've turned into a gardener.'

Sarah slipped her sandals off and slid her feet into the gumboots. They fitted perfectly. When she raised an eyebrow at Dan he told her, 'I borrowed a pair of your shoes to take with me.'

'They are absolutely perfect in all ways.'

'I thought so.' His phone buzzed with an incoming text. 'Excuse me.'

Sarah dropped back onto her chair, staring at the red and yellow creations on her feet. Laughter bubbled up her throat. Laughing at herself. She was changing so much. Gumboots. They'd look way out of place back in her apartment. Face it, there wasn't any gardening to do there either. Over the week she'd started tidying up the vegetable patch that had gone to weeds. She planted seedlings for salads and soups later in the year. Most of them she wouldn't be here to pick unless… She looked at Dan, love pulsing through her. Unless she committed to staying. Her laughter died.

Did she know Dan well enough to take the risk? How would he react if she said yes to Charlie? Did he expect her to consult further with him about that first? When she'd mentioned it the other night he'd said they needed more time. He needed more time. She didn't. She was ready to stay.

But if Dan wasn't ready for that then maybe he wouldn't be ready to face the cystic-fibrosis issue either. And she definitely couldn't cope again with the dillydallying about having that test done. Oliver had become a dab hand at putting it off every time she'd raised the subject. He'd assured her he could deal with the consequences, whatever they were, but as time had gone by and he hadn't spoken to his GP, she'd had to question that. Oliver had blamed her, saying if she left him alone he'd have done it months earlier. Said if she hadn't nagged him he wouldn't have turned to someone else for comfort. Yeah, right.

Now she wondered if he'd been afraid of learning he wasn't perfect. That would rock him, big time. His image was important to him, his ego huge. Something like being a gene carrier would punch a hole in that ego. And a sweet little obliging nurse wouldn't question his perfection.

Dan had intimated he'd had problems with Celine, although he'd never elaborated to her what they had been. Problems he only now seemed to be coming to terms with. Could she ask him to deal with hers so soon? How would he respond if she asked him to take a test for the gene? Probably very well. He was an empathetic man.

Was she willing to test how compassionate Dan really was? There was a risk he'd walk away from the whole issue, walk away from her. She shuddered. Like Oliver had done before him.

CHAPTER TEN

'WE'RE going horse riding,' Dan told Sarah on Saturday morning. 'Bea wants to give the horses a bit of a workout. Want to come with us? We could tell the hospital where you are in case you're needed.'

Sarah glanced out the window. The rain had finally played ball and disappeared, leaving a sparkling day. 'As long as I don't have to mount a horse, I'm all for it.'

Unfortunately Dan appeared to have selective hearing. Bea had three horses waiting when they pulled into the yard.

'Look, Sarah, there's Flicker and Jumbo and Sammy.' Leah's arm shot in front of Sarah's face, her little finger pointing to the massive animals.

Sarah gulped. 'Bea going with you?'

Dan climbed out of the Land Cruiser and slapped a hat on. 'Not that I know of.'

Another gulp. 'You haven't got me out here under false pretences, have you, Daniel Reilly?'

'I never said you wouldn't be riding. You did. It's my job to change your mind.'

'Not this side of Christmas, you're not.' Sarah stayed in the vehicle, staring through the window at the big beasts, their backs a long way from the ground. 'I'll wait here for you. In case the hospital phones.' Her knuckles were white in her lap.

Leah had already climbed the fence and was petting one of the horses. 'I presume that's Flicker.' Leah looked so tiny beside the horse. How could Dan even consider letting the child ride it? 'Don't you worry about Leah getting thrown off?'

'Yes, which is why someone always goes with her.' Dan stood at the door, his hand on her shoulder. 'Sammy's the smallest of the other two, if you change your mind.'

'He's enormous. My feet won't be anywhere near the ground.' Her heart was racing.

'You're confusing this with the merry-go-round.' Dan leaned in to give her a kiss. 'At least come over with me to give Leah a leg up. We can walk around the paddock with her.'

Bea came out from the house, surrounded by children, some of whom Sarah recognised as Dan's nieces and others she'd never seen before. 'Crikey,' Sarah muttered, beginning to feel inundated as they all crowded around.

Dan laughed. 'It's always like this out here. Bea's kids have a lot of friends and half the reason for that is Bea is so good with them.'

'Hi, there.' Bea waved over the many heads. 'What do you think, Sarah? Want to have a go? Sammy's so quiet you'll struggle to get him moving.'

'No, thanks, I'm into spectator sports.' Wimp. Sarah moved closer to Dan. When he took her hand she hoped he wouldn't notice how much she shook. 'I don't mind going up and patting horses, but that's as far I go.'

'Fair enough.' Dan grinned and slapped her bottom lightly. In front of his sister?

Who, when Sarah glanced at her, had definitely noticed the gesture and was smiling at them both. Great. Why were Bea and Jill so keen for Dan to get friendly with her? Hadn't they read the bit in the contract that said she was only here for three months? Did they want to see him get hurt again?

Everyone, including Sarah, climbed the fence to join Leah. Dan hoisted Leah up into the saddle, helped her slide her feet into the stirrups.

Sarah marvelled at Leah's poise. 'Like a pro.'

Bea agreed. 'Born to it, I reckon, same as with all my kids.'

Dan mounted and followed Leah around the paddock. Sarah couldn't take her eyes off him. Sitting straight and tall, his hands firm yet relaxed on the reins, his thighs pressing the horse's flanks, it was a sight she'd never forget. Simply beautiful.

'Have you ever ridden?' Bea's question scratched against the image holding Sarah enthralled.

'Once. The ride lasted all of three minutes before I was unceremoniously tossed off over the horse's head and into a blackberry bush. Definitely not my thing. Trust me on this.'

Bea smiled in sympathy. 'I can see how that could put you off. But who knows, one day we might get you in a saddle again.'

'What is it with the Reillys that none of you will take no for an answer?' Sarah smiled to take the sting out of her words.

'Guess we only see things from our point of view, and because we know how much fun riding is we want to share it with you.'

'How about I take your word for it?'

Dan trotted over to them. 'Want to try?' he asked Sarah. 'Trust me. I won't let anything happen to you.'

'No, thanks.' Why did he look at her as though she'd

hurt him? Of course she trusted him to look out for her, but so what? It wasn't as though riding a horse was the be-all and end-all.

Dan shrugged stiffly. 'Okay.'

She watched him trot back to Leah. They looked good riding together. Family. But it was only half a picture. There should be a wife, a mother, with them. She was sure she could be there, if she learned to trust again. But she'd sensed over the past week there was something Dan was holding back from her and until he told her, how could she trust him?

'Come and have a coffee,' Bea nudged her. 'Dan and Leah will be a while. The rest of the kids are going eel-ing and I'd love some adult female chat. At the moment all anyone around here wants to talk about is the camping trip we've got planned for next week.'

'I think you're just being kind, but coffee would be great.' Even an instant one. Which went to show how much she'd changed.

The hours flew past. After the horses had been wiped down and put out to graze Bea put on a simple lunch for everyone, including all the extra kids. John arrived home from the mine where he drove a front-end loader, in time to have a beer with Dan before they ate.

Sarah helped set out the food on a huge outdoor table, watching Bea handle the kids with an ease that made her envious.

'Families, eh? Aren't they great?' She hadn't noticed Dan coming up beside her. Her usual radar had failed. Even the scent of his aftershave was absent today, overlaid with the tang of horse smell.

'Yours seems to have it all worked out. Everyone gets along so well.' Even the children helped each other, despite bickering occasionally.

Dan placed his arm around her shoulders. 'You could still have all this. With the right man.'

Turning, she looked up at him. With you? Was he offering her something she daren't hope for? Did she want to spend the rest of her life with him? Yes, darn it, she did. She loved him. Then start by being honest with him. 'There's something I haven't told you.'

His hand traced a line down her cheek, rested on her chin. 'Go ahead. Fill me in on Sarah Livingston and what makes her tick.'

She pulled away from his warm, heavy arm, took a few steps into the paddock. Stopped. Clenched her hands in front of her, and spun around. 'My brother died of cystic fibrosis. I carry the gene too.'

Three long strides and Dan was before her, taking her cold hands in his. 'Sweetheart, I'm so sorry. Now I begin to understand some of the things I felt you left out when talking about your family.'

'You did?' Was there nothing this man couldn't get right with her?

'Yep.' His hand brushed her hair off her face. 'Thank you for telling me.'

Did he get it? Understand he'd have to be tested for the gene if they were taking this relationship to the next stage. He was a doctor, he'd get it. Was she rushing him? But she had to know. 'There's more. I'm not sure what you mean when you say I can have the whole nine yards, husband and family, but if we're heading anywhere together then you'd have to be tested for the CF gene.'

Dan's smile was so tender she nearly cried.

'Sarah, trust me, I understand that.'

Did he understand she'd like him to do it sooner rather than later? That she needed to know the answer before she could make other decisions about their future together?

Because if he had the gene she'd have to walk away and forget about having his babies. That would be doing the right thing by Dan. She could do it. But leaving would be so hard. Dan and Leah had shown her she could love and, more importantly, they loved her back.

Tuesday night and their lovemaking was unhurried, and exquisitely tender. Sarah had never known that desire could uncoil so agonisingly slowly that every cell in her body was dancing as they waited for the promised release.

'Pinch me,' Sarah whispered. 'I'm not sure that wasn't a dream.'

'Oh, it was real, every last bit of it.' Dan wrapped her in his arms and kissed the top of her head.

Every muscle in her body refused to move. Her mind was a cloud of spent desire. How Dan could take her to the edge and hold her there for so long, tantalising her, making her almost beg to be released.

He said into her hair, 'Wish I hadn't agreed to go camping tomorrow.'

'How long will you be away?' Because the trip had been put off for so long she'd begun to believe he wouldn't be going away.

'Four days at the most.'

'What?' she cried. 'You do what you've just done to me and then tell me you're gone for days?' She'd miss him like crazy. 'Where is this camp site?'

A deep chuckle erupted somewhere above her head. 'You're stroking my ego something terrible. Keep going like that and I'll believe anything's possible.'

'Like what?'

Dan slid down the bed until his face was opposite hers. 'Like coming camping with us.'

'Me?' What a ridiculous idea! She had a job to do in

town. 'Do you think the others would appreciate being kept awake by your passionate cries throughout the night?'

'I can do quiet.'

'For sure.' Sarah snuggled closer. 'I am going to miss you, and not just because of the sex.'

Dan stroked her back. 'Do you think you might like to try camping some time? We could go for a night one weekend while you're still here.'

'Me? In a tent? No hot and cold water, no coffee, wearing clothes I wouldn't be seen dead in?' She poked him lightly in the ribs. 'Get real.'

'I was.'

She chuckled. 'I guess anything's possible given enough time. After all, I do wear gumboots these days.' This guy made her do and say things she'd never have believed a few weeks ago. Now caution and excitement mingled in her veins.

'I'd buy you another pair of gumboots, this time with possum fur.'

'Now you're bribing me.'

'That was only an opening bid. You gave up too easily.'

She grinned. 'What else was on offer?'

'My body.'

'Doesn't count. I can get that with one touch.' And she proceeded to show him how easily persuaded he could be.

Further into the night Sarah lay on her side, Dan spooned behind her with his arm over her waist. Despite her languorous body, she was wide awake.

Dan was out of it, so soundly asleep a ten-ton truck driving through the front door wouldn't have woken him. She was storing up all the sensations from his hand splayed across her tummy to his breaths on the back of her neck, from his hard thighs against the back of her legs to the occasional light snore.

She hugged herself. She loved Dan. What more could she ask for?

Dan's love, that's what. And for him to take that gene test. It was starting to burn at her that he hadn't said any more about it since her revelation on Saturday. It had been hard to tell him, then she'd got nothing back since. *Patience*, she warned herself. But she didn't do patience, not when she was desperate to know his take on the situation. Not when this same scenario had backfired on her with Oliver. When would Dan have the test? Would he have it at all?

She tensed. Why should he? They hadn't made a commitment to a joint future. He didn't owe her anything. She was getting way ahead of herself. Comfortable in Port Weston, in love with Dan, desperate to have children.

She rolled over and looked at his sleeping form. Way, way ahead of yourself, Sarah. This is the affair you wanted to have with him. Nothing more, nothing less. Dan may have helped you move on from Oliver, he may have shown you how to love again, but there had never been any promises beyond that. He hadn't even promised that much.

She had less than three weeks left here. Did she spend them in Dan's bed? Or alone in hers?

The sound of a vehicle in the drive woke Dan next morning. The bedside clock read six. 'Who's that at this god-awful hour?'

He rolled over. Where was Sarah? His hand groped across the other side of the bed. The sheets were cold. He sat up. 'Sarah?'

The house was silent, ominously silent. He leapt out of bed and ran, naked, to her bedroom, then the bathroom still warm from the shower having been run on hot, the kitchen where the blinds had been raised and the kettle was warm to his touch. Sarah was nowhere to be seen. Outside her car had gone.

'Strange, I didn't hear the phone.' He'd check with the hospital to see if she'd been called in for an emergency.

'Sarah's not here,' the A and E nurse informed him. 'And we haven't called for her. It's been the quietest night on record.'

Then where had she gone? Walking the beach had become a regular habit for her now but the sky was bucketing down. Not looking good for camping, though John had assured him it would be fine by midmorning. Dan banged the phone down. That cold side of his bed bothered him. Had Sarah gone back to her room after they'd made love? He shook his head. She never did that. She reckoned the after-match cuddles were almost as good as the sex. The lovemaking. Sex sounded too...too impersonal, uninvolved. No, they made love.

Love? Making love didn't mean he was in love. Did it? Gulp. He'd been thinking it might be time to find a woman to share his life with but this was for real. He wanted Sarah, in his bed, in his life, alongside him as he dealt with all life's vagaries.

But was he ready? What if Sarah wanted to return to the city? Could he go with her? Leave his family behind? He sucked air through his teeth. Could he really do that? He'd hate it, no doubt. But asking Sarah to stay here meant asking her to leave her family behind. A family who had let her down big time. But still her family. How did she feel about leaving Auckland and her dad? If she didn't want to then he was prepared to give the city a go.

He flicked the kettle on and spooned coffee granules into a mug. A new mug that matched the other new mugs and cups in the cupboard. Piece by piece Sarah was making her mark on his home. Which had only been a place to grab some sleep and feed his daughter until Sarah had come along.

Last night their lovemaking had been even more magical than ever. Sarah had seemed very happy as they'd lain talking afterwards. He'd sensed she didn't want him going away today. So wouldn't that mean she'd be here to say goodbye to him with a few hot kisses to last him until he got back? What about Leah? Surely Sarah would've wanted to give her a hug before they disappeared for a few days?

Now dressed in jeans and nothing else, Dan stood at the window, his coffee growing cold as he watched the rain pelting down on the drive and paths. Had he missed something? Had Sarah gone from the house to get away from him? So she didn't have to see him until he got back from up the valley?

He ran the previous couple of days through his mind, looking for any clues. She'd been a bit preoccupied at times, but he'd put that down to work. She'd had a busy weekend almost from the moment they'd returned from Bea's, with a couple of tricky procedures that had had her phoning specialist surgeons she knew in Auckland.

For the first time in ages Celine popped into his mind. She used to stop talking to him, go out for a day without telling him where she'd gone. His stomach began churning. All the old guilt bubbled up, threatened to overwhelm him. He'd struggled to get through to her when she'd been like that, thinking the depression had had something to do with her reaction to him. What if he was the problem? Sarah was not depressed and yet she'd left the house this morning without a word to him.

No, history could not be repeating itself. Last night Sarah had been so loving, so willing. And afterwards she'd wrapped her body around his, holding him against her like she'd never let go. What had happened, what had entered her mind in the early hours of the morning that had driven her out of his bed?

Cystic fibrosis. The gene she carried. Should he have talked more about that with her? It would be a major issue in any lasting relationship Sarah was involved in. His heart squeezed for her. How hard had it been for her to tell him? Had she told him now in case they took this affair to the next level? Giving him time to digest it, make his mind up on how he felt? Had she been let down in the past? By Oliver? Questions banged around inside his skull, and the lack of answers raised his anxiety level.

When she'd told him he'd filed it away, something to think about in the future if they continued together. There'd be tests for him to have done, decisions to make if the results showed him to be a carrier as well. But Sarah would've wanted to have some indication on how he felt immediately. It would've been hard for her to tell him. Damn it, he hadn't been very understanding. At least he could rectify his blunder, starting this morning, before he headed away.

So where was she?

Sarah pushed her plate aside and reached for the coffee George had just made. 'That was excellent. I should start every day with a cooked breakfast.'

Opposite her Jill finished the last of her scrambled eggs. 'This baby sure gives me an appetite.'

Sarah laughed. 'At how many months?'

'Who's counting?' Jill buttered a slice of toast, smothered it in marmalade. 'Seriously, I'm always hungry at the moment. If that doesn't stop soon, I'll have to start being careful. Don't want to end up looking like the Michelin Man.'

Sarah rolled her eyes. 'No chance.'

'So...' Jill eyed Sarah over her toast. 'How's things going with my brother-in-law?'

'Fine.' Sarah's muttered understatement earned her a wink. 'Truly.'

'We all know that,' Jill drawled.

'All? Who's all?' Did the whole town about their affair?

'Oh, you know, family.' Jill shrugged her shoulders, but as Sarah tried to relax, Jill added, 'And the theatre staff, Charlie, these guys.' She glanced over at George and Robert working behind the counter.

Sarah gulped. Definitely the whole town. 'Tell me you're joking.'

'Everyone cares about you two, wants to see you both happy.'

'They don't know me.'

'They know you've made Dan smile again, that Leah loves you, that you're a superb surgeon who cares about her patients enough to go in before hitting the pillow late at night so she can make them feel better.'

'Like any surgeon would do.' Patients liked reassurance, especially at night when pain kept them awake and the doubts started rolling in. But she hadn't done a lot of that back in Auckland.

Jill's phone gave a muffled ring from the depths of her handbag. 'Odd,' she muttered when she read the incoming number. 'A and E. Why are they calling me before you?'

Because my phone's not switched on in case Dan tries to call. She didn't have an explanation for not being there this morning, not one she was prepared to give him anyway. But her pager should've gone off. Tugging it off her belt, she was surprised there was no message.

'Sarah's with me. We're on our way.' Jill snapped her phone shut. 'That was Tony. You're needed in the delivery suite. Like now.'

'What's up?'

'It's Cathy. She went into labour late yesterday but apparently everything's progressing too slowly. She has a history of pre-eclampsia, and Tony's considering a Caesarean section.'

'That's why he wants me.' She'd done sections, but not recently.

'Let's go, then.'

George stepped in front of her. 'Sarah, would you like to come to dinner tomorrow night? Not in the café but upstairs in our flat. The three of us.'

She blinked. 'I'd love that.' What was that about?

'See you around seven for a drink first.'

Dan's vehicle was in the car park when they pulled up at the hospital. Guilt tugged at Sarah. Would he be angry at her? That was the last thing she wanted, and yet she couldn't blame him if he was. She'd have been hurt if he'd done the same thing to her. But she'd needed to put space between them before she blew up and said things best left alone. Things like he couldn't be trusted to do the one thing that was ultra-important to her, just like her ex hadn't. Never mind that Dan hadn't known about the gene for more than a couple of days, she felt desperate to know that he could be relied on.

But there wasn't time for him right now. Jill had said Tony sounded very worried.

Tony was waiting outside Cathy's room. 'Thanks for coming in so quickly.'

Sarah got straight to the point. 'Details?'

'Cathy's blood pressure is 170 over 120, and rising. She's got excessive fluid retention and protein in her urine.'

Sarah frowned at the abnormal results. 'And the baby?'

'Prolonged tachycardia. Heart rate of 138 beats per minute five minutes ago.'

'Doesn't sound like we've got any choice but to retrieve the baby.' A racing foetal heart rate was serious.

Tony looked behind Sarah. 'Hi, Dan. Have you come in to help with this one?'

Sarah's heart thumped as she turned. 'Morning, Dan.' He looked wary, not angry.

'I'm available if Sarah needs me. I'm not going up the valley until after lunch.' Dan's eyes didn't leave Sarah's face and she could feel her cheeks heating up. 'I missed you this morning. You left very early.'

'I was restless and you were sleeping soundly.' Disbelief gleamed back at her. 'Jill and I went for breakfast at the café.'

'I tried phoning you to say have a good week, but I kept getting voice mail.'

Her tongue licked her dry lips. 'Sorry, I forgot to turn it on.' The lie was rancid in her mouth. 'Did you come to see Cathy?'

'Brent called me so I decided to drop by, offer him some support,' Dan said.

There was a huge question in his eyes, making her feel mean. She turned away, following the GP in to see Cathy. 'Hi, Cathy. Tony has filled me in on your details. He's called me in for your Caesarean.'

Cathy's eyes widened. 'Sarah, thank you for coming in. I'm really pleased you're doing the operation. Hey, hello, Dan.'

'Hey, how's my favourite cousin?' Dan leaned down to kiss her cheek before turning to a very worried-looking Brent and squeezing his shoulder.

'Not so flash right now.' Cathy had indentations in her bottom lip from pressing her teeth down, presumably during contractions. Her face was grey, another indication that things were not right. She looked to Sarah, a plea in her eyes. 'Is my baby going to be all right?'

Sarah winced inwardly. As yet she didn't know all the details so she wasn't about to make a promise she mightn't be able to keep. But she understood Cathy's fear. 'I certainly intend doing all I can to help ensure that it is.' Then she turned to Brent. 'How are you coping?'

'I'm feeling as useless as snow-boots in the desert. If only I could do something for Cathy.' His voice rose, and his Adam's apple bobbed in his throat.

Poor guy. 'It seems harder for the fathers in these situations.'

Cathy's eyes squeezed tight and her hands clenched Brent's. Her knuckles were white as pain racked her body. Beads of sweat popped out across her brow and the midwife sponged her face. Her breast rose and fell rapidly as she struggled to breathe. 'Pain. It's...not...the...contraction.'

'Take your time, breathe through the contraction,' the midwife instructed.

'Not a contraction.' Cathy struggled to speak. 'In my chest. Pain in my chest. I can't get air.'

The midwife glanced at the GP, then Sarah, one eyebrow slightly raised, before she slipped an oxygen mask over her patient's mouth and nose. Cathy's breathing deepened, not back to normal but better than it had been before the intervention of the oxygen supply.

Sarah finished perusing the notes Tony had handed her. 'Let's go. I'll page Hamish now.'

'He's here somewhere. His car's outside,' Dan informed her. Then he leaned close and whispered, 'Do you want me to assist you?'

A wee sigh of relief slid through her lips. Despite everything, having Dan there made operating so much easier. 'Definitely. That chest pain makes me wonder if something else's going on here.'

'I agree, but we'll take it one step at a time.'

Sarah wanted to touch Dan, hug him, but that would be giving him the wrong message after that morning. It was confusing her. How could she stay away from him during her last weeks here? 'Let's go scrub up.'

Everything happened in a rush. Hamish arrived almost before Sarah had finished paging him, and went straight to see Cathy.

Sarah told Dan, 'Antenatal patients are not my forte. They go to the obstetricians and gynaecologists, not to our clinic.'

Dan nodded. 'I guess I do have the upper hand in this case.'

'I'm quite okay about you taking the lead.' She wasn't about to stand on her high horse about his leave when two patients relied on her.

'How about I talk you through the procedure? Then if another case comes your way over the next few weeks, you'll have this one behind you.'

It wasn't likely to happen but Sarah acquiesced. 'Good idea. Let's get moving. Cathy can't afford to wait longer than necessary.'

Standing beside the operating table, Sarah picked up the scalpel and asked everyone, 'Are we ready?' Then she was pushing down into the swollen flesh that protected a little life.

Michael Ross was born with the umbilical cord wound around his neck. Sarah held him while Dan expertly removed the cord. Their reward was a shrieking, ear-piercing squall. A woozy Cathy watched him hungrily through tear-filled eyes. 'He's beautiful.'

By the time Sarah finished repairing the incision she'd made to retrieve the baby Cathy was alert and eager to hold the precious bundle a nurse had wrapped in a tiny cotton blanket. Thankfully nothing had gone wrong and her earlier concerns had disappeared. Sarah watched as the mother held her son for the very first time.

Cathy had eyes only for her son. The world could've imploded right then and she wouldn't have noticed. She certainly wasn't aware of the orderly wheeling her out into Recovery, where Brent waited anxiously.

Sarah followed, and told Brent, 'I don't think I need to say anything. Your wife and son are doing well.'

'He's a noisy little blighter,' Brent said around a face-splitting grin. He leaned over and kissed Cathy on her cheek, then carefully took his son's tiny fist in his.

Sarah watched them, enthralled. Along with Cushla, they made a perfect family. They'd be busy but she didn't doubt they'd cope.

'You okay?' Dan touched her arm lightly.

'Yes. Isn't this the most beautiful sight?' She nodded at Cathy holding her baby. What did it feel like to hold your baby that first time?

Dan nodded. 'It is. I still remember Leah's birth. The moment I saw her, holding her tiny body, so afraid I'd break her, the instant love that overwhelmed me. It's magic.'

The wonder in his voice made Sarah's eyes fill. She'd love to have Dan's child. She'd love to give him that magic moment again. Would he have that test done? Did it matter if he didn't? Ah, hello. Where had *that* weird idea come from?

'We'll call in later,' Dan told the happy couple.

'Thanks.' Both parents barely lifted their heads from their son to acknowledge him.

Dan took Sarah's elbow and led her out of the room.

'I'm heading home to pick up the tent and other things.' He paused. 'Is there anything you need, Sarah?' His thumb traced a line down her cheek, along her jaw. His eyes were dark with confusion.

Yes, a test result. A hug. Some understanding of why I'm so impatient and tense. 'Not at the moment.'

'I guess I'll get going, then.' He stood in front of her, searching her face. Looking for what? An answer to her behaviour?

'Have a good time. Don't let the sand flies bite too often.' She started to lean in to kiss him, thought better of it, and backed away. If she was going to cut the ties then now was the time to start.

Dan watched her stride away. Her shoulders were tugged tight, her back ramrod straight, her steps a little longer and louder than usual. He was definitely on the outer and none the wiser about why. Deep inside a dull ache began to throb. With it came memories of trying to understand Celine, trying to help her when she hadn't wanted to be helped. Was this the same scenario?

Had Sarah come to a decision about returning to Auckland at the end of the month? If she had, could he blame her? He hadn't given her any indications about his feelings. Because he was only beginning to understand them himself. And needed to know exactly how he felt before he made a move.

Jill appeared at his elbow. 'You okay?'

'Yes, of course.' Dan turned to his sister-in-law, saw the concern radiating from her eyes. 'Actually, I haven't got a clue.'

'She needs you as much as you need her. Don't let the past get in the way.' Jill stood on tiptoe and kissed his chin.

And then she was gone, heading for Theatre and the next patient.

'Easy to say,' Dan murmured. But he had a plan. Sarah had been hurt in the past, and so had he. One of them had to make the first move, break the mould that held them both tied to their pasts. So he went to find Tony.

CHAPTER ELEVEN

'SINCE it's such a beautiful evening, we'll sit out on the deck, if that's all right with you.' George told Sarah when she arrived the next night, a huge bunch of summer flowers in her hand.

'Perfect.' Sarah sighed. 'This is heaven.' Well, it would be if Dan were here to share it with her.

'Isn't it? We took a long while to settle here after the pace of Christchurch, but now we'd never leave. This is a little piece of paradise and the locals are delightful.' Robert sat in the chair beside Sarah. 'Port Weston grows on you, if you let it.'

Looking out over the rooftops of the main street shops to the ocean beyond, Sarah was startled to realise she agreed. 'Auckland seems so far away.'

'It is.'

Throughout the meal Sarah found her mind wandering back to that thought. Odd, but she hadn't missed anything or anyone from home. Not the social events, not the restaurants, the shops, or the clinic. She had been born and bred in the city, so when had she shed that persona? Or was it lurking, ready to take up again the moment she pointed the Jag northward?

Robert placed coffee and Cointreau in front of her. 'Port Weston's got under your skin. Already.'

Not Port Weston, but the people living there. Especially one man. Sipping the liqueur, she savoured the heavy orange tang on her tongue, and asked, 'So what do I do now?'

'Stay. It's as simple as that.'

'And as complex.' She couldn't stay if Dan didn't want her.

George leaned across the table and touched the back of her hand. 'Only you make it complicated. It's hard, shedding all those commitments you have in your other life, but if you want to, you'll find a way.'

'Thanks a bundle.' She knew he was right but this feeling of having found her place could be false. It could evaporate as quickly as it had taken her over. And if Dan didn't want her here then she couldn't encroach on his territory.

'We know what we're talking about,' Robert added.

The three of them sat in comfortable silence for a few minutes. Then George drew a deep breath. 'Sarah, we invited you here for a reason. Not that we didn't want to have a meal with you, of course.'

George spoke so quietly Sarah looked at him out of the corner of her eye. He was watching Robert with such tenderness she felt her heart squeeze. They were very lucky to have found each other.

Quietly, in a flat voice, Robert told her, 'George wants me to have my leg operated on. The pain's getting progressively worse and I don't sleep much at nights. I try not to disturb him but I know I do.'

Her heart blocked her throat. Was this what she thought it was? She said nothing, just waited.

'I'm having the operation done.' A quiver rattled his voice and the eyes he raised to her were heavy with fear. 'And I want you to do it.'

'Thank you for your trust in me.' Wow, Dan had said she could get Robert to change his mind, and it seemed she had without saying a single word. She asked softly, 'What went wrong last time?'

'I nearly died. Twice. My heart stopped while I was on the operating table. Then my leg got infected and they couldn't control it.' He reached for her hand, gripped it hard. 'It was terrifying.'

'You're not going to die.' Sarah squeezed his hand in return.

'I hope not.' The smile he gave her was twisted and sad and filled with fear.

'Robert, I'll need your authority to talk to your previous surgeon and to get your files.'

Sarah shivered. Was she up to this? The surgery didn't faze her, but helping these two men worried her. They'd become friends. She closed her eyes and hoped Dan's belief in her was realistic. Then she had an idea.

'George, Robert, of course I'll do the operation unless I find it is beyond me. But how would you feel about Dan assisting me?' She held her breath, not knowing why they'd come to her, a relative newcomer, and not gone to Dan, whom they were very close to.

The men looked at each and nodded. 'We'd be very happy,' George told her. 'You two are a team in everything you do. I'd have been surprised if you hadn't wanted Dan there.'

Some of the tension that had begun tightening her muscles slipped away. She might have personal issues to sort out with Dan but she needed him by her side when she performed this operation. Robert had become a friend and his fear made her nervous.

'Right,' she said. 'Let's talk.' And she spoke quietly, knowledgably, drawing on all her experience with distressed patients.

* * *

Sarah tentatively scheduled Robert's surgery for the evening two days away, worried to leave it any longer in case he changed his mind. Every spare minute of the next day was spent talking to specialists, calling in Robert's medical records to study and discussing with his previous cardiologist what had happened during the first operation. Hamish agreed to be the anaesthetist and she kept him appraised of everything.

She dropped into the café at lunchtime to reassure Robert. Over a double shot, long black, George tried to voice his gratitude for Sarah getting his partner this far already.

'It's unbelievable. I've been hoping and praying he'd have this done for so long now, and here...' He stopped, unable to finish his sentence.

Sarah leaned forward and touched his hand. 'It's not me you have to thank, it's Robert. He's a very brave man.'

It was nearly six that night when she tossed her theatre scrubs into the laundry basket and changed into jeans and a T-shirt. Outside she waved the key at the Jag to unlock it and slid behind the steering-wheel. A dull ache throbbed behind her eyes as she smoothed out the rough map Jill had drawn for her.

Finding the camping site was unbelievably easy, even for a city girl. Six tents were clustered along the flat grassed area above the river. A fire flickered within a circle of rocks. When Sarah pushed her door open, the harsh pitch of crickets filled the air.

'Sarah?' Dan approached the car. 'What brings you out here? Is something wrong?'

Darn, but he looked so good. Big and strong, his hair a riot of curls, his shorts revealing those muscular thighs she loved to run her hands down. How could she even think about heading north? Leaving Dan?

'Sarah?' Fingers caught her shoulders and his large hands shook her gently. 'What brings you up the valley?'

She swallowed. 'Firstly, there's nothing wrong.' She felt him relax. 'I need to ask something of you. It's important.' She looked up into those eyes that missed nothing, and silently begged him not to walk away as she deserved.

'Sure. Just let me tell the others we're taking a walk.' Was that hope lacing his words? Did he think she'd come to explain why she'd left his bed during the night last time they made love?

'Sarah, Sarah!' Leah exploded out of a tent, making a beeline for her.

Sarah's heart rolled over as she bent to catch the human speedball. 'Hey, gorgeous. How's my favourite girl?'

'Have you come to stay in our tent? Daddy takes up all the space. I have to curl up tight.' Leah's nose pressed into Sarah's neck, and Sarah inhaled her scent.

'It's so good to see you, sweetheart. I've come to talk to Daddy.' Then Sarah looked up and saw a shadow cross Dan's eyes. Had she made a mistake? Would he prefer she didn't act so affectionately with his daughter if she was leaving town? How could she not?

Within moments Sarah was surrounded by Bea, John and everyone else. It took a few minutes before Dan could persuade Leah to stay with Bea while he and Sarah went down to the river for a walk.

They sat on a large flat rock, their legs dangling over the water. Sarah batted away a mosquito and looked across at Dan. 'Robert's asked me to operate on his leg.'

'I knew you'd persuade him.' Disappointment and admiration mingled in Dan's eyes, making her feel sad and proud at the same time. She hoped he didn't feel peeved he hadn't been the one Robert had asked.

'No, you're wrong. He came to me.' She held his gaze. 'Dan, I need your help with this. Will you assist me? Tomorrow night.'

He looked away, looked back. 'Of course. But why? It's not difficult surgery.'

Everything her life had come to mean in Port Weston—friendship, love, belonging—was tied up in this particular operation. And, unusually, she feared failure. Sarah laid her hand on Dan's. 'Not difficult and yet the hardest I've had to do because he's a real friend. That's what this place has done to me. I know I'll be fine if you're there with me.'

His eyes sharpened, his hand under hers tensed. But he only said, 'I'll come back with you now. Leah will be happy staying with Bea. They're back the day after tomorrow.' He stood and looked down at her. 'We'll split tomorrow's theatre list so that you're not exhausted for Robert's surgery.'

He understood. He was coming to help her. And yet she knew she'd let him down. Had he been hoping for more? She wanted to explain her actions but couldn't without sounding like she was begging him for a place in his life. A place with conditions.

Because Dan had taken over half the surgical list Robert's surgery was brought forward to early afternoon. There were no problems, only one nasty surprise. When Sarah opened up the leg, she exclaimed in horror. The offending tendon had somehow got twisted before being rejoined.

'Working with you is a treat,' Sarah told Dan as they finished up. 'We seem to understand each other instinctively.'

'Not only in Theatre.' His eyes glowered back at her over his mask.

'I know.' But at the moment there were things they had to sort through to understand each fully.

In Recovery she told a groggy Robert, 'Your foot will take some work so you can walk without a limp, but at least the pain will be gone.'

Robert smiled the blank smile of a patient coming out of anaesthesia and promptly vomited into the stainless-steel bowl Jill held below his face.

'That's gratitude for you.' Sarah patted Robert's shoulder. 'I'll see you later.'

Outside in the waiting room she found Dan reassuring George that the operation had been a success and that there'd been none of the complications of last time.

There were tears in George's eyes when he gripped Sarah's hand to thank her. 'You don't know what this means to both of us.'

'Yes, I do. Great coffee, and lots of it,' she quipped, before giving him a hard hug. It was unbelievably good to have done something for people she had come to care about.

'I've got to go and pick Leah up from Bea's. It's been raining up the valley all day so they packed up camp,' Dan said.

'Give her a hug from me.'

'You can give her one yourself tonight. Unless you've now found somewhere else to stay?'

'Not at all. I'll see you later, then.' Sarah watched him go, her heart breaking. They were well matched, if only she could believe he wanted more than an affair.

'Sarah, we've got a man coming in from the mine.

Something about a head injury,' Hamish called from the door.

'On my way.' At least she wouldn't have time to think about Dan for a while.

Dan stopped in the doorway. His heart blocked his throat. Yearning stabbed him.

Sarah sat on the edge of Cathy's bed, baby Michael in her arms, a look of wonder on her face. Deep longing was in her eyes, in the careful way she held the precious bundle, in her total absorption with the wee boy.

Dan's feet were stuck to the floor. This was what he wanted too. With Sarah. He'd told her once she'd be a great mum, and he believed it even more now.

'I want to hold Michael.' Leah's voice cut across the room, jerking Dan's attention away from this beautiful woman to find Jill and Cathy watching him with smiles on their faces.

Sarah's head came up, her eyes seeking his. 'Hi,' she whispered.

'Hi,' Dan replied softly, love winding through his gut.

Jill sat Leah beside Sarah and took the baby, helping Leah hold the enfant. They all watched Leah, saw her face light up as she peered down at Michael. Then she looked up at Dan and Dan stared back. He knew what was coming, could see it in her innocent eyes. And, like standing in the path of an oncoming avalanche, there was nothing he could do to stop it.

'Daddy, why can't we have a baby?'

Dan stepped forward, not sure what to do, what to say. 'Leah, we just can't, okay?' And he glanced at Sarah.

Her face had paled. Her hands were fists in her lap.

'Why?' Leah persisted. 'I want one.'

Sarah turned to Leah. 'You've got to have a mother to have a baby.'

Leah's eyes widened. 'Why?'

'So the baby can grow in her tummy.' Sarah grimaced.

Leah gazed at Sarah, adoration in her eyes. 'You can be the mummy. Please, Sarah, please.'

'Leah,' Dan cut across the suddenly still room. 'That's enough.'

Sarah leapt up, her face drained of all colour, her eyes wild. She shoved past Dan in the doorway and was gone, tearing down the hall.

Dan snapped at Jill, 'Watch out for Leah,' and he was racing out after Sarah.

An ache grew in Sarah's chest. Mummy. That's the only word she could hear, bouncing around in her head. Bing-bong. Mummy. Mummy.

'Sarah, wait.' Dan's deep voice boomed out behind her.

She didn't slow down at all. Hauled the outside door open, charged out into the rose gardens.

Then Dan was running beside her, matching her step for step. His hand folded around hers, but he didn't try to stop her. Instead they kept running until they reached the car park on the other side.

'Sarah,' he gasped, and then he spun around in front of her and gripped her shoulders, absorbing the force of her forward momentum as she ran into him. His arms encircled her and he held her tight, his chin on her head, his fast breaths stirring her hair.

She tried to pull away. He tightened his hold.

'Let me go.'

'Only if you agree to come with me.'

What? Where? 'Why would I go with you? If you're gong to give me a hard time for getting Leah's hopes up then do it now, get it over with.'

'Sarah.' He leaned back at the waist to look down at her. 'I want to show you something.'

'Why?' She didn't understand. What did that have to do with what Leah had just said?

His finger lifted her chin so she had to look him in the eye. 'Will you trust me on this?'

Totally perplexed, she could only nod.

Within moments they were in the Land Cruiser, tearing down the drive and out onto the main road. She sat frozen while a million questions whirled around her brain. And then the vehicle slowed, turned in through a gate, the wheels bouncing over the rough terrain.

She jerked around to stare at Dan. His finger settled over her lips. 'Shh. Save all those questions. I asked you to trust me, remember?'

She nodded slowly. What the hell was going on?

Then he was delving into the back of the vehicle, bringing her gumboots to her door. 'Put these on.' He swapped his shoes for boots. He took her hand and began leading her across the ankle-deep, wet grass.

'Here.' Dan pulled her to a stop, turned her around and dropped his arm over her shoulders. 'Look at that view. Isn't it spectacular?'

The air was misty, and behind them the sea pounded the shore. Her breath caught in her throat. 'Simply beautiful.' But?

'Imagine a house built right here, a long house with this view from every room.'

Her heart began a steady thumping. 'A house?'

'Our house, Sarah. With lots of bedrooms for all those children we want. And a huge vegetable garden over there by that old pump shed. We'd have paddocks for horses, plenty of room for a dog to run around.' His hand tightened on her shoulder, pulling her closer to him. 'What do you say?'

The thumping got louder. Her tongue slid across her bottom lip. The picture he'd just painted was so real she could taste it in the air, see it in every direction she looked. It was everything she wanted with the man she loved. She wanted to say, shout, *What about those children?* What about the CF? But he'd asked her to trust him. And she knew deep down he'd never hurt her, never abuse that trust. And if she couldn't return that trust then she shouldn't be here.

She turned, slid her arms around his neck. 'I say yes. Yes, to all of it.'

Those blue eyes lightened, that wide mouth stretched into the most beautiful smile she'd ever seen. 'I love you, Sarah, with all my heart, and then some.'

'I love you, too. You sneaked in under my skin when I wasn't looking.' She stretched up on her toes, reaching her mouth to his.

Then he stopped her short. 'I had a sample taken and sent away to be tested for the cystic fibrosis gene the other day. The result will take a while to come through.'

Her heart slowed. She'd been right to trust him. He'd never let her down, never hide from his children's needs. 'Thank you,' she whispered against his mouth before her lips claimed his.

A kiss filled with promise. Not matter what the future brought them, their love would get them through.

EPILOGUE

SARAH stopped what she was doing to stare out across the lawn of their new home down to the pounding surf on the beach beyond. Those resolutions and new beginnings she had thought impossible almost a year ago had multiplied tenfold, making her happy beyond her wildest dreams. Today would tie everything, everyone, together perfectly.

A light kick on her hand made her smile, and she looked down at the most precious gift of all. 'Hello, gorgeous.' She bent over to kiss the fat tummy in front of her.

Davey gurgled back at her and kicked her chin.

'Thanks, buster.' Now for the job that had others in the house running for the beach. Holding her beautiful, healthy son's feet, she lifted his bottom and wiped it clean.

'Ooh, poo. That's gross.' Leah danced beside her. 'Boys are disgusting.'

Dan laughed from the safety of the doorway. 'We are not.'

'Not you, Daddy. You're not a boy, you're old.'

'Thanks a lot, missy.'

'Not as old as Santa.' Leah bounced all the way across the lounge to the huge pine tree in the corner, looking sweet in her lovely gold dress. She bent over, hands on hips, inspecting the bounty underneath.

Decorated in white and gold bows, glittering balls and

curling ribbons, their Christmas tree was perfect. Many presents lay around the base, constantly being shifted and sorted by a certain impatient young madam.

At a second change table Jill snapped plastic pants in place over baby Amy's clean nappy. 'Give Leah a few years and Dan will be wishing she still thought boys were gross.'

'I'm sure you're right.' Dan ventured close enough to drop a kiss on Sarah's brow and tickle his son's tummy. 'Can I get you two ladies a drink? One for the nerves, so to speak.'

'Oh, right, now he comes near. Brave man.' Sarah grinned as she handed him the bucket containing the offensive nappy. 'And by the way, my nerves are rock steady.' But her heart ran a little faster than normal, and she hadn't been able to eat breakfast. 'I'd love some wine but guess it will have to be OJ.' Breastfeeding had put a halt to some pleasures but had given her a whole heap of new ones. Four weeks old and growing by the minute, Davey had a voracious appetite for someone so small.

Dan didn't carry the gene but, while relieved, Sarah had discovered she'd have been more than able to cope if the test result had gone the other way. With Dan, anything was possible.

Jill lifted Amy into her arms and came to stand by Sarah. 'It's going to be a long time before I'll be touching anything remotely alcoholic.'

'I thought you were giving up feeding—' Sarah saw the glow in Jill's eyes. 'Oh, Jill. You're not? When?' She hugged her closest friend, careful not to squash Amy between them.

'September again.'

'You don't waste any time, do you? What wonderful news.' Sarah turned to dress Davey in a clean nappy, then tugged on his black pants and a white shirt to match his father's.

She glanced around, looking for Dan, expecting to see him caught up talking to a guest. But, no, there he was, walking towards her, two long-stem glasses held between the fingers of one hand. Her heart rolled over, her tummy did its melting thing. Dressed in new, fitted black trousers and a crisp white shirt, he looked absolutely wonderful. Mouth-watering. Sarah pinched herself, still struggling to believe how lucky she was that she'd found this man, the one man in the world guaranteed to make her weak at the knees. And even better, a man who loved her as deeply as she loved him.

He winked at her, a long, slow wink designed to make her helpless with desire.

'You shouldn't have done that.' She smiled back the kind of sweet, wide, tip-of-teeth-showing smile that got to him every time.

Dan laughed, loud and, oh, so carefree. 'Touché.'

Jill spun around to gawp at him. 'I still can't get used to you being so relaxed that you laugh at everything.'

Picking Davey up, Sarah glanced outside again. The lawn was filling up with people. The marquee to the side also contained its share of visitors. 'Who didn't Dan invite?'

'Old Joey.' Dan answered her rhetorical question from beside her. 'Actually, I did invite him but he had to catch a trout for Christmas dinner tomorrow. That's his way of saying he doesn't like to socialise.'

'That's sad.'

Dan raised those imperious eyebrows at her. '*You* think?'

She chuckled. 'Yes, I know. I remember that night I

came home to find a party in full swing. I wanted to head out of town.'

When she'd arrived in Port Weston she'd known no one and now look at all these people. She saw Pat, Malcolm, George and Robert. Bea and John. Family, friends, the new surgeon and his young wife who'd moved into the hospital house last week in preparation to working alongside Dan and her. Never in her wildest dreams, when she'd muttered 'new beginnings' that first day parked on the cliff top, had she envisaged being part of something so wonderful, of belonging to such an extensive and caring family.

And even more surprising were those two people sitting on the couch—at opposite ends—listening earnestly to Leah's explanation about how Santa would be squeezing down the chimney that night. Sarah gently nudged her son's cheek with her nose. 'Let's go and talk to Grandpa and Grandma.'

'Here you go, Dad. Your grandson wants time with you.' She handed her father the baby, and stood with her heart in her throat, watching the awe grow in her father's eyes. Her mother shuffled along the couch to be close to Davey. Or was it to be close to Dad?

They'd come separately, but were staying in the same motel in town. George had informed Sarah her parents had been for brunch at the café—together. And that they'd talked for ages. Good, happy talk, not acrimonious stuff. George's words. Sarah could only hope her parents might find their way back to each other.

Her father looked up at her, clearing his throat. 'I did my best for you at the time.'

'I know that now, Dad.' It had taken years, and Dan, for her to learn that.

He swallowed. 'But it wasn't good enough. I'm sorry.'

No, it hadn't been, but that was all behind them. Sarah

knelt down and hugged her father and son to her. 'I wouldn't change a thing, Dad. I really wouldn't.' Otherwise she mightn't have met Dan.

A warm hand on her shoulder. Dan's breath was warm on her cheek as he leaned down to kiss her. 'Have I told you today how much I love you?'

'Hmm, let me see. Once in the shower, again after breakfast.' She stood and slid her arms around his waist. 'And definitely when you were trying to get out of changing a particularly stinky nappy.'

Dan kissed her ear lobe. 'Are we ready?'

'I've always been ready.' It had just taken a while to realise that.

'Then let's do it, Dr Livingston.'

Sarah stepped back and smoothed her ankle-length white silk dress where it touched her hips. She straightened the gold sash around her waist and leaned down to do up the straps of her pretty, thin-heeled gold sandals.

'Leah, sweetheart.' Sarah held a hand out to her daughter. 'It's time.'

Dan lifted Davey onto one arm, and took Sarah's other hand in his. He led his family outside and down the lawn. They stepped over the scattered rose petals, heading to the marriage celebrant waiting for them. On either side family and friends cheered and clapped and blew them kisses.

Tears blurred Sarah's vision and she stumbled.

Dan tightened his grip, held her from falling. 'Silly sandals. What's wrong with a pair of gumboots?'

* * * * *

SECOND CHANCE WITH THE SURGEON

ROBIN GIANNA

Thank you to Dr Ray Kobus for putting my wrist back together again!

Also thanks to the wonderful occupational therapists who helped me take it from useless, post-surgery, to close to normal. Kathy, Janet, Paula and Heather – you all are fun and fabulous! I would have expected to be thrilled, walking out the door of the therapy clinic for the last time after three months of visits, but knowing I wouldn't be seeing you anymore made it bittersweet. You all are the best! xoxo

CHAPTER ONE

"Down! Down, Hudson. *Down!*"

Apparently the dog decided he didn't need to take her seriously because she was laughing, and he enthusiastically licked her face. She gave up for a moment and hugged his big body. How was it possible he'd grown so huge, when the shelter had guessed he'd be about average-sized? She was pretty sure that average-sized dogs couldn't slap their paws on your shoulders in greeting, but then again she'd known he was special the second she'd met him.

"You're such a good boy. I'm happy to see you, too." She grinned and shoved at his paws to take a quick step sideways—only nearly to trip when her other dog, a Yorkshire Terrier not much bigger than a city rat, bit down on her pant leg.

"No snagging my pants with your little dagger teeth, Yorkie. *Off.* Off, please!"

She yanked her leg loose and the slight unsteadiness of the movement didn't embarrass her anymore, the way it had when she'd been a child and even for a long time after she'd had surgery as a teen. Growing up with her legs different lengths hadn't exactly helped her fit in with the crowd, and had invited the kind of nasty teasing bullies were infamous for. Good thing those days were over. Now most people couldn't even tell she'd been a misfit for much of her life.

She crouched down to give Yorkie a hug, too, and the rambunctious greeting from her pups made her smile. Nothing like the unconditional love of dogs, was there? You didn't have to worry whether they really wanted to be with you, or were disappointed in you, or embarrassed by you. They just loved you, period.

"All right, I know you two are bored after being stuck in here all day. But working the early shift means I'm home early today! Plenty of time for a walk before it's dark."

The word *walk* incited yipping and excitement as Jillian walked the six steps it took her to get to the tiny bedroom in her New York City apartment, where she'd barely managed to squeeze in a double bed and a small dresser. It was an apartment that hadn't been designed to hold two dogs—especially one nearly the size of a motor scooter.

Familiar pain and regret stabbed at her heart when she thought about why she was living there instead of in the much more spacious apartment she and the pups had lived in before. The place they'd shared with her ex-husband until, after barely a year, their marriage had disintegrated. The place she'd heard through the grapevine he'd sold in order to move into an even bigger penthouse apartment in an even more exclusive area of the city. A place she'd fit into even less than she had before.

But there was no point in thinking about that anymore, was there? Her short marriage was over and done with.

From the first second her eyes had met her ex-husband's she'd felt as if the ground beneath her feet had shifted. It had been an earthquake like nothing she'd experienced before and she hadn't been able to escape.

It had taken only two dates for her attraction to morph from starry-eyed to head over heels in love with the man, and they had eloped into a dizzyingly fast and wonderful wedding even as her worried inner voice had told her all along it was too good to be true. She had always known, deep inside, that she wasn't the kind of woman who could measure up to being the wife of a man like super-surgeon, jet-setting, workaholic Dr. Conor McCarthy.

Unbidden, a vision of his dazzling smile, his messy thatch of blond hair and his heartbreakingly handsome face came into her mind. She squeezed her eyes shut, willing all that sexiness to go away. The fact that she just might have to see it for real every day made her stomach physically hurt.

How could she face having to work with him again?

Last week her boss at Occupational Therapy Consultants had told her she had to go back to the company where she'd met and worked with Conor, and the horror of it had made her feel so woozy she'd had to sit down. Apparently OTC was shifting its focus to work exclusively on lower body therapy, instead of hands and wrists, which meant she had to transfer back to HOAC, the hand and arm orthopedic center owned by Conor. She knew that seeing him all the time would rip off the scab on her heart that was still healing, and she feared it might start bleeding all over again if that had to happen.

Escape was the only answer, and she prayed the job interview she had set up for next week in Connecticut would get her out of New York City and away from

Conor. Housing there would be a lot cheaper, too, which would mean a bigger place for her and the dogs. And, while she'd miss the city and her friends, a move there would be a good thing.

At least she hoped it would be good. But, regardless, there was no way she could work again at the place where she'd have to see and sometimes share patients with Conor McCarthy.

She drew in a calming breath. No point in worrying about it this second.

Banishing all those scary thoughts from her head, she quickly changed from her work clothes into leggings and sneakers and a snug jacket. It was a surprisingly nice day for December in New York City, and she planned to take advantage of every moment of it before gray skies and cold and snow blanketed the city. To enjoy every minute of this crazy and wonderful place before she had to move away.

When the dogs saw the leashes in her hands their tails wagged so hard their entire rear ends wagged along with them, and Yorkie briefly danced around on his short back legs, helping her smile again. At least she still had these two. The two puppies she and Conor had chosen together at the shelter the very first week after their honeymoon.

Her heart pinched all over again at the memory of that day, and of their seemingly idyllic perfect days together until it all had fallen apart.

"Come on, you two!" she said, practically jogging them to the elevator in her hurry to breathe in some fresh air and banish the depressing thoughts that seemed stuck on repeat. "It's warmer today than yesterday, so this walk will be a nice long one. Happy about that?"

Tongues hung out in doggie smiles as they moved out to streets still lit by the low evening sun and all walked briskly toward the park, a few blocks away.

When they turned the corner they came face to face with two black dogs almost as big as Hudson, accompanied by a small elderly man. Normally Hudson and Yorkie were good around other dogs, but the second the other two saw her animals they growled and bared their teeth, which sent Yorkie onto his rear legs, barking furiously back.

"It's okay. Okay, guys," Jill said.

She turned to see if there was any way they could quickly cross the street. But traffic streamed through the green light, and just as she was tugging the dogs around the light pole to head in a different direction, the aggressive dogs lunged.

Hudson leaped away, pulling Jill with him into a stumble, and Yorkie rushed under his legs toward the other dogs.

Trying to firmly plant her feet, she felt a slight feeling of panic fill her chest as she worked to get her two dogs reined in. She could hear the man shouting, see him trying to control his dogs, but her two had got their leashes wrapped around the light pole, and as she tried to unwrap them she was yanked off her feet.

In one split second she went from standing to slamming onto the hard concrete, catching herself with her right hand, and the moment she hit the sidewalk she cried out at the intense pain radiating up her arm.

Damn it! Squeezing her eyes shut at the searing pain and the reality of the situation, she clutched the leashes with one hand and knew, just *knew*, without a single doubt, that her wrist was broken. How was she going to handle her dogs now?

"Sorry!" the man said breathlessly.

Jill blinked up at him and could see the light had changed. Thank the Lord he was now hurrying across the street, putting distance between her dogs and his. Gingerly, she rose to a sitting position and frowned down at her already swelling wrist.

A woman leaned over her, grabbed the dogs' leashes and finished untangling them from the pole and each other. "You okay?"

"Maybe not."

Shaking now, Jill struggled to get her bag unzipped to fish for her phone. Then she realized she had no one who could come and get the dogs while she went to an ER or to urgent care. Not her OT friends, who never answered their personal phones when they were working. Not her parents, who still lived in her home state of Pennsylvania, nor her sister, who lived in New Jersey and was out of town for work.

And not Conor. Not anymore.

"I need to get home."

"I'll help you with your dogs. You live very far?"

"No. Just a couple blocks. Thank you… I… Thanks so much. I've hurt my wrist and the dogs might be hard to handle on my own."

"Happy to help. Come!" The woman gave a quick tug on the dogs' leashes and they both dutifully came to stand quietly next to her.

"You're obviously an experienced dog-handler," Jill said, trying to smile. "And at this moment my guardian angel, I think."

"Ways to be a guardian angel don't come by too

often, so you're making my day. Except that you're hurt, which I'm sure sorry has happened," she said. "I'm Barbara Smith. You need help getting up?"

"No, I... I'm okay."

Using her good hand to awkwardly push herself to her feet, Jill knew she was definitely not okay, and prayed it was a simple break. Nothing that would require surgery or weeks of the kind of therapy she helped her own patients with.

But, looking at the odd angle of her wrist, and the fact that it was already discoloring, she had a bad feeling she wouldn't be that lucky.

"Then show me where you live, dear, so you can get that wrist looked at."

"It's just a couple blocks north. I'm Jillian Keyser, by the way."

"I'd say it's nice to meet you—but the circumstances aren't very nice, are they?"

"Unfortunately, no."

Pain still radiating up her arm, she held it protectively against her stomach as they walked the few blocks to her apartment building. She didn't feel much like talking, which worked out fine because Barbara kept up a cheerful monologue about dogs and the city and the parks she often took her own animals to.

Beyond glad to finally get her pets inside the door, Jill turned to her guardian angel in the flesh. "I can't tell you how much I appreciate your help. Truly. I... I'm not sure what I'd have done if you hadn't been there when it happened."

"No thanks necessary. I was lucky to be in the right place at the right time."

"Thank you again."

The door clicked closed. Jill drew several steadying breaths before she struggled one-handedly to get the dogs fresh water, then debated what to do next.

The surgery center she'd worked at before her divorce had some of the best hand and wrist surgeons in New York City. One of them being her ex-husband. She'd been at her job at OTC for ten months, which had given her some idea about the other surgeons out there, but the truth was she felt more comfortable reaching out to someone she knew well. Someone she knew would fit her in right away for an X-ray, and who wouldn't blab about it to Conor McCarthy if Jill asked her not to.

She grabbed her cell phone, drew another deep breath, then dialed HOAC. The awkwardness of doing it made her think about how hard it was going to be to function with only one usable hand. Her years of working as an occupational therapist had told her a lot about how handicapping it was, but she had a feeling that having her own struggles would be eye-opening.

"Hi, this is Jillian Keyser. I used to be a OT there. Hey, Katy! Yeah, long time no see. Um…can I speak with Dr. Beth Crenshaw? Believe it or not, I'm pretty sure I've broken my wrist."

"Looks like a fairly light surgery schedule today," Conor McCarthy said to the two other orthopedic surgeons in the men's locker room as they changed into scrubs.

"Yeah. Glad the snow and ice season is coming. It's good for business," Bill Radcliff joked.

Conor couldn't help but chuckle, knowing Bill was kidding. "Don't let your patients hear that, or it'll be all over social media how you like to see people slip and fall so you can fix them up."

"It's an unfortunate reality that our jobs entail being there for people after they hurt themselves, and my patients love me for it." Bill grinned. "Always confounded, though, by the folks who decide to take up running in the winter, instead of getting into the groove while the weather's nice. Wouldn't you love to know what percentage end up falling and breaking something?"

"Yeah…"

The mention of runners made Conor think of Jillian, which sent all amusement from his chest, leaving it feeling hollow. A vision of her slender body in running tights or shorts that showed her shapely legs immediately came into his mind, along with her beautiful smile and the cute messy bun she always wore her hair in when she ran.

He'd loved seeing that bun bounce as she ran out the door almost every day, probably trying to make up for not being able to run for so many years. She'd told him that after the leg-length discrepancy she'd been born with had been surgically repaired in her teens, running had been the first thing she'd wanted to do. He'd always admired the hell out of her for her determination to overcome what some would have thought a handicap.

The ache in his chest almost physically hurt, and he dropped his hand when he realized he'd been unconsciously rubbing it over his sternum, as though he could somehow soothe his stupid broken heart. He'd have expected that after nearly a year apart he wouldn't be reminded of her by the least thing, but obviously he was nowhere near getting over Jillian Keyser.

"You close to finalizing that deal with Urgent Care

Manhattan to partner with us? That would be huge, if they could move in next door now that the space is vacant," Bill said. "We're all counting on you making it happen."

"I have a meeting with them today, as a matter of fact. Hoping to close on it soon—before our competition woos them with an offer they think they can't refuse."

"I know you have a lot on your plate, but you're still planning to be chairman once the companies merge, right? With you there, making sure they're both managed the way they should be, I've got my check already written as an investor."

"Believe me, I'm going to make it happen and I'll have them running as smooth as a Wall Street banker. So get your checkbook ready."

Conor took a last swig of coffee and headed toward the OR to find his surgery schedule. Studying the paper in his hand, he walked past several patients being prepped for surgery in cubicles only partly curtained off—and then the sound of a woman speaking caught his ears and he stopped dead.

He turned to see the owner of the melodic voice and felt his heart drop into his stomach. Her body was wrapped in a hospital gown, her usual sweet smile was on her face, and her hair tumbled across her cheek as she exchanged comments with the prep nurse and an anesthesiologist.

"Jillian? What the...?"

She looked up and his eyes met the gorgeous ones he'd missed so much. A mesmerizing mix of green and gray and gold—like clouds on the horizon with the sunlight shimmering through.

Damn it. The connection between them was still

there. In spite of everything he could feel the electric zing of it, and his breath caught in his lungs.

Then she blinked, and her gaze shifted to the hallway behind him. Her smile flatlined and her lips twisted into a grimace before she looked at him again, cool now, all that feeling of connection gone.

"Oh. Hi, Conor. I… I broke my wrist. Distal radius fracture. Beth is putting in a plate and screws this morning to put it back together."

"How? What happened?"

"I took the dogs for a walk. A couple of big dogs weren't very friendly, Yorkie freaked out, and we got all tangled up—next thing you know, I'm flat on the sidewalk."

"Ah, hell. Is it your right hand?" He stepped closer to reach for it carefully, and the feel of her soft hand in his felt so good his heart got all twisted up—which bothered him no end.

What was wrong with him? No matter how hard he'd fallen for her, he should never have married Jillian in the first place. He'd learned the hard way that he wasn't husband material any more than his father had been, obviously having inherited his bad DNA. He'd had a selfish, cold father and a mother who'd twisted herself into knots trying to somehow make his father happy—until the day he'd left. Which had made a bad home situation dramatically worse.

Their eyes met again, and he knew the pain and sadness he saw there had nothing to do with her wrist and everything to do with him. God knew he'd wanted his own marriage to be different. But she'd been right to leave. The last thing a special woman like Jillian needed was to be tied to a man who made her miserable.

Except he couldn't lie to himself. In the ten months since she'd been gone he'd thought of her every day and every night, missing her even as he'd forcibly reminded himself how much he'd hurt her. Disappointed her.

"Yeah. No fun, but I'll get through it."

"Titanium time!" Dr. Beth Crenshaw appeared in the curtained doorway with a grin that faltered a little when she saw Conor standing there. "Hey, Conor. Surprise, surprise, huh?"

"Definitely a surprise." It took some effort to release Jill's hand before he folded his arms across his chest. "Why is it no one has told me this happened? That Jill is having surgery here today?"

"Because I asked her not to tell you," Jill said in a stiff voice. "No reason for you to know."

The truth of that stabbed his chest all over again. "Maybe not, but I would have liked to know anyway. Who's taking you home post-op?"

As soon as he asked the question his heart jolted. If she had a new guy Conor hoped and prayed he wouldn't have to see him with her in Recovery.

"I asked Ellie next door. She's the only person I know who has a car."

"Wait. Isn't she the one who's about eighty and has a bum knee?"

Her lips twisted again, this time in a wry smile. "I know it's not ideal, taking advantage of her good nature when she has a tough time getting around. But they won't let me take a taxi by myself, as you well know."

"You should have told me you were having trouble finding someone," Beth said. "I can take you home. You'll just have to hang around in Recovery until the end of the day. You'll still be partially out of it for a bit, anyway. I assume you have a friend to take care of you tonight? You know you shouldn't be alone."

"I think Kandie from the other office is planning to stop by and check on me at some point. And my sister's coming sometime later this week. But she's got a big project at work and can't take off right now."

"I can't believe you haven't figured all this out already." Conor looked from Jill to Beth, then back. "She'll be coming back tomorrow to get the cast off, right? And what about the dogs? Plus, your sister's work schedule is almost as bad as mine, so how can you count on her to get here soon?"

"You know, I appreciate your concern, but frankly I don't see how this is any of your business," Jill said, her chin jutting out with that mulish look he was all too familiar with. At the same time he could see plain as day that she felt anxious about how she was going to manage everything post-op. "The dogs and I will be okay."

"Considering you've seen hundreds of patients, and know how they feel the day the cast comes off and you work with them to make a splint, I'm pretty sure you know how much pain you'll likely be in. How completely non-functional your arm and hand will be at first. Hudson's a big lug—not to mention there's no way you can take them outside for a walk. Not for quite a while—until your bones and the titanium plate and screws have fused. If you fall again before that happens it could be a disaster."

"I won't fall. And there are dog-walking services, you know," Jill said. "I… I didn't think to look one up before surgery, but I'm sure I can find one. And, like I said, Briana is coming as soon as she can."

"Let me check to see if there's a nurse or one of the

office staff who wouldn't mind making some cash by helping you tonight and bringing you back tomorrow. Walking the dogs, too," Beth said, looking from him to Jill, then back. "Meanwhile, we have to get you into twilight sleep and to the OR—or the whole day's schedule will be messed up, which nobody wants."

Obviously Beth's calm tone was designed to keep Conor from getting upset about this, but it wasn't working. Jillian might not be his anymore, but that didn't mean he didn't still care about her. Wouldn't worry about her.

"I have a light surgery schedule this morning, so I can take you home," he said. "Though I do have a—"

Abruptly, he closed his mouth. He'd almost followed his comment about taking her home by telling her he had an appointment at one o'clock with some of the decision-makers from Urgent Care Manhattan, to go over the details of the potential collaboration with HOAC. Telling her that he'd take her home when the meeting was over. But his work and business schedules had been part of the reason why she'd left and how badly he'd failed her.

But this was an emergency, damn it. Much as he hated any delay in getting the deal closed, his competitor shut out and the urgent care department up and running, he'd just have to reschedule the meeting.

"I'll come to Recovery as soon as I'm done with my last surgery and I'll take you home. Get you settled."

"Conor, no." Despite her obvious need, her beautiful eyes widened in clear dismay. "I—"

"Perfect," Beth interrupted cheerfully. "I'll meet you in Recovery. And now, Jill, it's time for Dr. Fixit to fix you up."

Jillian opened her pretty lips to protest more, which tightened his chest. Was it really that horrifying for her to have to spend a few hours with him?

Conor watched the anesthesiologist administer twilight anesthesia through Jill's IV. Her long lashes swept her cheeks as her lids slid closed, and he forced himself to turn away from her beautiful face in sweet repose. She looked very much as she had back when he'd held her in his arms every night as she fell asleep.

Damn. That ache pressed in on his chest again, but at the same time his heart strangely, bizarrely, lifted. He was going to get to be with her this evening for the first time in nearly a year. Drugged up and in pain, she wouldn't be like the smiling Jillian he'd loved. But knowing that she needed help, that he could be there for her at least for a few hours, made him feel better than he'd felt in a long time.

And never mind that the hollow loneliness he knew he'd experience when he went back to his regular life without her in it might feel every bit as bad as when she'd first left.

CHAPTER TWO

CONOR DOUBLE-PARKED IN the loading zone outside Jillian's apartment building and prayed he wouldn't get a ticket—or, worse, towed. Presumably it wouldn't take long to get her into her apartment and comfortable, and he could get the car to the parking garage down the street after that.

He jumped out of the car and ran around to open the passenger door. "Okay, I know you're still feeling weak and weird, so I'm going to hold you up in case your legs feel wobbly."

Her eyes blinked up at him and she nodded. He reached into the car to place his hands around her waist, pretty much lifting her out of the seat—which wasn't easy, considering she couldn't help much and he was worried about jostling her arm. Not that he needed to be concerned that he'd hurt her. It was covered in a cast and an elastic cover and would stay totally numb from the nerve-block for at least twelve hours.

"You're doing great," he said as she walked slowly beside him to the front doors of the building, keeping his arm wrapped around her waist to keep her steady.

Thank God he'd had the foresight to get her keys before they got out of the car. It would have been a serious juggling match trying to get them out of the pocket of the jacket he'd draped over her shoulders without her falling down right there on the concrete steps.

Once they were in the building, maneuvering her to her apartment wasn't difficult. He'd only been there once—the day he'd brought the dogs over to live with her after she'd moved out—but he remembered exactly where it was. Had often pictured her there when he was lying in bed at night. Wondering how she was doing. Wishing he was a different kind of man. Wishing things could have gone differently for them. Wishing she hadn't stubbornly refused any money from him so she could live in a bigger place. He had hoped she was happier now, even as the thought of her being happy with someone else tore him up inside.

The moment he unlocked her door he heard the dogs running across the hardwood floor. Worried that Hudson might accidentally knock her over in her current wobbly state, he turned her sideways and put his body in between them as a buffer, reaching to scratch the dog's head.

"Sit, Hudson. That's a good dog. Good boy."

It tugged at his heart that the dog obviously remembered him, whining and thrashing his tail back and forth so hard his hind end went along with it. Yorkie leaped up and down on his short legs, too, equally excited to see him.

Damn it. Letting down Jillian had been the worst, but the dogs' happy greeting reminded him he'd let them down, too. She'd wanted them to have dogs and he'd gone along with it. Had wanted her to be happy. Wanted to know what it would be like to live a completely different kind of life from the one he'd grown up in. To love someone who loved you back and have a family that was always there for one another.

Instead he'd turned out to be a bad husband and bad dog dad, incapable of giving any of them what they needed. Thank God they hadn't had children for him to hurt, too. He'd failed at being there for his mother the way he should have been, and he had failed at being there for Jillian.

That dismal reality had shown him that the focus of his life had to be only on what he was good at—and that was surgery and business and building his bank account and portfolio. Lonely, maybe, but at least he wouldn't hurt the people he loved. He believed providing for them financially, for their future, was the best way to show his love.

Jillian hadn't agreed.

"Sit. Sit, you two."

He held up his hand to signal that he meant it, the way the dog trainers had shown him and Jill when they'd first gotten the puppies. Jillian tripping over the excited animals on their way to the sofa would *not* be good, and he was both glad and surprised that they actually did as he told them to.

"Jill, we're going to walk to the sofa. I'll be holding on to you, so try not to trip over Yorkie if he jumps around again."

"Okay. I'm not as unsteady as you think I am."

"That's good. But I'll hold on to you anyway."

Because the feel of her body in his arms felt better than anything had in a long time, even as the ache of his failures burned in his chest.

He eased her down on to the sofa. "You feel like sitting for a while? Or do you want to lie down in bed?"

"I feel okay. Just groggy. But I want to wake up, not go to sleep. Once I'm feeling more alert you can head on home. Or back to work, probably."

"I don't have any surgeries or patients to see this afternoon. And I canceled a meeting I had scheduled, so I'm all yours."

Or he had been once.

But for today, at least, he had this chance to be there for Jillian in a way he hadn't during their marriage, although at the same time he somehow needed to keep a cool head and an emotional distance. Except looking at her now, with her arm in its huge cast, her hair all messy and her expression a little vulnerable, he wanted to scoop her into his arms, sit on that sofa and hold her close. Kiss her face and stroke her hair until she relaxed against him.

Bad idea for both of them.

He cleared his throat. "You hungry? How about a little soup and toast, or something like that?"

"Maybe in a little bit. I'll just sit here for now. Why don't you take the dogs out? Their leashes are in that basket by the front door."

"Okay. Come on, you goofs."

Wagging tails and little leaps from Yorkie had him smiling despite the weight he felt in his chest at being here. At the memories of him and Jill during happy times together. He'd never expected to be a dog person, but he had loved spending time with them. Loved seeing how much Jill enjoyed them. In some ways that seemed like a long time ago, and in other ways it seemed like yesterday that they'd lived together and loved one another until it had all imploded.

Heaving a sigh, he took the dogs outside. They were

better behaved on their walk than he remembered them being as puppies, and he had time to ponder how it was going to work out, him helping Jill. He was pretty confident that she'd be okay on her own most of the time, so long as he saw her every morning and evening and took care of the dogs until her sister showed up.

Problem was her apartment was a long way from work, while his was just a couple blocks away from the surgery center. Somehow he'd have to find extra hours in the day, or look for someone to walk the dogs.

The animals were panting by the time they got back to Jill's door, and he pulled her key from his pocket and tried to open the door quietly, in case she was sleeping—then wondered why he'd bothered when both dogs leaped into the room, making all kinds of racket on the wood floor.

Her eyes were closed when he looked across the room at her, but her lids lifted and she sent him a surprisingly sweet smile. Probably because the drugs hadn't worn off enough for her to remember that she didn't like him much anymore.

"Seems like you just left. Were the dogs good?"

"Really good. You've done a nice job training them."

"Don't think I can take a lot of credit. They just needed to mature a little bit. But they still have their moments, believe me."

"Moments like when they get upset at other dogs and get tangled up and make you fall and break your wrist?"

"Yeah. Like that."

Her lips curved even more, into the kind of laughing smile he'd fallen for like a ton of bricks when they'd first met, and it felt good to smile back.

He stepped closer and crouched down in front of her. "How you feeling?"

"Arm feels like someone attached a log to me. Can't feel it at all yet. Sometimes I forget and lean down, then it swings out and I have to grab it back. I know you always tell patients that's what it'll feel like, but I've gotta tell you... Much as it makes me want to laugh when I lose control of it, it feels super-weird."

"It'll be numb like that for at least another eight or nine hours. Then it'll feel tingly, like you've laid on it funny and it's gone to sleep. Then it'll finally feel normal."

"I think you mean my *new normal*—for now. Painful and immobile."

"Yeah." He stood and shoved his hands into his pockets so he wouldn't reach out and tuck those wisps of hair behind her ears, as he would have before. "You feel like eating something now? I can get some soup from the deli? Or does something else sound good?"

"Something light, like soup and crackers, sounds perfect."

"You got it."

It would be good to have something to do besides talk with her and look at her. From the first moment he'd seen her in the occupational therapy room two years ago, he felt like he'd been smacked in the head by some unexplainable force. She'd stood up from the table, her athletic runner's body in a slim-fitting dress, and her laughter at something her patient had said slipped into his chest. When her beautiful gray-green eyes had lifted to meet his he could have sworn his heart completely stopped.

Looking down at her now, he felt waves of tenderness mingle with memories of that day. He wished that he could take away the pain he knew she'd be in as soon as the brachial plexus block wore off. Felt the desire to pull her close, to take care of her, to make all that pain go away.

"I'll be right back."

He made himself turn away before he reached for her, and then left for the deli. He chose two kinds of the soup he knew she liked, and a bagful of crackers. When he came back and opened the door to her apartment he stopped abruptly when he saw she wasn't on the sofa, and neither one of the dogs were in sight, either.

No way would she have decided to venture out while still half drugged up. Would she?

A panicked sensation rose in his chest and he strode to the galley kitchen, shoved the food onto the counter, then moved to her bedroom. "Jill? Jilly?"

One of the dogs whined before she answered. "In here. The bathroom. I... Go ahead and come in."

He pushed open the door. Was stunned to see both dogs and Jillian sitting on the floor of the tiny room. Her sweatpants were twisted around her thighs and her good hand was held to her forehead.

He dropped to his knees. "What the hell happened? Did you hurt yourself?"

"Kind of. I'm so stupid. I had to go to the bathroom, and while I was sitting here I dropped the new roll of toilet paper. I leaned over to get it. Forgot all about my arm. It flung forward and dragged me off the toilet. I landed right on my cast and hit my head on the wall. Kind of funny, really."

She sent him an adorable crooked smile and his heart

squeezed even tighter. He grasped her wrist to lift her palm from her forehead. "Let me see."

"Just a bump. Not a big deal."

"Maybe not compared to your broken wrist, but it still hurts, I bet." He wanted to lean down and kiss the offending red lump, and drew in a deep breath to quell the urge. "Let's get some ice on it."

He wrapped his arm around her back to help her up, and realized she was having trouble standing.

"You hurt your leg, too?"

"No. I just... I couldn't get my stupid pants pulled up using only one hand while sitting on the floor."

He lifted her to her feet. "Hang on to the sink while I finish pulling them up so you can walk."

"This is ridiculously embarrassing," she said, her face now stained pink and no longer smiling. "My ex-husband having to pull up my pants."

"Just think of me as your doctor. Not a big deal."

Logically, it shouldn't be. But the truth...? The sight of the smooth skin of her thighs, of her round rear peeking out from beneath her panties and all the memories it conjured, made him want to tug those pants down, not up, and touch her and kiss her until neither of them could breathe.

He gritted his teeth and pulled up the sweatpants as fast as possible, before lifting her into his arms to move them toward the sofa. The scent of her wafted to his nose and he breathed her in. Who'd have thought the woman could smell so good after being in surgery and then Recovery half the day? But it wasn't perfume, it was simply her, and he remembered it so well it seemed they'd been holding one another just yesterday.

Damn it.

"I can walk," she protested.

"Yes, but this is easier and faster, and there's no risk of additional injury." He sat her on the sofa again. "I'll get some ice for your head, then you can have some soup."

"I don't need ice. It's just a little lump."

"Trust the doctor. You need to ice it."

"I see Dr. Bossy is alive and well."

Her pretty lips tipped into a smile as she rolled her eyes and the tightness in his chest loosened. He had to grin, remembering all the times she'd given him that look.

"I consider the nickname Dr. Bossy to be a compliment. Where are your plastic bags?"

"In the second drawer, next to the refrigerator."

Once a bag was filled with ice and wrapped in a towel he sat close beside her. Slipped strands of hair away from the bruise before he placed the bag on it. Their eyes met and he nearly forgot to place the bag on her injury, wanting so much to kiss her instead.

"That's cold!"

Thank God for that distraction.

"Ice generally is cold. It'll help with the swelling and make it feel better."

"Yeah, well, right now my forehead hurts way more from the ice than the bruise."

"Once your skin is numb it won't hurt anymore."

"Says the surgeon who lies to his patients about pain every day."

"Lies to my patients? I never lie. I may downplay what they're going to experience so they don't freak out, but I never lie."

"You forget I've heard you talk to patients when

they're in occupational therapy." Her voice went into a bass tone. *"Well, sir, your bones are healing nicely and the ligaments are stretching out well. In no time your fingers are going to be playing the piano again. You don't play piano? Well, because of my magical surgical skills now you will."*

He had to laugh at her words and her cutely ridiculous expression. "I don't believe I've ever said that to a patient."

"No? I do sometimes. It's an occupational therapy joke that most people enjoy."

"And that's one of the many reasons why your patients think you're wonderful."

He knew they did. Her numerous thank-you notes and high patient satisfaction scores proved that. He'd always thought she was pretty wonderful, too, even though she hadn't believed it.

"Feeling any less painful?"

"Um…yes, actually."

He watched her lids slide closed and held himself very still so he wouldn't stroke her soft cheek or lean in to kiss her, which he suddenly wanted to do more than he wanted to breathe.

"Thank you. I'll take over holding it now." Her hand covered his on the ice before he slid his away.

"I'll warm your soup. Which do you want—chicken noodle or tomato basil?"

"I love both—as you know." She opened her eyes and turned to him, her expression serious. "I appreciate all this. I do. It's…awkward me being here with you, and I know it's awkward for you, too. I'm sorry about that. But I realize you were right. You bringing me home was lots better than trying to have my neighbor do it.

She wouldn't have been able to steady me the way you did. Or pick me up off the floor and bring me food, and walk the dogs and all. So thank you."

"No thanks necessary. I…we might not be together anymore, but I'll always care about you."

And the truth of that made his throat close and sent him to the kitchen to busy himself and get her some food before he showed her exactly how much he still cared.

He helped her move to one of the two chairs at the tiny table placed at one end of the living room. "You comfortable enough to eat here? Or do you want to sit in your armchair and drink the soup from a mug?"

"This is okay. Smells wonderful."

"I'll take the dogs out again while you eat. Don't try to get up until I get back, promise? We won't be gone long."

She nodded, and he escaped with an urge to kiss the top of her head before he went, as he often had when he'd left for work or meetings in the past.

The dogs were excited to be outside again, and he wondered how often Jill had to walk them. Did she take them on her runs sometimes? Probably only Hudson would be up for that. Yorkie might have a big attitude, but there was no way his short little legs could handle the miles Jill logged.

Probably he should keep the dogs out longer, but he felt an uncomfortable niggle, worrying about Jill and how she was doing all alone, and hurried back after only about twenty minutes.

Seeing her still sitting at the table when he nudged open the door had him smiling in relief.

"I see you're being a good patient."

"Did you doubt me?"

The smile she sent back held a hint of the mischievous Jill he'd adored.

"I'm limiting myself to one event per day of finding myself on the floor."

"How about trying for zero events? The first one about gave me a heart attack."

"I'm still sitting here, aren't I? By the way, Kandie called and she said she can stop by after work tonight to check on me, see if I need anything. How would you feel about taking the dogs to your place until Briana gets here? I mean, I know you're super-busy, but you can hire a dog walker to take them out while you're at work. It…it wouldn't be for long."

How much he didn't want to leave her or the dogs shocked him, and his feet seemed rooted to the floor even as he'd been thinking about how difficult it was to be here with her.

"Is Kandie spending the night?"

"No, of course not. She has a young son, and there's no reason for her to do that."

"Post-op orders are for you not to be alone tonight."

"I feel okay. Barely woozy from the pain meds now. I'll be fine."

"Is the woman who just fell in the bathroom actually saying this?" He stared at her. "You'll need to take meds when you go to bed, to help with the pain when the block wears off. And what if you fall again with nobody here?"

"That's not going to happen."

"It did happen—and, since you're a smart woman, you know that's not something you can assume."

He folded his arms across his chest, ignoring her

mulish expression. Two could play at the stubborn game, and he had no intention of losing because the thought of her lying hurt and alone chilled his blood.

He realized there was only one solution that would solve the problem, difficult though it might be.

"You and the dogs are coming home with me, and staying there until your sister comes."

CHAPTER THREE

JILL'S HEART BUMPED hard against her ribs, then seemed to stop for a moment before revving up again. Stay at Conor's place? Be close to him for hours on end, reminded of all the good and bad parts of their marriage and why it had fallen apart?

"No." A feeling of panic filled her chest. "I'm not doing that. Period."

"It's the only thing that makes sense. I live just a couple blocks from HOAC. Tomorrow morning you'll get your cast off and have a splint made, then you'll be able to easily go back to my apartment and get some rest."

"*No*. There's no way—"

"Listen to me."

He pulled the other chair close to her and leaned forward. His expression was earnest and determined, and she'd learned from the past that trying to fight him when he'd made up his mind would be like beating her head against a brick wall, bringing another bruise. But that kind of bruise wouldn't hurt nearly as badly as the one on her heart.

"I get that you want to limit how much time we spend together—I do, too, to be honest. But remember my work hours that you hated so much? I'll hardly be around—just enough to make sure you're okay overnight. To walk with you to your appointment tomorrow morning. I'll find someone who wants to make some extra cash by checking on you when I'm not there and walking the dogs. It'll work out until your sister gets here. By then you'll be off the pain meds and able to stay alone."

She absorbed his words. The logic behind them. Her apartment was a good half-hour trek away from the center on the subway. When the numbness wore off and her cast was replaced by a splint she'd be in pain and still a little drugged up. Plus, she knew from talking with her patients that the challenge of trying to function with one hand wasn't going to be easy—especially with no one around to help.

Time for her to act like the mature and reasonable woman she was trying to be. The one who was fighting her insecurities and who didn't want or need a relationship until she'd dealt with all the baggage her marriage to Conor had proved she still carried around.

And maybe it wouldn't be too awful. He worked so much she'd probably hardly see him. Finding someone else to help her and take care of the dogs, with him basically an overnight watchdog for the next few days, was the logical solution.

Rock versus hard place. That described the situation to a T. She couldn't deny that trying to stay here alone, with her arm still in the nerve block, and then somehow making her way to the orthopedic center all by herself in the morning wouldn't be easy, even if she took a taxi.

"All right." She heaved out a resigned sigh, shoving down the dread that came along with it. "I know you're right. I shouldn't be alone right now. Just for a day or two, though. Then I'll come back here, and you can keep the dogs until Briana comes."

"Thank you." He stood and looked down at her, his expression hard to read. "I'll clean up the dishes while you rest."

Hating this whole scene, she reached for her spoon but managed to knock it off the table instead. Apparently clumsiness was part of this whole experience, and she sighed as she leaned over to pick it up off the floor. As she did so, her stupid dead arm swung out.

Yorkie had been standing there, waiting to see if some treat might be offered, and her arm in its heavy cast hit the poor pup right on his little nose, knocking him sideways to the floor as he yelped.

"Oh, dear! I'm so sorry! Aw, come here, Yorkie." She reached out her good hand and was glad he came over to let her pet him, clearly not holding a grudge.

"Damn. That thing is a lethal weapon," Conor said as he stepped away from the sink. He reached for her numb arm, currently held in a sling, and placed it back against her stomach. "Poor dog. And poor you."

He gathered up Yorkie, tucked him under his arm and scratched behind his ears, with an indulgent smile on his face which sent another stab to her chest.

This was the sweetness she'd fallen head over heels in love with. The thoughtful and considerate man who had treated her like a princess during that brief month they'd dated before they'd impulsively, excitingly, got married. The man who hadn't even particularly wanted the dogs, never having had a pet, but who'd wanted her to be happy. And then had seemed to so enjoy playing with them for the few hours a week he'd been free.

A thick lock of blond hair tumbled onto his forehead

as he talked to Yorkie, and remembering how they'd felt about each other not too long ago made her heart pinch. How in the world were they going to handle spending time together again?

A deep fatigue crept through her bones and she found herself folding her good arm onto the table and leaning her head on it. Tonight and the next few days couldn't go by fast enough.

A large hand rested softly on her temple, its fingers caressing the top of her head. "You've had a big day. Let's get your overnight things packed up. The sooner you can get to bed, the better."

"All right. But you don't need to help. I can do it."

"Three hands are better than one." He sent her a lop-sided grin. "Show me where your suitcase is and we'll get it done."

It seemed to take longer than it should to pack a few clothes and toiletries, but of course there were the dogs' things to get, too. Their beds, with Hudson's being a big armful, their food and bowls, their leashes... Finally Conor had everything stowed in the car and had come back to help her to the curb.

"You want me to water your plants before we go?"

"Water my plants?" She stared, astonished he would have thought of that. "You never even liked all the plants I brought to...to our apartment before."

"Just wasn't used to having living things around that needed attention." His smile disappeared. "And that was a poor choice of words, wasn't it?"

She knew he was referring to her. To her neediness and insecurities during their marriage. Something she wasn't proud of. "Accurate choice. And I'm working on all that."

"Nothing you ever needed to work on. I told you that. It was all me."

Not true, and she knew it, but it was ancient history. "Anyway… I just watered the plants a few days ago, so they'll be fine until I get back."

"Let's go, then."

He helped her down the narrow stairwell of her apartment, then eased her into the plush front seat of his car. "It's going to be a tight squeeze to get both dogs in the back seat, but they'll be okay, don't you think?"

"They haven't been in a car since…you know. When you brought them here." Lord, this was feeling more awkward by the moment. "But I think they'll be fine."

In minutes he'd returned with the dogs, who bounded into the back seat with excitement. Jillian had to laugh at how comical it was to see Hudson pretzeled in there, but his doggie grin showed he didn't mind a bit.

"This reminds me of a clown car," she said, glad to have the dogs to talk about. "How many Hudsons can you fit in a luxury sedan?"

"I believe the answer is one." Conor grinned as he slid into the driver's seat. The purr of the powerful engine competed with the sounds of the city as they drove through streets now brightly lit through the dark night sky.

Jillian wanted to ask where his new apartment was, but decided to stay silent, since she'd be finding out soon enough. Besides, he'd said it was close to HOAC, and that was only one block away from Central Park.

The car came to a stop in front of an old stone apartment building and Jillian's throat closed. Yes, the man had upgraded all right. As though his last apartment hadn't been prestigious enough…

"Your new apartment is off Fifth Avenue? Wow."

"It's a good location for work and a good investment."

He slid out of the car as a valet came from the building. She could see him talking to the man, who nodded and opened the back door to get the dogs as Conor helped her from her seat.

"Alfred will bring your suitcase and the dogs' stuff up, then get the car parked."

"You've really been slumming it, having to juggle with illegal parking in front of my place and walking up and down a bunch of crooked steps, haven't you?" she said, trying to bring some levity into this distinctly uncomfortable situation.

"I slummed it for plenty years of my life," he said quietly. "And *you're* the one who wouldn't accept any money from me after our divorce. Which still upsets me. I wanted you to live in a better and bigger place, but you hated me too much to take even a cent."

"I never hated you. I just felt there was no reason for you to give me anything. Our marriage was a mistake for both of us and I just wanted to move on, like it didn't happen."

"But it *did* happen." He held her hand and looked down at her. "And I'm more sorry than you'll ever know that I made you so unhappy."

If felt as if her heart was shaking inside her chest. They'd both contributed to their mutual miseries, hadn't they? Definitely not all his fault. Something she'd come to see even more clearly over the past ten months.

"Conor, listen. I—"

The dogs leaped from the car, with Alfred holding their leashes, and Conor stepped over to take them. She wasn't sure exactly what she'd been going to say, but was glad the dogs had interrupted. Everything had been said that needed to be said—or at least most of it. Hashing over it again would make both of them sad or mad or critical or defensive—just like before. None of those emotions would accomplish a thing—especially considering she had to stay at his apartment for a night or two.

Cool and calm was the way to go. Starting now.

Conor led the way to the elevator, which opened on to a floor with only two doors in the hallway. Obviously his new place was way bigger than even his other apartment. He unlocked one of the doors and gestured for her to go inside.

"I'll keep the dogs out here for a second, so they don't knock you over on the way in."

"They're not that bad. Though it's true that they seem pretty excited to be checking out a new place."

It was like stepping into something from a magazine. He'd clearly decided to start over completely, since not a single thing in the entire space looked familiar. Modern furniture in neutral tones sat near floor-to-ceiling windows that looked out over the twinkling lights of the city, and beyond the curve of the windows was a huge kitchen with an island and bar stools. It was surprisingly as comfortable-looking as it was breathtaking, and she wondered how his designer had accomplished that feat.

A familiar hollow feeling weighed down her stomach. The same weight she'd carried to every highbrow event they'd attended, knowing she'd never fit in to Conor McCarthy's life.

"It's…beautiful. Really gorgeous. Congratulations."

"Thanks. I like it." He unleashed the dogs, who instantly ran around, sniffing the room, then grasped her elbow. "How about sitting down until Alfred brings your things? Then you should take your pain meds and get to bed."

"Okay. I admit I feel pretty tired."

"I'd offer you a glass of the wine you like, but it's not a good idea to mix it with drugs," he said, a slight smile curving his mouth.

"Are you sure? Because a glass of wine sounds pretty good."

She was kidding, though at that moment she thought maybe mixing alcohol and painkillers would be a good way for her to completely pass out and not have to deal with how strange this felt.

He shook his head, probably knowing exactly how she was feeling since he doubtless felt the same way. Soon Alfred brought everything up, and Conor placed the dog beds at one end of the room, then filled their water bowls and placed them on the stone-tiled kitchen floor. Enthusiastic slurping by Hudson left puddles all around it.

"Being the neatnik you are, I guess you're glad to not to have to deal with doggie messes anymore."

"I got used to the messes. The dogs were always fun to be around."

But she hadn't been so fun to be around, which was why he'd been gone all the time.

The words came into her head but she fiercely banished them. This was the baggage she had to unload. These damned insecurities that flew into her head with the least provocation. Making a simple statement about the dogs, making small talk, didn't mean she should take it personally, the way she had before. That had to stop.

"I...um...guess I'll go to bed now."

"Good idea. I'll show you your room. Mine's at the end of the hall. If you need me for anything in the middle of the night, just yell."

"I'll be okay." And even if she wasn't she wouldn't call for him unless it was a dire emergency.

He carried her small suitcase as he led her down a hallway covered with lush carpeting, then went through the door of yet another beautiful room with a different view of the city. Two chairs and a table formed a small sitting area in one corner, with a large bed in the center, and another door that doubtless led to a bathroom.

He set her suitcase on a folding thing obviously designed for that purpose. "Okay if I get your things out? I want you to take the pain pills right now, so they're working when the plexus block starts to wear off. Then I'll help you undress."

Her eyes lifted to his. They held only a cool detachment. No sign of what the words had made her feel, which was her belly jumping, her breath catching and her heart beating a little harder.

"I'm sure I can get ready by myself."

"Yeah? With that thing on your arm and it held in a sling? No way."

"Then I'll just sleep in what I'm wearing," she said. "I won't be the first patient to arrive at the clinic wearing the same clothes they wore for surgery."

"Suit yourself. But you're going to be overly warm and uncomfortable in that sweatshirt. And you'll need something with no sleeve to wear over the cast tomorrow when they take it off." He shrugged, seeming to not care one way or the other.

She knew he was right—damn it. "Fine. Can you pull the sleeve off over my cast?"

He did as she asked, carefully removing the sling, then pulling the sleeve off her arm before reaching for the bottom of her sweatshirt. He gently slipped it up and over her head, exposing the camisole she wore beneath. He seemed to be concentrating on the sweatshirt, but when his eyes met hers for a long, suspended moment his expression made it hard to breathe, and she was beyond glad when he turned to grab her toiletries bag from her suitcase.

"I'll get you some water for the pain meds."

The speed with which he strode from the room told her she hadn't imagined it. This crazy situation was reminding both of them of things better left forgotten.

He returned with a glass of water and wordlessly handed it to her. "Take a drink, then I'll hold the glass and you can pop the pills."

Even taking pills with only one hand required either help or juggling, and she hoped and prayed her hand would be usable sooner than some of her patients experienced.

"Thanks."

"Think you'll need help to go to the bathroom?"

"I'm sure I'll be fine. Goodnight."

Her face burned all over again, and she could feel his eyes on her as she went into the chic bathroom and closed the door, leaning back against it. She stared at her toothbrush and toothpaste, sitting on the counter, and wondered how she was going to manage to put paste on the brush with only one hand, or wash her face.

Lord. How had her world gotten so messed up in one

split second? No doubt about it—the next few days, and longer, were going to be misery in more ways than one.

And being close to Conor again was definitely at the very top of the misery list.

Thank heavens Conor had insisted she take the pain medicine. At about two a.m., when the nerve-block began to wear off, the intense tingling pins and needles sensation accompanied by pain surging through her whole arm was way worse than she'd expected—even though she'd had plenty of patients complain about it.

Another dose of medicine to get her through the night left her feeling a little woozy in the morning and, as uncomfortable as she was being in his apartment, she had to acknowledge—again—that Conor had been right. If she'd tried to take the subway in to HAOC all by her lonesome to get the cast taken off, or even taken a cab, it would have been hard going, possibly even unsafe.

Except there was one significant problem she had to deal with right now. When Conor had simply and without expression stripped off her oversized sweatshirt so she could sleep comfortably in the camisole and sweats she'd worn yesterday it had been in a fairly low light, and quick enough that she hadn't had to endure feeling embarrassed, or whatever it was exactly that she'd been feeling, for very long.

This morning. Though… After struggling for a few minutes trying to get a loose short-sleeved shirt on over the giant cast, she huffed out a frustrated breath. Clearly not going to happen. What was it going to be like, trying to get dressed and undressed after the cast was off and a splint had been put on instead? Regardless, she was absolutely not going to ask Conor for help—even if it meant wearing the same clothes for days until her sister came.

Not going to cross that bridge until she came to it. But this bridge had to be crossed right now—because she couldn't exactly show up at her former workplace with only her thin camisole covering her torso.

"Um... Conor?"

She heard the rattle of cups and walked into the kitchen, ridiculously holding the shirt over her front even though he was facing the sink. As though the man hadn't seen her half naked last night and totally naked a hundred times in the past.

But they weren't together anymore, and she just couldn't feel comfortable walking around with her breasts visible through the thin fabric as if it was no big deal.

"Can you slip this over my head? Can't quite manage it."

He turned, his eyes meeting hers for a long moment, and she could tell he was thinking the same thing she was. That they were in a kitchen together, with him making coffee and her strolling in a few minutes later, just like old times. Except she wouldn't be wrapping her arms around him and kissing his back, and he wouldn't turn to pull her close, giving her a long kiss that would have the air shimmering with love and desire and sometimes would mean a quick trip back to the bedroom before they had to leave for work.

Wordlessly he stepped close, to take the shirt from her hands, and his gaze briefly slid to her breasts before he quickly tugged the shirt over her head. Gently, he took her big bandaged arm in his hand and carefully drew the short sleeve up and over it.

"How's it feeling? I assume the nerve-block has worn off?"

"Yes—and to say that did *not* feel good is an understatement. We have to be more sympathetic when patients come in to get their cast off."

"I'm always sympathetic. It's you occupational therapists who make them do stuff that hurts the very first day."

"That's our job. You get to play the good cop who does the miracle repair surgery, putting them back together, and we have to be the bad cop, making them do stuff to help them get it usable again. Which unfortunately means some pain."

"I'm sorry you're going to have to go through that pain yourself now."

For several seconds he skimmed his fingers across her cheek, before dropping his hand to his side, and the tension between them faded a little as he gave her a small smile.

"You being the bad cop when you were on the PT side of the table is maybe true, but you were always a very sweet bad cop. What do you want to eat before we go?"

"I'm really not hungry."

"Have to eat something." He rummaged in the refrigerator. "Have some yogurt and a banana."

"You're offering me a black banana to spur my appetite?" She held it up and chuckled. "Thanks."

"I've learned that if you stick them in the fridge they keep longer, even though the cold turns the skin dark. I'm too busy to go to the store much, so it's been good to know."

She often wondered how he'd survived before they'd

married, when she'd taken over the grocery shopping and cooking. Later, she'd also wondered if that had made her an enabler of his workaholism, but probably he'd just have eaten out most of the time. Presumably he did that now.

She silently ate the food he offered as he got the dogs fed and took them out for a short time. When he came back inside, so they could walk the couple of blocks to HOAC, it struck her all over again how tall and beautiful the man was, and she looked away to grab her purse, not wanting to feel the surprising skip of her heart and the ache in her chest that kept showing up uninvited.

Walking into HOAC was another strange moment of feeling as if the past was the present all over again. It felt like she'd worked there just weeks earlier, instead of leaving for the occupational therapy center ten months ago, after she and Conor had divorced.

It had been her decision to leave. Seeing Conor every day had been like a stab in her chest, and she was sure he'd breathed a sigh of relief, too, when she'd gone.

But she had friends here. People she still met with once in a while and missed working with. Several looked up in surprise when she came in, and her old pal Michelle Branson widened her eyes and then widened them even more when she saw Conor behind her.

"Jillian! What happened?" Michelle asked.

"Fell on the sidewalk. Distal radius fracture. Beth did the surgery yesterday."

"Oh, no! I'm so sorry to hear that." Michelle stood to give her a hug, and her side-eye toward Conor was obvious before she looked back at Jillian and gave her a sympathetic smile. "You always were one of the most dedicated PTs around here. Did you decide you had to know firsthand what it's like to deal with one of these injuries? I'm very impressed with your commitment to your work."

"Very funny. Not something I ever thought would happen to me, I've got to admit. But hopefully it won't disrupt my life too much."

Except it already had, with her having to be with Conor for a few days of torture which she knew were going to be far worse than any physical pain and inconvenience she might experience.

"Jillian is living in a fantasy world," Conor said. "She thought she could go home and stay by herself last night, then get here alone this morning. I don't remember her being stubborn like that before—do you, Michelle?"

"I think I'll stay out of any conversations about that." She gave them both a half smile. "But maybe going through this *will* help you understand your patients better, hmm? You can give a talk about it to all the other therapists after your arm and hand are normal again."

"Maybe… I'm trying to remind myself that this will be a good experience in terms of sympathy and understanding for my patients. Already is, in fact."

"That's the way to see a silver lining. Here, have a seat at my table." Michelle gave her another hug. "I didn't realize that my patient this morning was *the* Jillian. Let's get that cast off, then Dr. Crenshaw will be here to talk to you."

"I'm going to take a look at my schedule," Conor said. "I told them I couldn't do any surgeries until later this morning, but I want to make sure I have plenty of time to take you home."

Home. His home. And yet he'd said it the same way he had when they'd been married…

Jill swallowed hard and couldn't help but watch him as he left, until Michelle leaned close and spoke in a low voice.

"I couldn't believe it when I saw Conor with you. What's the scoop there?"

"No scoop. He saw me getting prepped in the OR, asked a bunch of questions, and decided he had to play hero by taking me to his place and looking after the dogs and stuff until my sister is able to come help for a few days."

"Because he's a *good* man."

"Just not good to be married to."

"Jill. I get that your man—*ex*-man—works too much and keeps ridiculous hours. But he's also—"

"I know. I do. I shouldn't have said that."

Immediately she regretted the bitter words. She'd thought those negative feelings weren't still festering in her, but being around him seemed to stir them up. Clearly she had a long way to go to get herself whole.

"It wasn't a party for him to be married to me, either. For a lot of reasons we just weren't right for one another."

"Well, maybe spending a little time together again means you can part as friends this time." Michelle gave her a hopeful smile. "I hear they're changing up at your office. Are you coming back here to work?"

"I have to—until I find something else. Working with Conor would be too uncomfortable long-term, you know? I need to start somewhere new. I have a job interview in Connecticut—though that might be delayed because of my stupid wrist."

"Well, we miss you, and would love to have you back with us permanently, but I do understand. And we're going to do everything we can to get your hand working again."

Michelle gave her a warm, sympathetic smile, then got to work removing her cast. Beth came to take a look at the surgical site, check the stitches and talk with her, and all that was the perfect distraction to take her thoughts away from Conor.

"Looks good, Jillian. Pretty great stitching, if I do say so myself." Beth grinned. "As you know, the stitches will dissolve on their own. I'll want to see you again in two weeks for another X-ray, to see how it's doing. And of course you can call me anytime if you need to."

"Thank you, Beth. I hope I'll be the kind of patient who astonishes everyone with her amazing progress."

"So do I. I love to brag to the other docs that I'm the best surgeon here—especially Conor. Speaking of which…is he taking care of things? Do you still need me to look for a dog walker and helper?"

"Uh…maybe. I'll be working on that today, I think. I'll let you know—thanks for the offer."

Beth nodded, gently patted her swollen hand, and moved on to her next patient. It felt strange to be on the other side of the therapy table, watching as Michelle expertly began fitting the temporary splint to her wrist and hand.

"Swelling's not too bad," Michelle said. "Hopefully it'll become semi-usable more quickly than some."

"Here's hoping… I need to be functional as soon as possible."

"That's the goal." Apparently satisfied with her work, Michelle sat back. "Still, I have a feeling this is going to be a whole lot harder than you think it will."

"Yeah…" And hardly being able to pull her own

stupid pants up and down just might be the least of her worries.

"What are you going to do about work? Your hand isn't going to be usable for quite a while."

"I was thinking about that. I figure I'll take a couple days off, then come here and help as I can, since I was being transferred anyway. I know the bosses would give me time off with my current disability, but I can't just sit around at home twiddling my thumbs. Or thumb, as the case may be."

"You never were the type to just relax. And twiddling one thumb sounds very unsatisfying." Michelle chuckled. "But how can you do any work?"

"There are things I won't be able to do for my patients, but I can get them into heating pads or set up in the dry whirlpool. Help with evaluations. Bring everyone the therapy tools…keep them clean. And some things I can do with one hand, right? Like massage scar tissue, manipulate fingers and wrists, take measurements."

"Obviously you've thought a lot about this already. Sounds difficult, but if anyone can do it you can." Michelle squeezed her good hand. "My next patient just came in, but I'll see him at the other table. You can wait here until Conor comes back."

A good thirty minutes went by, which left Jill wanting to get up and help, proving that she wasn't cut out to take time off—especially since she couldn't carry on training for the marathon she'd signed up for now. No running while her wrist bones and the plate and screws weren't even close to fused. It was another depressing consequence of her injury, since running always helped clear her head of worries.

Fifteen more minutes had her thinking she should just head on back by herself. Conor was known for squeezing in patients who needed to be seen in the office right away, which could mean another hour or more. And why not? His apartment was close, and he'd given her a key. The pain meds had mostly worn off, which meant her arm hurt some, but she didn't feel woozy anymore. Not having the use of one arm didn't make her a cripple, right? And the break was protected by the new splint. She had to learn how to live this way for the foreseeable future, and there was no time like the present to start making that happen.

She walked to Michelle's second table, where she was working with her patient. "Looks like Conor got held up. Can you let him know I'm going back to his apartment?"

Michelle frowned. "I don't think that's a good idea just one day post-op. Grab a magazine and relax. He said he has all surgeries scheduled this afternoon and wants to get you home first, right? He'll be here soon, I'm sure."

"You know how his schedule can be. Could be forever till he's done. Plus, it's a nice day out. I'll be fine."

Maybe it was the thought of being close to Conor as they walked, enduring the awkward discomfort between them, that suddenly made her want to run out the door and get to his apartment. Not to interrupt his normal workday anymore. To take a nap and breathe at being alone again, not having to stare at Conor's handsome face and sexy body and think about what used to be between them.

She waved to her former co-workers and left. Outside, the December breeze against her skin helped soothe the chaos in her chest. Soothe all the bittersweet feelings that kept surging up every time he came close, or held her arm to steady her during those uncomfortable moments of him helping her get dressed and undressed.

How was she going to handle this? And would it be as hard on Conor as on her? Probably not, since his work had always been more interesting to him than she'd been.

She forced herself to walk slowly even though she wanted to get there and see the dogs and maybe lie down for a minute. She nearly took the stairs, as she would have at her own place, but remembered she should take it easy for a few days. Last thing she needed was to trip on the steps, landing on her newly put back together wrist and splinted hand.

The second she opened his apartment door the dogs greeted her excitedly, and much as she wanted to hug them she used a stern voice when she spoke to Hudson, making sure he didn't throw his paws onto her shoulders and knock her flat before she'd healed for even one day.

Her poor night's sleep once the nerve-block had worn off, combined with the events of the day, had left her feeling so tired she'd expected to conk out right away. But a half hour of trying to rest on the super-comfortable guest bed just sent her mind to places she didn't want it to go. Places like Conor's bedroom, which she hadn't let herself peek into, and wondering if he had women there with him sometimes. Of course he did. He might work a hundred hours a week but he was a hot-blooded man, wasn't he? And hot was an understatement.

Thinking about their fabulous sex life, and what

other women he must be enjoying that with now, made her feel a little sick. She jumped out of bed and began pacing the gorgeous apartment. She stared out at the amazing view of the city and Central Park and decided she had to get out of there.

Surely she could walk just one of the dogs? Yorkie was the obvious choice, because he was small and couldn't pull her along the sidewalks and pathways like Hudson could if he chose to chase a squirrel, or something else grabbed his attention. She and Yorkie would both get a little exercise, and maybe that would clear her mind of all the unsettling thoughts that kept poking at her.

She grabbed the dog's leash and headed down the elevator and out through the door, managing to smile back at the doorman even as she wondered how many women the man saw coming and going from Conor's place.

Breathing in the crisp air and doing something as normal as taking a walk felt good, and it helped bring back her equilibrium. But once she and Yorkie had explored the park for only a short time a new fatigue began to settle in her bones, and she realized that maybe she was overdoing it for the first day after surgery.

After resting for a while, on a bench tucked beneath an old oak tree, she decided she should head back and take the kind of nap she'd felt too restless for before.

"Time to go, Yorkie. Okay with you?"

She'd barely taken ten steps, concentrating on not tripping over the uneven sidewalk, when Yorkie leaped forward with a yip and she looked up. She was stunned to see Conor McCarthy heading toward them, eating up the pavement with long strides, a thunderous expression on his face.

For some reason her heart started beating harder. She wasn't sure if it was the look on his face or the way he kept coming so fast, but she stopped dead and stared at him.

"What the *hell* is the matter with you?" His hands reached for her shoulders and he pulled her closer, anger practically radiating from him.

"Nothing. I just… I wanted a little fresh air, that's all."

"That's *all*? So you do whatever you want, not caring that it scared me to death? I was worried and mad when Michelle told me you left. How do you think I felt when I went in my apartment and you weren't there? I didn't know if you'd even gotten there until I saw Yorkie was gone, too, and Alfred told me you'd left. And then you didn't answer your phone! *Damn it*, Jill!"

His expression was fierce, but deep inside the fury in his eyes she could see how worried he'd been. Scared for her. Guilt stabbed, because she'd left without thinking it might worry him. And didn't that make her the kind of person she'd accused *him* of being when they'd been married? Telling him that he didn't care how it made her feel when he was hardly ever home?

"I didn't hear my phone… I forgot to turn the sound back up, I guess. And it didn't occur to me that you'd be worried, but it should have. I'm sorry."

He stared at her for a long second before his mouth came down on hers, hard and possessive. The shock of it had her swaying, leaning into him, loving the taste of him and the feel of his lips on hers that she'd missed more than she'd admitted to herself until now.

The tone of the kiss changed, softened, his mouth slowly moving on hers with more than a hint of the kind of tenderness they'd shared when they'd first fallen in love. His hands moved to cup her cheeks and her good hand lifted to his chest, curling into his jacket as her knees weakened and her heart began to thud in heavy strokes against her ribs.

"Jilly… Jill…" he whispered against her mouth, before he kissed her again, still soft, still slow, but deeper now.

Her focus narrowed to just him. The feel of his hands holding her face, his hot mouth on hers, his chest rising and falling as his breathing quickened. Only one thought was in her head. How had she lived without him in her life, kissing her like this? Making her feel like this?

The sound of Yorkie barking finally got through the mistiness of her senses, and she opened her eyes to see Conor opening his at the same time. His gaze was still fierce, his blue eyes dark, his face taut. In slow motion his hands slipped from her cheeks and he took a step back. Without a word he reached for the dog's leash with one hand and linked his fingers with hers before he turned to walk back down the path.

They didn't speak—and, really, what was there to say? Him scolding her some more? Another apology from her? A conversation about why kissing each other was the worst idea ever and how it was going to make staying in his apartment together even harder than it already was?

Now that his mouth wasn't on hers, short-circuiting every rational thought, she remembered that his kisses and the touches that had made her feel treasured and desired had happened less and less as he'd been gone more and more. His absence had tormented her, bringing every insecurity to the forefront of her brain, until living together was misery instead of joy. For both of them.

And now they were living together again, bringing all those wonderful feelings and those awful feelings, the guilt and the pain, to the surface. Even if it was only for a day or two, he couldn't want to revisit all that any more than she did.

They had to find a different solution.

When they stepped inside his apartment the large, lovely space felt excruciatingly oppressive. She squared her shoulders and turned to him.

"Listen. I don't think this is going to work. I'll figure out what I can and can't do and find solutions to problems. I'll be fine at my place and we'll find someone to walk the dogs. They can stay with you until Briana—"

"No. I get that this is strange and awkward. For both of us." He shoved his hands into his pockets and looked down at her, nearly expressionless now, compared to the anger and passion etched on his face ten minutes ago. "But you need at least a few days to get your bearings. Your hand is swollen and sore and in a splint, and you can barely move your fingers. Doing everything with one hand is going to take practice. I'm sorry about what just happened. I was freaked out and worried but it won't happen again. I promise."

"I think I'll be all right if—"

"No," he repeated, in a quiet voice that felt far more compelling than his angry tone of a moment ago. "I'm asking you to please stay. For me. So I'm not worried and anxious about how you're doing. You shouldn't be alone right now. We're adults and we can make this work—in spite of…everything."

"Conor—"

"Please."

She found her gaze clinging to the entreaty in his eyes.

"I know there's no reason for you to do anything for me. But please do it for yourself. For your safety. Please."

"I just… All right." How was she supposed to argue with him when he was looking at her that way? "Briana will be in New York soon, I'm sure. Just a couple more days and I'll be out of your way."

"You could never be in my way."

The soft sweep of his knuckle against her cheek seemed to shake her heart before he dropped his hand.

"Why don't you rest while I take Hudson out. I'll bring you something to eat before I go back to work."

"If you're working until ten I don't see how that's any different from me being alone at my place."

The sadness she heard in her voice wasn't supposed to be there. And the bitterness she was trying to banish for good.

She rushed to sound less pathetic and needy. "But, thanks. Some food would be good."

"I won't be working late. I've rescheduled my evening meetings until next week. So I'll be back as soon as surgery is over and I've finished the paperwork. Go lie down and I'll be back soon."

Maybe it was the big emotions of the past twenty minutes, but suddenly that deep fatigue seeped through her bones again. All she wanted to do was lie in that comfy bed, close her eyes and do nothing but start to heal.

She watched him get Hudson's leash and walk out

the door, then sat for a long time staring out the huge windows. Admiring the amazing view of this city that was like nowhere else. Being together with him in this apartment, feeling her heart squeeze and tug every time she looked at him, already felt like torture. And there was no way that working with him again would be anything but painful, too.

Much as the thought of leaving New York made her feel more than a little sad, she knew a new job in a different state had to happen. Being far away from here would be the next necessary step in really addressing her insecurities once and for all and getting over Dr. Conor McCarthy.

CHAPTER FOUR

Leaving Jill at his apartment all alone had felt strange and uncomfortable, despite her assurances that she wouldn't try to go anywhere. Maybe he was being stupidly overprotective. Having only one hand was a handicap that would keep her from fixing her own lunch and give her other challenges, but she could still get around. So why couldn't he get the niggle of worry out of his head?

Was she in pain? Was she coping okay or was she miserable? When would her sister be able to come and stay with her, and for how long? The woman had a pretty demanding job in the advertising business, so he couldn't imagine she'd be able to stay with Jill for very long. How was she going to cope after that?

Not his problem, he reminded himself for the fiftieth time. She'd once been his everything, other than his work, but she'd seen soon enough that he wasn't the kind of man she wanted. And she'd believed she wasn't the kind of woman he needed in his life, that attending charity balls and galas and making small talk with work associates wasn't something she could do. That he didn't really desire her—which he still couldn't believe. No man touched a woman and kissed a woman and laughed with a woman the way he had if he wasn't crazy in love with her.

But she'd been right about the rest. He'd wanted a different kind of life from the way he'd grown up. Financial security, a special woman, children, stability... The first moment he'd set eyes on Jillian his heart had fallen at her feet. A month of delirious fun and lovemaking had had him rushing her into marriage, not wanting to wait one more day for them to be together forever.

Forever hadn't lasted even a year.

He'd made Jillian miserable. Not the same way his father had made his mother miserable, but still...

He hadn't realized until his monumental failure that the way he'd grown up had left him damaged, somehow. Anxiety about their financial security, so intense it had made him sweat and have trouble sleeping, had sent him working long hours, the way he had since he was a boy. He'd tried to ratchet it back, to make Jillian happier, but much as he'd loved her, loved being with her, the back of his mind had always been full of all the things he might be dropping the ball on. All the ways his businesses might fail and their future tank, leaving them destitute.

To him, providing for her future was the best way to show how much he loved her—but she hadn't seen it that way.

He'd begun to realize that intense worry and anxiety was some kind of mental health thing from his childhood, but in the end it had become clear that he had no clue how to be the kind of husband she wanted and deserved. When she'd walked out the door he'd accepted it, because the last thing he'd ever wanted to do was hurt Jilly any more than he already had.

He closed his eyes at the memories. It was over and done with. But seeing her in such pain from her broken wrist after surgery had about killed him. And being physically close to her, touching her through necessity as he'd helped her dress and eat, being near her soft skin and hair, later knowing that her warm, sweet body was asleep in the next bedroom over, had seriously messed with his equilibrium all over again.

Which was the best explanation for why he'd kissed her in the park. He'd been filled with an overwhelming fear when he'd seen she was gone with Yorkie, and he'd practically run from the apartment to find her. His relief had been joined by anger, and he'd kissed her before he'd even known he was going to.

Then the taste of her, which he'd missed more than he'd realized, the feel of her in his arms, the sweet scent of her, had robbed him of breath. Taken over his senses until he'd felt delirious with it. It was a good thing it hadn't come over him that way in his apartment, because he just might have picked her up and carried her to the bed, begged her to make love with him, broken wrist or not.

And what a terrible mistake that would have been. He absolutely refused to do anything that would hurt her any more than he already had.

He rubbed his hand down his face. Time to somehow get his mind off of her—and the best way to do that was to take care of the tasks in front of him. Paperwork on patients. Checks on his investments and stocks. Looking at the financials for some of his businesses. A few phone calls and emails to the Urgent Care Manhattan decision-makers to set up a new meeting—which had to happen soon.

Thinking about it not working out added another layer of stress to the turmoil already swirling in his head so he tried to refocus. Pulled up some X-rays for patients he'd be doing surgery on in the morning.

And then just as he'd thought he was nicely back in the work groove, he found himself texting Jill.

You doing okay?

She didn't answer, which probably meant she was sleeping. Or at least he hoped so.

The niggle of worry that he knew was ridiculous had him finishing up as quickly as possible. He strode through the teeming crowds on the sidewalk to get to his apartment, and when he saw a family waiting for the elevator he ran up the nine flights of stairs to get there faster.

When he shoved open the door, his relief at seeing her quietly sitting there reading, with the dogs on either side of the chair, weakened his knees.

"Hey. How are you feeling?"

She looked up and her eyes met his. It seemed impossible that just that simple connection made his heart beat harder, but he knew hurrying through the crowds and running up the stairs wasn't the reason he felt breathless.

"I'm okay. Feeling antsy to get out of here and take the dogs for a walk, but I figured you'd go ballistic if you came back and I was gone again."

"And you'd care about me getting upset?"

"I'm an occupational therapist—that means I care about people. So of course I don't want to worry you—though why you get worried about me, I don't know."

She *should* know. He tried hard not show it, but he worried about a lot of things. And, since he would always care about her, he worried about her, too. But he wasn't going to go there.

"Are you hungry?"

"I ate the last black banana and found some granola in a bag in your cupboard, so, no. Not yet. Though how you keep your healthy physique without any food in your place I have no clue."

"I eat out a lot. As you know." He watched her gaze slide down his aforementioned physique and tried not to get aroused by her unexpected perusal. "What do you think about walking the dogs together? So we can both get some fresh air?"

"I was thinking I'd walk Yorkie by myself. Then you can take Hudson out. Before you go back to work."

"I'm not going back to work."

"You're not?" She looked at him as though she found that incredible, but her being here was a special circumstance, wasn't it?

"Not tonight. I'll hold their leashes and you can stroll along at whatever pace feels good to you."

"Didn't we just talk earlier about how it's weird and uncomfortable to be around each other again? I want to enjoy being outdoors, not feel nervous."

"I make you nervous?"

"You know you do. Or uncomfortable…or sad…or… I don't know, exactly, but I can't say I enjoy the sensation."

He wanted to lean toward her, touch her soft cheek and put a word to what she felt, what sensation might be happening to both of them, but forced himself to stay put. "I know I wasn't a good husband, Jillian. That I let you down. I do. But it would be nice if we could be friends. Or at least not enemies. Wouldn't it?"

"I… I suppose this time together could help us be a little more friendly than the last time we saw each other. And a walk sounds nice." Her troubled expression lifted a little. "You can't let dogs off-leash in Central Park until after nine, or before nine in the morning. But there's a small dog park not too far from here that a friend told me about. I take them to the one close to my apartment and they love running around there. Plus I read that there's a burger shack right around the corner from there, where we can grab some food and a milkshake."

"I remember how much you love a vanilla shake." Without thinking, he reached out to stroke the bump on her forehead. "You can hold the cold cup against your head before you drink it."

"Or not." She sent him an adorable crooked smile. "Okay, that's the plan. Give me five minutes to try to look presentable. Though I learned today that's pretty impossible, since my hair ended up looking a little like I'd stuck it in a blender after I washed it."

"I noticed it wasn't in its usual smooth, sleek fall down your shoulders, or in that messy bun you like to wear the rest of the time."

"Yeah… I also learned there's no way I can get it in a bun one-handed, and drying it without using a brush in my other hand does not turn out well."

"Are you taking notes? These are good things for a hand surgeon and occupational therapist to know."

"Don't laugh, but I actually am. I figure I'll give a presentation to the OTs after I've gone through all this.

Maybe come up with some new ideas for patients as I go along."

"Not laughing at all. It's a good idea."

He'd been to a few of her professional talks in the past, both about her work and how she'd become a runner after her leg surgery. Her energy and warmth made her the kind of speaker who held everyone's attention, and he remembered feeling proud of her when others had told him how impressed they were.

"Make sure us surgeons hear it, too. Sometimes it's easy to focus on the bones and forget how surgery affects a person's everyday life. You're such a good speaker—I know everyone would get a lot out of it."

She sent him a smile so pleased it was as though in simply speaking the truth he'd given her a gift, and his chest expanded the way it had back when they were together. Back when she'd looked at him as if he was some kind of superhero.

That thought deflated the pleasure filling his chest, because it hadn't taken too long for her to totally change her view about that.

"Thanks. That's a nice thing for you to say. I'll be back in just a few minutes."

He decided to stay in his scrubs for their visit to a dog park, and sat to scratch the pups' ears while he waited for her. When she stepped back into the room he smiled at her only slightly less messy hair, but decided it would be better not to comment on it. No reason to have her irritated with him before they'd even started their agreed-upon friendly outing.

"Ready?"

"As ready as is currently possible."

Once they were out on the sidewalk, he reached for her hand to keep her steady, but she tugged it away.

"I'll be fine. I'm learning to walk a little more slowly than usual, paying attention to make sure I don't somehow stumble and fall. You helping me isn't going to accomplish that."

He nodded, but the truth was that steadying her hadn't been the foremost thought in his head. Memories of all the times he'd held her hand had made it seem like the most natural thing in the world to reach for her that way.

He stuffed his free hand into his pocket as they walked the few blocks to the dog park. Both were mostly quiet, enjoying the crisp December air. He found himself enjoying being close to her, strolling along as though the ugly past between them hadn't happened. As if they were the two people they'd been for that wonderful short time, wildly in love. He tried to shove down how bad that made him feel now.

"It's good we're taking them to the park today," he commented when the silence had stretched on a little too long. "Supposed to get colder and rain later in the week."

"Well, that's a bummer. Rainy New York is not my favorite."

"It's nobody's favorite. Except for that time we were under an umbrella in Central Park, walking through that downpour. Laughing at how our shoes were soaking wet and yours were making loud squeaking sounds. Squeezing close together to try to stay dry as the wind blew rainwater all over us. Kissing and holding one another." Without thinking, he wrapped his arm around her shoulders and pressed her close to his side. "That was probably my favorite day ever in the city."

Her eyes shadowed and she pulled loose from his hold and looked in the other direction, which made him want to thrash himself. Why had that stupid memory come out of his mouth? Probably because the mention of rain as they'd walked close to one another had brought that day into vivid recollection, and his chest physically hurt, because he knew it would never happen again.

"There's the dog park," she said abruptly, pointing. "They can play first, then when they're tired we'll get some food and sit on a bench to eat."

"Whatever you want."

To take his attention from Jillian's sad expression, and the way his heart was squeezing in his chest, he looked around the area at all the people with their dogs. "I've never been in this park before. It's nice. With Central Park so close to work and my apartment, that's where I usually go."

"You take time to relax in Central Park? Doesn't sound like you."

"You got me started on running to clear my head. I do that sometimes."

Talking about his focus on work and his other failings wasn't his favorite conversation to have with her, so he was glad the dogs had started pulling hard on their leashes and wagging their tails.

"They're pretty excited, aren't they? Do you put Yorkie in the little dog area, or keep him with Hudson?"

"Is that a real question?" She grinned up at him. "You know as well as I do that Yorkie has a big personality inside that little body. He does fine with Hudson."

He opened the iron gate to the park, unclipped their

leashes, and both dogs took off across the gravel surface, excitedly running with the other animals there.

"Good thing you're wearing your scrubs instead of nice pants. Benches are usually none too clean in a dog park, which is why I wore these old sweats," she said as they sat.

"I figure old sweatpants will be your uniform for a while, until you can use your bad hand to zip and button again."

"Hey, I have new sweatpants, too, that don't make me look so ratty. I figure I'll mix up the tattered and un-tattered days."

"Old ones are looser—easier to slide up and down. The newer ones I helped you pull up yesterday will take more work."

Memories of seeing her smooth skin, touching it as he helped her dress, and the entire conversation about dressing and undressing, made him feel short of breath.

Maybe she could tell where his mind had gone, because she turned away and pointed down the street. "You know, I've never been able to decide if I like the design of the Guggenheim or not so much. What do you think of it?"

"I like it. But my favorites are the Flatiron Building, Grand Central Terminal, the New York Public Library... And I can't leave out the Empire State Building, and the—"

"Are you going to name every iconic building in the city?" She laughed. "But I agree—and I've taken pictures of all of them. Along with Brooklyn Bridge and St. Patrick's Cathedral and a lot of others. After we... we broke up, I decided to take a photography class. I really enjoyed it. And now I just realized that's yet another thing I won't be able to do for a while. Can't hold a camera and take pics with only one hand."

"It won't be too long until you can manage that." Her frustrated frown had him reaching to cup her cheek in his hand, until he realized what he was about to do and dropped it. "I noticed a few photos on the wall of your apartment but I had no idea you took them. That's awesome. Could I talk you into letting me buy a few for my office wall?"

He'd love to have some photos she'd taken, to remember her by.

As if he needed anything to look at for that.

"I don't sell them—it's just for fun. But if you'd want a few I'll print them out."

"Thank you. Tell me about the class and where you took it."

The subject was a safe one, and she chatted about it as they watched the dogs run and play. Eventually both animals slowed down, tongues hanging out, and when Jillian stood up he went to retrieve them.

"There's a hose and a bowl for water over there," she said. "After you get them something to drink we can go to the burger shack."

"Dying for that vanilla shake?"

"Been thinking of nothing else for the past half hour."

He got busy getting the dogs some water. "Where's this burger place?" he asked.

"I think just around the corner. And they have…are you ready?…chicken ice cream for dogs. They love it."

"Chicken ice cream? You're kidding."

"Nope. Being next to the dog run, they sell a ton

of it. Maybe you should give it a try, just so you know what they're eating."

"Think I'll stick with a burger, thanks all the same."

They shared a laugh, and Conor again had that urge to put his arm around her shoulders. They sat on a bench to enjoy their treats, and just as Conor was feeling as relaxed as possible around Jillian his phone rang. Digging it out of his pocket, he saw it was the lawyer who'd put together all the legal papers to present to Peter Stanford at Urgent Care Manhattan when they discussed becoming partners.

"Conor McCarthy."

"Hello, Conor, it's Sam Smith. I met with the new investors you told me about, and I've revised the paperwork accordingly. Thought you might want to read through it as soon as possible, since I know you're planning to reschedule your meeting with the Manhattan Urgent Care people soon. I faxed it to your office, and your secretary told me she'd put it on your desk."

"Appreciate that. Definitely want all the numbers to be up to date when we meet. I'll call you as soon as I have the date and time finalized."

He hung up and looked at Jillian, enjoying the soft, relaxed look on her face as she lounged near him, hoping it wouldn't get all disdainful when he told her he needed to stop into the office.

"Would you mind walking to HOAC with me? You don't have to if you're tired. I can take the dogs there and meet you back at my apartment. Or you can come with me and we'll grab a taxi to take you home while I walk back."

"I'm not tired. And I'm enjoying this dry weather

while it lasts. Anyway, I need to get my strength back to start running again."

"Okay, but promise me no running for eight weeks to make sure the plate and bones are fused?"

"Yes, Doctor."

His heart got that funny feeling again, squeezing and expanding at the amusement on her beautiful face, at his memories of better times together.

He didn't trust himself to speak, and they walked mostly silently together the five blocks to HOAC. It was past seven, and long closed for the day, but as they approached he could see a boy of about ten pounding on the door.

"Need something, buddy?" Conor asked as they stopped next to him.

He turned with a grimace on his face and panic in his eyes. "I need a doctor who can fix my arm."

Conor's gaze moved to where he was pointing. The misshapen elbow joint and swelling were impossible to miss.

CHAPTER FIVE

JILLIAN WATCHED CONOR carefully reach for the boy's injured arm and lean closer to look at it. "How did this happen?"

"Part of the sidewalk was cracked and raised up and I didn't notice. My skateboard banged into it and I flew off into the corner of a building. Hurts real bad. I knew this place was here, so I came."

"Do you have a phone? Did you try to call your parents?"

"Don't have a phone."

"Here." Conor dug into his pocket. "I'll call them for you and you can talk to them. You need to go to an urgent care department to get this taken care of."

"I want to go inside this place and have them fix it. Why can't I do that?"

Jillian's and Conor's eyes met. His lips twisted. "It's not open right now. And you need your parents' consent before anyone can get X-rays and take care of you."

"I don't know if my mom'll answer. This time of day she's probably in a bar somewhere."

Jill's heart hurt for this boy whose mother apparently wasn't always there for him—something which she couldn't imagine, having been raised by wonderful, supportive parents. She looked up and saw that Conor's lips were pressed together.

"How about your dad? He wouldn't need to come here—we just need to talk to him and get permission to take you to get some care."

"I don't have a dad." Looking even more worried, the boy jerked his thumb at the door. "You sure this place is closed?"

"Yes. But I'm a surgeon here. Maybe there's something I can do." Conor's eyes met hers again. "Let's try to call your mom and we'll go from there. What's your name?"

"Noah Thomas."

Conor dialed in the number Noah gave him, then handed the boy the phone. After many rings Jill was about to give up hope when someone apparently answered.

"Mom, I hurt my arm. You need to say it's okay for me to get treated by an urgent care department, or something."

Her words in reply weren't decipherable, but the loud and angry tone was more than clear.

Conor reached for the phone. "Let me talk to her."

"Ma'am, this is Dr. Conor McCarthy. Your son Noah needs medical attention. I'd like permission to send him by taxi to an urgent care facility, and to call ahead to let them know to expect him."

Jill looked up at his grim face, not catching everything the woman said except the fact that she wasn't about to pay any urgent care fees and wanted Noah to just go home.

"All I need is your permission to treat him. I will take care of him here at my orthopedic center with no charge, but I need you to give your consent, which I will record."

There was more brief conversation, then Jill got the distinct impression the woman had hung up on Conor. "Did you get her permission?"

"Yes."

She could see him work to relax his expression into a smile before he looked at Noah.

"I'm an orthopedic surgeon, which means I specialize in bones. Since I can take care of you here, without charging your mom, I guess we'll go ahead and do that. Okay with you?"

"Yes! That would be awesome."

For the first time since they'd run into him the boy's expression lightened and he even almost smiled.

"All right." Conor punched a code into the keypad to unlock the door, and turned to look at Jill as the three of them and the dogs piled into the elevator. "I think Hudson and Yorkie will do okay in the storage room. You think they'll be tired enough to sleep a little after all that running?"

"Definitely. They'll rest while you and I find out what's going on with Noah's arm."

"What did you do to yours?" Noah asked, staring at her splint as he clutched his own arm to his belly.

"I fell and broke my wrist. Hopefully your arm isn't broken, but we'll find out. Dr. McCarthy is a really good orthopedic surgeon, so you're in good hands."

"It hurts superbad and it looks awful. It has to be broken. Doesn't it?"

"Nope," Conor said. "Could be a dislocated elbow—that's a real possibility. Could be something else. We'll find out with an X-ray, then go from there."

They both quickly got the dogs settled, with more bowls of water, then moved to the X-ray room. "Sit down there, Noah, and put your arm on the pad just like that."

Jill stood behind the wall and watched Conor gently and expertly place Noah's arm in several different positions before stepping next to her and pushing the button to take the pictures.

"All done. Let's go take a look and see what they show, hmm?"

They moved to an office off the main hallway that held computer equipment and Conor pulled up the images.

"Take a look, Noah. See how the ball of your elbow has shifted out of the socket? That's called a posterior dislocation. And that's good news."

"It is?"

"Yep. It means it's not broken. I have to reduce it, which means put it back into place. It'll hurt, and we'll have to put it in a splint and a sling for a few days. Then check on it again. But it's much better news than if it was broken."

Conor sent him a warm smile that would have reassured even the most frightened patient.

Noah smiled back at him, and her heart pinched at how sweet Conor was with the boy. She'd seen him many times, meeting with a patient in the therapy room after surgery, but had rarely had the chance to see him talking with people prior to surgery—especially a child.

Conor patted the boy's back. "I'm going to give you something to make you feel sleepy when I reduce it, because it does hurt. But the medicine, which is called conscious sedation, will help you not really be aware of what I'm doing. Then, afterward, you'll wake up again in no time."

"Okay."

Noah looked up at Conor with a look of utter trust on his face and Jill drew a deep breath. Conor might have been incapable of being emotionally available the way she'd wanted and needed during their marriage, and unable to make her a priority ahead of his work, but in his own way he was still a good man.

She turned away. "I'll get the sedative."

When she returned Conor was carefully examining Noah's arm and hand, speaking calmly to him and telling him what to expect.

"Your circulation seems fine, which is more good news. No veins pinched in there, causing poor blood flow. Should be a simple procedure. Are you ready for me to give you the shot that will make you sleepy? It'll sting a little."

"Ready."

Cursing her one useless hand, Jill helped Noah get comfortable on the clinic bed before Conor injected the conscious sedation into the boy's thigh, and in moments his lids slid closed.

"All right," Conor said, looking at Jill. "I'm going to reduce the elbow. Are you able to hold on to his bicep with one hand while I manipulate it back into place? If not, I'll do it solo."

"I'll do my best."

Jill gripped the boy's arm as strongly as she could with her good hand, and watched in fascination as Conor grasped the wrist and forearm, slowly pulling and twisting. She'd never actually seen this procedure done in person, just in videos at therapy school. It obviously took skill to know exactly what to do, but in less than thirty seconds a loud popping sound came as the joint slipped back into place.

"Impressive, Dr. McCarthy," she said. "That was amazing to watch."

"Well, I *am* pretty amazing. Glad we were able to be here for him." He sent her a pleased grin and she smiled back.

"I think it was meant to be. I mean, we got to the door right as he was banging on it. I wonder what he would have done if we hadn't shown up?"

All amusement left Conor's face. "Struggled. Gone home to a mother who's only half there and barely able to take care of herself, probably, let alone a kid."

Something about his tone, which was not just grim but sad, too, had her wondering if there was something about his own childhood he hadn't shared with her. She knew his father had left when he'd been only five or six years old, and that his mother died when he was barely eighteen. He hadn't told her much more than that, other than saying she'd been ill for a long time.

Should she ask, or let it be, since they weren't a part of each other's lives anymore?

She opened her mouth, not exactly sure what she was going to say, but stopped as he turned to Noah and gently shook him.

"Hey, Noah. All done. You can wake up now."

The boy blinked up at him. "Huh?"

"Your elbow's back in place. Jillian here is an occupational therapist, and an expert at making splints for people. When you're feeling alert again we're going to make one for you. I want you to come back in two days. Let me know when you're feeling up to walking."

Noah nodded and Conor turned to Jill, his expression impassive. "Will you keep an eye on him as he wakes up? I'm going to find that fax I need. Be back soon."

By the time Conor returned Noah was feeling well enough to go to the therapy room with both of them.

"Sit right here, Noah. I'm going to fashion a splint for you out of this cool thermoplastic stuff," she said, holding up the sheet of hard material. "When I put it in hot water it softens, so I can form it to your arm. What color do you want?"

"I like that green."

"Green it is."

She dipped the sheet into the hot water bath, wondering how she'd manage with one hand. But with Conor holding one end as she placed it over Noah's arm she found she was able to form it to fit.

"Hey, I'm not as handicapped as I thought I was!" she said triumphantly. "My first success post-surgery!"

"I'm glad—but try not to be impatient and push it. You need time to heal just like Noah does," Conor said, smiling at both of them. "I'll cut the Velcro straps. I'm sure you can do it, but having two hands will make it a little easier."

"True. Not to mention that it's probably good for a high-and-mighty surgeon to do some therapy work once in a while."

"High-and-mighty? Is that how you think I come across?"

"No…"

And she didn't. He'd always treated everyone in the surgical center with respect, whether they were cleaning staff or a nurse or a worker in the office. Something not true of every surgeon—especially one who owned the whole place, like Conor did.

"Except when there's just one cup of coffee left in the clinic kitchen and you call dibs because you're heading into surgery."

"Well, I admit that's true. Wouldn't be good to fall asleep in the middle of cutting and drilling bones, right?"

His amused eyes met hers and they shared a long smile before he turned back to Noah and attached the Velcro straps.

"No skateboarding while you're wearing this," he said. "Your arm is going to feel sore and you don't want to be falling again while it's healing."

"I never fall."

Conor laughed. "You and Jillian. Both of you claim you don't fall, and yet both of you did. Stubborn and more stubborn."

"Not stubborn," she said, having to laugh a little, too. "Haven't I been good? Watching my step and walking slowly?"

"Yeah. You've been good."

His blue gaze met hers for another long, connected moment that made her heart race and her breath feel short until he broke the contact.

"You need to be good, too, Noah. I'm going to send you home in one of those ride-sharing vehicles. Then I want you to come back here after school in two days— and walk if you don't have somebody to drive you."

"I don't have any money for a ride-share," he muttered. "I'll walk and take the subway. I won't ride my skateboard."

"I have the ride-share app on my phone. So you

don't have to worry about that." Conor reached to pat the boy's shoulder again, then gave it a squeeze before handing him a card. "Here's my cell phone number and the office number. If you're in a lot of pain or worried about your arm, call me."

As Jill finished adjusting the Velcro on the finished splint the boy stared down at the card in his hand before lifting serious eyes to Conor's. "Thanks. I... Thanks a lot for doing all this. Fixing me up and everything." He turned to Jill. "You, too."

She gave him a smile and small hug. "I'm glad we were here to help. You can take the splint off to have a shower, but otherwise I want you to leave it on until you come back to see Dr. McCarthy."

"All set?" Conor looked at her, his eyes still serious, and at her nod gave another quick pat to Noah's shoulder. "Okay, tell me your address and we'll call for a car. Jillian can wait outside with you while I get the dogs. And I'll see you here in two days after you get out of school. What time is that?"

"Three-thirty."

"I'll expect you here at four, then. Will that work?"

"Yes. Okay."

The boy shared his address and Conor typed it into his phone, then headed for the storage room.

Jillian and Noah took the elevator down and went outside, where the evening sky was now fully dark. He fidgeted a little awkwardly, and she made some small talk to relax him, talking to him a little more about the splint and how to be careful with his arm.

In mere minutes the car arrived and she opened the door for the child.

"Hang in there. I think you'll be fine until you see

Dr. McCarthy again—but, like he said, if you have any worries, call."

"I will. Thanks again."

She waved, and as he waved back she could feel Conor's warmth behind her, the dogs on each side.

"That was your good deed for the day. Actually, maybe for the whole year," she said, smiling up at him.

To her surprise, he didn't smile back. "I hate that his home life is so bad. Did you hear what part of town he lives in? I wonder why he was so far from home to begin with? Probably doesn't want to be there with no-body else around."

"I didn't hear. But it *is* terrible that his mother didn't come for him. Didn't even want to send him to urgent care."

"Yeah… Maybe I'll talk with him a little about that when he comes back." His gaze seemed to focus on something in the distance for long seconds before he turned his attention back to her. "You've walked a lot, and it's dark now. I think we should take a ride-share of our own. Request a driver with a big enough car for the dogs."

"I admit I do feel a little tired now, but it's only a few blocks. I'll be fine." She pressed her hand to his arm and squeezed. "I want to say I think you're pretty wonderful, doing what you did for Noah."

He shook his head. "You of all people know work is the one thing I am wonderful at—which includes fixing up Noah. In another couple days you'll be rid of me for good."

She nearly protested, because there were so many things he was wonderful at, even if wanting to be with her during their marriage hadn't been one of them. In the end, though, she stayed silent, deciding there was no point in going there. As for being glad to be rid of him again…? The way her heart clutched and her stomach squeezed told her that a part of her didn't feel glad about that at all.

Early the next morning Jillian peeked out through her bedroom door, her heart bumping around in a ridiculous pitter-patter. Expelling a relieved breath that Conor wasn't visible, she shut the door and moved to the spacious bathroom.

Being in his apartment with him had sent all kinds of mixed feelings swirling around her chest as they'd watched mindless TV last night, sitting a respectable distance apart as he did his usual reading emails and texting, until she'd excused herself to go to bed, hyperaware that he was just down the hall.

The discomfort of her wrist had made it hard to sleep, and the emotions swirling in her chest had added to her insomnia. Sorrow. Relief. A longing for the delicious past that she'd thought they'd have forever, until her insecurities and her inability to fit in with his wealthy cronies, combined with his workaholism, had proved that impossible.

His sweetness with Noah, the way he'd obviously been moved by and even upset about the boy's sadly less than optimal home life, had both tugged at her heartstrings and made her wonder about what Conor's own childhood had been like. Since he'd said so little she hadn't thought much about how had it might have affected him.

After last night she saw that she should have wondered. Should have asked. Their relationship was over, but maybe she should reach out anyway. Try to be his friend, as he'd suggested.

Was that possible?

And was it something she even wanted?

Confusion and uncertainty about all those questions gnawed at her, and she heaved a sigh as she undid the splint from her arm to step into the shower.

She held her wrist close to her body to protect it from getting bumped as she tried to make herself presentable for her therapy appointment this morning. Dumping shampoo directly on her head did not work well. Just like yesterday, even when she tried to distribute it at least a little evenly on her head, before rubbing it through her hair with the fingers of her good hand, there were serious globs in some places, and absolutely no shampoo in others.

She tipped her head back beneath the shower, trying to rinse out the soap. Apparently simple things like washing her hair weren't going to be simple for a while, and she just had to accept that.

Same with washing her body. Laying the washcloth open on the seat at one side of the shower, squirting body wash on it, then picking it up again, seemed incredibly inefficient, and all of it made her shower take about ten full minutes instead of the usual five.

Conor had asked if she wanted help getting ready. The thought of him walking in to see her naked in the shower made her feel both horrified and tingly and warm all over, which she knew had nothing to do with the water temperature. Proving that being close to him was making her crazy.

Flashbacks to them showering together popped into her head. Back when they'd been briefly happy, living in his old apartment. Where they'd laughed and made love and where they had seemed, for a very short and delusional time, to be perfect for one another.

Squeezing her eyes shut against the memories and the soap, she hurried to get the stupid shampoo fully out of her hair so she could dry off, get dressed, and stop thinking about how near Conor was and how much the part of her that kept forgetting their sad past wanted to drag him into the shower with her.

Yep. Crazy and crazier were good descriptions of her current headspace.

She twisted the knob so that colder water would rain on her head, which put a chill on that very wrong thought and motivated her to get out of the shower fast. One-handed toweling off was a different kind of challenge, and it took long minutes to blot her hair and get most of the moisture off her skin.

Finally giving up on being able to get it much drier than semi-sodden, she ran a hairbrush through the wet strands, put her splint back on and looked through her clothes options.

She'd already learned that getting a bra on and hooked was impossible, so it was a good thing her breasts were modest and she could get away without wearing one if the shirt fabric was thick enough. Pants were a different problem. She had tried to pull tight-fitting leggings on with only one hand yesterday... After wriggling and tugging and not even getting them past her thighs, she'd huffed out an aggravated breath and accepted that it was impossible. Zipping up and buttoning jeans? No way. Dress pants? Possible, but not easy.

She chose an oversized sweatshirt and managed to

wriggle it on, which made her feel slightly better. Then she held up two pairs of sweatpants. Both had dog hair on them, with yesterday's nicely adorned with dirt from the dog park as well. Feeling bothered by the thought of not looking presentable around Conor, then annoyed that she should care about that, she flipped through the few other options, trying to find something that would work.

A knock on the door had her freezing in place and turning to stare.

"Can I come in?"

CHAPTER SIX

CONOR'S VOICE THROUGH the closed door sent panic through Jill's chest.

"I… I'm trying to figure out—"

Apparently he took her lack of an actual answer as permission, and came into the room. His gaze immediately slid to her rear, which was currently clad only in the bikini underwear she'd wrestled on, but at least her sweatshirt covered it a little bit.

"Uh…you need some help?"

"Well, actually…" Her voice trailed off but truthfully she did. And he was already in the room, staring at her half-dressed body, so what was the point in shooing him out now? "Yes. Can you help me put these pants on? Then blow-dry my hair? 'Cause I can't do that without looking like I've been in a wind tunnel, as you saw yesterday."

He came to stand next to her, seeming to study the contents of her dresser drawer very intently. "Which pants?"

"I guess these." She held out some black dress pants. "They're not tight, like my jeans or leggings, which are too hard to get on. But I can't get them zipped and stuff."

He reached for them, and when their eyes met his held a familiar expression that darkened his eyes and made her face feel warm.

Lord, this was embarrassing—and at the same time it was absurdly arousing. Apparently her libido hadn't caught up with the fact that they were completely wrong for each other, and divorced, and that she had zero interest in a relationship with anyone until she'dgot herself together first.

"Put your hand on my shoulder," he said as he leaned down. "Then lift your leg."

She'd almost forgotten the wide bones and muscular strength of his shoulders, and forced herself to hang on and focus on her balance instead of how his body felt beneath her hand. She slipped one leg, then the other, into the pants, but had to keep holding on to him to keep from toppling over.

He pulled them up to her hips, the backs of his fingers touching her skin. Their warmth slid around to her belly button and down to the zipper, then pressed into her flesh a little as he worked the button. Absurdly, she had to bite her lip to keep an unexpected sigh of pleasure from escaping. If the feel of just his fingertips on her stomach was enough to make her want to grab him and throw him to the bed, she was in serious trouble.

"Okay." He pulled her shirt down over the pants and their eyes met again, his dark with the same desire she felt pumping through her blood. "Not your usual combination. Dress pants with a big sweatshirt. Want me to help you with a blouse? I figure the sweatshirt was all you could handle on your own?"

"No," she managed. "I can't get a bra on, so I'm... I'm naked under it."

A soft groan left his lips and the hands that were still on her pants button moved to tighten on her waist. "Did you tell me that just to torture me?"

"No. Of course not."

Had she? Or had it been because being this close to him, with his hands on her clothes and her body, made her think about what it would feel like for him to strip off the stupid sweatshirt and lick her bare breasts?

"Okay," he said again, lifting his hands to run them through his hair before turning toward the bathroom. "I have no idea how to blow-dry your hair, but I'll try."

"Can't do any worse than I did with one hand."

She followed him, seriously pondering just letting it air-dry—except she didn't want to show up at her appointment looking like she was wearing a fright wig. Lord, this was awkward—especially because being so close to him made her feel stupidly quivery.

"Sit here," he said, pulling out the plush seat beneath the vanity. "Where's your dryer?"

"In the bottom drawer."

Trying to feel as if she was just sitting at a salon, she ran the brush through her hair again, then handed it to him. "Put it on the high setting, then brush while you point it at my hair."

He did as she asked and she watched in the mirror as he frowned down at her, his focus on the job so intense that the tight feeling loosened and she had to chuckle.

"You look like you're about to do surgery. Something like brain surgery that you've never done before."

"Because I *haven't* ever done this before. And I think it's clear I have no clue how, since I wash mine, comb and go. I mean, what exactly am I supposed to be *doing* with the brush?"

"Just sort of smoothing it as you dry. Didn't you ever watch me when we…? Never mind." Bringing up more memories of when they'd lived together was *not* a good idea. "So, brush the part you're aiming the dryer at. Just drying it, as I learned when I simply pointed it at my hair and left it flying around, makes it look like an eggbeater has been at it."

"Okay. No eggbeater look. I'll try—but, just so you know, I'm not promising how it'll turn out with me at the helm."

"Hey, I have an idea!" She turned to look at him, wondering why she hadn't thought of it before. "How about I use my good hand to brush, while you aim the dryer?"

Their eyes met and held, until he broke the connection by looking down again. "Good idea. Probably would work better than me brushing. Take this."

His voice sounded a little strained. Their fingers touched as she took the brush, and the buzz in the air between them practically crackled. She tried to focus on her reflection in the mirror, to see exactly where he was aiming the dryer and how her hair was turning out, but her attention kept being captured by him.

His shoulders were broad in the dress shirt and tie he always wore to see patients or for business meetings when he wasn't in his scrubs. His profile looked more as if it should belong to a male model than a surgeon. His strong jaw and sexy lips…

"I thought you were going to brush your hair while I dry—is your arm tired?"

'Um…no." She flushed. The distraction of his physical beauty had her completely forgetting to brush. "I just…you know…"

"Yeah. I know."

The blue eyes meeting hers were deeply serious, and at the same time the heat between them shimmered. Her breath caught as she felt his hand slide the brush from hers, then slowly sweep it through her hair. He turned off the dryer and placed it on the counter. His fingers dipped into the strands he'd just brushed before he leaned down to press his lips to the bump on her forehead.

Her eyes slid closed as he moved to press his cheek against her temple and over her cheekbone, in a warm slide that sent her breathing out of whack and her heart beating harder.

"I'm so sorry you're going through this. I wish there was something I could do to take away your pain. To make things better."

"I—"

"Woof!"

"Yip! Yap!"

Hudson careened into the bathroom, with Yorkie hot on his tail, sliding a few inches across the tile floor to bump into the vanity seat, jarring them apart.

"Hudson! Yorkie!" Conor said, his voice a little rough. "Sit."

Trying to focus her attention somewhere other than on him, she turned to pick up the forgotten hairbrush and gave her hair a few strokes. A glance in the mirror showed that her hair was surprisingly presentable. It also showed that Conor stood behind her now, his eyes somber as they met hers.

"No wonder you got knocked down on the street. I thought they'd be roughhousing less now that they're not puppies anymore."

"They're still fairly young," she managed to say.

"I'm going to grab a cup of coffee before I take them out for a walk. You want one?" He sounded for all the world as though the aching connection between them a moment ago had never happened. "I'll help you get your shoes on, and whatever else you need, then we'll go."

"Sounds good."

She watched him leave the room and turned back to look at herself in the mirror. Blinked to rid her expression of the melancholy she saw reflected there. Somehow, for the next couple of days, she needed to look and sound like Conor just had. Show him she could think of him as a friend and nothing more.

Whenever Conor showed post-op X-rays to patients, then talked with them about the results and their treatment plan as they met with the therapists, it usually took his full attention. Today, though, Jillian being in the same room was a constant distraction—and never mind that the occupational therapy space was massive, taking up nearly half the entire floor of the tall building where HOAC had its headquarters.

The building where, with any luck, a new urgent care facility would soon exist, with him as part-owner. It would be good for patients to be able to go directly from diagnosis to meeting with surgeons, then to the OR, then back here for post-op care. And it would be good for his financial future as well. A win-win all around.

Which reminded him—he hadn't heard back from Urgent Care Manhattan's CEO, Peter Stanford, and needed to call him to get their meeting set up again. The longer the delay in getting the deal closed, the better the chance that another surgical center would woo the group to partner with them instead.

But even as he was thinking about what he needed to do to expedite the process Jill caught his attention again. Jokingly complaining and grimacing as she used the therapy equipment to try to improve her hand mobility. Then chatting and laughing with the OTs during each brief break. The bright overhead lights brought out the golden highlights in her beautiful hair, and even when the smile he loved was directed at someone else it sneaked into his heart anyway.

Despite the uncomfortable feelings rolling around in his chest he had to chuckle, noting that her hair looked fairly smooth. They'd definitely somehow avoided the eggbeater look she didn't want, but how that was possible he had no clue. They hadn't even managed to fully dry her hair before he'd found himself kissing her bruise and loving the feel of his cheek against hers. If the dogs hadn't run in right then he wasn't at all sure he wouldn't have forgotten everything and moved on to kiss her mouth—which he'd promised her he wouldn't do again.

He drew in a deep breath and strode to the computer to look up some charts, needing to get his mind off the intense desire he still felt for her. They'd both regret being intimate if they gave in to the sexual heat that kept shimmering between them, which probably surprised her as much as it surprised him.

With all the anger and disappointment that had led to their divorce, he'd figured all those feelings would have been snuffed out. But being with her, close together in his place, had proved that wasn't the case at all. Somehow, though, he had to make sure he kept his hands and mouth to himself.

He went to his office and pulled out his cell. "Peter? Conor McCarthy. I'm sorry I couldn't make our meeting, but I had a family emergency to deal with." Not exactly family, but he sure didn't want to go into that with Peter Stanford. "When would be a good time for us to reschedule?"

"Unfortunately I have a busy week. I'll take a look at my calendar and get back to you."

"Thanks. I'd like to get the details worked out as soon as possible, so please let me know what would work for you."

Conor's gut tightened as he hung up. *Not* good that Peter had sounded so vague. With another surgery center wooing Urgent Care Manhattan to become partners, he had to make sure his proposal was laid out to them pronto. And if it ended up not being the first one they saw, he'd just have to make sure it was the best one.

He blew out a breath and was glad it was time to see patients. Some as follow-up, and others who were there to see him with new injuries, discussing their options for future surgery and what to expect.

After a couple hours he decided he should check on Jill and suggest she head back to his apartment to rest. He scanned the therapy room, frowning when he didn't see her anywhere. Michelle Branson was working at her computer, not with a patient at the moment, and he moved to ask her if she knew where Jill had gone. Then his gaze caught the shimmering waterfall of silky hair that covered half of Jill's face, turned in profile.

Instead of sitting and relaxing, or talking with the people she used to work with, or trying to do the exercises, she was in the laundry room, standing at a table to fold the towels they used under patient's arms and elbows during therapy. Then she gathered a heating pad to take it to a patient who had just arrived, smiling and talking with them as she folded it over his arm in preparation for therapy.

He shook his head. She'd said she wanted to get back to work as soon as she could, but wouldn't taking a few more days off to rest be a good idea? She'd had her own therapy session, and he knew she had to be in pain after it.

Nonchalantly pretending to look at his tablet, he watched her work with the patient. The stressed look on her face was obvious, even as she smiled. When she moved back to the laundry room he followed her there.

"Something wrong?" he asked.

"No. Why do you ask?"

"I thought you looked stressed."

"I am stressed. Worried that this—" she held up her arm "—is going to take forever to be normal again."

"It is going to take a while—which you know. So why are you working? You know you need to be resting, instead of messing around distributing towels and heating pads."

"I'm only using one hand and resting my other one."

"Why won't you take just a few days off?"

"Now, isn't that the pot calling the kettle black?" She rolled her eyes. "The surgeon who works fourteen-plus hours a day is annoyed that I'm bored and want to do something productive."

"I don't always work fourteen hours a day, and I'm not injured. You are."

Even though his chest felt tight with concern for her, he couldn't help but feel a tinge of pride that this amazing woman, the woman he'd thought he'd love forever, was such a tough dynamo, with zero interest in lying on a couch and watching movies for the next however many weeks as she healed.

"What's wrong with putting your feet up and letting people take care of you?"

"I'm hardly doing a thing. Mostly because I can't. Punching you in the nose isn't even an option." With a teasing smile, she waved her splinted hand toward his chin. "You can't imagine how frustrating it is only being able to manage a little of the work I usually do. To feel dependent on other people for things I'd never dreamed I'd need help with. As *you* are unfortunately aware."

Her voice held a joking tone, but he could see deep inside her beautiful eyes that glum and forlorn were good words to describe how she felt. And, yeah, despite working with patients for a long time now, it was true that he didn't really know exactly what it was like to be temporarily or, in the case of some unfortunate patients, permanently crippled.

"Hey…" He reached to gently draw her into a corner, standing close enough that they could talk quietly. The frustration he'd felt with her just moments ago melted into sympathy and warmth, even as he tried to shore up the protective shell around his heart. "It's going to be okay. You'll get where you were before—I'm sure of it. It's just going to take time, patience and effort. Like you always tell your own patients."

"I know. But I'm not going to be able to run. I'm meant to be in training for a marathon, and I really thought I'd be able to beat my best time. I'm not going to be able to run at all for a couple months—which I hate."

"You're training for a *marathon*?"

"I started running marathons just after we broke up. It was cathartic. Now I'm addicted."

"Wow. Good for you."

He could just picture her training, driven despite the small handicap of her leg, working to achieve her best time. Her hair flying as she ran. He almost told her he'd like to watch her run, but stopped himself. After she was on her own again having any contact outside work wasn't a good idea.

"I'm sorry it's so frustrating that you can't run and train right now."

"I can't even tie my sneakers. Can't get dressed... I—"

The tones of a muffled "William Tell Overture" chimed in his ear and he knew it had to be her cell phone—because who else had that as their ring tone?

"That's you. Where's your phone?"

"In my purse."

She took a few steps to grab it off the counter and began fumbling to unzip it one-handed. Seconds stretched on, and he finally reached for her bag.

"I'll get it."

Digging inside her purse, touching her lipstick and her wallet and other things, felt strangely intimate, bringing memories he hadn't even realized were there. When he finally pulled her phone out from under a small notebook he was glad to be able to hand her purse back, so the smell of her perfume stopped wafting to his nose.

Despite telling himself not to, he glanced at the screen to see if it was some guy she might be dating, but it was just a number with no name. Of course if there was a guy, wouldn't he be around to help her? If she had a guy who wasn't here for her when she needed him he deserved to be dumped to the curb and never thought about again.

Though he'd been that guy, hadn't he? And she'd left.

"Here."

He passed the phone to her. Maybe it was a friend who was ready and available to help her out—he should be hoping that was the case. That would be good. Really good for both of them. Except his heart didn't seem to be wishing for that at all.

Carefully watching her expression as she glanced at the phone, he saw that it first held surprise, then concern.

"Hello?"

She moved to the other side of the small laundry room, her back to him. It was ridiculous that it bugged him that she obviously wanted to keep the call private. They weren't married anymore, and she had every right to keep whatever she wanted from him.

"I understand. Please let me know if there's another opening in the future. Thanks again."

Her shoulders visibly slumped and she ran her hand down her face before turning back to him with a grimace.

"What's wrong?"

"Nothing. Not important."

"Jill? What don't you want to tell me?"

He tipped up her chin to make her look at him, and all those conflicting feelings filled his chest again. More than anything he wanted to lean down and kiss her, to take away her worries. To taste her and fall into her and forget all the negativity between them. But he managed to stop himself.

"I had an interview for a job in Connecticut next week. I let them know about my wrist when it first happened, but it wasn't a problem because they didn't expect me to start work for six weeks. Now someone's left and they need a replacement immediately. So that means I'm out of the running—at least for now."

"A job in another state?" His heart jolted, then sank to the pit of his stomach—which made no sense.

She'd left to work at the occupational therapy clinic after their divorce ten months ago, and he hadn't seen her even once in all that time until now. So why did it feel as if her moving to another state would shove wide open the cracks in his heart that were barely beginning to heal?

"I'm sorry. But you know your job here is secure, regardless of how much time you need to heal?"

"Well..." Her lips twisted again. "For reasons I'm sure you can understand, I don't want to work here, have to see you all the time. It wouldn't be good for either of us."

Damn it. So he was the reason she wanted a new job in another state?

"We can figure it out. Maybe work on that friendship we talked about?"

"I've thought about that," she said softly. "And I think we both know we can't really be friends."

"Okay, I get it." He drew a deep breath. "But there are other jobs out there. Regardless, I don't want you to feel you can't work here because of me."

"Don't worry about it." She gave him a crooked smile. "I'll find something—and moving away from the city makes sense. You know I need more room for the dogs. I can find a bigger place a lot cheaper if I get a job in Connecticut, or somewhere else. Maybe even in Pittsburgh, since my parents are there."

"Will you please reconsider letting me buy you a place to live? You never believed it, but all I wanted was for us...for you...never to have to worry about money ever."

"Money isn't the answer to everything, Conor."

Her smile turned sad and wan, and he wished he understood why.

"Sometimes it just complicates things and makes them worse."

"I know money isn't the answer to everything. But it is—"

"Never mind." Her suddenly bright voice was at odds with her expression. "I've got to get back to work. I'll text you if I get tired and decide to go back to your apartment."

"Thanks."

Obviously the conversation was over, at least for now.

"Noah is supposed to be here in an hour. If you feel up to it maybe you could take a look at his splint with me, since he knows you."

"Noah? Oh, my gosh, I'd forgotten today is when he's supposed to come back to see you. Of course I want to help. I'll meet you right here."

CHAPTER SEVEN

JILLIAN PRETENDED TO focus on folding towels and tidying up the therapy space, but she was really watching Conor. An hour past the time Noah was supposed to show up, but hadn't, Conor was practically pacing the floor. He'd go into his office to do some paperwork, then come back to see if Noah had arrived, then pull up some charts on the computer, then check back again. Finally he came straight up to Jillian, a deep frown on his face.

"I'm going to Noah's house. If he comes, let me know and I'll get back here as fast as possible."

"You know where he lives?"

"His address is still on my ride-share app. It's pretty far, so I'm going to drive."

"What if he's not there?"

"He might not be. But I have no other way to find him, so I might as well start there."

The depth of concern on Conor's face surprised her. "I wish he'd come to see us, so we could look at him, but he's probably okay, don't you think? If he wasn't he would have come back."

"Can't count on that. Will you be okay getting back to the apartment by yourself?"

"Of course. But if you're worried about him I want to come with you."

"Not necessary. And his neighborhood is pretty rough. I work at a free clinic there every few months, and you have to watch your back."

"If it's safe enough for you, it's safe enough for me. And I'm the splint expert—not you. So let's go."

Their eyes met for a long moment before he finally nodded. "All right. I'll get the car from my apartment parking garage and meet you out front in fifteen minutes."

It was rush hour as they made their way through the city, though when it came to New York it felt like rush hour pretty much all the time. Horns blared and taxis swerved in and out of lanes.

As they got closer to where Noah lived the debris on the sides of the road increased and the buildings looked more dilapidated, some even boarded up. People looked up and then slipped away between buildings as Conor's powerful car nosed down the streets, finally stopping when the GPS told them they'd arrived.

Conor turned to look at her, his expression grim. "I have the address, but not his apartment number. Guess I'll have to knock on doors. Why don't you stay put in the car until I figure out which apartment it is and if he's even there?"

"It'll be a waste of time for you to knock on doors alone. We'll do it together, different doors on the same floor, and go from there."

"Why do I feel like that's a bad idea?" He sighed. "But all right."

The hallway of the first floor was pretty dark as they approached each door. A few knocks were answered, but nobody knew Noah. They went to the next floor, and by the third both of them felt discouraged.

"Can we find out what school a child living here would go to? Maybe we can do that, then contact the school tomorrow," Jillian said.

"Good idea. This isn't working out too well. Sorry."

"Don't be silly. I think it's wonderful that you care about him, and want to see how he's doing. I know a lot of people would be stunned to learn that you're taking a big chunk of your day to look for a little boy you took care of."

"Let's finish this floor, and if he's not here we'll head back."

The next door opened and a young man stood there, looking suspicious.

Conor held up his medical badge, which showed his photo and name. "I'm Dr. McCarthy and we're looking for a boy named Noah. He hurt his arm a couple days ago and I want to check on him."

The man studied both of them for what felt like a long time, until he apparently decided they weren't the police, or whatever it was he was concerned about.

"He's up one floor. 409, I think."

"Thank you."

They moved to go up the next set of stairs, and Conor paused. "You okay to climb another flight of steps? You can always go back to the car."

"I might not be able to use one arm, but the rest of me is in good shape, Dr. McCarthy."

"Don't I know it?" He flashed her a grin before heading up the steps.

After several knocks on the door there was still no answer, and Conor turned to her, his lips twisting.

"Looks like a wild goose chase. Let's—"

The door cracked open and Noah's face appeared. His eyes widened before he swung it open. "Dr. McCarthy! Why are you here?"

"You didn't come to your appointment today. So we came to you."

"I… Wow." After a quick glance behind him, he turned back. "I'm doing okay. It hurts, but you said it would. So I figured I'm fine."

"Still want to take a look. Can we come in?"

Obviously nervous, he glanced over his shoulder again. "I don't think that's a good idea. My—"

"Who are you talking to?" A woman's annoyed voice came from a back room.

"It's the doctor who…who fixed my arm."

"What?"

A woman, presumably Noah's mother, emerged from the back room, looking as if she'd just woken up.

"Who the hell are you?"

"I'm Dr. Conor McCarthy. I believe it was you I spoke with on the phone about Noah's arm."

Jillian was amazed at his calm tone in the face of obvious hostility.

"We want to check to make sure it's doing okay."

"He's fine. I've got no money to give you, so don't be coming around expecting any."

"We're not wanting any money. We just want to look at Noah's injury."

"I don't believe you. Everybody wants something." She crossed her arms and glared. "Noah's dad left us high and dry, without a penny, so you're wasting your time."

"Mom, Dr. McCarthy took good care of me and I

want him to look at my arm again. He didn't charge me anything first time, right?"

"Then he shows up at the door? Ha! You've got a lot to learn, boy." She grabbed her purse from a worn chair. "I'm outta here. You want to pay your doctor friend, that's your problem—though I know you're as broke as me."

Jillian wondered if Conor would stop her, try to convince her he was offering his services for free and reassure her that he had Noah's best interests in mind, but he didn't look back as she left. Didn't even mention her as he placed his hand on Noah's back and led him to the sofa.

"How about you sit here while we take a look? How's it feeling?"

Jillian watched, amazed. For all the world you would have thought the two of them were sitting at HOAC having a normal doctor/patient visit. Was this something he did often? How had she never known he was used to working in communities like this and dealing with the various challenges involved?

"It hurts. Still really swelled up. But okay, I guess."

Conor took the boy's arm in his hand and carefully removed the splint, gently feeling all around his elbow, talking with him the whole time. He asked him questions and smiled, joking a bit, and the look of total trust and admiration on Noah's face made her heart fill with something warm and fuzzy.

Appreciation for this side of Conor she hadn't often seen. Pride in the man he was, even though he was no longer a part of her life.

In their brief time together she'd felt frustrated that Conor McCarthy had such an extreme need to make more and more money, through hard work, investment and business acquisitions. He'd made that the number one focus of his life. And yet this Conor McCarthy was a different person. This Conor cared about only one thing right now, and that was the health of this boy.

Together they adjusted the splint and refastened it, and then, to her surprise, Conor sat on the sofa next to Noah. "Tell me about your mom. Does she take care of you or is she not around much?"

"Sleeps most of the time when she's here. Otherwise she's not around much. She seems…sad a lot. I think I make her even sadder, so she goes places with friends."

"I doubt you make her sadder. Sometimes when people feel sad it's hard for them to see how the things they do affect others," Conor said quietly. "Was she sad before your dad left, too?"

Noah shrugged. "I don't really remember. That was a long time ago."

"Okay." He put his arm around the boy's shoulders. "My dad left us, too, and my mom was sad afterward. Really sad. So I know about that, and how it feels. I'd like for us to be friends and get together to talk—about ways you can help your mom and about other things. Can we do that?"

"Sure. If you want."

The way Noah looked up at him said a lot more than those casual words. It said that having Conor be his friend and talk about the problems in his life was the most amazing thing that had ever happened to him.

"Good." Conor stood, and handed him another business card. "Call me next weekend. We'll get lunch or something. And don't forget this time."

"I won't." Noah stood and grinned. "I won't forget. Thanks for coming to see me."

"Good luck, Noah," Jillian said, fighting a lump in her throat. "And if you need help with that splint let Dr. McCarthy know and we'll get you into the office to adjust it."

"Okay."

Conor gave the boy another pat on the back before he opened the door and ushered Jillian out.

They didn't speak until they were in the car, heading back into traffic.

"I'm not sure what to say to you," she said quietly. "Except that you were wonderful with that child. Do you often mentor kids like him?"

"Sometimes. When the opportunity is there."

"How did I never know this? Why didn't you tell me?"

He didn't answer at first, then sighed. "Easy to move from surgery to seeing a kid to a business meeting before I came home without making a big deal of it."

"I would have liked to hear about it. The children you mentor and why."

Again he was quiet for a long time. "Another one of my failings, Jill? I don't know how to talk about things like that, so I just don't. Didn't think you'd be particularly interested."

"I was your wife. Of course I'd have been interested in anything you were doing. Anything you were interested in. Anything that impacted your life from the past."

He turned to look at her, his eyes filled with regret. "Another thing I did wrong. Not explaining where I was after work sometimes. I know you wondered why

I wasn't with you. Felt hurt by it. I wasn't smart enough to understand it. But we already know there's something big missing inside me, don't we? I proved that over and over again. I'm just sorry you were hurt by it. Sorry I didn't learn soon enough."

She opened her mouth to say that wasn't entirely true, that she wanted to talk more about what he'd just said. More about her own failings and issues, and what she'd learned about herself since their divorce. But he looked so grim. Melancholy. Was there any reason to go over it at all when their relationship was history?

"Conor, I—"

"What do you want to eat?"

He stared through the windshield and the interruption showed loud and clear that he didn't want to talk anymore. "I'll call and order something so it'll get to my apartment soon after we do."

"Um…pizza would be good. Something I can eat with one hand."

"Pizza it is. With mushrooms, as I recall?"

"And pepperoni. Got to have some greasy meat to help my bones heal."

A small smile curved his lips and she smiled, too, glad he wasn't feeling so bummed out anymore.

"Nothing better than mush and pep."

They didn't say much on the elevator ride to his floor, and then the dogs were a good distraction, jumping around excitedly when they came through the door. Conor laughed, and roughhoused a little with both the dogs, and Jillian's throat closed again. Why had she always focused on his absence and not paid enough attention to all the good things about the man?

She knew why. His glitzy life and wealthy friends

and expensive apartment demanded a woman who'd fit in to all that, and she wasn't that woman. Focusing on his failings and inadequacies had been easier than focusing on her own.

"I'll feed the dogs, then take them for a walk while you wait for the pizza," Conor said. "That work for you?"

"Sounds good. I'll do that resting you keep nagging me to do."

"You've had a long day. And you know as well as I do that your body is putting a lot of energy into healing, which *has* to make you feel tired. It's not a weakness to let yourself rest—it's smart."

"I know, I know. And if you ever injure yourself, I'll have to remind you, the energetic Dr. McCarthy, of the same thing."

Their eyes met and she wanted to smack herself. Why had she said that? First, he'd hopefully never break any bones, and second, if he did, she sure wouldn't be around to remind him of anything.

"I'll be back soon."

Apparently, he'd decided not to react to her comment. The dogs gulped down their dinner, then excitedly left for their walk. The pizza came just as they returned, and Jill moved to the kitchen to get the dishes.

"Let someone else do the work while you can," he said, shaking his head. "You'll be faring for yourself soon enough. How about we sit on the balcony and look out over the park? You'll have to wear a jacket, but it's a really nice night. Pretty soon it'll be raining and snowing and freezing cold, so we should enjoy it while we can."

She figured there was no point in saying it would

likely be the *only* night they'd enjoy his balcony together, regardless of the weather. "Sounds nice."

He carried plates and slid open the French doors to the balcony. Two chairs sat on either side of a small table, with chaise longues at the other end. Car headlights moved in both directions on Fifth Avenue, and the glittering lights of the city lit the panorama below. Beyond that, a half-moon hung above the dark silhouettes of the trees in Central Park.

"Wow," she breathed. "This is just beautiful. I see why you moved here."

"It is beautiful. But that's not the only reason I moved here."

"Because you're close to work? Because it's a good investment?"

"All of those reasons. And one more. Because I couldn't stand living in the place we shared together without you there with me."

His admission made her throat close, and she had no idea what to say in response. Their eyes met for a long moment until he moved back to the French doors.

"I'll get everything else."

He returned with the pizza, a bottle of wine and two glasses, pouring each of them a drink.

"Wine?"

"Your favorite—Chardonnay, as I recall. Since you're only taking your pain meds at night, now, I figured it would be nice to enjoy a glass."

"I'm not going to argue about a glass of wine with pizza. Sounds wonderful."

Without conversation they sat and ate and drank as they stared out over the park. For quite a while the silence was oddly comfortable, until it stretched out too long.

With the pizza finished and a second glass of wine in her hand, Jillian decided she was going to talk with him about Noah. About what he'd told the child about his own mother being sad, which he'd never mentioned to her. About why he'd never talked to her about what he did when he wasn't home during their marriage. Keeping it to himself. Feeding into her insecurities and fueling the belief that he didn't really want to spend time with her.

That was partly her fault, she knew. But she wanted to understand it better.

"Tell me about your mom," she said. "You said she was sad. Why?"

He kept on looking out over the park, his handsome profile seeming etched in stone. "Not worth going into, Jill."

"I think it is," she said softly. "How did you feel when your father left? How did it affect your mom, and your lives? Was that why she was sad?"

She'd begun to think he wasn't going to answer when he finally turned to look at her.

"I suppose I may as well tell you, so you know some of the reasons I was such a lousy husband." He sighed. "My father left when I was in kindergarten, but I still remember it well because my mother freaked. Which I didn't understand since he wasn't very present at home anyway. By that I mean he was gone a lot, and when he was home he didn't talk to me or my mom much anyway. So when he left it didn't really matter to me, because he obviously already didn't care about me one way or the other. But it mattered to my mother a lot. Changed our lives completely."

"In what way?"

"Well, number one was that we had no money after he disappeared, and he couldn't be tracked by the courts to pay child support. My mother stressed all the time about how to pay the bills, and once I was old enough to help I did what I could to get odd jobs. Mowed lawns, scrounged the neighborhood for cans to recycle, walked dogs—whatever a ten-year-old could do. Once I was a teenager I was able to get regular work, bagging at the local grocery store in addition to the other stuff, and help more. But paying the rent and everything was always a worry. When I heard her crying at night I always thought that was why."

"Oh, Conor." Jill reached for his hand. "I can't imagine how hard that must have been."

"I'd lie there and wonder what to do. Try to figure out other ways to earn a few bucks." He looked down at their twined fingers and she tightened her hold. "I vowed that once I was able to make real money we'd never be in that situation again."

"I see." She'd always wondered why the money he made had never seemed like enough to him, and tried to understand it better now. "Did your helping out that way eventually help your mother feel less stressed?"

"No—and I didn't get it. I hated that she was sad, but the horrible truth is I was focused on myself way more than her. My jobs. Friends. School. I resented when she'd go out at night, thinking, *What the hell? I'm working two jobs and going to school, and she's out having fun?* I didn't see what was happening. Didn't understand. Until it was too late."

"What didn't you understand?"

"That she had a mental illness. Was in a deep depression. Her escape from the pain of my dad leaving, of being alone except for me, who was hardly ever around, of the money worries—all that sent her to bars to drink. To forget. To be with people who were just as sad and miserable as she was."

He lifted his gaze to hers, and the anguish she saw there made her throat close.

"I don't want to tell you the rest, but you deserve to know."

She dreaded to hear what was coming. "What happened?" she whispered.

"I didn't open my eyes to the depth of her pain. Her depression. Wasn't there for her emotionally. Then one night she drove home drunk, lost control of her car and hit a tree."

"Oh, Conor." Her fingers tightened on his, her heart in her throat. "And that's how she died?"

"That's how she died. And if I'd been paying attention to her, instead of just myself, maybe I could have gotten her help. Maybe I could have talked with her, been there for her. Maybe if I had she'd still be alive."

Jill stood and squeezed next to him in his chair, wrapped her arm around his neck and pressed her cheek to his. "I'm so, so sorry. But you know it wasn't your fault. Alcoholics rarely listen. Drinking buries what hurts and numbs the pain."

"I don't know it. After she died I made myself face all the signs I'd ignored. All the ways I'd let her down. All the things I could have done to be there for her. And when it turned out she had an insurance policy—a pretty good one that got me through college and medical school—it about broke my heart. Made me feel like the worst human in the world. Because I'd convinced myself she was self-centered, that she wasn't there for me just like my father. But all along she had been—as much as she could be. She'd been paying that policy when we barely had money to buy food, to make sure I was taken care of in case something happened to her. Truth is, it was me who wasn't there for her. Just like I wasn't there for you."

"Conor." She pressed her mouth to his cheek, her heart aching for the boy he'd been. "You were a teenager. Every kid that age is focused on themselves. You can't beat yourself up for being normal. Can't take responsibility for your mother's drinking problem. When you think of what you've accomplished with your life you have a lot to be proud of, and I know your mother would be proud of you, too."

He didn't respond for a long time, then finally shook his head. "Anyway. So now you know. All that made me think that I'd like to have what I never had. What my parents never had. A woman to love forever, to be a good father, to provide for my family." His hand lifted and cupped her face in his palm. "I fell crazy in love with you the minute I met you, Jilly. I didn't know then that I couldn't be the kind of man I wanted to be. That you wanted me to be. Bad genes, probably."

"Conor—"

His finger moved to her lips. "It's just the truth. I thought providing a solid future for us, making as much money as possible, was all I needed to do. The way to show how much I loved you. But once I saw how miserable I made you I knew I'd been wrong. That it wasn't enough, and that I'm missing something inside. That I can't be the kind of husband you want and deserve. I'm a one-dimensional guy, as sad as that is. And I'm more sorry than you'll ever know that I hurt you."

Her heart shook. She wanted to tell him he was wrong. But the truth was, everything she'd seen in the months they were married had shown he was right. No matter what she'd said or done, working and making money had been his priority. He hadn't been capable of, or even interested in, changing that. And she hadn't been who he needed, either. A wife who was comfortable mingling with people she didn't know, going places she would never fit in.

She wanted a normal life, doing normal things with normal friends. She wanted a husband who loved to be home, and Conor had proved he just couldn't be that man. Even if he'd thought he wanted to be.

She stared at him for a long moment, her heart hurting for both of them, until he wrapped his arms around her, pulled her onto his lap and kissed her.

Jillian slipped her fingers into his hair and let herself feel the emotion in his kiss. All he felt from his youth, from his belief that he'd let his mother down. His resentment over his father's abandonment. His grief. And tangled with all those big emotions was what they'd had together. The giddy passion, the deep love, the pain of failure—all of it hung between them as their mouths fused together.

He held her so close, her legs straddling his hips, that it almost felt as if they were one, and then the kiss began to change. It felt less about those big emotions and more about the connection they'd always had. The kiss softened, deepened, and the tenderness of it made Jillian's heart flip inside out, reminding her of the brief time when it had been amazing between them and how much she'd loved him—how she'd believed, for a time, that there was nothing more perfect than the way they felt about one another.

"Jillian..." His mouth separated from hers just long enough for him to breathe her name. "Jilly..."

The kiss changed again. Hotter, wetter, sending her blood pounding and heat pumping through her pores. His arms tightened around her—until sharp pain had her crying out.

"God, Jillian!" He leaned back, looking horrified. "Did I hurt you?"

"My...my stupid arm."

"Damn it! I'm so sorry. I can't believe I forgot to be careful." He reached carefully to grasp her splinted wrist in his hand, staring down at it.

"Not your fault." She stroked his cheek with her other hand and kissed the top of his head, not wanting him to feel guilty all over again. "I'm the one who forgot about it and wrapped it around you. You'd think the splint would protect it from getting jostled, but I guess not. I suppose that's another thing for me to understand better and learn to talk to my patients about."

"How to make love while wearing a splint?" He looked up at her with a crooked smile, then lowered his mouth to her hand, gently pressing his lips to each swollen finger. "If you give that talk I'll make sure I'm not there. Wouldn't want to be in a public place while being reminded of how it feels to touch you and make love with you."

"We're not making love. Are we?"

"No. Because that would be a bad idea...wouldn't it?"

She nodded, but at the same time she could see the

eyes meeting hers held something hot and alive, and before she could decide exactly what to do next he'd swung her into his arms and was carrying her back into the apartment and down the hall to his bedroom.

"Um… I thought we weren't sure if—"

His mouth dropped to hers again as he flicked the covers back and deposited her on the big bed. His talented surgeon's fingers had the buttons of her shirt undone in a blink, before he opened it, then slid it down and off her good arm. Getting it over her splint forced him to separate his lips from hers, and their eyes met as he slowly stroked his hands from her shoulders down her arms.

Jillian quivered, and she wondered if he could tell how he made her feel. Wondered if he felt as aroused and confused and uncertain about whether or not this was a bad idea as she did.

"It's up to you if we make love or not," he said, his gaze on her camisole before their eyes met again. "But I think you need some occupational therapy, regardless. To make your pain go away."

"You're a surgeon, not a therapist," she said, and couldn't help it that her voice was breathy.

"Sure about that? I seem to remember you liking my therapy treatments in the past."

"Please don't use the words 'therapy treatments' as a euphemism for sex. I'll never be able to work again with that on my mind." She started to laugh, then gasped as his fingers slowly traced along the lace of her camisole and lightly across her nipples. "But I admit that I'm curious to see what you have in mind to help me feel better."

"I *definitely* have some ideas about how to make you feel better."

Her heart kicked hard at his sexy, teasing smile. He leaned down to cover her breast with his mouth, his tongue teasing her through the fabric, and her good hand held the back of his head as she gasped. His hands moved to her waist and she could hardly bear the delicious sensation of his fingers trailing across her skin. He flicked open the button on her trousers and unzipped them, his mouth moving down to her stomach as his fingers stealthily dipped inside her underwear.

"You're so beautiful, Jilly."

God, it felt so good. So wonderful. The way it always had with him. The incredible pleasure of it tossed aside any worries that this might be a bad idea and she arched toward him, wanting him. Wanting this. Wanting him to forget the sadness and guilt of just a moment ago. Wanting to forget her physical pain and her heartache over him and enjoy the delirious bliss of being with him one more time.

"Conor?"

"Mmm…?"

"Make love to me."

"What, you think this really is some unorthodox medical treatment? Maybe being away from you for almost a year has made me lose my touch." Smiling, he tugged her pants all the way off, then brought his mouth back to hers as he caressed her again. "Just taking it slow. Slow and easy, right? I have to, or I might lose control and hurt your arm again."

"*Is* something wrong with my arm? I don't remember…"

"Ah, good. Glad to hear the therapy is working."

He laughed against her lips but kept up the heat, and she arched against the talented fingers that were making her quiver and burn. She could barely breathe at the goodness of it, and she pulled her mouth from his because she wanted to see his face. His eyes were smiling, but glazed, too, and he looked like he had so long ago. As if she meant the world to him.

It squeezed her chest and sent another layer of emotion into the incredible pleasure of making love with him again after all this time.

She'd just placed her hand behind his head to bring his mouth to hers for another kiss when she realized she was doing all the taking and none of the giving. And that she was nearly naked except for her camisole, but he was fully clothed.

"We have a problem here. I'm naked and you're not."

"I don't see that as a problem." He nuzzled her neck, licked her earlobe, moved his mouth to the hollow of her throat.

"It…it is a problem." She could barely get the words out, so she needed to talk fast before she couldn't talk at all. "Because I can't undress you. And I want to feel all your skin against all of mine. Will you take off your clothes, please?"

"In a minute…"

His mouth continued its leisurely trek across her collarbone, down to her nipples again, and the orgasm sneaked up on her before she knew it was going to happen. Waves of pleasure skated across her skin and through her body and she let out a soft cry.

"Ah, Jilly…" He kissed her softly as his hands moved to cup her waist.

Somehow she managed to open her eyes and look

into his beautiful blue ones, filled with the same passion she felt. She waited to feel regret, the fear that this was a mistake. But there was no regret. Only want.

"Wow…" she breathed. "That was very…therapeutic. Thank you."

"There's more."

"That's what I was hoping," she said, reaching for his pants to wrestle with the button—until he stopped her.

"No. You're handicapped, remember? Tonight you're letting me do everything. Undress you…undress me. Kiss you and touch you and make love with you, while you just lie there and let me make you feel good."

"And here I was thinking that having a broken wrist was awful. Who knew it could lead to something so wonderful?"

"There's a silver lining for everything, I guess."

He smiled and kissed her again, softly and slowly, his mouth lingering so long she was torn between enjoying the bone-melting pleasure of it and telling him to get naked, already. Finally, he lifted his head and stood, stripping off his clothes until he was next to the bed gloriously naked.

She let herself admire his muscular body, his smooth skin, the jut of his erection. Thought about how she'd explored every inch of its beauty and how intimately she knew each small scar and imperfection.

Which reminded her of her own scars and imperfections. How she'd hated him to see them, and tried to hide them whenever they'd been naked together.

The thought briefly dimmed the excitement she was feeling—until he came onto the bed, kneeling above her. His gaze trapping hers, he slipped her camisole over her head, held her face in his hands, then began kissing her until everything was forgotten except how he made her feel.

"I think the safest place for your arms is over your head." He gently placed them there, and she shivered as he ran his fingertips down the soft skin of her inner arms, wriggled and laughed when he stroked down to her armpits, then gasped as he caressed her breasts. His fingers continued on, slowly tracing her entire body, then opening her legs and touching her *there* until she was making little mewling sounds she couldn't seem to control.

"I'm not sure if this is pleasure or torture," she said with a gasp.

"Pleasure. Only pleasure, I promise."

She was vaguely aware of him taking something from the nightstand and then he was inside her, moving, finding the perfect rhythm they'd always shared together. The pace grew faster, taking her higher, making her feel as if they were chasing the past. The best part of the past. Wanting to experience one more time what they'd had before they could never have it again.

His mouth crushed hers as they both moaned their release and her heart shook as hard as her body. Conor McCarthy was hers again, for this brief moment, and she would hold him close while she could.

CHAPTER EIGHT

JILLIAN SAT ON one of Conor's comfortable modern sofas and stared out over the city while she ate a banana that wasn't black this time.

The dogs were at her knees, nudging her and demanding attention, despite Conor having taken them for a walk early this morning, and she managed a crooked smile even as she inexplicably wanted to cry. She reached to scratch their ears, and when Hudson whined she rested her face on his big head.

"I know. I miss him, too. Which is *not* a good thing."

But, she reminded herself, she'd missed him even when they were married, hadn't she?

If only she'd known how things would turn out when she'd fallen so hard for him on their very first date. Except, if she was honest with herself, she had a feeling that nothing would have kept her from wanting to be with him, from marrying him, even if she'd known that her heart would be so deeply bruised when it was over.

After last night's conversation she understood him better. And that understanding made her heart hurt for him, made her appreciate why he hadn't seemed to want to change his ways even as their marriage had crumbled. It was good that she knew, and it would go a long way toward closure as she moved on to a new phase of her life.

The 'William Tell Overture' began so abruptly she jumped, then fished around for her phone. Finally finding it between the sofa cushions, she saw it was Briana.

"Hey, sis! What's the scoop?"

"I finally squeezed out some time to come stay with you," Briana said. "I'm really sorry I haven't been able to get there sooner. I'll be doing some work from there, but I figure that's not a problem, right?"

"Not at all. I have therapy sessions three times a week, and I even get a little work done for another hour or two. I'm not too functional yet, but you shouldn't have to stay very long. I'll be off the nighttime pain meds soon, and I am learning how to get along with only one hand until the other one starts to work again."

"Great to hear. I'll be there the day after tomorrow. I'll let you know what time. Can't wait to see you and the pups."

"Can't wait, either. Love you—and thanks."

Her fingers went limp with the phone still in her hand and she stared out the window again. This was it. Briana was coming. Time to say goodbye to Conor, except for the times they'd run into each other at HOAC. Besides getting her hand to work again, looking for another job would be her priority now, so they could say goodbye for good and never see one another again.

She should feel glad about that. Seeing him, and then making love with him, had seriously messed with her equilibrium and brought back some of the pain and heartache she'd been trying to move on from. It had also brought back wonderful memories of how much fun they'd had together when things had been good.

Which must be why her stomach felt hollow at the thought of never seeing him again. Of it truly being over with again.

But of course neither of them had any interest in going back in time. Conor was who he was, and she was who she was. Great sex was just that, and it had nothing to do with being right for one another in any real-life way.

She sighed and lay her head back against the cushions.

Apparently she'd dozed off, because the next thing she heard was the sound of the front door opening and Conor's voice saying her name. She felt his hand smoothing back her hair and opened her eyes to see him smiling at her as he crouched in front of her, wearing a suit and tie, crinkles at the corners of his eyes.

"Hey." He gave her nose a gentle flick. "How are you feeling?"

"Pretty good."

If she didn't count feeling confused. Wired from what had happened between them last night. A little sad that it wouldn't happen again. And relieved not to have to rehash all the bad things between them anymore.

"I'm glad. Because I don't have any surgeries scheduled today and I decided to get a bunch of business stuff done this morning and put the rest off until tomorrow so I could take the rest of the day off to spend with you."

"What?" She struggled to sit upright and his hands wrapped around her waist to help her.

"I know it's hard for you, being cooped up here when you're not at therapy or helping out there. Not able to run, or mess with your plants, or do all the stuff you usually do. Speaking of which…" He stood and walked to his doorway, then returned. "I figured the cool tones of the decorating around here needed a little warmth to make you feel at home. So I brought a couple of your plants to keep you company."

He set them on the coffee table and she stared. Reached out to finger one of the leaves as, inexplicably, a lump came to her throat. "That's...very sweet of you. Except there's no reason for me to try to feel at home anymore. Briana called and she's coming day after tomorrow. I'll be going back to my place."

His smile faded and their eyes met for a long moment before he put on a forced smile. "Well, that's good. I'm glad she'll be able to take care of you for a while."

"Yeah. It's good."

His chest lifted in a deep breath and neither of them spoke as their eyes met.

Finally, she made herself stand. "So, maybe you can help me pack?"

"You said she's not coming until day after tomorrow. And you know I never take an afternoon off. So let's enjoy it while we can."

She stared at his crooked smile and her heart bumped around in her chest. She couldn't believe he'd taken time off to be with her. Was that a good thing she'd be able to take with her when they parted ways? Or would it make her miss him even more than she would have?

"I... I don't know what to say."

"I hope you'll say yes," he said quietly. "I was thinking we could spend some time in the city, doing a few things we talked about but never got around to. Go to a couple of your favorite museums, since I never take time to do things like that. See the Rockefeller Center Christmas tree."

A bubble filled her chest, warring with the melancholy she'd felt earlier, balling up in there until she could hardly breathe. Incredibly, Conor had taken the afternoon off to spend it with her. Maybe it would be the best way in the world to put the chaotic feelings from their divorce into the past.

Her throat tight, she somehow managed to answer. "Well… Since I'll probably be moving sometime soon, that sounds like a nice way to say goodbye to both you *and* New York."

Conor let himself hold her hand, as he had from pretty much the moment they'd left his apartment. He'd convinced her he was making sure she didn't stumble and fall on the uneven sidewalk, but the truth was he wanted that physical connection with her for the short time he'd be able to enjoy it. What was the point of keeping his distance when they'd shared a kind of closeness last night that was bittersweet?

Sweet because they still obviously cared about one another, and immeasurably bitter because he couldn't be the man she deserved and he'd never put them in a position where he could ever hurt her again.

Jillian looked up at him as they left the last exhibit at the Guggenheim Museum and headed toward the coat check, where they'd stashed their lunch cooler. "This was fun. I feel silly that I've never come to this museum in the three years I've lived in New York."

"I haven't been here for a long time. And I'm still not sure about that weird exhibit that looked like giant cotton balls on pieces of wood and those big stones strewn around the floor—but, hey. What do I know about art?"

He loved the way she laughed, just like she had when

they'd looked at the exhibit. Lighthearted, the way she had been long ago when they'd been happy together.

"Enough to know it looks like overgrown cotton balls. I thought we might get thrown out, joking about it. Good thing we moved to the Kandinsky exhibit or we might have."

He grinned. "Yeah. Good thing… I enjoyed most of the other stuff, though."

"Me, too."

The way she smiled at him had his chest feeling lighter than it had in a long, long time. She'd been right. He should take time to enjoy the city in a way he rarely did. He'd be going back to the grind once she was out of his life for good, but he'd take this day with her while he had it.

"Ready to go to Central Park for our winter picnic? It's already mid-afternoon, so you've got to be hungry." Conor took the backpack cooler from the coat-check clerk and adjusted it on his shoulders before they headed out the door.

"I am. Studying fine art takes a lot of energy."

He had to laugh at her cute grin. "How about we sit here in the sun? Unless it's too cold for you?"

"I wore my parka so we could be outside as much as we wanted. So we can see the Rockefeller Center tree after it's dark."

"My coat is warm, too, so that's the plan." He tucked her chilly hand into the crook of his arm and drew her close as they walked. "After we eat maybe we can go to the Metropolitan Museum before we go to the Rockefeller Center—unless you have another idea."

"I hear they've kept the boathouse at the Lake open late this year, because the weather has been so mild. I think it's closing tomorrow for the winter. Maybe we could rent a boat and row around for half an hour before we eat? I've walked by the boats on the Lake a few times and always wanted to do it, but never have. A couple times I had the dogs with me, and I was afraid Yorkie would jump into the water, like the goof he is. Plus Hudson's awful big for a rowboat."

Another knife-stab of regret jabbed him in the chest. He wondered if she'd wanted to do that while they were married. If so, it was another example of the ways he'd failed her, leaving her alone most of the time.

"I'm sure the dogs love the park, but for today I'm glad we came without them. Hitting the museums and riding in a boat couldn't be on our agenda if we had them with us."

"Not to mention that Yorkie would be trying to steal our lunch whenever we weren't looking."

He'd always been a sucker for that smile of hers, and he shook off the melancholy that had sneaked into his heart again. He wanted this day with her to be filled with good memories for both of them.

"All right. Boat ride it is, and then we'll eat."

They walked in companionable silence to the Lake and rented a rowboat. Conor set the backpack in the bow of the boat, then reached for Jill's hand. "Step in. I'll steady you until you've sat on the middle bench. I figure you want to row?"

He grinned at her surprised laugh.

"I *do* want to row. Except we'll go in circles using only one oar."

"Well, if you're going to make me do all the work," he said with an exaggerated sigh, "you might as well sit in the back."

"How about we both sit on the middle seat and each take one oar?"

This time he was the one who laughed. "I think that would be really difficult."

"Let's give it a try, anyway. I need to keep at least one arm strong."

He found himself falling into her twinkling gray-green eyes, felt his own smile forming deep inside his chest even as all those mixed emotions tangled in there as well. "All right. Who knows? Maybe we'll be trend-setters and everyone on the Lake will follow our lead."

"Not too many people out here on a chilly December afternoon, with the boats about to shut down. Maybe they're smarter than we are."

"Or we're smarter than they are, having to sit close together to stay warm."

She laughed as he helped her onto the middle seat, then shoved the boat into the water and jumped in next to her. Their hips were smashed next to each other's and their shoulders bumped, too. Her beautiful face was so close her hair lifted to tickle his skin as he reached across to grab her oar for her, and suddenly he was incredibly glad she'd suggested this unorthodox and probably ridiculous way to row a boat.

"Ready?"

"Ready!"

They both dipped their oars, and for a few minutes they did fine. Then their rhythm got off-kilter and the boat began to move in a slow circle back to where they'd come from, making them both laugh and stop rowing.

"Seems to me we're doing what you said we'd do if you rowed alone," Conor teased. "Let's decide where we want to go, then we'll try again."

"How about over there by the rocks? Someone told me there are lots of turtles there. Maybe we'll see them."

"Okay. I'm going to row twice to turn us, then you're going to join me. Okay?"

She grinned up at him and nodded, and he got so fixated on her eyes and smile he forgot to start rowing. He leaned in to kiss her forehead, and let his lips linger there because he couldn't help himself.

"Your bump's almost gone."

"Probably that nasty ice helped it go away faster."

"Probably..." He let himself softly kiss her mouth and was glad she didn't pull away. "See? I do know what I'm doing sometimes."

"Sometimes. Especially when it comes to rowing."

She leaned up to press her lips to his again, and he closed his eyes to soak in how good it felt. Floating on the water with the sun on their faces and the cold breeze on their skin and the feel of her mouth on his. He wrapped his free arm around her back, wanting to keep kissing her. Wanting the moment never to end.

A loud splash nearby, along with some laughing, had them pulling apart, their eyes meeting. Hers seemed to be filled with the same longing and melancholy that kept threatening to ruin the day, and he resolutely shoved his own longing down. Appreciating and enjoying one another today would go a long way toward healing them both when they parted.

"All right, here we go. One, two, three, dip."

This time they managed to row in sync, slowly making their way across the Lake. Conor kept his arm around her waist, holding her close. Because it felt so good, because he wanted her to stay warm, and because he thought maybe it helped them move together in rhythm. Though that made him think about last night and...

He sucked in a deep breath. "Doing good now, aren't we?"

"Expert rowing, I must say." Her white teeth gleamed as she smiled up at him. "Though I haven't seen anyone else rowing like this. No trendsetting going on."

"Give it time. Next time you're here I'll bet half the people on the Lake will be doing it just like this."

"That might be a long time," she said, her voice tinged with regret. "If I move out of state I won't be coming to New York much."

He nearly told her that she didn't have to take the job if she'd miss the city so much. Then he remembered the reason she wanted to move and couldn't argue with it. He knew that it would be incredibly difficult for them to see one another regularly at work. When they'd been dating, and then first married, seeing one another there had been the highlight of his day. After their breakup it had been the worst torture in the world, and he knew she'd felt the same way.

Having no good response to her comment, he stayed quiet as they rowed across the water, glistening with late-afternoon sunlight on its gentle waves. They approached the rocky shoreline on one side and she pointed and exclaimed.

"Look! There they are—three of them, sunning on that rock. Wow, I didn't think we'd really get to see them."

"Pretty cool. Not too many places where you can see turtles on a lake with a skyline like that in the background."

"True. No place in the world like New York City."

There it was again. That tinge of sadness in her voice. He stopped rowing and reached to turned her face toward his. "Jill. If you don't want to move, you shouldn't. We can figure out a way to work near each other. Or you can stay at the OTC until you find another job in the city. I don't want to be the reason you feel you have to leave here."

"I know. But moving is a good solution in a lot of ways. The dogs will do better in a bigger place, and it'll be a lot cheaper for me to live. Those are pluses. And maybe up the road I'll want to move back. Or maybe I'll love it wherever I end up next." She stroked her fingers across his cheek and he could see the effort she made to smile. "Please don't worry. All things work out the way they're supposed to."

Did they? Maybe… Probably. Though he wasn't sure if that statement made him feel better or worse.

"Jill, I—"

"Let's go a little further—up to that pretty bridge," she said, interrupting.

Which was good, because he hadn't really known what he was going to say.

"Then we'll go have lunch?"

"All right."

He breathed in the lake-water-scented air, glad to move on from the subject even though he wasn't sure they'd fully talked it through.

After floating beneath the bridge, they turned around and headed back to the dock.

"You stay put," he said as he set the oars back in place and stepped out. Then he put out his hand. "Careful, now."

"I may be handicapped but I'm not an invalid, Mr. Mother-Hen."

The cute smile she sent him loosened the bands of guilt and regret tightening his chest. "That's *Dr.* Mother-Hen, thank you. And I'm just trying to keep you safe."

He helped her step from the boat, then retrieved the backpack.

"If looking at fine art made us hungry, rowing should make us feel starved. I know a good place not too far off. Should have some sunshine to keep us warm."

They walked through the park until he found the spot he knew she'd enjoy. He tugged out the thin blanket he'd rolled up and stuck in the backpack and laid it down on the ground, with Jill helping spread it out as best she could. They sat in the center of it, her knee touching his as he twisted to dig into the cooler.

"Turkey sandwiches—mine with hot pepper cheese and yours with that yucky Swiss you like."

"Swiss is a classic cheese that many people around the world love."

"Yeah, well, they'd like pepper jack better if they tried it." He loved to tease her, if only to see her roll her eyes and the way her lips tipped up at the corners. "Potato chips, carrots—and, of course, dill pickles just for you."

"You like pickles, too."

"Not the way you do." He held one up to her lips and she took a smiling bite. Without planning to, his lips followed, pressing hers, and he gave them a tiny lick. "Mmm… On second thought, maybe I *do* like the taste of them as much as you do. In fact, I like it lot."

Their eyes met for a suspended moment, and he was about to go in for another kiss when she turned her face away and gently shoved her shoulder into his. "Then I hope you brought plenty of pickles, because I expect my fair share."

"More than your fair share, I promise."

He pulled the rest of the food out of the pack as those mixed emotions kept on rolling around his chest. Sitting here with Jill so close to him it seemed every sensory sensation was heightened. The feel of the warm sun on his skin and the cold breeze on his face... The sight of her beautiful eyes smiling at him... It had him thinking about how wonderful she'd felt in his arms. About the taste of her mouth that he'd never get to enjoy again after today.

"I had them cut your sandwich in four pieces, so it would be easy to eat with one hand," he said.

"I have to tell you," she said, her suddenly serious gaze meeting his, "I would never have guessed you could be such a thoughtful caregiver. I mean, you're good with patients, and a great surgeon, but that's not the same as thinking ahead to someone's needs. You've really done that with me through all this."

"Can't claim to have spent much time thinking about other people's needs—which you know very well. But I've been glad to be here to help you as I could."

"Maybe it's time to rethink that about yourself," she said softly.

"Believe me, I—"

He saw her sit up straighter and stare over his shoulder, frowning, which had him turning, too.

"What?"

"Somebody just fell off their bike on that path over there. And they haven't gotten up yet."

CHAPTER NINE

CONOR COULD CLEARLY see the bike lying on its side, and someone flat on the ground next to it. After a full minute or so the person still hadn't got up, and Conor pushed to his feet. "I'm going over there to see if they're hurt."

"I'll come with you. But don't lag behind for me. I'll catch up."

He reached down to help her up, then strode to see what the situation was. When he got closer he could see it was a man lying there, clutching his wrist and staring at it as he struggled to sit up.

Conor covered the final distance at a jog until he stopped in front of the guy, instantly seeing that his index finger was turned sideways at the joint.

"I guess I don't need to ask if you're okay, because I can see you're not." He crouched down and helped him to a sitting position. "I'm Dr. McCarthy, an orthopedic surgeon. It's possible that it's broken, but my guess is that you dislocated your finger when you fell."

"Look at it!" The man looked up at him, his eyes wide, obviously distressed. "It hurts like hell and it's freaking me out."

"Dislocated fingers do tend to freak people out, but

hopefully it's not too serious." Conor gave him a smile he hoped would reassure him a little, because his skin had blanched to a pale gray and he was listing to one side so much it looked as if he might pass out. "Want me to take a look?"

"Oh, God." The guy stared down at his hand again and didn't respond to the question.

"What's…? Oh, I see," Jillian said, kneeling next to the two of them with the cooler bag in her good hand. She looked up at Conor, and as their eyes met it was clear that she, too, saw the guy was feeling seriously upset over the way his hand looked.

"Try not to worry. It's gonna be okay." Conor grasped the man's wrist and leaned in close to examine the finger as best he could, at the same time feeling for his pulse. "Jill? Can you get some ice out of the cooler? And maybe one of the paper lunch bags."

Their eyes met again, and hers telegraphed loud and clear that she knew exactly why he'd asked for the bag. The man's breathing was quick and heavy, and his pulse way too fast. Definitely beginning to hyperventilate. The sooner they could get it under control, the better.

"You'll have to help me get it unzipped."

"Sorry. You'd think I'd remember by now."

He shook his head and got it open for her, before he turned his attention back to the injured man, helping him sit more upright.

"Hang in there. I know it looks scary, but try to breathe a little slower, down into your belly instead of your chest. You feel lightheaded?"

The man nodded, and seemed to have listened as he obviously attempted to alter his breathing. But the way he started to lean to one side again made Conor worry that he might completely faint.

"You're starting to hyperventilate—which is totally normal when something looks as weird as a dislocated finger. I'm going to have you breathe into a paper bag. In and out…real slowly."

"How about you hold it to his mouth while I ice the finger?" Jillian said as she emptied a paper bag and handed it him.

Conor realized there was no way she could hold it to his face with her current handicap, so he worked to get it open and around the man's lips in just a few seconds.

"Breathe in, then out. Slower. Like I said, breathe all the way into your belly. That's the way."

The man nodded and breathed, and after a minute or so Conor was relieved to see some of the color begin to come back to his face. He glanced down to see that Jill gently held a bag of ice on his hand, and as their eyes met again he saw hers filled with a warm smile.

"Are you going to try to reduce it?" she asked.

"No. I think it's probably just dislocated, but we should get an X-ray to make sure before it's moved back into place." He slowly lowered the bag from the man's face, glad that he seemed calmer. "Feeling a little better?"

He nodded, and Conor gave him a smile. "Good. You're going to need to see an orthopedic surgeon. You can go to an ER and have an X-ray done there, or you can go straight to the hand and arm orthopedic center where I work. Honestly, that would be the most efficient thing, with less wait time, and I can call ahead to tell them you're coming. They're open for another hour, but it's whatever you want to do."

"ERs can have an awful wait," the man said, with a grimace. "Your orthopedic center sounds a lot better. Where is it? Close enough that I can walk?"

"Not a good idea for you to try to walk there when you're hurting and a little light-headed. You might even have your finger jostled by pedestrians on the way, and you definitely don't want that. Do you feel up to taking a cab, or do you want me to call an ambulance?"

"Seems stupid to call an ambulance for a messed-up finger." The guy shook his head. "I feel better now. I'll take a cab. But…can you lock up my bike? The lock's around the handlebars. I'll send my son to come get it later."

"Will do. I'll call HOAC to tell them to expect you, then I'll walk you to Fifth Avenue and make sure you get in a cab safe, give them the address. Okay?"

"Okay. Thanks so much. Sorry I was such a baby about the way my finger looks—but, *wow*. Never seen anything like it." The man managed a weak smile. "I appreciate all you've done. And for taking care of my bike, too. Very nice of you."

"Glad to be here to help. And I can assure you most people are distressed by dislocated limbs and the way they look."

Conor pulled out his phone to call HOAC, then grasped the man's arm to help him stand.

"Hold that bag of ice on there, okay?"

The guy was definitely a little shaky, but he held the bag against his finger when Jill let go of it, and seemed okay to walk with Conor close to him.

Conor turned to Jill. "I'll be back shortly."

"Okay. I'll get the bike locked up over there." She

pointed at a rack. "Will your son be able to find it, do you think?"

"Yeah. And if not I can come back myself, after whatever they're going to do to my finger—even if it's tomorrow."

Conor reached for Jill's hand and smiled at her as he gave it a quick squeeze. "See you in a sec."

After he'd got the man safely into a cab he came back into the park to see Jillian sitting on the blanket where they'd eaten their lunch. Her head was tipped back and she had her eyes closed, probably enjoying the warmth of the sun. The sunlight caught the golden highlights in her hair as it fluttered around her face, and his chest squeezed at how beautiful she was.

It seemed she must have felt his gaze on her as he stepped closer, because she opened her eyes and curved her pretty lips into a smile.

This would probably be the last time he'd see her looking exactly like this. Relaxed and appreciating the simple pleasure of being outdoors in Central Park. Enjoying being with him, almost like they'd used to be and yet not quite. They might have talked through their history and come to a new understanding, but some of the pain of those days still lingered. Probably always would.

Some of the love did, too. At least, it did for him.

As he approached and her smile widened the emotions pressing on his chest told him he would always love her. It was just too damn bad—crushingly pathetic, really—that he wasn't a different kind of man. There wasn't another woman in the world as special as Jillian Keyser, and a part of him wanted to grab her up and kiss her and beg her to come back to him.

But he wouldn't. He'd just hurt her again, and he

couldn't bear to do that to her. What he *could* do was cherish these last hours with her and then keep the many perfect memories close to his heart, accepting the ache that would follow.

His throat closing, he glanced at his watch. "It's going to be getting dark soon. How about we head to the Rockefeller Center now?"

"I'd love that."

"It's about two miles from here. You feel up to walking that far, or do you want to grab a cab?"

"As I said before, I'm no invalid." This time she was the one who tucked her hand into his arm and stood close. "And walking in the city is one of my favorite things to do—especially since I can't run at the moment."

"Then let's go."

Their trek down the crowded sidewalk felt perfect in every way. They laughed together about the dogs' antics, about funny things that had happened where she'd been working, about all kinds of lighthearted subjects—which was exactly what Conor wanted for their last day or two together.

As they approached Rockefeller Center the lights of the tree glistened all the way down the street, and a cute squealing sound came from Jillian's lips.

"It's so beautiful! I never, ever get tired of looking at it. Do you?"

She lifted her face to his, her wide and happy smile making him feel beyond glad he'd been smart enough to take the afternoon off. That she'd wanted to come here tonight.

"Never. I've lived in the city for a long time now, but it wouldn't be Christmas without this tree, would it?"

"No. It wouldn't. And I just might have to change my mind and come back to the city every Christmas after I move away. Just to see it again."

He knew she wouldn't want to see *him* again, but refused to let that thought ruin the rest of the night.

They joined the crowds around the tree, watching the skaters on the ice rink next to it and listening to a band that had just begun to play. For a long time they stood together and soaked in the moment without speaking.

Gusts of wind whipped through the streets, more than earlier, and he moved to wrap his arms around her, pulling her back up against his chest.

"Are you cold?"

"No. I'm perfect."

"Yes, you are."

He rested his cheek against her temple and thought about how true that statement was. Jillian Keyser was as perfect as a woman could be.

"I'm not, you know." She turned in his arms and looked up at him, her eyes deeply serious. "We've talked about your past and how that affected you. But I haven't confessed about my own past and how that's affected me. And I think I should, so you know that all that was part of why our marriage failed, too."

"What are you talking about?"

"You know about my leg surgery… But I only shared the basics with you—like how old I was when I had the surgery, which as an orthopedic surgeon you would have known anyway. You assumed I'd left it all in my past. But I never really did."

He wasn't sure where she was going with this, and decided to stay mostly quiet and let her talk. "So it was traumatizing?"

"Yes. Growing up with one leg a lot shorter than the other, living with that kind of abnormality, was horrible."

"Why didn't you talk about that when I asked you? You told me it was so long ago you hardly remembered."

"That was a fib." She sent him a rueful smile. "I guess I just didn't want to talk about it. Which proves I've never fully dealt with how that felt, even though I thought I had."

"Did other kids make fun of you?"

She stared up at him. "How did you know?"

"Kids can be mean little things. Somebody stands out in some way…it makes them a moving target for bullies, unfortunately." The wind lifted her hair, and he gently ran his hand over its softness. "What did they do?"

"Called me lovely names—especially on the playground, where I had trouble doing some of the things the other kids did. You'd think that being called *freak* or *peg-leg* would be the worst. Believe it or not, though, the ones that hurt the most were *Jumpin' Jill* or *Jumpy Jillian*. Isn't that silly?" She shook her head. "I mean, it's such a stupid nickname I should have let it roll off my back. But I hated it."

"God, that's horrible. Makes me wish I could find them now and kick their butts—if they were guys."

"Both boys *and* girls called me those names. And, since I'm going into true confession about this whole thing, when I was about fourteen, the year before I had the surgery, was the worst. Not a single boy was interested in me other than those who wanted to torment me and make fun of me—and you know how self-conscious teenagers are anyway. It was awful."

"Damn. What idiotic fools." He tightened his hold

on her, tucking her close. His chest tight for Jillian and what she'd gone through when she was young. "Why didn't you tell me this when I was giving my own true confession last night? We both had some rough times as kids."

"I know. Which brings me to what else I want to say to you."

He waited. Her beautiful eyes were so serious he wondered what could possibly be coming next.

"I blamed you for everything that went wrong in our marriage. Your working too much. Your extreme focus on making money. Your making me feel less important than all the other stuff in your life. It was all your fault—or so I convinced myself."

"We've already agreed I was a lousy husband," he said quietly.

"But now I'm admitting that I know that I was part of the problem, too. These past ten months I've thought a lot about what happened and how I reacted to it. I've come to see that all the insecurities of my physical abnormality have made me deeply insecure in a way I didn't understand. Didn't realize was still there. I was ashamed of the scars on my legs. That's why I always wore long dresses to the gala events we went to. Not just because some of the other women did, but because I didn't want those people—your wealthy, glamorous friends—to see them. To know how much I didn't belong there. That I didn't fit into handsome, wealthy Dr. Conor McCarthy's life the way your wife should."

"Jill…" He was so stunned at what she'd said he could barely speak. "I had no idea. You're always the most beautiful woman in any room. Your scars show nothing except that you're a warrior. That you dealt with something difficult and overcame it. Took up running. Trained for *marathons*, for God's sake! You—"

"Stop." She pressed her cold fingers against his lips as she leaned up to kiss his cheek. "I'm not telling you this to have you reassure me or compliment me. I'm telling you because I want you to understand that I know *my* issues were part of our problem, too. My insecurities had me wanting you to constantly prove that you loved me, that you found me desirable despite my scars. I'd lived with my wallflower status my whole life. I wanted to prove that I was the most important thing in your world, despite my inability to fit into it. I kept pushing you to let me do that, and when you didn't it dumped fuel all over those awful insecurities. Which made me push you harder about your work hours, which made you feel angry and frustrated. It was a vicious circle that couldn't possibly end well."

"I'm sorry." He pressed his forehead to hers, still reeling from all she'd said. "More than you'll ever know. I'm sorry I didn't give you what you needed. I'm sorry I can't be the man you deserve. And you deserve so much, Jillian. You deserve the world. You're the most special woman I've ever met. I don't know what else to say…"

"Don't be sorry." She pressed her palm to his cheek. "As much as our breakup and divorce hurt, it's helped me see how much I need to work on my inner self-confidence. Find it for real, in myself, and not expect to get it from anyone else. It has to come from me. That's the very important lesson I've learned from our relationship, so thank you for that."

He couldn't think of a thing to say that hadn't already been said, so he kissed her. He held her in his arms as the music swirled in the air around them, as people chattered and laughed, and he kept on kissing her.

Someone jostled them and he finally lifted his head. Their eyes met and he felt her shiver.

"You're cold." His voice was gruff. "Are you ready to go back to my apartment?"

She nodded, possibly finding it as difficult to speak as he did. Wordlessly, he took her hand and walked to Fifth Avenue to hail a cab. Sat silently next to her as the car whizzed past the lights and sounds and people of the city. Took the elevator to his apartment, where the dogs jumping around gave him a chance to fully gather his thoughts.

He got the dogs their food, and as they began to gobble it down he made up his mind. He'd failed Jillian in so many ways, but there was one thing he could do for her tonight—something that he wanted to do for both of them before they went to live their separate lives.

He strode to the sofa where she'd just sat down. "There's something you need to know."

He wondered what his expression looked like, because she looked slightly alarmed.

"What?"

He dropped to his knees in front of her. Reached for the leg of her loose-fitting pants and shoved his hand up to her thigh. Ran his fingertips down the long, white scars left from the surgeries she'd had, followed by his lips.

She tried to tug away. "Conor, don't. I—"

"You have to know that this is one beautiful leg. *Beautiful.* Soft and smooth and strong. It's a gorgeous shape and it does amazing things. Walks dogs. Runs marathons. Kickboxes." He lifted his face to see her staring. "I admire the hell out of you, and this leg, and what you've both done to overcome its start in life."

"That's...that's a very sweet thing to say. But I— *Oh!*"

She squirmed and gasped as he licked his way up her shin, tickled her knee, and began to move another couple inches up her inner thigh, until the sweatpants wouldn't roll any higher.

"What are you doing?"

"Showing you that you and your legs are sexy as hell. Showing you that I think you're wonderful in so many ways. Showing you that if anyone should have an abundance of self-confidence, it's you, Jillian. You are beautiful both inside and out."

"Thank you," she whispered. "And, though we weren't right for one another, you are special in so many ways, too, and I'll always care about you."

"I'll always care about you, too. And I'd be lying if I said I don't want to be with you now. Maybe it's a bad idea. But I don't care. I want one more time with you before we say our goodbyes."

Because that was true, he sat next to her, pulled her close and kissed her. Exerting a soft pressure, his mouth moved slowly on hers and she kissed him back.

"Just one more time," she breathed. "Once more..."

His heart thumped hard as the kiss deepened, and she gasped in protest when he broke the kiss and dropped to his knees again.

"Conor. What—?"

"Shh..." he murmured against her calf as he resumed kissing his way up her leg. "For once I can't be sad about your current handicap. Because I know these loose pants aren't going to be very hard to slide off."

His hands moved to her waistband, his thumbs slipping inside and tugging them down to her knees. This time his mouth followed the line of her scars on its way back down, and eventually he pulled the pants over her feet. Then he stood to tug her sweatshirt off and she gasped and laughed at the same time.

"No fair! You stripped me nearly naked in a nanosecond when I can't begin to get your clothes off you."

"Handy, then, that I can do it myself." He got out of his clothes as quickly as possible and loved the way she was staring at his naked body.

"Well, okay, then," she said, leaning back to look him up and down with a sultry smile. "I guess being handicapped isn't so bad after all."

He laughed, then decided that moving to his bedroom was the best option. She squeaked when he picked her up and carried her toward the bedroom. The dogs had been lying on the floor, and got up to follow.

"Sorry, guys. You're not invited."

He kicked the bedroom door closed behind him and laid her gently on the bed, his body following. He managed to remember her injured arm and lifted it over her head again before lowering his mouth to hers.

"Got to protect this," he said. "Things might get a little rough."

She laughed against his lips and wrapped her good arm around his neck. Their kiss got hotter, wilder, as he touched her everywhere he could reach, and the sound of her small gasps and moans was so arousing he had to fight to not dive inside her right that second.

"Conor... Conor, I need you inside me."

Obviously she felt the same way he did, and he gritted his teeth against the insistent desire. "I'm not ready. This is not nearly long enough to make love with you."

"I know. But I want you *now*."

She stroked her hand down his belly, grasping him and wresting a deep groan from his chest, and he knew he couldn't hang on much longer.

"We'll go slower next time," she said.

"There won't be a next time." He hated the truth of the words that had come out of his mouth, but they were the one thing that managed to cool the heat. "Remember?"

"I remember. Except maybe we can renegotiate that deal the way you do in the boardroom? I'm not going back to my apartment until the day after tomorrow. Right?"

"Right…"

He loved the tiniest of smiles that curved her lips as he grabbed a condom from the drawer and kissed her again. Smashed her body to his. And as they joined and moved together his heart lifted and soared in a way that obliterated any and all thoughts of the past.

He broke their kiss to draw in a deep, ragged breath. Stared into her eyes as her name left his lips. "Jillian. Jilly…"

She cupped his cheek in her palm and emotion clogged his throat. As he nudged her over the peak she cried out and pressed her mouth to his, swallowing the moan that followed.

He pressed his face to the side of her neck and breathed her in as his heartbeat slowly settled. Her soft hand slowly stroked his back, and the physical and emotional sensations got all tangled up in his chest as he held her close.

God, how he loved this woman. But he would never put either of them in a position where he could hurt her again. And he knew with certainty that her leaving his life a second time was going to feel every bit as terrible as it had the first time.

CHAPTER TEN

JILLIAN WAS FEELING happy that morning. Her therapy had gone even better than expected, and her hand and fingers were becoming a little more mobile every day. It had nothing to do with the magical day she'd spent with Conor and their night together. Nothing at all.

She inwardly rolled her eyes at herself as she folded towels in the therapy center's laundry room. She shouldn't be feeling so lighthearted. She'd be moving back to her own apartment tomorrow. It must be because she and Conor had come to a better understanding than they'd had when they'd broken up. An understanding that had made moving on from that unpleasant experience much easier.

As though she could feel his presence, she looked up from the folding table to see the man in question moving toward her. The overhead fluorescent lights made his hair seem even lighter, his features even more handsome, and the smile he sent her made her feel warm all over.

"Hello, Jillian." He moved closer and tugged her into a corner where curious eyes couldn't easily see them. "How did your therapy go?"

"Wonderful. I feel like I'm really making progress,

and I can even use a few fingers to help fold these towels now."

"I'm glad." He shoved his hands in his pockets and looked down at her, his expression now inscrutable. "I have a question for you—and please don't be too quick to answer...just think about it."

"What question?"

"I know you don't love—okay, don't even *like* going to charity events. But there's one tonight I've been asked to attend to represent one of my businesses which is sponsoring an adoption event for an animal shelter. Since you're an animal lover, I was hoping you'd be willing to come with me."

A charity event. The thought sent a chill down her spine. She'd always felt so awkward attending them when they'd been married. Now that they were divorced would it be even worse? Or would it be easier, since she wouldn't have to prove anything as Conor McCarthy's wife?

"I don't know. I—"

"Before you answer—" he held up his hand "—there's another part to the question. How would you feel about one more night out together on our anniversary?"

"Anniversary?" She managed a faint laugh. "Maybe you're thinking of a different ex-wife, because we got married in January."

"It's the anniversary of your first day at the OTC. Of the first moment I saw you. Of our first date. And, yeah, that's unbelievably sappy, but I thought of it and thought it might be...fun."

"I can't believe you remember that." Her heart flip-flopped as she stared at him. "I'm...touched. But I think we both know that prolonging our goodbyes isn't going to make it any easier."

"I know. And I'm not trying to make it easier, because nothing will."

His somber expression shook her heart.

"When we said goodbye the day you left—or didn't say it—we were both angry and upset and hurt. I guess what I want this time is a different kind of closure. A positive kind. A nice evening that celebrates all the things we liked about one another. A bookend moment to mark when we met, and when we said goodbye again."

"Well, I... That does sound...nice. And the charity does sound worthwhile..."

She wasn't sure it would be "nice" at all, but wouldn't one more night with him, and the closure he spoke of, be a positive thing? Better than just shaking hands with him after she packed up her stuff from his place and left?

"Thank you. How about I take you back to your apartment so you can get a dress to wear? It doesn't have to be anything fancy—just the usual for an event like this."

"All right. That would be perfect. I'll be able to get some stuff done there, too, like water my plants, and then I'll head back to your place on my own. I'll take a cab instead of the subway."

"Good." He glanced around, then leaned in to press his mouth to hers in a short but unbearably sweet kiss, his eyes gleaming as he drew back. "I'll drop you off at lunch. Then see you back at my place before the event."

It felt a little odd to be back in her own little apartment. She'd called it home for less than a year, and couldn't say she had any particular attachment to the place. Fussing with her plants and doing some photography work on her computer felt nice, but part of her couldn't wait to get back to Conor's place. So she could see the dogs, of course.

She flicked through the formal dresses she'd bought during their marriage, glad she hadn't gotten rid of them as she'd considered doing. She reached for a floor-length gown she'd always liked the color of, then stopped and looked at a different one she'd never worn. A beautiful shade of sea-green, with a chiffon skirt that stopped an inch above her knee.

She thought about all she'd confessed to Conor. All the insecurities she had about herself and her scars and how she'd never quite fitted into his world. She fingered the silky fabric and then, in a quick decision, pulled the dress out, slipped it into a zippered garment bag, and looked for shoes to go with it.

This was her first step toward the new and improved Jillian. If Conor thought her legs were beautiful, that they didn't make her undesirable or a freak, shouldn't she finally believe it, too?

That bubble of happiness filled her chest again as she packed up her things and went out to hail a cab to Conor's place.

She took Yorkie out for a short walk, though the cold wind had her wishing she'd brought one of the dog's sweaters to Conor's, so he could have worn it. Then again, with Briana coming they'd all be going back to her place tomorrow anyway, so what was the point?

Refusing to let those thoughts put a damper on the evening, she got ready for the charity event. She swirled the skirt a little in front of the long mirror in the guest bedroom, pleased with what she saw. Proud of what she felt for the first time in her life. Yes, her scars were visible. But Conor was right. From now on she'd think of them as war wounds that she'd earned, overcoming her limp as well as she possibly could.

Her cell phone rang and she hurried to grab it, not recognizing the number. "Hello?"

"Hello, Jillian? This is Mary Rodgers, from Therapy Centers of New England. I apologize for calling so late, but we have another opening and we would like to have you take the job. The board has already looked through all your credentials, and we don't feel you need to interview. Are you still interested?"

Jill's heart jumped into her throat. Was she? Did she still want to move to Connecticut? Start a new life there away from New York City and far from Conor McCarthy?

Just a few days ago she'd been sure the answer was yes. But tonight, after their time together, and learning about Conor's past, and after her own questions and revelations about herself, it was possible the answer might be no.

She opened her mouth, then closed it again, not sure how to answer, and worked to find her voice. "I appreciate the offer, Mary. I'm in a meeting right now, but can I call you back tomorrow?"

"Of course. I would appreciate hearing from you as soon as possible, because we need a replacement right away. Even with your injured hand we'd like to have you help train our newest therapists until you're able to fully work with patients."

"I understand. I'll definitely contact you tomorrow."

She hung up and slowly walked into the living room,

looking out over the twinkling city lights and knowing she didn't want to move from here.

Would it really be impossible to work with him again?

Would it be impossible for them to be together again?

The thought made her head swim, because she'd never considered that. But now, thinking of everything they'd been through in the past, and the things they'd shared with one another now, could they have a second chance to be together again?

Her phone rang again, and she looked down to see it was Conor. Her hand shook a little as she answered. "Hi. Are you on your way here?"

"I'm really sorry but I got held up. I've been trying to pull this meeting together for a month now, and of course they wanted it to happen this evening. But we're almost done. How do you feel about taking a cab and I'll meet you there?"

"Um…okay. I guess I can do that." The idea of walking into a fancy gala event all by herself sounded daunting. But she was working on being the new Jillian, wasn't she? She could do it.

"Thank you. I'll text you the address. See you there."

The phone went dead—he'd obviously been in a hurry.

She sighed and got her coat and handbag. Said goodbye to the dogs, went downstairs. Alfred insisted on getting a cab for her, even though she could have done it herself, and in minutes she was on her way.

The lights of the city seemed in full twinkle tonight, and she absorbed the way living in this city made her feel. It seemed as though the entire place had a pulse to it, alive and vibrant, and she realized *she* felt alive and vibrant here, too.

She wanted to stay in this city. And she also realized, terrifying as the thought was, that she wanted to try again with Conor, too. He'd said it was the anniversary of the day they'd met—couldn't that mean it was the perfect night to tell him she wanted to make that happen?

Walking into the hotel ballroom on her own didn't feel as awkward as she'd expected it to. A few people she'd known back when she and Conor had been married approached her with friendly smiles. She'd always found it hard to make small talk, to feel comfortable in large groups like this, but it turned out to be good that this event was about finding homes for sheltered animals. It was something she cared about, and she'd adopted two dogs herself, so making conversation turned out to not be torturous at all.

She'd planned to wait to eat until Conor arrived, but after an hour decided to try a few of the hors d'oeuvres. After another half hour she started to worry, and called Conor's cell phone. It went straight to voicemail.

She left a message. "I'm here, waiting. When do you think you'll get here?"

A text message pinged, and she hurried to look.

Sorry. Meeting ran late. Done soon, though. I'll be there shortly.

She blew out a breath. How late was he going to be? How long did she have to stand around and smile at people, feeling more and more foolish as time went on?

A man came and asked her to dance. She was about

to refuse until her brain pointed out that it would serve Conor right to walk in and find her dancing with someone else. Then she regretted her decision, because talking to only one person on the dance floor was even harder than talking to a group. She found herself looking over the man's shoulder every time she could see the door, but unfortunately there was no tall, handsome surgeon walking in, looking for her.

Another hour or more passed. Much of the food was gone now, as were many of the people who'd been there earlier. Sitting alone at a table, she swallowed down the tears thickening her throat, and then told herself to stop it. She should be mad instead. After all they'd talked about, after all the times he'd said how much he hated it that he'd hurt her, after asking her to come here on some stupid made-up anniversary, he'd left her high and dry?

Oh, yes, she was an idiot.

The pain searing her heart was real, but Conor wasn't at fault for the damage to that vital organ. This time he'd stated loud and clear who he was, and said that he couldn't be anyone else. She'd known it but apparently had forgotten it. Or hadn't wanted to believe it after she'd had a glimpse of what they'd shared in the beginning. Of why she'd fallen in love with him.

She closed her eyes and sat very still, letting herself go back in time to when they'd first met. Those glorious early months of falling head over heels in love with each other. When every day together had seemed better than the last and the future had looked bright and brilliant.

But it hadn't been bright or brilliant. And now it was history. Over. Her wanting it to be different this time, believing it *could* be different, had been nothing but a foolish pipe dream.

She got up and headed out the door. Hailed a cab, slid inside and shut the door. As she struggled to put on her seat belt she saw a tall blond figure running to the front doors of the hotel—only to stop and stare at her. Their eyes met, and then he quickly strode toward the cab as her heart lurched, her stomach roiled, and the tears threatened all over again.

"Can we get going?" she said to the driver. "I need to get out of here. Now."

Conor leaped up the steps to Jill's apartment, his heart beating hard both because he'd been running, and because he feared how upset she might be. He'd blown everything sky-high, hadn't he? Hadn't shown up for the charity event. Just like so many times before.

He tried to tell himself she hadn't been miserable there alone. Probably hadn't cared if he was there or not, since it had been supporting a cause she believed in. And she didn't want to rekindle their relationship anyway, did she?

But he knew he was a damn liar. It *did* matter. It all mattered. They'd grown close again—so close that he'd begun to wonder if maybe they could try again. If maybe he could be a different man.

Making love with her, seeing her beautiful smile, being with her and sharing her joy in life, had had him feeling the best he'd felt since the day they'd married. And yet here he was again, being the jerk he'd known he couldn't help being. Letting her down like he'd let his mom down. Like he'd let her down so many times before. Just like he'd told her he would.

The meeting had dragged on with important business that couldn't be put off. He'd been so focused on the debate and conversation he hadn't even realized how late it had gotten until it was over. His heart had nearly stopped when he'd looked at his phone, and he had known he had no excuse to offer that was even close to good enough.

Hard as it would be, he owed her a face-to-face apology. And he owed her his assurance—again—that she was the most amazing, most beautiful woman in the world, and it was only his massive failings that had ruined everything between them. Both in the past and tonight.

He'd hoped for a closure between them that would be on a better note than the last, terrible one.

He'd sure demolished the chance for that, hadn't he?

If she screamed at him and told him what a loser he was he'd give her the chance to vent—because he deserved it.

He heaved a fortifying breath and knocked on her door. Knocked louder when she didn't answer. "Jillian?"

Still nothing. Would it be wrong of him to use the key he had? Would it scare her?

His heart was beating so hard he thought it might burst out of his chest, and anxiety churned in his gut. He had to see if she was there. See if she'd let him apologize one last time.

He slowly opened the door—then stopped cold when he saw her sitting on the sofa, wrapped in a robe, the arm with the splint resting in her lap. The eyes that met his didn't hold the anger or condemnation or disgust he'd expected. No, they simply looked tired and beyond sad, and his throat closed at the defeated expression on her beautiful face.

"Jilly…" He sat close in front of her, reaching for her

good hand, and the soft feel of it in his made his chest hurt, knowing he'd never get to hold it again. "I'm sorry. I'm just so damn sorry."

"I know. I'm sorry, too. You should go now."

He had no idea what to say or do next, but getting up to leave before he'd let her know how he felt wasn't an option.

"I hope you know it's me, not you?"

"Yes, we've gone over this."

"And that you're the most beautiful, amazing woman in the world and I love you." It was true, and saying the words made his throat close again, but he forced out the rest of what he had to say. "I wish I could be different. But obviously I can't. I don't deserve you. I'm not good enough for you. You deserve so much more than a man like me."

"We've gone over this, too." Her lips curved in a smile that didn't touch her eyes. "Don't worry, Conor. I understand. It's simply time to say goodbye."

Her words were exactly what he'd been about to say, but they punched a hole in his chest and he couldn't speak for a long moment.

"If you stay in New York I promise I'll keep my distance from you at work. It…it won't be easy to be in the same building, but I want you to feel comfortable there. I don't want you to leave on my account."

"I've been offered a job in Connecticut. I'll be moving there soon."

He didn't know what the weight in his chest meant, because he should be *glad* she'd found a new job. But the finality of not seeing her again felt unbearable. Somehow it was almost worse than ten months ago, which he wouldn't have dreamed was even possible.

But it was.

"Do you…do you need help moving?"

"Conor."

Her lips twisted and she looked at him as if he was pathetic, which he clearly was.

"If I do, I don't think you'll be the person I call. We agreed earlier that this would be our last evening together, anyway. Let's stick to that. I… I don't want our goodbye to drag on any longer than it has to, you know?"

He looked down at her hand in his and nodded. He should feel the same way, but knowing he'd be leaving this apartment in a matter of minutes and never seeing her again shoved the knife blade currently sticking into his heart another inch deeper.

He lifted his gaze back to hers and stood, and was surprised when she stood with him.

"Remember, always, how special you are," he said.

"You, too," she said softly, shocking him by resting her hand against his cheek and giving him that sad smile again. "You're special, too, Conor, in so many ways. And I hope you find happiness someday that is more than just work. I truly do."

Emotion clogged his throat. She didn't hate him the way she had the last time they'd said goodbye, despite him deserving it. He wrapped his arms around her and held her close against him, just to feel her there one last time. When he made himself let her go he saw the sheen of tears in her beautiful eyes.

He knew there was nothing else to say that hadn't already been said. Somehow, he forced himself to turn and get ready to leave—until she reached out to touch his arm.

"I'll have Briana come get the dogs tomorrow."

"Okay. Have her give me a call." More words felt impossible, and he stepped to the door before he turned to look at her one last time. "Goodbye, Jilly. I hope your life brings you everything you want."

She nodded, and as she did so a few tears spilled from her eyes. "I hope yours does, too, Conor. Goodbye."

And with that he somehow made it out the door before a few tears of his own slipped down his cheeks.

CHAPTER ELEVEN

PACKING UP HER apartment proved to be difficult. Jillian was thankful that Briana had gotten quite a bit done for her before she'd had to leave, and that now Michelle had been willing to stop by after work to help with the things she couldn't possibly do with one hand.

"I really appreciate this," Jill said, running the packing tape dispenser across a box as Michelle held the flaps closed. "Clothes and stuff weren't hard, and even putting things into the boxes just took me some extra time. But getting them secured and stacked? No way."

"Happy to help." Michelle lifted the box and put it on top of the others waiting for the moving company that would arrive at any minute. "But you know I'm still wondering if this is really what you want to do."

"It is. I'm sure."

Well, maybe she wasn't completely sure she wanted to leave New York. But did she want to have to see Conor's handsome face and infectious smile and think about how good it had felt to be together again for a few wonderful days? Think about how much she still loved him?

She briefly closed her eyes, picturing the face she missed so much, and swallowed down the stupid tears that threatened. Just as Conor himself had said, sometimes love wasn't enough. It just wasn't. He had demons that he didn't seem to want to battle, and she had her own. And even if she got a grip on hers, and felt she was making progress, she knew for certain now that if they tried once more it would end up in heartbreak for both of them all over again.

Not a place either of them wanted to go.

"I know from stuff you've said that you'll miss the city," said Michelle. "And I think it's wrong to let Conor McCarthy run you off if you don't want to go."

"He's not running me off. I'm choosing to go."

"Uh-huh? You're not kidding me. There was a new smile in your eyes when you two were seeing each other again—until he acted like an idiot, as usual."

"He's not an idiot. Just a guy with some issues. And I'm not sticking around to try to fix him, getting hurt all over again in the process. I'm going to concentrate on fixing myself. You should be glad about that."

"I don't know how much fixing you need, Jill. I think you're already there. As for Conor? He may have those issues you talk about, but he's more than worth fixing, in my opinion."

Yes, he was. But he didn't believe he could be fixed. And shoring up her own confidence had to be her priority—not trying to help a man who didn't believe he could be helped.

"It's too late for us," she said softly. "It just is."

Michelle sighed and moved another box. "What about leaving the city? You love it here."

"I do love New York. But the new place has lots of good things going for it."

She glanced out her front window and knew it was

true that she'd miss this city. Yes, it was expensive, and crowded, and sometimes crazy, but there was no place like it and it felt like home to her. Even more after she'd moved into Conor's apartment for those first months they'd been deliriously, happily, married.

A sprinkle of raindrops began hitting the window and streaking down, and she held in a sigh. How appropriate that the unusually warm early December weather she'd enjoyed with Conor had given way to cold, gray drizzle this past week. It definitely reflected her mood. Hopefully the movers would have a way to keep her things dry as they packed them into their truck.

She turned back to Michelle and forced a smile. "Anyway, I can come back and visit New York any time, right? Expect me to bunk in with you about every three months or so."

"Uh...with the dogs?" Michelle shook her head and grinned. "Don't know that my roommate would be willing to share her bedroom with *them*—and there's only room for you and me in mine."

Jill laughed, glad to move the subject to safe ground that didn't make her heart hurt for something that couldn't be. "I'll find a kennel where they'll be happy before I visit, don't worry."

"Ready for us?"

She turned to see two guys in her doorway, wearing matching shirts with the moving company's name on them. "Yes. We have a couple more boxes to close, but you can start to load up things while we do that, right?"

"Absolutely." He leaned down to scratch the heads of the greeting committee, known as Hudson and Yorkie, who were nosing the man's legs and wagging their tails. "Great dogs. The big one reminds me of mine."

"They *are* good dogs. Most of the time."

"So, the plan is to store your stuff in the truck overnight, then we leave in the morning. Right?"

"Right."

Tomorrow morning. The first day of her new life.

She managed to smile at the man before she and Michelle got busy packing the last few things in the kitchen as the men moved boxes and furniture.

Jill suddenly remembered the small bag of Conor's clothes he'd accidentally left that first day, when he'd brought her here after her surgery. She wanted to give it to Michelle, to take to work with her so she could return them. She didn't want to just give them to a charity shop, but also she definitely didn't want to call Conor to come get them. Their goodbye had been utterly final, and seeing one another again even for a moment would just dredge up those sad feelings all over again.

She moved into the bedroom and picked up the bag, then hesitated. The old T-shirt that he'd worn to exercise and walk the dogs poked up from the top of the bag and she tugged it out. Held it to her nose and closed her eyes to breathe in his scent. The smell she loved and that she'd never get to enjoy again.

Even as she told herself it was pathetic she opened the suitcase she'd packed, so she'd have the basics handy at her new place, and folded the shirt inside. Zipped it closed even as she scolded herself that the last thing she needed was his shirt to wear. Something that would remind her of him at her new place and in her new life.

But she'd be thinking of him anyway, wouldn't she? Maybe in some strange way wearing his shirt would be a source of comfort instead of sadness.

With a sigh, Jill carried the bag holding his other

things to the living room. "I just remembered I have some of Conor's stuff. Will you take this to work and give it to him?"

Michelle looked at her for a long moment, then nodded. "Sure. I've finished the last of the kitchen utensils. I think that's everything."

"Thanks."

She watched Michelle stack the box next to the door that was still propped wide open after the men had carried out the sofa. Then she realized that Hudson was lounging in his bed, but there was no sign of Yorkie.

"Where's Yorkie?"

She and Michelle looked all around the small apartment, and when it was clear he wasn't there a feeling of panic welled in her chest.

"Oh, my God, could he have gotten out?"

"I'll look in the stairwell," Michelle said.

"I'm coming, too." Jill shut the door behind them so there was no chance Hudson would follow.

When there was no sign of Yorkie on any of the staircases her hands began to shake and the feeling of panic grew.

"He must be out on the street! Who knows where he'll run? And he's so tiny…he could easily get hit by a car."

"Where do you usually walk him? Maybe he'll follow that route."

"I don't have a specific route, really," she said, trying to think through the cold fear clouding her mind. "I wonder if Conor did? He walked them a few times the day he was here."

"I'll call Conor and ask. Maybe he can give you some insight."

Jill's heart jolted. The last thing she wanted was to have to talk to Conor, but this was an emergency, and her feelings weren't nearly as important as finding Yorkie.

"Conor's not answering his cell. I'll call the answering service," Michelle said.

"Yorkie! Yorkie!" Jill hurried to the moving truck, calling to the men inside. "My little dog got out when the door was left open. Do you know where he is?"

"No. Damn—sorry about that. I didn't see him if he followed us."

Jill ran up the street, craning her neck and calling the dog's name with Michelle by her side, her phone still pressed to her ear.

"I need to speak with Dr. Conor McCarthy immediately," Michelle said. "It's an emergency."

"Here are the numbers I believe we can generate in the first year," Conor said as he handed everyone assembled in the boardroom the folders holding the calculations and projections he'd worked on for over six months. "The location next to HOAC is perfect for Urgent Care Manhattan to become well established as *the* place to go for non-life-threatening injuries and illnesses. No other urgent care clinic is situated within a twenty-block area, but there's a hospital only a few blocks away. If you needed to refer your patients there for things you can't take care of it would be easy to do."

"I agree the location is perfect," Peter Stanford said, addressing everyone in the room. "For all the reasons Dr. McCarthy just noted and because we can send patients directly to HOAC if they need to see an orthopedic surgeon. I believe that when we advertise that advantage a lot of patients with possible broken bones will want to come to Urgent Care Manhattan instead of our competitors."

Conor listened to the board members as they asked Peter various questions. Also asked their accountants about the numbers Conor had presented, and addressed some contract questions to their lawyer. For some reason he found he had to keep making himself refocus on the conversation. How that was possible he didn't know, because he'd worked on this project for so long he should be zeroing in on every word. Instead thoughts of Jill kept drifting into his mind, adding to the ache that still hung in his chest from the night they'd said goodbye.

He'd heard through the grapevine that she was leaving New York today. Taking the dogs and moving to another state. It was unlikely he'd ever see any of them again.

It was what he wanted. For her to find a new life and a new beginning that made her happy. The kind of happiness he'd failed so miserably to provide. So why did his heart feel every bit as heavy as the night he'd walked out her door?

He didn't know. And it made him wonder how long it would take for him to feel even a little more normal. Which was the best he knew he could hope for, because he was absolutely certain he'd miss Jillian's lovely face and warm smile and beautiful heart forever.

He managed to focus his attention long enough to answer some of the board members' questions, but as two of them started to disagree over a few of the details his cell phone buzzed with its emergency call chime. He never answered his phone during meetings and he frowned, wondering what the problem could be, since he wasn't on call.

"Excuse me a moment," he murmured as he grabbed the phone and stood to step to the other side of the room.

"Conor McCarthy."

"Conor! It's Michelle."

Her voice sounded breathless and scared and his heart dropped straight into his stomach before it began racing. "What's wrong? Is Jill hurt?"

"No, it's Yorkie. He got out of the apartment when the moving guys were taking out the furniture. We're out here looking for him and Jill wondered if you'd taken him on any specific route when you walked him. We thought maybe he'd follow it if you did."

Damn! "Is she there? Let me talk to her."

"Okay—here…"

A muffled sound, then Jill was on the line.

"Conor? Oh, God, I'm so worried. Do you have any idea where he might go?"

His fingers tightened on his phone, because even sounding tense the voice he'd thought he'd never hear again slipped inside his wounded heart. "I don't. But let me think a minute."

"Call me if you come up with anything. I've got to go."

"Wait."

He stared out the window at the rain streaming down the glass, at the bright flash of lightning in the sky. Heard Jilly's voice sounding so panicked. Without another thought, he knew he had to help her through this scare. Help find little Yorkie, lost in this storm. The dog had been his once, too, and he had to be there for both Jillian and Yorkie when they needed him most.

"I'll be right there to help you look. I'll call after I park the car and find out where you are."

"Okay."

She hung up and he strode back to the meeting. "I'm afraid an emergency has come up and I have to leave. Please continue to go over the numbers and call me with any questions you might have."

"We'd hoped to finalize this tonight—it's important that you be here to answer those questions," Peter said, his eyebrows raised. "If it's a patient, surely there's another surgeon who can take over for you?"

"It's not a patient. It's my dog. He's lost and I have to go help find him."

Everyone in the room stared at him with varying degrees of surprise and disbelief on their faces.

Peter sent him a thunderous frown. "Your *dog*? Surely someone else can look for it?"

"They need my help."

"It seems to me perhaps you shouldn't plan to be president of this new company we'd be creating with the merger, then, if this meeting can't take priority over a pet."

"Maybe that's true. Sorry, Peter, but I've got to go."

Conor bolted to his car, waiting to be singed by gnawing regret. By worry that the deal that had been his priority for so long would fall through because of this. That all his hard work, all the money he and others would make as they improved and expanded patient care, was about to go straight out the window.

It didn't come. Even though his chest was tight with worry for Yorkie, it felt strangely light, too. As if he'd thrown a thousand-pound monster from his shoulders and was finally free of it. A monster that had been hanging there, controlling him, for way too long.

He wasn't sure exactly what that meant, but figuring it out had to take a back seat to the current emergency.

Right now Jillian and Yorkie were his priorities, and he drove as fast as he could through the traffic and rain, parked in the garage near her apartment and ran out to the streets.

"Yorkie! Yorkie!"

He strode toward the nearby park that the dogs liked, though he assumed Jill had probably gone there first.

He pulled out his phone to call and find out. "I'm near the park close to your apartment. Where are you?"

"Michelle and I were there maybe fifteen minutes ago. Didn't see him. We're a few blocks over. I don't know how we're going to find him."

Her voice ended on a near-sob, and if he hadn't already wanted desperately to find the little pup her distress would have made him even more determined.

"I'll look here again, then call back, and we'll make a plan. Hang in there."

He strode through the small park, looking beneath the many shrubs and trees around its perimeter and in the thick groups near a few benches. "Yorkie! Yorkie!"

Bending over, he peered through a hedge that lined the brick wall, then did a double take, blinking the raindrops from his eyes. He looked again, and there, shining within the leaves, was a set of beady little eyes staring at him.

He crouched down and held out his hand. "Yorkie! It's me! Come on—you're okay. Come out now."

Conor held his breath as the dog just stared at him.

He worried that Yorkie might be afraid and disoriented after he'd run off, and schooled his voice into a croon.

"Come on, now, big guy. Your mama is trying to find you. How about a treat? A nice treat?"

He drew the syllables out, the way Jill did when she talked to Yorkie, and sure enough the dog took a few halting steps closer. Close enough that Conor was able to quickly reach in, grab him, and pull him close to his chest.

A giant breath of relief whooshed from his lungs. The poor, wet dog was shivering, and he tucked him inside his coat. "There you go. You need to warm up."

Yorkie whimpered, and Conor knew there were two priorities—one was to get the dog dried off and warm, and the other was to let Jillian know he had him safe.

Making sure he had a tight grip on the pup, he used his other hand to fish his phone from his pocket. "Jill? I have him. He was hiding under some shrubs in the park. Yes, he's okay. Just cold and wet. I'll meet you at your apartment."

"Oh, my gosh!" Her voice came on a new sob. "Thank you! We've doubled back toward my apartment building, thinking he might have tried to go home. So we're almost there now."

Conor talked to the dog as he walked and, now that he had him safe, spared a rueful thought for his clothes. A wet and muddy dog, not to mention pouring rain, just might ruin his suit—but he couldn't worry about that. He could buy a new suit, but finding the dog he loved and keeping the woman he loved from being scared and sad...

That was worth anything.

As he approached the front door of Jillian's apartment building he could see her running toward him through the gray rain and his heart jolted.

"Don't run! You could easily slip and fall on the wet pavement! I've got him and he's not getting away, I promise."

"Oh, Conor!"

She flung her arms around him and he wrapped his free arm around her and pulled her close. Both of them were soaked, but apparently she didn't care anymore than he did.

Water dripped from her sopping hair down her forehead and cheeks as she leaned up to press her wet mouth to his. "I can't believe you came. I can't believe you found him. I was so scared he'd be lost forever. I owe you so much."

"Don't be ridiculous. He was my dog once, too, and I care about him as much as you do."

It was true, and as he stood there holding her in the rain it was all he could do not to tell her how much he loved her, and that he'd learned something beyond important tonight. That work could never, ever replace the love her felt for her. His need to be there for her. With her.

His fear for Yorkie, and for her, had been so powerful it had taken precedence over anything else—including the meeting he'd so stupidly thought was everything. It might have taken him way too long to see that bright truth, but he'd never make that mistake again.

Except standing in the rain, with a wet dog tucked into his coat and a shivering woman held close in his arms, wasn't the best time to tell her all he'd learned and seen during the past hour.

"This reminds me of my all-time favorite moment in New York. Holding you in the rain in Central Park."

"Except that day we had an umbrella. And we didn't get soaking wet. And it wasn't freezing cold."

"True." Her smiling eyes met his, and it was all he could do not to lean down and kiss her. "Let's get inside out of this weather, hmm?"

She nodded, and when they got to the door a rained-on Michelle stood there. "Wow, you are *amazing*, Conor! I'm so happy you found him. I hope it's okay with you, but I'm going back to my apartment to get dry clothes." She grinned. "I admit I really want to just stay there and get warm in my jammies, but if you need me to come back and help finish packing in the morning, let me know."

"Thanks, but I think it's pretty much done," Jillian said. "I appreciate all your help so much, and you looking for Yorkie. I'll be in touch."

The two women hugged, then Conor and Jillian took the elevator to her apartment.

"There's a small problem," Jill said, shoving her wet hair from her eyes. "All my stuff is packed in boxes on the truck. Towels, clothes—you name it. I don't have any way for us to dry Yorkie, or you and me."

"Well, that *is* a problem."

He pulled Yorkie from his jacket and held him up. Both of them laughed at the way the poor pup looked as if he'd lost ten pounds, with his wet fur lying flattened against his little body, resembling an opossum more than a dog.

"You're a troublemaker, you know that?" Conor told him.

The dog licked his wet nose and yipped, and both

Conor and Jillian laughed again—until Conor sobered, knowing the things he wanted and needed to say to her might be coming way too late. But knowing his future happiness, his life's happiness, depended on it.

"I... I have a lot of things I want to say to you."

Her eyes met his for a long moment before she gave him a slow nod. "All right. But first let me see if there's anything other than clothes in my suitcase to get York cleaned up."

"Let's use my shirt, first." He set the dog on his feet and pulled off his suit jacket, then began to unbutton the shirt that was mostly dry except for where York had been held against his chest, leaving a muddy stain. "It's probably ruined anyway."

He rubbed the dog all over, and being as small as he was, the shirt and Yorkie's repeated shaking, flinging droplets of rain around the room, seemed to do the trick.

"There. Bedraggled, but dry enough, I think."

"Oh, Conor. I'm so sorry about your clothes." She gave him a rueful smile. "Good news is I have a bag of things you left here."

She picked it up and handed it to him, then bit her lip. "Um...there's not a shirt in there, though. Let me... get it."

He dug in the bag and saw sweatpants and socks and a few other things, before she came back holding his T-shirt. Their eyes met as he reached for it, wondering why it wasn't in the bag with everything else.

"I kept it," she blurted, as though she'd read his mind. "I know it's stupid and silly, but I wanted to keep a little piece of you with me. Sorry I was going to steal it."

He dropped the clothes, wanting so much to reach for her and hold her close, wet or not, but he knew he had to tell her what he'd learned first and see if she'd possibly believe him.

"Stupid? That would be *me*, Jillian. A man who loves you more than anything in this world but still walked away."

"Conor…" she whispered. "It's okay. We—"

"Let me finish." He pressed his finger to her cold lips. "I let you go because I thought it was the best thing for you. Was sure it was because I'd proved over and over that I couldn't be there for you the way you deserve. That there was something wrong with me— something missing inside. And then tonight I finally got a hard hit to the head that made me open my eyes. Made me see that wasn't true at all."

Her eyes were wide on his now, but she didn't speak, and he reached for her shoulders and forged on.

"I was in the middle of a meeting with all the Urgent Care Manhattan board members, among others. About to close a deal I've been working on for a long time and that I thought was the most important thing to concentrate on. Critical to make it happen. But I was sitting there thinking of you, instead. Thinking of you moving today, and thinking how much I'd miss you, and how much I love you, and how much I wished I could be a different man."

"And then…?"

"Then I got Michelle's call about Yorkie. It scared me. And when I heard how scared you were I saw with an instant blinding clarity that I've been utterly wrong about so many things. That I'm not like my father at all. That *you* are the most important thing in the world. Way more than any work or money or investments could ever be. And that providing monetarily for you isn't the best way to show my love for you. It was like lightning struck me, and burned into my brain that if I let you go that would be the one thing that would truly make me a failure."

"You left the meeting?"

"I left the meeting," he confirmed. "And as I did all the things I believed about myself and my life fell away, and I knew with absolute certainty that all I need in life is you. Not more businesses, not a bigger portfolio, not a bigger apartment. Just you."

"Oh, Conor." Her lips trembled and she wrapped her arms around him. "I'd told myself our relationship being over was a good thing. A chance for me to believe in myself, be confident in a man's love for me someday, when I was ready to try a relationship again. But, listening to you now, I know for certain that you finally coming to believe in yourself was a process, the way mine was. And I believe we're both there now in a way we weren't before."

Her words made it hard for him to breathe, and he had to try twice before he could speak. "I know I am. I know that I love you, Jilly. I know that I'll always be here for you, and that I'll never be that guy who failed you ever again."

"And I'll never be that woman who wonders if you really love her. Because I can *see* it, Conor." Her voice wobbled as she smiled up at him. "I see the love I feel for you reflected right back. I see it so clearly I can hardly breathe from the happiness I feel right now. I love you. So much."

Unable to speak, he pulled her close and buried his face in her wet hair, not caring that her clothes were damp and cold against his bare chest. They stood there for long minutes before he pulled back and kissed her sweet lips, and the taste of them made his throat close all over again.

He lifted her wet sweatshirt away from her skin before reaching for her cold hands. "I know you need to get into dry clothes, but I can't wait even a few more minutes." He swallowed down the emotion in his chest so he could ask what he desperately needed to know. "Will you marry me, Jill? Again? This time I'll be the husband you deserve. I'll be the man you want. I'll be the man who is always there for you and who gives you everything you need—and I'm not talking about money. I'm talking about myself. I promise."

"Yes, I'll marry you. Again." Her fingers tightened on his. "I'll believe in you and I'll always be there for you. I promise."

Relief weakened his knees and he pulled her close, kissing her until the moist air around them seemed to steam and their wet clothes weren't even close to cold anymore.

When they finally separated he smiled down at the beautiful face smiling back. "How about we get these wet clothes off before you catch a cold? Then a warm shower."

"Sounds like very good medical advice, Dr. McCarthy."

She gave him the impish grin he loved so much, and the fact that he'd get to see it every day of his life weakened his knees all over again.

"And here's something you'll be pleased about. I have my hair dryer in my suitcase, since you're so good at using that."

He tugged her shirt off over her head, grasped her

hand and headed toward her bathroom. "I *am* pleased about that. And I'd like to show you other things I'm good at, too. Prove that I'll always be good to you. What do you think about that?"

"I think being good to one another is the perfect way to begin our second chance together. Starting right now."

EPILOGUE

Jillian finished the measurement of her patient's hand strength and mobility, entered the numbers in the computer, then sat back with a smile. "Looks like you've hit all the required markers, Sandy. Congratulations! I'm graduating you from occupational therapy."

"I'm so glad! This sure hasn't been fun, except for working with you, Jillian. Thanks so much for everything. You've made a painful and frustrating process a whole lot better than I expected it to be. And my hand really works again! I almost can't believe it."

"I always knew you'd get there—and making therapy less miserable is one of our goals. If you keep up with your exercises at home you'll be almost as good as new in a few more months."

"I will. Thanks again."

Jillian stood and raised her voice. "Sandy's graduated, everyone! Time for her clap-out!"

All the therapists cheered and clapped their hands as Sandy laughed and waved on her way out the door.

Jill cupped her big belly and took a moment to stretch her back before shutting down the computer and grabbing her purse.

She paused to look at her scarred wrist. The surgical

line had faded to a pale pink, no longer obvious, and she smiled, thinking of how Conor sometimes still kissed and nibbled at it the way he did the scars on her legs, making her laugh until things morphed into another kind of kissing, then into making love, which brought so many emotions.

Feeling cherished. Feeling loved. Feeling blessed.

He was right. All her physical scars were simply life scars that everyone had, both inside and out. Things that showed she'd been through some tough battles and prevailed as the warrior Conor said she was.

He'd helped her see that, and had helped her work through the internal scars, too—the insecurities, that she no longer felt. And she, in turn, had helped him with his internal scars—and wasn't that what a close relationship was all about? She was grateful every day that they hadn't lost the chance to do that for one another forever. The chance to feel truly whole for the first time in their lives.

Jillian took the elevator to the fourth floor and walked through the glass passageway that connected the HOAC building to Urgent Care Manhattan, now Conor had successfully merged the two companies. Business for both had grown, even with Conor working only on the board and not as president, which had been his original plan.

She turned the corner and smiled to see all the children playing in the daycare center HOAC now offered their employees. Running and laughing, climbing the small plastic jungle gym, crawling on the floor, playing with toys. And sitting on the floor with them was a handsome man with familiar thick blond hair, playing and laughing, too.

Her smile widened and she shoved open the door to the play area. "Isn't Dr. McCarthy going to get his pants wrinkled, sitting on the floor like that?"

"I thought about leaving on my scrubs—but, since we're going out to eat before we see the Rockefeller Center Christmas tree being lit tonight, I figured I'd wear actual clothes and look presentable." He smiled down at their daughter and rubbed his hand down her small back. "You excited about that, Alyssa?"

"Yes!" Beautiful blue eyes looked up at Jillian, and she reached to slip the toddler's blonde hair out of her face. "Hi, Mama!"

"Hey, sweetie! What are you and Daddy doing?"

"We're pwaying cars and twucks and doctors. My twuck just smashed into his car and now the doctor has to come and fix the daddy's bwoken leg." Looking very serious, she held up a little plastic doctor figure.

"I see." Lowering herself to the floor wasn't easy at eight months pregnant, but she managed to get there. "I'll bet the doctor will do a very good job."

"Yes, a *vewy* good job."

Alyssa concentrated on the toy doctor and the car and the other small doll figures, and Jillian turned to Conor. "It's so wonderful that you insisted on having this daycare center built here. Thanks for convincing all the board members it would ratchet up employee satisfaction scores by making their lives easier and better."

"Well…" He leaned in to press his cheek to hers. "A certain person I'm crazy in love with showed me that having a work/life balance is important."

"Yes, it is." She wrapped her arm around his neck and tangled her fingers in his hair as she soaked in the warmth of his skin.

"Having daycare here benefits everyone—including me. I get to sneak over and visit my daughter for a minute if a patient doesn't show, and neither of us is struggling through the city to drop her off and pick her up from an offsite daycare. What's the point of owning a business if you can't make everyone's life better?"

"Making money would be one point..."

He moved his cheek until his lips slipped across hers. "That *is* an important one—making sure our family is financially secure. But my beautiful and wonderful wife has helped me see that it's not quite as important as a few other things."

They smiled at one another, their eyes meeting in a long connection, before he stood. "Let's get going. I'm hungry and I bet Alyssa is, too—aren't you, pumpkin? Then we're going to see the tree lit! Are you excited about that?"

"Yes!" Alyssa tossed aside the toys and stood, a happy smile on her face. "Weady to go?"

Conor grasped Jillian's hand to help her up off the floor and they both grinned. "Are you ready to go?"

"Yes. More than ready."

"Are we bwinging the dogs?" Alyssa asked.

"Not this time. But we'll take them some other day. Maybe they can watch you learn to ice skate with me helping you? What do you think about that?"

"Ice skate? Yes!"

Conor got Alyssa's coat and hat on, swung the child into his arms, and then the three of them headed into the city. After dinner at their favorite restaurant they walked the few blocks to Rockefeller Center. The place was jammed full of people, and Conor placed Alyssa on his shoulders so she could see everything.

A light snow began to fall and Jillian pulled Alyssa's hat down a little farther, to keep her ears warm. Excitement was in the air, and the countdown finally began.

"Five! Four! Three! Two! One!"

The rainbow of lights covering the giant Christmas tree blinked on, illuminating the night sky, and everyone cheered.

Little Alyssa clapped her hands and cheered along. "It's so pwetty! I love it!"

"I love it, too." Conor held on to the toddler's leg as he wrapped his arm around Jillian and looked at her. "And I love *you*."

"Love you, too. So much."

They kissed, then kissed some more, until the music began and people started to dance.

Alyssa wanted to dance, too.

Conor lifted their little one from his shoulders and she danced around for a few minutes, before reaching for Jillian's round belly and placing her hands on either side of it, her mouth pressed against it.

"You like the music, baby bwother? You like the lights? I *love* the lights!"

"He can't see the lights yet, Alyssa, but I bet he can hear the music," Conor said, looking down at their daughter with such adoration on his face it made Jill's heart fill to bursting. They had this amazing life together. The life they'd both wanted but thought would never happen.

"I'll bet he's dancing inside Mama's belly. What do you think?"

"Yes! He's dancing! Just like me!"

She began to bob up and down and back and forth so vigorously that both Conor and Jillian laughed.

Conor placed one hand on Jill's back and the other on her abdomen, leaning in for another kiss. "Does it feel like he's dancing? If he is, I hope he's not dancing quite as hard as she is."

She chuckled. "At the moment he's quiet but… Oh! Did you feel him kick?"

"Wow. I did." His eyes lit, then he sobered. "My third miracle. Alyssa was the second…"

"And the first?"

"*You*, Jillian. You're my forever miracle. You didn't give up on me even when you should have."

"And now you've given me everything I ever wanted." She placed her palm against his cheek as their mouths met again. "You, our beautiful babies, and New York City and the Rockefeller Center at Christmastime. What else could anyone need?"

He swept the snowflakes from her nose and smiled before he kissed her again. "I can't think of one single thing."

* * * * *

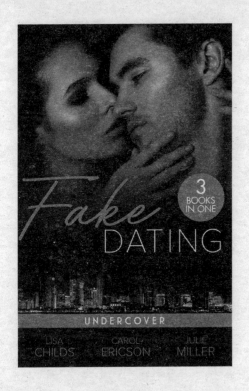

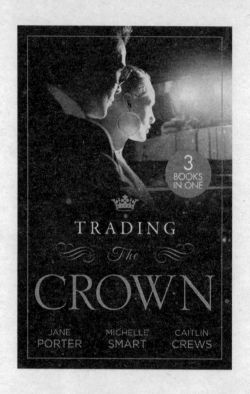

LET'S TALK
Romance

For exclusive extracts, competitions and special offers, find us online:

 MillsandBoon

 @MillsandBoon

 @MillsandBoonUK

 @MillsandBoonUK

Get in touch on 01413 063 232

MILLS & BOON

THE HEART OF ROMANCE

A ROMANCE FOR EVERY READER

MODERN

Prepare to be swept off your feet by sophisticated, sexy and seductive heroes, in some of the world's most glamourous and romantic locations, where power and passion collide.

HISTORICAL

Escape with historical heroes from time gone by. Whether your passion is for wicked Regency Rakes, muscled Vikings or rugged Highlanders, awaken the romance of the past.

MEDICAL

Set your pulse racing with dedicated, delectable doctors in the high-pressure world of medicine, where emotions run high and passion, comfort and love are the best medicine.

True Love

Celebrate true love with tender stories of heartfelt romance, from the rush of falling in love to the joy a new baby can bring, and a focus on the emotional heart of a relationship.

Desire

Indulge in secrets and scandal, intense drama and sizzling hot action with heroes who have it all: wealth, status, good looks…everything but the right woman.

HEROES

The excitement of a gripping thriller, with intense romance at its heart. Resourceful, true-to-life women and strong, fearless men face danger and desire - a killer combination!

To see which titles are coming soon, please visit

millsandboon.co.uk/nextmonth